# Radhika Rages at the Crater School

Radhika Rages at the Crater School

Chaz Brenchley

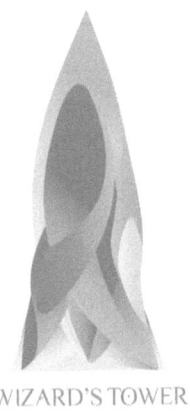

WIZARD'S TOWER

Wizard's Tower Press

Rhydaman, Cymru

Radhika Rages at the Crater School

A Crater School Novel

Text © 2025 by Chaz Brenchley
Cover art & design by Ben Baldwin
School badge designed by Elizabeth Leggett
Book design by Cheryl Morgan

First published in Great Britain
by Wizard's Tower Press, June 2025

Paperback ISBN: 978-1-917950-01-5

http://wizardstowerpress.com/
http://www.chazbrenchley.co.uk/

# Contents

CHAZ BRENCHLEY

*"This one's for Cheryl*
*with love, gratitude and not a little awe"*

# Praise for Radhika Rages at the Crater School

"No fear of Brenchley's inventiveness flagging. A new arrival sets a test that lays bare the school's hitherto hidden flaws for the reader. If the Cratereans cannot see this for themselves, they risk failing their latest pupil."

*Juliet E McKenna*

# Praise for Mary Ellen, Craterean!

"The Crater School series offers glorious nostalgia and escapism and old-fashioned plucky girl values From a Simpler Time, only without the racist/jingoistic undercurrents that usually accompany the original works. It's like reading your childhood fave again, but without the constant fear of stubbing your toe on hidden rocks. And as such, I will take as many of these as the author can be persuaded to write."

*KJ Charles*

"We see Old Mars and the Crater School through an intriguingly different lens, as Mary Ellen, scholarship girl, finds herself in this alien environment. Thus Brenchley deftly offers fans of the series a fresh perspective while new readers share her discoveries and will surely be drawn into this fascinating world."

*Juliet E McKenna*

8

# Praise for Dust Up at the Crater School

"Only in the laboratory of Chaz Brenchley could the British school story be lovingly sutured together with the Old Mars of the pulps, animated with the crackling static of a planetary dust storm, and sent lumbering down to the village. No — **skipping** down to the village, with a beret, and a paper bag full of bulls'-eyes, and a wholesome desire to excel at lacrosse."

*Francis Spufford*

# Praise for Three Twins at the Crater School

"What a brilliant wheeze, to transplant a girls' school story to a steampunk Martian colony. Chaz Brenchley performs a pitch-perfect quantum shift that's full of plums. If you're a fan of Brent-Dyer or Brazil or Blyton, you will love Three Twins at the Crater School."

*Val McDermid*

"All the earnest charm of a British boarding school story, plus aliens! I wish I were a Crater School girl."

*Marie Brennan*

# RADHIKA RAGES AT THE CRATER SCHOOL

"Three Twins at the Crater School is splendidly full of peril and charm. It calls forth very particular memories of books and mountain schools and the adventures of teenage girls."

*Gillian Polack*

"In a past that isn't ours, in a world of aether ships and an Eternal Empress, the Crater School embodies all the values, passions, high jinks and adventures of the classic girl school stories of the first half of the twentieth century. For every fan of The Chalet School, Malory Towers, Dimsie or the Abbey Girls, this is a guiltless pleasure."

*Farah Mendlesohn*

"Who would have thought an English boarding school story and a science fiction adventure mashup would work so spectacularly? This is a one-sitting page-turner!"

*Sherwood Smith*

"The British Empire has met its match in Chaz Brenchley's Mars. Mysterious aquatic aliens have transported humans to the Red Planet by means unexplained, and the Brits, willingly taking on the colonizing of this new world, establish themselves well. The Crater School brings to mind the rigidity of Aubrey Upjohn's Malvern House, the rowdiness of Stalky's Coll, and the resourcefulness and sheer heart of St. Trinian's. Brenchley had me at 'British girls' school on Mars.'"

*Jennifer Stevenson*

"If Angela Brazil and Edgar Rice Burroughs had decided to write a story together, Three Twins at the Crater School might have been the delightful result. Friendship, family ties—good and bad—and schoolgirl shenanigans set against the backdrop of a Mars straight out of early science fiction makes for exciting and yet cozy reading. I was especially intrigued by the hints of alternate history—the deathless

Queen Victoria, a Great War fought between Britain and Czarist Russia—there's much to explore here, and I sincerely hope there will be further instalments."

*Marissa Doyle*

"In this inventive combination, Brenchley offers readers an entertaining opportunity to revisit the school stories and planetary romances of days gone by. Along the way, he interrogates the assumptions and attitudes of those books and their era with charming ruthlessness. Highly recommended."

*Juliet E. McKenna*

"A rollicking good read from start to finish! Move over, Enid Blyton, there are new girls at school—they fight monsters!"

*Ellen Klages*

"Twins we will never forget and cool Mars creatures."

*Miranda and Talia, age 9*

# PRELUDE

"I won't go. I won't, I *won't*!"

"Child, you will go. It is quite decided."

"Not by me! You didn't even *ask* me!"

"No, of course not. It was my decision to take, Radhika. Even you must see that." Her father gazed at her with a weary implacability.

"But, but, but it's not *fair*!" Even she knew she was on weak ground there, but it was too late to recover.

"Is it not? Perhaps it isn't. Life is very often unfair, you will find. Especially so when you're too young to choose your own direction, and a figure of authority has to take those decisions on your behalf." He made a deliberate effort to soften the sternness in his voice. "Don't you want to be near Mama-ji, Radhi? It's the reason I chose this school, so that you'll be right there for her when she wants you."

That checked Radhika's temper, if only for a moment. Her tiny and beloved mother was desperately ill, with what had only recently been diagnosed as Meyerboehn's Syndrome, or Martian Paralytic Fever. The marvellous doctors who had made that determination, and were fighting even now to bring her safely through that dreadful and often fatal disease, worked far and far from Marsport, high on a crater's lip, almost at the edge of Charter lands.

Radhika was frantically worried about her—but even so, the notion of being sent away to boarding school without any consultation of her own feelings enraged her. The fact that it was her adored father who had chosen to do so only made things worse, for she was an only child and had always been a daddy's girl. On top of all the other injustices that had brought the family to Mars in the first place, it was just too much to bear. Hence this outburst, even in the face of her father's obvious exhaustion.

"I can't keep you here without her," he went on, when she made no reply to his question. "It isn't fitting, it wouldn't be proper; and how would I keep you safe, when I must work all night and sleep at least part of the day? No, no. Far better that you go—"

"I could work too," she offered instantly. "That would help, wouldn't it? I could be a, a chambermaid, I'm sure Mr Garrard would find work for me, and then I'd be under the housekeeper's eye all day, and quite safe here."

"*No*, Radhika. You will absolutely not abandon your education, for this reason or for any. It is our sacred trust as parents, to see you properly educated to the full degree of which you are capable. In your case, that means school through the sixth form, and university after. I may have wasted my own life and opportunities"—he gazed rather bleakly around the seedy attic room of this seedy and somewhat worse than seedy hotel, if his daughter only knew the truth of it—"but I am determined not to allow you to waste yours. Let me hear no more arguments now. You will be going to the Crater School next week, when term begins, and that is that."

"I'll hate it. Don't you care about that? I'll run away."

Unexpectedly, that raised a smile in him. "No, you won't. Oh, you'll go there determined to hate it, I'm sure. I did just the same, when I was sent away to public school in England. But you'll buckle down and apply yourself anyway, you'll try to do everything right, because that's what you do when you're angry and upset, you just focus on the task at hand—oh, don't gape at me like that, girlie, give me credit for knowing my own child—and you'll find yourself making friends regardless, and finding interest in the lessons, and exploring a whole new side of Mars and a whole new life you haven't had a glimpse of yet. The Crater School has a splendid reputation, and there are young and not-so-young women all across the colony who relished their time there and never wanted to leave. You'll do far better there than you ever could at St Dymphna's."

"But, but..." But she liked the easygoing nature of her day-school, and the way she could shine at her lessons without really trying; and she loved skipping out of school when the bell rang at four o'clock and ranging at will through the streets of Marsport with her friends, until she had to come back to the Blue Dolphin for supper and bed before her father's shift started in the evening. He was the Night Manager here, which sounded grander than it was, especially as Mr Garrard the real manager would always wake up and take over in any real crisis.

"No, Radhika. No more 'buts'. Your name has been entered in the school rolls, and you will join the train on Tuesday morning, no doubt with many another Crater School girl. Now come along, there is much to be done before then. We must get you fitted out with new uniforms, and a new trunk, and everything else that falls needy to a boarding-school girl. The school matron has sent me a list, and woe betide us all, my *jaan*, if we fail to meet it in every particular..."

# CHAPTER ONE

## Strangers on a Train

The platform was, of course, a seething chaos of schoolgirls swirling around isolated adult figures. But this was the Crater School, so it was at least a somewhat organised kind of chaos. Only the new girls were entirely bewildered. Experienced hands knew more or less where they were expected to go, which prefect or staff they should be looking for: Juniors gravitated towards the near end of the platform, the goddesses of the Sixth Form some halfway along—*some* part of the train must after all be left for civilian traffic—and everyone else in between.

The train was in already. The first three carriages bore printed signs in their windows, *RESERVED FOR THE CRATER SCHOOL*. Clutching her father's hand rather more tightly than a rising-fourteen-year-old perhaps ought to do, Radhika found a moment's distraction in pondering the extreme unlikelihood of St Dymphna's ever reserving even a single carriage, for any reason whatsoever.

Only for a moment. They were approached by a tall, graceful girl Radhika might have taken for a mistress, if she hadn't been dressed in the same gold-and-green outfit as herself.

"Excuse me, sir—I think you must be a new parent, as I don't believe I recognise your daughter?" with a welcoming smile to Radhika somehow tossed into the mix.

Papa-ji snorted with laughter. "In my day, it was the child that was reckoned new. But I do see what you mean," as other parents all around were conducting their young hopefuls to their proper places, or else brutally abandoning them at the platform gate to sink or swim alone. "So yes, I am indeed, very new to all of this. My name is Captain Harvey, and this is my daughter Radhika."

At his side, she tried to stand as straight and proud as he did. He had never lost his military bearing, nor ceased to use his rank even in civilian life, even in the awful circumstances of that life. She might still be furious with him for despatching her to the far end of this farther world, but she would never, ever shame him, nor stand still to see him shamed.

Also, he had never lost the defensiveness with which he had introduced his daughter, all her life long.

If this girl had any reaction to his statement, she showed none of it. She simply glanced down a list in her hand, and ticked one name off with a pencil. "Radhika Harvey, yes. All present and correct. This is your trunk? Splendid. Thank you, Mr Jennings," as the porter bore the trunk away without another word needed. "No, no, sir," as Papa-ji rather help-lessly held out a sixpence for the man, "no need for that. The school sees to all that's necessary. It would be a free-for-all, else." *A bazaar*, Radhika thought she meant, a marketplace where wealthy parents could outbid the less fortunate and reserve the porters' business to themselves. Growing up as she had, she couldn't help noticing such things. "Trust me, the men won't feel themselves hard done by. They're old friends, to most of us who make this journey. Now, my name is Arie Bunker, and I am the official interceptor of all the first-timers; you have officially been intercepted, young Radhika, your trunk attested to, your night-case noted," with a nod to the little suitcase Radhika had insisted on carrying herself. "In your person, you look neat and trig, and pass inspection with great credit. I do like the nifty way you have with a tie—oh, but your father's a military man, of course. Naturally a soldier's daughter would take care with her turn-out. Sir, if you'd march Radhika over to Miss Hendy, in the rather fetching toque there, she is the official welcoming party for new folk. I must dash, I spy a mother all at sea..."

"...Toque?"

Radhika giggled, despite herself. "Cap, Papa-ji. See, the lady with the cute cap and the battle-worn tweeds."

"Ah! Thank you, Radhi." Tweeds at least he understood.

They marched as directed, and were greeted with another smile, another list, another tick against her name. "Now, Radhika," again with no hint of a reaction to the reality of her, "if you'll say goodbye to your father and let him get away, it'll be all to the good. Don't worry, I'll see you're not stranded on your own, but we do like to chase parents off quickly, for their own good..."

It was a brief and awkward parting, between two who were not currently friends. He kissed her cheek, while she clamped her hands tight together behind her back to be sure not to hug him, not to cling. Nor did she watch his tall figure disappear through the crowd. She turned away to be sure of it, in case he happened to look back, and found herself face to face with two girls more or less her own age, the one honey-blonde and the other a scorching redhead.

"Hullo!" The blonde held her hand out, and a rather startled Radhika took it and shook it mutely. "I'm Marigold, and this is Charm." Another startlement—who calls their daughter *Charm*?—and another handshake. That must be the custom of the school, she supposed. She couldn't actually remember ever shaking another girl's hand before. "Miss Hendy says you're likely to be in our class—"

"—and you're *certain* to be in our house," Charm, cutting in firmly, "because she's our housemistress so of course she knows. She's asked me to be your sherpa," with a stern glance at Marigold and something of a stress on *me*, "which means that I get to look after you and show you around and answer all your questions until you've found your feet. I was new myself a year ago," she added confidentially, "and Marigold sherpa'd me, though she *wasn't* asked to, she only took it upon herself because that's what she does. So she'll probably do it with you too, and so I warn you. Don't be misled, though; I'm in charge."

Marigold snorted at her side. Charm ignored her friend loftily, tucked her arm through Radhika's and led her towards the train. "We're Upper Third this term, and we've pretty much bagged this end of this carriage. Miss Hendy says we can go ahead and find seats, so long as no actual fistfights break out," with a giggle. "Blessedly it's a corridor train, of course, not individual compartments like the funicular. What? No, you'll see when you get there. Nobody gives the game away, about the funicular. Well, except that it isn't a funicular. We're allowed to say that much and no more. *Any*way, *as* I was saying, our set has grabbed some facing benches, with a table in between. It may be a *bit* of a squeeze, with one extra," surveying Radhika's slim hips consideringly, "but I think we'll all fit."

Fit they did, in that way that Martian adolescents can, being far more about length than width; and so Radhika found herself in the midst of a cheerful crush, friends catching up with each others' news and opinions, memories of times past, wonderings on the term to come, "because we're *Middles* now, and you know what that means."

18

Wise nods from all. Radhika seized the opportunity of a moment's silence to murmur in Charm's ear, "Please, I don't know," and it might matter, if she was to be one of them. "What does it mean?"

"Oh! No, of course you wouldn't, would you? Well, you see, it's kind of a tradition that the Middles, um, have the most fun they can manage at school, regardless of whether it's actually against the rules or not. Is that fair, Marigold?"

"Quite fair," Marigold said judiciously. "The most important thing, of course, is to outdo what the forms ahead got up to in their turns. One has to be inventive."

"We could make a list?" someone else put in. There had been a positive storm of introductions around the table, and Radhika didn't quite have everybody straight yet. Was that Maeve, or Janna? She wasn't sure. Well, no doubt she would sort them all out in time.

"Well, we could—but it'd be death if a pree caught sight of it."

"No, but we could make a list of what we *can't* do." This from a bright young hopeful she was fairly sure to be Cate. "Then they'll be totally confused and expecting everything wrong, while we, um, define our parameters by ruling out the obvious."

"Brilliant," Marigold declared. "Pencil and paper, someone? Right, then. Charm, you've read all the books there are, so you're in charge. We can't do what our own predecessors have done, obviously, but we shouldn't just copy the girls in the books either. Top of the list, Charm?"

"Midnight feasts," decidedly. "Boring, old hat, bad food, Lower Fourth did it last year, and it's an insult to Mrs Bailey's cooking."

"Seconded," from Marigold, writing in bold capitals. Who's next?"

It was almost fun, almost, to be squashed in with these girls and listen to their mischief. Radhika reminded herself firmly that she wasn't here to enjoy herself. She was bitterly angry at her father and the world, and she meant to loathe and detest the Crater School from first to last, and every moment in between.

As the new girl, she had been shuffled through to the privilege of a window seat. It was a gesture of pure generosity, and she took advantage of it now by turning her face away from her giggling cohort and staring out, trying not to listen to their bright clear voices, trying to find some interest in the emptying platform.

The train's steam-whistle sounded, twice. A guard came along the platform edge, closing doors and calling, "All aboard!"

She couldn't see him wave his green flag, he was long gone from her sight; but she did hear the shrill blast of his whistle when he blew it. The train replied with one more blast, the carriage jerked, and slowly, slowly began to roll away, carrying her with it. Away from everyone and everything she knew on Mars, the only home she'd had here.

She could hear the locomotive at its work, heaving effortfully, pulling them along faster now; she could feel the rip in her heart as they came to the end of the platform and there was one solitary figure standing there, watching her leave, raising his arm in farewell.

She did not, did *not* wave back.

"Radhika?"
            "Don't *poke* me!"

The whole table fell quiet, and Charm seemed thoroughly taken aback at the snarl in her voice.

"Well," she said, "it was more of a nudge, really; and I am sorry, but it's hard not to, with us all sardined together like this, and Chrissy was offering her butterscotch around, only you seemed to be in a bit of a brown study, so..."

"Oh! I, I'm sorry I snapped," because honesty was branded into her very soul, and she really was sorry. She might rage against the school and everything it stood for, when what it stood for most in her mind was this utter abduction; but there was no value in making enemies of her classmates. She had no intention of making *friends*, mark you—she didn't mean to be at the Crater School long enough to let that happen; Mama-ji would get well, very soon now, any day now, and the two of them could travel home together, and Radhika would take the very best care of her frail mother and even Papa-ji would see that she was essential to his wife's recovery—but for the moment, manners and good breeding would do no harm, and she did after all have the very best of breeding, the very *best*, whatever other people might say or think or believe. "You're right, of course, I was miles away." *Back in Marsport, with my family*, a mile further with every minute that passed, as the train came up to speed. "And thank you, Chrissy, I'd love a piece of butterscotch, if I may."

She was beamed upon, and butterscotch'd to the satisfaction of all; and she-thought-it-was-probably-Janna who said, "Radhika is such a pretty name, but I don't think I've ever heard it before. What does it mean, can you say?"

There were chuckles all around the table, and Charm said, "Janna"—ah, she'd been right, then!—"collects names, it's a sort of hobby of hers."

"I don't *collect* them," Janna protested. "I mean, not written down in a book or anything. They're just int'resting, that's all."

And now everyone turned back to Radhika again to hear her answer, and she could feel herself flushing darkly at the attention. "It's a Hindustani name, and Mama-ji says it means 'one who is filled with joy.'"

"I'm sorry, *who* did you say said that?"

"Oh! Mama-ji—it's what I call my mother. The -ji bit is a, a sign of respect; we say it to all our elders and superiors."

There is an unwritten rule all through the Red Raj that it's impolite to ask personal questions, particularly about someone's life before they came to Mars. On the other hand, the patient silence all around the table was a question in itself. Radhika could feel the weight of it pressing down upon her.

She sighed, and gave in to the inevitable.

"Papa-ji was an officer in the Indian Army. He met my mother there," *obviously.* There was no hiding that; it was why she wore the name she did, two cultures proudly on display. "So I was born in Benares, and grew up in army camps and barrack quarters all across the country. I loved it there," *until I lost it, until we lost it all.* "Only my father's time there came, came to an end," which still felt like a lie every time she said it, but it was the least-dishonest way of words that she could come up with, "and we came to Mars to make a fresh start."

"Ooh, did he transfer to the Double Reds?"

That meant the Empress's Own Twelfth Borderers, of course. It was … Maeve? … who asked the question, but from their rapt interest it was clear that every one of her listeners had some private investment in the regiment, be it a parent, an uncle, a brother, a pen-pal…

Also, it was one of the questions that you could always ask of a Martian, be they born or new-minted in the colony. Patriotism trumps manners, at least in that particular context. They held the Double Reds very close to their hearts for many reasons, many of which were painful.

"No-o. He left the army altogether. He, he's a hotel manager now."

"Oh." There was a slight, probably inevitable slump around the table, a let-down kind of feeling. Only for a moment, though, before the girls recalled themselves to their duty in making the newcomer welcome.

"We've had Indian girls in the school before, of course," Marigold said. "Indeed, we've a pair of sisters with us now, so if you want to have the Hindustani and want to keep it up, I'm sure they'll be happy to natter away with you. They're Mars Indians, though, born and bred up here." Mars was always *up*, and Earth was *down*. "I don't know if we've ever had a girl from actual India, from the Raj proper. Anyone...?"

A general shaking of heads; but they had none of them been at the school particularly long, nor of course had they ever thought to enquire of their elders, whether or not they could find a way to do it mannerly.

That was enough of an interrogation, they clearly felt, for now.

"Do you realise," Marigold said—Radhika was starting to suspect that Marigold would always take the lead, unless someone else stopped her—"that in our new and glorious capacity as Middles, we will be sharing a common room with both the Fourths, those very Fourths who have been jeering at us as Juniors all this time?"

"They still will," Charm said gloomily. "They'll call us Junior Middles, and sneer just the same. And my sister will be one of the worst."

"Oh, come on! You two are thick as thieves, you know you are. And I don't believe Levity has ever sneered at anyone in all her life, never mind her own kid sister."

"Well, maybe not—but school is making her awfully bossy, when she never was before. She'll be keeping an eye on me the whole time, when we're in the same room together. It's going to be awful. Same house, same common room—how am I ever going to get away...?"

Being an only child, Radhika had no particular notion of the pressures and strains of sisterhood. Even so, she thought perhaps that Charm protested a little too much, and somewhat unconvincingly.

"*And,*" Charm went on, being in an apparently grumbly kind of mood, "she and Mamma are always going to be my only company on my birthday, because it's slap-bang in the middle of summer. It's never going to be in term-time, like most people's birthdays are."

"Well, but at least we can send you cards and things," Chrissy said, taking out a neat little pocket diary. "What date, Char?"

Charm giggled. "Don't ever let Mamma hear you calling me that. Liv tried it once, and got *roasted* for it. Me, I like it, but just 'tween ourselves, yes?"

"Yes, yes. No grown-ups, no prees. Date?"

"The last day of June, the thirtieth."

"What?"

Once again, the whole table was staring at Radhika. She flushed again, and cursed inside again in fluent Hindustani, because that could only ever draw more attention to what these nicely brought-up girls were so steadfastly ignoring, the colour of her skin.

"Sorry," she mumbled. "I didn't mean to shout. But, it's just, that's my birthday too."

"Wow, really? How old will you be this year?"

"Fourteen."

"Me too! We're twins!"

Charm seemed ecstatic. Now it was Radhika's turn to stare. "What? No—"

"Oh, not really, not *blood* twins. Not like the twinses in the Crew. But birthday twins is definitely a thing! I've decided! We were born on the exact same day, even if on two different planets, so it's obviously fate that Miss Hendy asked me to sherpa you."

24

With a sinking heart, Radhika realised that what she really meant was that they were obviously destined to be best friends.

Well, she supposed she could play up to that for a while—*for a short while, please, please...?*—if it made Charm so particularly happy.

She managed a smile and said, "Twins it is, then, through space and time," *if a pale-skinned redhead really wants to twin up with a dusky half-caste. We'll see how long it lasts.* Cosmopolitan Marsport had been a blessed relief, after a lifelong experience with the British Indian Army and its all-white officers, their all-white wives and children, Mama-ji and herself the only exceptions. She wasn't expecting to find the same relief at a colonial boarding school.

Still, she went on, "And you won't have to be totally alone with your family, your *blood* family, if you don't want to. My father said I'd have to stay here all through the holidays too, at least until Mama-ji can leave the Sana—"

The word died half-born in her throat; she had been so determined not to say that, never to say that.

Too late now. Every girl at the table had a sorrowful, sympathetic air; Charm even took her hand, and squeezed it encouragingly.

"Lots of girls at school have relatives in the Sanatorium," she said. "It's one of the reasons we come here. I mean, not us specifically, I don't think anyone here—?"

Heads were shaken, all around.

"No, but plenty of others. And of course some of us have been there too, when we're really ill; and we all like to visit when we can, even if we don't have anyone particular to see. We sing for them and all sorts. You'll see. Miss Hendy can arrange for you to go over on Sundays; I expect she knows already, doesn't she? I expect it's why your father sent you to us..."

# CHAPTER TWO

## The Dread Simoom

The train had run for hours, all morning and into the afternoon. It would run for hours more, Radhika had learned, before they reached their destination, a town with the somewhat doom-laden name of Terminus.

They had eaten and drunk while the locomotive did more or less the same, coaling and watering at the previous stop, readying for a dash across an incursive arm of the true Dry. Now they were as far from civilisation as you could come, anywhere in the province; this was old Mars, Mars untouched even by the Builders. No canals reached out this far, in this direction. Radhika had never seen anything like it. Soft red Martian cliffs had been wind-sculpted into outlandish pillars of stone, that were as good as clouds for letting people see different figures in their wild distorted shapes.

When they had tired of that and Marigold produced a couple of packs of cards, Radhika politely cried off and went back to her window, fascinated beyond measure. She kept recalling some of the wonders she had seen in India—the Taj Mahal, the Red Fort, Mehrangarh—but those had all been works of man, not natural as this landscape was.

26

"Incredible, isn't it?" Thus Charm, out of the game and not interested in following it further, looking over Radhika's shoulder to share the view. "I was just awestruck, the first time I saw this. I was only a little kid at the time, but I thought giants had made it, or something like that. Not just wind. Well, wind and sand, I suppose, working together."

"Speaking of which," Radhika said, "what's that out there, some kind of dust devil?"

She pointed, Charm squinted—and then Charm scrambled hastily up onto the table, scattering cards in all directions and drawing half a dozen protests at once, drawing the attention of everyone in the carriage as she reached up and pulled the communication cord, signalling the driver to bring the train to an immediate emergency halt.

Brakes squealed; so did a number of girls. One of those terrifying figures known as "prees" or prefects came barrelling down the aisle to confront the guilty party as she jumped back down to ground.

"Charm Buchanan, I know you will have had a very good reason for doing that, yes?"

"Yes, please, Melanie. Look." Charm pointed, as Radhika had before her.

Melanie frowned, following the finger out into the Dry; and then she gasped, and said, "Simoom?"

"I'm sure so. Radhika saw it first, but she didn't know what it was. We've seen it before, Liv and me. Been caught up in it before, and it's the horriblest thing, and that, that is exactly what it looks like as it comes."

"Very well." For once in a way, Melanie made no attempt to correct a younger girl's egregious grammar. I'll alert the staff; someone sensible—you, Lise, yes—run forward and make sure the men on the engine understand and come inside. Everyone else, keep calm, close all those windows and pull down the shades. Take off your blazers, if you haven't already, and loosen your ties. If you have anything to drink, then drink it now."

With which sequence of strange instructions she was gone, pelting down the aisle at a speed that would have led to any other girl being pulled up in short order; but Melanie was Head Girl, and this was indeed a true emergency. Every Crater School girl of any experience understood that when Mars offered one of its own particular suite of dangers, even the strictest rules could and would be set aside, in favour of survival.

Radhika was gaping rather, utterly bewildered.

"It's the dread simoom," Charm completely failed to explain. Then she caught herself with a giggle, and said, "Sorry, that probably didn't help much, did it? Let me try again. It's a windstorm that happens sometimes in summer, out here in the Dry, and it picks up tons of sand and throws it every which way, and it's *hot*. Not just the sand, I mean, the wind itself is hot. It's peculiar, and really, really scary. I had to stop the train so the driver and the stoker could get to cover. They could have died, else. We should be all right now, but stand ready. It's probably going to be awful. And if anyone tells you to do something, don't hesitate, just do it."

As a military brat—her father always insisted that stood for British Regiment Attached Traveller, but she thought he was having her on—Radhika was quite accustomed to taking orders. She nodded acquiescence, but said, "Why did we have to pull the shades down? I'd love to see—"

"You wouldn't love to see the windows break," Marigold said. "Which they could. The shades will keep the glass from flying everywhere, if they do."

"That," confirmed Charm, "and they'll help keep it a tiny bit cooler. Though you probably won't notice. It'll get scorching in here, if it passes right over us."

28

People had been scurrying busily up and down the aisles, conveying news and making arrangements between one carriage and the next. Now the doors were firmly closed, to isolate each from each; and a woman who must be a member of the school staff clapped her hands firmly for attention. She had it, immediately; you could have heard a pin drop, Radhika thought, remembering a teacher in Lucknow when she was little who would literally hold up a pin and ceremonially drop it to quiet the class down.

"Thank you, girls. Now for those few of you who don't know me, my name is Miss Peters, and I teach English. I know a few of you have encountered a simoom before; well, so have I. It can be quite a terrifying experience, but please trust that we are as safe in here as we can be. As I'm sure you will have gathered by now, it's about to grow very hot in here, as the storm passes over. Do not try to peek around the shades, those of you near the windows; that would certainly be dangerous for you, and could be dangerous for us all.

"The simoom is also remarkably loud, so be prepared for that." Radhika thought she could hear it already, indeed, a hissing sound, and that even before any of the blown sand could yet have reached the train. "If the carriage shakes, don't be alarmed; there has not been a simoom born that could overturn a masterpiece of Martian engineering like this train."

That brought a subdued cheer, which won them a smile before she held up a hand for silence once again.

"It should be over in twenty minutes or so; they are brief phenomena, the dread simooms. And yes, I know you all want to know why we always say "the dread simoom", and now I am going to tell you—or rather I am going to reveal the answer to you, through the performance of my party trick. When I was more or less your age, in my wicked youth—yes, I too was a Middle, once upon a time," which brought another cheer, significantly louder, "and I too committed sins without number against the school body and the rules thereof—on one particular occasion, and no, I am not going to tell you what I actually did to deserve it, I was condemned to learning the entirety of Felicia Heman's poem "The Caravans in the Deserts"—which, I may tell you, is very, very long—and then to recite it to the entire school at assembly.

"I threw myself into this task body and soul, which I advocate to you all as the only proper way to approach a punishment. I gave a performance that was hailed to the skies, and won me reprieve from all penalty else; and since that day, try as I might, I have never been able to forget a single word of the wretched thing. It is not a poem that I teach to my own girls, ever. However, on occasion, I can still call it forth; and what better occasion than this? Hark, I hear the rattle of pebbles on glass even now; I said, the simoom will be loud. However, I will be louder. I will endeavour to boom, rather than to shriek. Hold yourself in readiness to be awed, girls, at my achievement. I begin.

> "Call it not loneliness, to dwell
> In woodland shade or hermit dell,
> Or the deep forest to explore,
> Or wander Alpine regions o'er;
> For Nature there all joyous reigns,
> And fills with life her wild domains..."

There was, as she had promised, an awful lot of it. But she did indeed give it her all, parting imaginary trees as she explored the deep forest, shielding her eyes with her hand against the snow-glare of the Alpine regions as she looked about. It was glorious fun to watch her; the whole carriage was riveted by this most unlikely of poems.

"But he whose weary step hath traced
Mysterious Afric's awful waste,
Whose eye Arabia's wilds hath viewed,
Can tell thee what is solitude!
It is, to traverse lifeless plains,
Where everlasting stillness reigns,
And billowy sands and dazzling sky
Seem boundless as infinity!"

The girls too trod that awful waste, in her guiding foot-steps. They all but forgot their own predicament, in worry for that lone traveller that she portrayed.

When she came to

"What meteor comes?—a purple haze
Hath half obscured the noontide rays:
Onward it moves in swift career,
A blush upon the atmosphere;
Haste, haste! avert the impending doom,
Fall prostrate! 't is the dread Simoom!"

there came a cheer so loud in reply that not even the most dreadful of the dread simooms could have outblasted it, though that one outside was blowing its hardest and doing its best; and still the poem rolled on and on. Every mention of camels brought another cheer, and cries of "Good old Mabel!" which Radhika didn't understand at all, but never mind.

It was a marvellous, ecstatic performance, and the girls erupted in applause when at last, at long, long last, the poem came to its inevitable melancholy end.

"No stone their tale of death shall tell,
The desert guards its mysteries well;
And o'er the unfathomed sandy deep,
Where low their nameless relics sleep,
Oft shall the future pilgrim tread,
Nor know his steps are on the dead."

Miss Peters subsided into a seat, fanning herself with both hands. One by one, bench by bench, group by group, the girls realised just how hot it had grown in the carriage, and how bad the air. Their hair clung damply to their heads and necks; every breath they drew was uncomfortably, unpleasantly hot.

But the dread simoom's roar which had underscored Miss Peters' epic portrayal had died away to a whisper, to a hiss. A door at the far end of the carriage opened unexpectedly, and there was Melanie to say that all was safe now and no one hurt, that it would be perfectly in order to pull up the shades and throw the windows wide, that the men would have the train moving again as soon as humanly possible, and what on earth had been going on in here, to raise quite such a cacophony that it could be heard even above the aforementioned dread simoom?

Miss Peters raised a guilty hand. "I'm afraid that was me, Melanie, all my doing."

"Miss Peters, for shame! I expect you to know better, at your time of life!"

It was sheer joy, to hear a mistress scolded and to see her meekly submitting to it. Radhika gathered that this too was part of the fun, and that very likely Melanie had known exactly what was going on before she made her entrance. Or else they were both simply improvising, for the girls' entertainment.

Light and air were blessings indeed. The excitements of the last hour had raised the girls' energy to a fever pitch, to the extent that not even Melanie could keep them quiet. She stepped out of the carriage, somewhat surprising Radhika and a number of girls else, to judge by their comments and expressions, only to return after a minute with another girl, taller even than herself and perhaps a little older, a striking blonde not wearing the obligatory uniform but none the less surely not a member of the staff?

She was greeted with further good cheer, cries of "Rowany!" that almost, almost could withstand the solemn expression of displeasure on her face. They died in the end, though, as they had to do.

The presumptive Rowany nodded. "That's better. Honestly, Middles, what a rabble you are! I'm sure we were nothing so dreadful, were we, Mel, when we were scruffy fourths?"

"Sure?" Melanie asked, with a glint in her eye that overrode any objection to the word "scruffy".

"Here comes a story," Charm murmured to her neighbour. "They'll tell it between them, against each other, and it'll be the funniest thing you ever heard, and one more thing we will *not* be getting up to, because it's already been done. Rowany is a classic of her kind, a pillar of the school; she was Head Girl in my first term here, a year ago, and she was supposed to go up to Oxford after, only they sent her back to do an extra year of study. She is a joy and a delight, but you do *not* want to get in her bad books..."

Time passed, as it does on trains: both slowly and suddenly, in distracting spurts. They stretched their legs, roaming the aisles of every Crater School carriage, burying poor Radhika under a flood of names she could never hope to grasp, never mind remember; picnic foods were somehow produced from nowhere, sandwiches and fruit-filled pasties

33

and lemonade that wasn't simply delicious, the best she'd had, but also miraculously, impossibly cool; girls played cards, read books, chatted quietly amongst themselves or else gazed out of windows thinking their own thoughts— Radhika among them when she was allowed, when the table wasn't pulling her into yet one more game or argument or reminiscence—while the iron wheels beneath them ate away the distance, bringing them ever closer to journey's end.

The day had been an adventure, a voyage of discovery, all kinds of unexpected things. Radhika eyed herself askance, wondering if she had already been wooed away from her anger. It was a relief to find that no, that was still firmly in place, burning at the heart of her, a fierce glint of rage at her father and the school and the world and even God, for bearing down so cruelly upon her poor Mama-ji and thus causing all this in the first place, this, this personal dread simoom that had o'erswept her life and carried her away.

The actual simoom had delayed the train long enough that dusk was falling before they reached their destination. Lamps illuminated the station sign, *TERMINUS*. Radhika still thought that sounded a little ominous; but then, why not? This really did spell the end of the line, in more ways than one. She thought it was the end of everything she had loved, all her life long.

"Stay in your seats, please, girls. We will disembark in order, row by row. When your turn comes, stand up, take down your night-case, make sure you're leaving nothing behind you, and file out quietly. Line up on the platform; I want to see a march, not a mob."

Thus Miss Peters, who had stayed with their carriage. The girls obeyed her implicitly, shuffling out of the carriage in line astern to find prefects waiting on the platform, gesturing them into formation, two abreast.

"School, attention! March!"

At least Radhika knew how to march—she and the other army brats she grew up among had soaked it into their bones, throughout their long childhoods—though she'd never before done it with schoolgirls.

They marched to the end of the platform, wheeled left, and came to another, shorter, where a strange little compartment train was waiting for them, steam up. Lights glowed throughout, and every door stood open ready.

Charm steered Radhika by the elbow into the compartment Marigold had already claimed. All her other companions of the day piled in after them, and again there was—just—room enough.

"*Now* we can talk!" Charm exulted. "Maeve, close that door in a hurry, before some pree decides to join us, or worse, break us up."

The door slammed, the girls grinned at each other.

"I've never ridden the funic in the dark," Chrissy said. "I wonder if it's less scary because you can't see, or more scary because you can't see?"

"Why should it be scary at all?" Radhika asked. "And, come to that, what's a funic?"

"Funicular railway—which this one actually isn't, it's a rack-and-pinion," Charm didn't quite explain. "We call it the funicular anyway, because we always have, it's a school tradition; like greeting Miss Tolchard by that name every time, even though she's been Mrs Mackenzie for ever."

"Every time you tell me something," Radhika grumbled around a giggle, "I end up more confused than I was before."

The whole compartment laughed. "Welcome to school!" Marigold said. "But seriously, you'll get used to it all soon enough. And you've got Charm to sherp for you, and all the rest of us to help. We'll see you straight. And don't worry about the ride being scary; it's only Chrissy who needs to hold someone's hand when we go up the crater wall."

"It's so *steep*," Chrissy said, not at all abashed. "I always worry what would happen if we fell."

"And we always explain to her that it can't fall," Cate added, "and she worries anyway. She can't help it; Sister Anthony says it's a nervous condition. So I sit one side and Marigold sits the other, and we both take a hand each when we start to climb, and everyone's fine."

"Here we go!" Marigold declared as the guard's whistle blew and the little train jerked into motion. "Just one more lap, people, and then it's school again!"

Radhika could not imagine being that enthusiastic about going to school, never mind a school like this, that took you away from your parents, from everyone and everything you knew. She sat and seethed at the unfairness of it all, as the train trundled on into the dark.

# CHAPTER THREE

## Radhika's First Morning

Radhika lay in bed with her eyes closed, wishing she could close her ears too. She knew exactly where she was; the problem was sorting out her memories of how she came to be here, when it had been such a long, strange day and the end of it such a muddle. She remembered a most unlikely march along a lakeshore in the dark, following a lady with a lamp; she remembered a meal of some kind, eaten in one corner of a great and otherwise empty hall, in a most unlikely and utterly empty building. Then she remembered another brief march through the dark, to a big house where lights burned here and there, just exactly where they were needed for girls to find their way upstairs to dormitories, bathrooms and beds.

Miss Hendy the housemistress had been there at the door to welcome them all in, with quiet words for each, but it was Charm at her side who showed Radhika how to find whatever she needed—on tiptoe and in whispers, because earlier arrivals would already be asleep—and how to unpack and stow away her night-case, exactly where in her cubicle everything should go, "and don't ever leave anything out of place, because Sister Anthony is a *Tartar* who won't think twice before calling you out of lessons to put it straight, and there's no mistress likes you when she does that..."

No one would come to chivvy the latecomers out of bed, they had been assured; they were to have their sleep out, and come downstairs only when they were properly rested. But that same unusual leniency did not, of course, apply to any-one else. There were six girls in this dormitory, not counting the prefect, and three of them—Radhika herself, Charm on one side of her, Marigold the other—had licence to lie in. That left just three more, to make noise enough to rouse all the devils in hell, under the stinging whip of the prefect's voice: "Lauren, *will* you show a leg? Elana, you'll be late for your bath if you don't make haste, and I'm the one who follows you, remember, so don't you dare delay me. Agnosia Pratt, do you seriously mean to tell me you intend to leave your cubicle curtains looking like that...?"

Radhika was an only child, and had never shared a bed-room in all the years she could remember. She treasured peace and quiet, especially in the early morning, when she was accustomed to think over the previous day and put it all into order in her head. She'd never minded the distant bellows of drill sergeants on the parade square, or Tommies calling to each other around the camp, but this racket was impossible. Even holding her pillow tight over her head didn't help.

So when Charm thrust a tousled, outrageously red head through her cubicle curtains to take the measure of her charge, it was a scowling, irate Radhika she found sitting up in her pyjamas.

"I say! What's gone wrong for you?" Charm slipped inside the cubicle, taking the new girl's dressing gown off its hook and draping it around her shoulders. "We're not allowed to sit up in bed without a gown on. It does something terrible to our constitutions, according to Sister Anthony."

38

"You're not actually allowed to visit one another's cubicles either, Charm Buchanan." That from outside, the dorm prefect's ominous voice.

"No, Sophie, but she'll need my help this first morning. And prefects are always kind to new girls and their sherpas, early-doors."

That was met with a chuckle, and, "Very well—but where on Mars did you pick up that expression?"

"I heard a farmer use it, out on the Planum; I've been saving it up. Oh dear, is it slang?"

"Well, probably not exactly; more dialect, I should say. But if I were you, I should *not* say it in front of a staff, or a prefect. Or me," with another laugh. "And if I hear it spreading through the school, I'll know whom to blame, will I not?"

"Oh, but we have lots of girls from the Planum, any one of them might—"

"They might; but they have wisely chosen not to, at least in my hearing. Enough. Less arguing, more helping, young Charm."

"Yes, Sophie. Now, seriously, Radhika, what's got your goat, and how can I help?"

"Is it," Radhika tried to swallow down her bile, not to bite a girl who was only trying to be friendly and useful, "is it always so *noisy* here in the mornings?"

"Oh lord, yes." Charm sat on the new girl's mattress, all uninvited. "Too many girls with not enough baths between them and nowhere near enough time, prees at our heels like, like vigilant watchkeepers," correcting her course hastily, remembering the older girl outside. "It's Babel and Bedlam combined, and it'll be worse tomorrow. Don't worry, you'll get used to it soon enough. Now I think we might as well get up, don't you? Seeing as how we're both wide awake anyway, and you don't want to start off thinking you're allowed to dawdle. Not at the Crater School, not ever. Every minute is accounted for, you'll find. Put your slippers on, pick up your washbag, and I will explain the Holy Order of the Bath as we go..."

Twenty minutes later, Radhika knew which bathroom she was to use, whom she was to follow in its use, and who would be waiting to follow her. She knew what a frantic rush it was, to be in and out in time, and leaving the bath running for the next girl; she and Charm had had a trial run, and even a military brat with a no-nonsense father had never sponged herself down so quickly, and in cold water too. Sister Anthony approved of cold baths, apparently. Quite who Sister Anthony might be, and quite why—he? she?—they had such a peculiar name, she had not yet found breath or time enough to ask, as Charm hurried her this way and that about her morning ablutions.

Now they were coming downstairs, spruce and groomed and their cubicles left just so, with Radhika despairing of the notion of doing all that by herself in half the time; and here was Melanie Fitzwalter in all her head-girl glory, waiting at the foot. With, Radhika was unsurprised to see, a list.

"Good morning, girls! We're too late for breakfast up at the Castle, of course, so Miss Hendy has been kind enough to summon us all to eat with her. Charm, was there *any* sign of Marigold when you left Curie dormy? She is the last of us, and Lord knows I don't want to go up there and personally stir her stumps, but we're keeping Miss Hendy waiting."

Charm grinned. "Don't worry, she was splashing and dashing just moments ago; I expect—yes, here she comes," loud footfalls on the stairs above announcing her friend's hasty arrival.

"Excellent." Melanie ran a critical eye over the newcomer, nodded a little reluctantly, and said, "You'll do, Marigold— but you'll do better tomorrow, or I'll know the reason why. Come along, all. A feast awaits."

A feast indeed awaited. Radhika was reluctant to admit it, but the sideboard did look tremendously attractive, with its chafing-dishes of bacon and eggs, its mounds of rolls and plates of butter, bowls of glistening marmalade; and there was even more. Her eye slid on, then jerked back.

"Oh!"

Yet once more she had seized everyone's attention, all unwillingly.

"Yes, Radhika?" Miss Hendy was laughing at her kindly, knowing exactly what she'd done.

"You, you made *rava uttapam*!"

"I did indeed. I shared rooms in Oxford with a girl whose father ran a successful import and export business in Madras. She taught me many an Indian dish in our time together. Also, I am extremely proud to tell you that Geeta Anand became Mrs Peter Hendy, and thus my sister-in-law; and that they asked me to act as godmother to their firstborn daughter Lakshmi. Who is already enrolled on the books here at the Crater School, you may depend on that, as and when she comes of age."

Was it Radhika's imagination, or was Miss Hendy sending her a message, to say that her mixed blood and dark skin mattered not at all here? She wasn't sure, and she didn't quite dare to hope.

Besides, she was going to hate the place. She hadn't forgotten that.

"Now, girls," to the assembled throng. "Take plates, help yourselves and each other, find seats at the table. It's a bit of a squash, but you'll all fit. Those of you who are bold enough, let Radhika show you the proper way to roll *rava uttapam* and dip it in the chutney. Yes, Marigold, in this one instance you may eat with your fingers, as is only proper. That does *not* mean you may make an egg-and-bacon sandwich, no..."

After they had feasted and washed their fingers in lemon-scented water and cleared away and cleaned up after themselves, Miss Hendy chased them all back to their responsibilities, "for the school day stops for no girl; no, Marigold, not even the first day of term, you know how hectic this day is for everyone, so go on, be about it, shoo"— except for Radhika and Charm. "You two stay a minute, please. Step out into the garden with me, it's such a lovely day…"

Miss Hendy was a gardener. Radhika knew it, the moment she paused by the back door to don a hat and pick up a trug of tools. Every camp and barracks Radhika had known housed such women, who patrolled their patches with the diligence of sentries at the gate, and could never step outside without a trowel or a pair of secateurs, in case of need.

Miss Hendy led the girls to a rosebed, and began to deadhead those blooms that had gone over. As she worked, she talked:

"Our headmistress Miss Leven will see you later in the day, Radhika, to welcome you formally to the Crater School, but I always like to speak with my new girls first. You're the only one I have this term, and I know you came under special circumstances, just as Charm did a year ago, for reasons beyond anyone's control.

"Of course you'll want to visit your mother, as often as you're able. I will see what I can do to arrange that. Sunday is the usual day for our girls to cross the water—oh, but you arrived in darkness; you won't have seen it yet, our great Sanatorium on the other side of the lake—but I do need to take counsel with her doctors first, to learn when they think would be best for you to see her. We may not contrive to do that this week, so don't set your hopes on the coming Sunday. Be patient, and know that everyone is working to make it happen as soon as may be, yes?"

"Er, yes, Miss Hendy. Thank you..."

"Now, on to other matters. I don't think you've been away to school before, have you?"

"No, Miss Hendy." Barrack schools and camp schools: some years she'd hardly been to school at all, only the occasional lessons in drawing or music from a bored army wife. Those had been the best times, when she could run wild with friends of any colour and any caste, quite unsupervised.

"Well, you'll find it different from anything you've experienced before; but everyone here knows that, and will be prepared to make allowances, so long as you're obviously trying to find your feet. You've come to a happy house, or I like to think so. As your official sherpa, Charm should be your first port of call when you run into trouble, as you inevitably will; but if there's ever anything you need help with that you don't want to discuss with a classmate, then either take it to a prefect—you've met Melanie, I know; she has an ever-open ear for schoolgirl troubles—or bring it to me if you want to talk it over with a grown-up. You do know what *in loco parentis* means, yes? Good, good. It's the literal truth here, you'll find; I stand in for both your parents at once. Anything you'd say to them, you can say to me, and I'll do my best to respond as I believe they would wish me to."

"Um, yes, Miss Hendy." She doubted that, really, after some of the things she'd said to her father in recent days. Or some of the things he'd said to her.

"Meanwhile, a word to the wise—which in Latin is *verbum sapienti sat est*, if you're curious. We do not allow slang at this school; we expect our girls to speak brightly, clearly and the Empress's English, except when studying or practising another tongue. I have a cousin who grew up as you did, in military India; when he was sent Home to public school, his language was so riddled with Hindustani phrases and a kind of pidgin English that his masters had literally to beat it out of him.

"We will not be threatening you with corporal punishment, of course; but if, as I guess, you have a tendency to slip into a similar argot unthinkingly, try to keep a curb on your tongue until you have learned to think about it and choose another phrase. I'm sorry to play the harsh taskmaster, but we really cannot have that or any other patois spreading through the school, and I know very well how certain tricks of the tongue can catch on among teenage girls."

"Oh!" Indignation burned like fire in her soul—they wanted to take her own *language* away from her now?—but very well, then. "I will try," she promised, and she would indeed, quite grimly, "but I should tell you I have already used *Mama-ji* and *Papa-ji* to the girls on the train, and explained what they meant."

Miss Hendy smiled. "I doubt any of the girls will adopt those as terms of use, dear; and I don't believe we've ever tried to regulate any girl's way of addressing her parents. We hear such a range across the school, that would be an impossible task, besides breaking lifelong habits and their parents' own wishes. No, you may keep those; but if you could keep them largely within your family, it might be best. And Charm will help to remind you, if she hears you say anything untoward. Won't you, Charm?"

"Yes, of course, Miss Hendy. Um, I did say that Radhika would be free to speak to Maya and Samira in Hindustani, if she liked to. I hope that was right?"

"Oh heavens, yes. It's mingling words from the Raj into English that we would need to stamp on. Oh, and we may wish to offer you elocution lessons, Radhika, because I do hear a certain—subcontinental lilt—in your voice, that is not really appropriate to English speech. That would be an extra cost, of course, so I must take it to your father; but there is a woman in Terminus who helps a number of our girls to speak properly."

Oh, so now she didn't even speak English properly? Radhika seethed, her hands in fists behind her back. She said nothing, though—well, she wouldn't want to offend Miss Hendy's ears with her impure *lilting* voice, now would she?

"Now, you have a busy day ahead of you, and we're late getting you started. Sister Anthony will supervise your unpacking personally, this afternoon; I'm afraid the rest of your morning must be spent head-down over a number of tests that the staff has set for you, to help us determine which class you should be put in. Charm will take you up to the Castle now, so that you can buckle down to it. We've set some tables aside in Hall, Charm, with Rowany overseeing. Off you trot now."

"Yes, Miss Hendy."

It was possible that her fury was showing on her face. One glance, and Charm bit back her usual cheerful chatter and led Radhika in silence up towards the main school building.

This was Radhika's first time, seeing it in daylight. When she stopped glowering at her new school shoes for long enough to raise her head and look at it—well, she stopped walking too, and simply stared.

"It, it really is a castle!"

"Well, not *really* really," Charm said, relieved that the new girl had found her voice at last. "It was built as a hotel, just made to look like a castle; only it failed, and it was all kinds of other things before Miss Tolchard found it and bought it for our school. Now, we go in this way," through a tall gated archway in what was clearly the back of the building, with high narrow stained glass windows on either side. "That's the library on our left, and the chapel on our right. You can go in and out of the library through that door, but only if the library is where you're meant to be, you can't use it as a shortcut to the rest of the school, though of course everyone does. And the chapel door you mustn't use at all, and that one honestly nobody does. 'T'wouldn't be respectful, really. Mostly we come through here," into a sunny courtyard. "That's the main way in," a flight of stairs leading to an imposing studded-oak double doorway, "but today we go this way," a shorter run of steps up to a pair of French windows, "into the dining hall. The staff all call it Hall, with a capital H, as if we were a proper Oxford college, but mostly we just say the hall. Staff are silly sometimes. Rowany," as her flood of words carried them through the open windows—or were they doors when they stood wide, Radhika wondered, and only windows when they were closed?—and into a high, long space where tables stood in tidy rows, each with benches either side and a chair at one end, "I've brought you a new victim."

Two of those tables were in use, a dozen girls or so bent over papers, scribbling furiously. The extremely tall girl from the train—who had told that *ridiculous* story about the samovar and the trumpet mouthpiece, and Radhika did *not* believe that could ever have worked, not in a million years— was supervising casually from a chair, if leafing through a magazine could count as supervisory in any sense whatever. She glanced up at their entrance, and smiled.

"Ah, you must be Radhika Harvey, yes? Splendid. Here is your spot on the bench of pain," with an airy, elegant gesture, "and here are the instruments of torture," a stack of typed papers, lined writing-paper, pens and pencils. "Ah, don't look so alarmed, girly," with a sympathetic laugh, "it isn't as bad as it looks. One hint I will share: use the neatest hand you can. They never say, but that's one of the things they're looking for. This school is very fond of elegance in all things. Now off you go, and do not pause for breath. Milk and biscuits at eleven. Thank you, Charm; you may rendezvous with your victim again at noon. Scatter off about your own occasions now, pet, there may be one or two other things expected of you today, one or two..."

Charm groaned, turned on her heel, and ran.

Radhika took her seat, drew the first test towards her— English, of course, now that she knew how they looked down on all her spoken versions of it—and gritted her teeth, and began.

# CHAPTER FOUR

## Assessments

"So. We come to Radhika Harvey, then. Thoughts?"

It was the evening of their first full day back, and Miss Leven the headmistress had as usual been invited to join the mistresses in their Staff Room to talk over any issues arising, and particularly any new girls.

A series of grunts and chuckles ran around the room. Miss Leven raised an eyebrow. "I see. Like that, is it? She seemed a perfectly nice girl when I interviewed her, if a little ... reserved?"

"*Reserved* is not quite the word," Miss Harribeth murmured, "for someone who can only speak through clenched teeth."

"Oho! Do go on."

"Well, I can tell you this, that after a brief examination on paper I learned that like many of her kind, she knows a great deal about the Empire in India, and precious little history else; and after an oral investigation, I gathered that she is intelligent and willing to work, if only to catch up with her cohort and not be put to shame in a lower class—and also that her beloved father is a traitor, a brute, a tyrant and an oppressor, and she holds us and ours in derision and contempt."

"Demeter Harribeth, she did not say that!"

"Not in so many words, I grant you, but she would scorn to hide it behind anything more than a veneer of manners."

"Oh, dear! Well, but we've had plenty of girls before who did *not* want to come to us, and made their feelings about the matter perfectly clear, and yet they all settled within a term or two. I don't believe any of them failed to serve out their time here, in the end; nor, blessedly, have we ever yet had to send anyone home." Miss Leven reached out a superstitious hand to touch the coffee-table at her elbow, just in case. "A fit of the sullens is something we are experienced in and well equipped to deal with. Who's next?"

"I wouldn't say she's sullen, so much as sheerly angry." Thus Miss Tattersall, the mathematics mistress. "There's a hot focus to her, a core of fire within. Also, my dears, I am here to tell you that she has been woefully undertaught in all areas that touch my interest, except in those that have touched hers. She could, I am sure, lay a barrage to a nicety; I'm tolerably sure that some gunnery sergeant found her the opportunity to do so, or at least to fire a single gun at a target, with a devoted squad of Tommies in attendance. Also she could plan and lay out a campsite, and many another military task that involves the use of numbers on the ground. Beyond that, she is entirely at sea."

"Oh, dear. Again, though, this has not been uncommon in our experience, and we can probably catch her up. Miss Whitworth?"

"She knows cricket, of course; what army brat does not, especially coming from the Raj? If any of that heat in her comes out as energy, I might like to look at her for the Senior interschool matches, at least as twelfth man; you know I like to blood them early, if they show any signs of promise. Otherwise, she has played street-games with urchin children, and very little organised sport at all."

"She may take to it like a duck to water; we can hope so, at any rate. Miss Llewellyn, what does she know of music?"

"Much, and little. Which is to say that all the teaching she has had came from her mother, whom I gather to be quite an exceptional musician, in her way. Unfortunately, her way is not our way. Young Radhika has been trained to that curious nasal Indian style of singing, in Lydian scales and worse, scales far beyond my humble understanding. I find her musicianship quite remarkable—and I have absolutely no idea what to do with it. Of course I will introduce her to Western music, and I make no doubt that she can master it; but I don't want to spoil what she has, because it's quite extraordinary."

"Pair her off with Lois Shannon," a suggestion from the corner, from the art mistress and far-famed sculptress Isobel Buchanan. "One special talent with another. Let them … explore each other's knowledge, if you see what I mean. Mayhap they'll find some musical common ground where they can stand together."

"Yesss… Yes, that I can certainly do. Thank you, Isobel. And then there are the Pandit sisters, of course. I don't know if their experience has crossed at all with Radhika's, but it would be interesting to find out."

"Good!" Miss Leven said cheerfully. "We make progress. Who else?"

Miss Peters groaned softly. "Me, I suppose. Her written English is … well, Indian, in inflection and vocabulary, where it is not pure Army. I can throttle that back, at least somewhat; it may still be flowery, but at least not perfumed. Her handwriting, on the other hand, I despair of. It's immaculate, and thoroughly legible—and as ornate as temple Arabic inscriptions, if you've seen those. Worse than her language."

"I'll be interested to see that," Isobel Buchanan again, musingly. "If it's as intricate as I think you mean, I won't touch it; but I can probably train her in another hand altogether, to bring her down from the ethereal to the merely human."

"That would be a blessing. Again, thank you."

Isobel bowed her head gracefully, amusement dancing in her eyes. She was looking forward to her first encounter with this particular prodigy.

No one offered anything particularly new thereafter, until they came at last to Miss Hendy, Radhika's housemistress as well as the school's passionate instructor in Natural and Native Sciences.

"I fear I may have inadvertently provoked that ire that others among you have encountered," she confessed. "I did drop a couple of hints this morning, firstly about that awful polyglot slang we've heard from other Anglo-Indians, and then about the singsong tone that you may have heard, those of you who have spoken to her in person. I meant no harm, I only wanted to ease the child into the tenor of our ways before she encountered her first prefect in their wrath; but I could see immediately that she took it much awry. We may be in for turbulent times, I fear, in that regard. *Mea culpa, mea maxima culpa.* I will do what I can to make amends.

"As to my own subjects, I never expect Earth girls to know much if anything about Martian flora and fauna; but she does know a respectable amount about the same in India, as you might expect, and I hope to light another kind of spark in her, over time; that's an interest that may readily transfer.

"Otherwise—well, as her housemistress, I have undertaken to query the Sanatorium about when she may be allowed to visit her mother there. You all know, I take it, about—? Yes, I presumed so. I think we need to take that into account in all our dealings with her, until she settles here. Though I confess to being curious, as to why she has taken so much agin us from the start. What girl doesn't want to be close to her ailing mother, when offered the chance? Especially one with Radhika's upbringing, with her father away much of the time on duty and only her mother for family?"

"One who has idolised her father all her life," Miss Leven said wryly, "and seen him broken, and remade as a poor imitation of himself. No, I will say no more about that; I have heard nothing more than whispers, and I'm not sure it would be proper to pursue those. But there has been trouble in their past, that much I'm sure of, down on Earth; and he at least is troubled about the life he's been able to build for them here, even aside from his wife's dreadful sickness. Well, well. Enough for now. Matters will play out as they must, over time, and we will learn a great deal more about Radhika Harvey, I deem, before term is out. Some of it may well surprise us, as our girls so often do. Might there be more coffee in that pot, at all...?"

Two sisters, both alike in flame-haired glory, making their way up the hill in cricket whites after an exhilarating house match, Stokes versus Jopling:

"I must say, Charm, your ... sherpee? ... Radhika is really quite something, isn't she?"

Charm glanced around, to be sure the girl in question was not in hearing. "That would be an understatement," she said, with a little groan.

Levity cocked her head consideringly. "Obviously, I've only really had to do with her on the pitch so far, but she was like a young demon this afternoon: batting like a girl possessed, bowling like a fury, chasing every ball that came anywhere near her and hurling them back hard enough to break a stump... If that's what they teach them in India, maybe we should send all our prospects down for a season. Radhika of the Raj: it has quite a ring to it, don't you think?"

"Radhika of the Rage, more like it," Charm said gloomily.

"Well, I grant you she will need to cut back on the yelling at her own teammates, when they don't play up to her satisfaction, or Miss Whitworth is going to have some serious words with her. 'Tain't gentlemanly, for one thing; and I am not sure all those words were quite according to Hoyle, even in British India. You might drop her a gentle hint, to save trouble later. Otherwise Melanie will do it, and then it won't be gentle at all."

"No, you don't understand, Liv. The point is, she's like that all the time. Not yelling at people, I don't mean, just, just seething inwardly. I mean, I like her, I think, or I want to; but she's so cross about everything, it's hard to keep up."

"Ah, I think I see. Is she like Rachel Abramoff, just very much not wanting to be here?"

"Oh, so *very* much. She's furious about it, and so she's furious at her father for sending her, and at all of us for being here, and at the school for existing. I think she's even furious at her mother, for being in the Sanatorium and so causing all of this in the first place."

"Hmm. Is she unfriendly to you, or rude to the staff or the prees, or anything like that?"

"No-o. Sometimes she's snappish, sometimes she's offhand, at least with us; but nothing out of the way. And if she'd cheeked a staff or a pree, I think we'd have heard about it. From her, most likely, as something else to be angry about."

"Oh, lor'. Sounds like you've got yourself a handful, kid. And your first time sherping, too."

"I don't suppose you have any brilliant ideas, do you, Liv? I think I need help."

"Well, I don't, not just off the cuff—except for the obvious one, I mean, and I don't suppose you'd care for that."

"What's that?" Briefly, there was a spark of hope in Charm's eyes.

"Ask for it, you goop. Take this to Mamma. Or to Rowany, or Melanie, or Miss Hendy. They're always telling us to go to them with our problems, aren't they, if we can't resolve them on our own?"

"Well, yes, I know—but I don't, I don't want to seem to be giving up, not this early, and as you say, my first time being asked to sherp anyone."

"That's what I thought. We Buchanans are an independent lot, by and large. All right, kid. You carry on muddling through as best you can, and I'll see what I can come up with meantime. And see if you can't burn off more of that furious energy of hers with sports and games. Try her with the ponies, too. If she's Raj-bred and Army too, I'm willing to bet she rides."

"Oh, Liv! That's brilliant! Thank you so much! I'll go and ask her right now...!"

Charm had been pony-mad her whole life, and would have moved bodily into the school's stables if allowed. She skipped off down the hill again in search of her errant charge, leaving her elder sister to watch after her with a lingering smile on her face.

"That," Radhika said decisively, "is not a pony."

Charm giggled, while Elle and Pete grinned at her from either side of the couched and cud-chewing Mabel, where they were brushing dust and mud from her coat. Mabel herself ignored the newcomers loftily—but only for a moment, as Radhika stepped confidently forward to meet the camel eye to eye.

"Um, be careful," Charm murmured, as Elle reached hastily for Mabel's head-rope. "She has been known to bite..."

"She won't bite me. Will you, *Rani, meri jaan...*?" she cooed, as she lifted a hand to Mabel's nose.

For a wonder, Mabel didn't even grumble, never mind lunge. She sniffed at Radhika's fingers, then gazed at the ceiling in an open invitation to scritch her under the chin.

Radhika obliged, still murmuring endearments, while the other three girls gazed upon her with varying measures of disbelief.

"I have never," Elle said slowly, "*never* seen her behave that way with a stranger."

"Ah, but I'm not a stranger," Radhika said, laughing, ducking aside as Mabel swung her head like an amiable cudgel, wanting more attention to be paid to her ears now. "There's a camel sisterhood, and I've been a proud member all my life. Well, all until we came to Mars; but camels still know their own. How, though, is there a camel here?"

She gazed about the loose box as though she might suddenly spy an answer for herself, but nothing availed. There was a well-worn saddle, yes, and empty saddlebags, ropes and harness, all the appurtenances you might need to ride a camel even across the Dry; but never a hint as to cause or origin.

"She's mine," Elle said, a little awkwardly, possibly even blushing. "I, um, rode her here. From a mining camp."

Wait, she really had ridden her across the Dry? "That ... must have been quite a journey." Radhika had had some acquaintance with deserts, as well as with the camels of her father's troop.

"In the middle of that dreadful duststorm last year," Pete added, to make the occasion even more impressive.

"Oh! Oh, my—we caught some of that, even in Marsport. Out in the Dry, it must have been ... epic." She could think of no word else that would suit.

Elle shrugged, and turned back to her brushing. "She looked after me, the way she always has. She's an easy ride, if she likes you; want to try? She won't let you fall."

"Of course she won't, will you, bright-eyes?" That saddle was nothing like the Army's that she was used to, but she'd manage. She was young yet, and flexible. "I don't suppose there's time now, but..."

"*Definitely* no time now," Charm interrupted, before either of the older girls could do so. "We have to get back for prep, and you haven't even *met* the ponies yet. I don't quite know how it is, but everything you do in the Crater School always ends up being done in a terrible rush before the next thing's due. There's never any loose *time*..."

"You were absolutely right, Liv, of course you were; only that you were righter even than you know. Radhika isn't only a horse person, though she did pretty much grow up in the saddle, she says; but she's camel-crazy too, and she and Mabel fell in love at first sight, if you can believe it, and we're all going to go out riding together with Elle on Sunday, and..."

As it happened, Levity had heard all this already from Elle herself, but she was perfectly happy to let her younger sister bubble on to her heart's content. Charm had been such a worried little person just a few hours ago, and now she seemed to have shed that burden entirely and be back to her normal cheerful positive self.

"...And she'd been ever so much a nicer person since, she hasn't snapped at me once since cricket, or at anyone else either, that I saw."

*Work a girl hard and then find her a reward she'll actually value, and she won't have time or inclination for temper tantrums.* That was one of their mother's wisdoms, for Isobel Buchanan was fond of showing her daughters the very mechanisms of their raising. Human nature was all her subject, and she thought perhaps the proper subject of all art; the more they understood it from the inside out, the better young humans they would be, and the more they would find in themselves to offer to the world. That was her philosophy, at least, and she did think it was working out rather well so far.

"Well, but don't go expecting any overnight miracle, kiddo. Chances are she'll understand  soon enough that she can't spend all day and every day in the stables any more than you can, and then she'll add that to her list of grudges against all and sundry, and be just as grouchy as before."

"Still, at least we do know now that she can be nice, and even happy here," Charm said. "That's something, isn't it? Something we can work on."

"It absolutely is. I'm just saying, you will need to put in the work. It took us half a term and more to bring Rachel around, and even then it didn't really happen until her sister appeared out of the blue that way."

Charm grinned. "It's funny, isn't it, that out of the nine of you in the Crew, two of them both ran away *to* the Crater School?"

"For very different reasons, but indeed it is. Run along now, brat. Your bedtime is looming, and if your little friends aren't looking for you to plot mischief, my name isn't Levity Buchanan..."

# CHAPTER FIVE

## Letters Home, and Lessons out of School

From Radhika Harvey at the Crater School, to her mother at the Lowell Crater Sanatorium, translated (somewhat freely) from the original Hindustani:

*Dearest Mama-ji,*

*My housemistress Miss Hendy has spoken to your doctors on the telephone, and they say it's too early for me to visit you yet, but perhaps next week so long as you continue to improve; so mind you eat all your meals and take all your medicines and focus on getting better, because if I have to wait any longer before I see you I will surely die.*

*It's ever so frustrating being this close to you—just over the water!—and not being able to see you, but at the same time it's still the best thing about coming here. I can look across the lake and imagine that you're doing the same, that we're both thinking of each other at the same time. And I always wave you goodnight before we're sent to bed. Which is far too early, by the way. Grrr!*

*You'll never guess what, Mama-ji—they don't only have a pony-stable here, they have a camel too! Her name is Mabel, and she's the sweetest thing. She belongs to an Upper-Fourth girl named Elle, who rode her here, by herself, all across the Dry! Through that dreadful haboob earlier this year! People say that she wanted to come here to learn how to be a girl, which seems daft to me, but never mind. Her best friend is called Pete, and tries everything she can to be as boyish as possible. They're very funny, but rather nice, I think. We're all going on a ride together this afternoon, and Elle says I can Box-and-Cox with her, swapping pony and camel rides on the way out and coming back again. I can't wait to be on the back of a camel again!*

*Oh, and there's something else in the stables, two something-elses (or do I mean somethings-else?)—sandkits! A girl here found them abandoned, and we think their mother must have been killed by a farmer protecting his lambs, so they've been raised here at school. They earn their keep by patrolling the vegetable gardens at night and keeping down the sand-rats, so they're always really sleepy when we take them their milk in the mornings, but they're awake and active after school, and when we've finished looking after the ponies—and Mabel, of course!—we can play-wrestle with them. They're very good, and always play paddy-paws so nobody gets scratched. I think they understand what weak and fragile creatures we are...*

*All of that is great fun, but otherwise—and apart from being so near to you—I really wish I was back in Marsport with Papa-ji and my friends at dear old St Dymphna's. Do hurry up and get well, so we can go home together! Pretty please!*

*The teachers here—we're supposed to call them "mistresses" or "staff", though I don't know why that matters—are horribly strict in lessons. You get scolded for looking out of a window, or for whispering in class even if you're only trying to borrow a pencil, or for half a hundred other things. And I get in trouble just because I don't know things I was never taught before— "Great heavens, child, have you never been taught to reason from cause to effect?" Well, no, actually, I haven't. I didn't know what she meant at all. So she had to stop and explain it to me, and then I was scolded again for holding up all the rest of the class, as if it was my fault that lessons at St Dymphna's were so very different from here.*

*So no, not everything is sunshine and roses here—or even camels and sandkits!—but don't you worry about me. I'll just buckle down and do better, and show them that I'm not as stupid as they think, and that St Dymph's is just as good a school as this place even if it's not so grand.*

*I said not to worry about me, and I meant it—but you're not to worry about anything at all, do you hear me, Mama-ji? Your only job is to get better, and get us both back home. If it helps, you could think of that as rescuing me, like the princess trapped in the castle from that old Persian fairy-tale you used to tell me when I was little. I mean, I may not be a princess, even if you did call me your little rani, but I really am living in a castle here. Or a pretend one, at any rate. This place is crazy, it has towers and battlements and a drawbridge and a portcullis and everything, if you can believe it...*

*[...]*

*Anyway, I have to stop now; there's never time enough for anything here, before you have to dash off and do something else, though woe betide you if you leave anything unfinished, ever. The prefects are even worse than the teachers, if you can believe it, and one of them—the Head Girl, as it happens—has her beady eyes on me right this minute...*

*Write back if you're well enough, Mama-ji, but otherwise, just concentrate on getting better and rescuing your poor languishing daughter from her trials and tribulations...*

*With ever so much love,*

*Radhi*

\* \* \*

"My heavens, Radhika! No wonder you were last to finish, that's quite a packet you've written there!"

Melanie took the envelope with a friendly smile, ticked Radhika's name off her list, then glanced casually at the address before adding it to her box of sealed letters.

The smile shifted to a puzzled frown. "Wait a minute, though; I thought your people were in Marsport?"

Radhika stiffened. "My father is. I wrote to my mother."

"But, my dear child, this is supposed to be your weekly letter home."

"How is my mother not my home? I have two parents, not in the same place. And my mother is in hospital, so of course I chose to write to her. Is that not allowed?"

"Well, I suppose... But your mother is a few scant miles away and you have every hope of seeing her very soon, while your father is far from here and no doubt anxious to hear from his only daughter, how she's settling in and so forth. When we say "letters home", we do commonly have in mind the address you live at, the parent or guardian who sent you here."

"Am I not to write to my mother, then?"

"Oh, don't be ridiculous, Radhika! Of course you may write to your mother. I do feel that something is owed to your father too, however. Perhaps you'd better find time this afternoon. At least write him a quick note, and I'll pass that on this occasion, if I have your promise that you'll send a proper letter next week."

"I'm going riding this afternoon."

"Yes, well. Nevertheless. Write it immediately after lunch, and you won't delay your friends too long. There's plenty else to distract them in the stable yard."

\* \* \*

From Radhika Harvey at the Crater School, to her father at the Blue Dolphin Hotel in Marsport:

*Dear Father,*

*I am told I must write to you instead of Mama-ji.*

*I have arrived safely, although we were caught in a Dread Simoom which might have proved fatal to us all.*

*I have not been allowed to visit Mama-ji.*

*I am not to be permitted to use our own Anglo-Indian language, which I have spoken all my life; it is slang, and unladylike.*

*Also you are to be asked to pay for elocution lessons for me, as I have an unpleasant singsong accent. I expect I picked it up from Mama-ji.*

*I am healthy, and the food is good.*

*The teachers are dissatisfied with my work. I will try to improve.*

*Now I must run.*

*Your daughter,*

*Radhika Harvey.*

\*　　\*　　\*

"Radhika, you've been an age! You've missed all the fun of tacking up, and we had the sandkits out here to help, which was hilarious if not exactly terribly helpful, and what have you been *doing* all this time?"

"Something Melanie Fitzwalter said I had to do."

Wise in her generation, Charm recognised the scowl on her charge's face and backed off hastily. "Well, never mind, then. When Melanie says to jump, we ask how high—and this is Mars, of course, so we jump higher than you ever did on Earth. Anyway, we're all ready to go, and we'd best go now, if we're to get all the way around the lake before suppertime. We've picked out the three liveliest ponies—because honestly, you never heard me say it, but some of them are just *puddings*—to give us the most fun rides, and Elle says if you just let her start Mabel off and get her settled, because she is a *little* noisy and disgruntled when she first gets rousted out of her nice comfy loose-box, you can swap as soon as you'd like to..."

The ponies were little round tubs, full of fun and frolics and no apparent brains at all. Mabel was a thoughtful, deliberate creature, a slow swaying ride who placed her feet with care, gazed down on all her company with scorn, and absolutely declined to be hurried.

She was saddled desert-style and ridden with a simple head-rope, rather than the military saddle and reins that Radhika was accustomed to, so it took a little while for each of them to adjust to the other. They soon enough settled to each other's habits, though, and Radhika revelled in her first camel ride on Mars, her first for years.

The girls called to each other in high, clear voices and raced their ponies ahead, and then waited till Radhika caught up at Mabel's steady amble.

"Want to swap back?" Elle asked, looking awkwardly leggy in a pony-saddle, even with the stirrups let down to their furthest length. She saw Radhika's face fall at the suggestion, and laughed, and said, "No matter, then. You enjoy Mabel; I'm having fun enough. Look, there's the San ahead. There are safe to be patients out on the lawns, it's such a lovely day; those who can't walk, the nurses wheel them out onto the terrace still in their beds. Maybe you'll see your mother! We always give them a wave in any case..."

Peer as she might, Radhika couldn't quite persuade herself that she could actually see her mother's tiny figure among the distant patients. They were strictly forbidden to go any closer than the lake path without special permission, "and there's always prees and staff there on Sunday afternoons, so they'd know, sure as eggs is eggs," according to Charm. Radhika contented herself with waving wildly from atop Mabel, and hoping against hope that her mother might be able to see her and to know her.

A number of cheerful hands waved back, some clad in Crater School colours, some in hospital whites. Riding on, Radhika tried to feel boosted, as though anywhere that took such kind care of their patients must surely be able to find a cure for Mama-ji; but again, her native honesty overrode any such special pleading. Chances of recovery from this particular disease were low, and not noticeably improving despite the good doctors' work here and elsewhere in the province. It was too rare to have been studied much; they still didn't even know how it was passed on, let alone how best to treat it. Papa-ji had told Radhika that her mother might never return from the Sanatorium, and that if she did, it would likely be in a wheelchair, if not an iron lung. It was a terrible thing— but it did of course make it certain that they couldn't leave Radhika here at school, because Papa-ji could never take care of a bedbound patient on top of all his work at the Blue Dolphin. He'd have to depend on her help, he'd simply have to.

Coming back over the playing fields—skirting the sacred cricket square, of course: Mabel might not do much damage with her padded feet, but pony-hooves would tear the pitch to rags—they found a tall, tall, very tall figure in the stable yard, playing not-exactly-fetch with the sandkits. They had a knotted rope's-end that they loved to chase if you tossed it for them, and then wrestle over and tug-of-war between themselves, until one would aggravate the other just a little too much and they'd abandon the rope in favour of fighting each other for a spell. They never had caught on to the idea of bringing it back to the human element in the game, so said human was obliged to cross the yard and fetch it herself, before waiting till they were ready to chase again.

"Rowany!"

She was too tall and they were too few in number actually to mob her, but Radhika's three companions did their best nonetheless, staying mounted for the sake of a few extra mobbing inches. Radhika herself held back, and slid quietly down from Mabel's back to watch.

"Calm down, you wretches! I'm hardly a rare sight hereabouts. And it's not you I'm here for, anyway." Piercing blue eyes turned in Radhika's direction. "I am charged with a mission to our newest member. Radhika Harvey, we meet again." A cool hand, at the end of a long arm; a slow, considering handshake, while she felt as though those eyes penetrated to the very core of her soul, while revealing nothing of what they saw there. "Come and walk with me awhile."

"Oh, but I can't! I, I've got to see to Mabel..." Even where there were grooms and stable hands available—or, more commonly in her case, a barracksful of devoted Tommies— she had always understood that a rider's first duty is to their mount, to see the animal clean and comfortable and settled, fed and watered.

"On this occasion, my sweet, you must render up to Elle that which is Elle's, while Pete and Charm tackle three ponies between the two of them. I don't believe for a moment that will put either of them out, so don't even pretend, you two."

"No, Rowany."

"No, Rowany."

"Thank you. Radhika, you and I will corral those wild beasts," the sandkits, who were summing up their chances of pouncing on a pony without getting kicked, "and take them up to their place of employment, and talk along the way."

The kits interacted with humans in a state of amiable neutrality. They were certainly in no sense tame; but they liked their accommodations here, they liked their company, they liked regular meals and regular games, and they were creatures of habit, fond of routine. They were quite accustomed by now to having heavy chain leashes clipped to their harnesses, and padding quietly along beside their wardens on the path up to the walled vegetable garden for their night-long patrol.

There was no doubt in anybody's mind that had they wished, the kits could have scaled that eight-foot wall with ease and vanished into their native hills. The fact that they'd never tried was largely taken as a compliment, though a few cynical souls did hold that the beasts were merely grown lazy and preferred the easy life offered at the school.

This was Radhika's first time on this particular errand, and she thrilled rather at the sense of power and purpose in the animal pacing along at her side, its flank occasionally rubbing against her leg.

"Are, are they boys or girls?" It was her first time speaking solo with a legend of the school too, and she wasn't quite sure which she was more nervous about.

"One of each." Rowany grinned down at her. "You have the boy there. Officially, please note, they have *not* been given names, being neither pets nor property. However, unofficially, that is Thomas and this is his litter-sister Alice. Tell no one."

Radhika giggled, assuming quite rightly that everyone knew already, from Miss Leven to the bootboy, from Melanie Fitzwalter to the youngest girl in the school. The kits seemed to respond to their names, glancing up at the speaker in turns before resuming their steady progress.

They came to the walled garden, and to its wooden gate; Rowany opened that, and waved Radhika through.

"Oh! *Oh!*"

A chuckle behind her, a hand on her shoulder gently urging her forward, so that Rowany could step through in her turn and close the gate at their backs. "First sight of it? Take your time, drink it in."

There had been little to see from the outside, only the solid red stone of the wall and a few tree-tops showing above. Inside, though, the garden was ablaze with colour and heaving with life, every bed full of growth and busy with bees and butterflies and insects of all kinds, flitting from flower to flower.

"This," Radhika murmured, "is *not* just a vegetable garden." She knew those of old, Army-style, with their rigid measured rows and labels.

Rowany laughed. "Well, it absolutely is a vegetable garden—but all right, no, not *just* that. It keeps the school in fresh flowers too, most months of the year. Mrs Bailey grew up in the cottage-garden tradition, and firmly believes there's room for everything, if you just plant them a little closer, mix and match throughout, and let them all run riot."

Voices hailed them. Startled, Radhika looked around to see two black-curled, olive-skinned lads in rough work clothes tying lengths of bamboo into pyramids for climbing beans. They waved, greeting Rowany with as much enthusiasm as the girls had in the stable yard. She beamed, waved back, and called something incomprehensible. Well, it was incomprehensible to Radhika. The boys were quite wrecked with laughter.

"What, what in the worlds was that? I've never heard anything like it!"

"Nor shall you; for that was Basque, and there is nothing like it in all the worlds together. Their people came here as refugees, of course, because the Kings of Spain have never liked independently-minded people within their borders; but the Basques are shepherds to their souls, and you will find little communities of them in sheep-country all across Charter lands. We try to find jobs for the young folk, either among us or nearabouts; the village is desperately poor, and some families depend on this extra help. Now, set Thomas free, come here," guiding her firmly to a bench in the waning sunlight, "sit down with me, and let me explain why I want you.

"Your cricket, I hear, is something of a wonder, unless it was a terror; my correspondents were not entirely clear on that point. Splendid stuff, though, either way. Also, I am pleased to learn that you ride a camel as to the manner born. It's a skill I'd like to see inculcated into every Martian girl, in case of need.

"However, games and jaunts and jollies are not, or not entirely, the point of school; and your mistresses are a *leetle* bit concerned about your progress in class. Oh, don't get on your high horse, you goop; you are not in trouble even with them, never mind with me. And no, I am not one of them. I am neither fish nor fowl nor good red herring, as it happens, which is why I'm currently seeing out my final term for the second time.

"Supposedly, I'm here to pursue my own work, before going up to Oxford for the Michaelmas term. However, the staff here do keep finding extra work for me, and it's been suggested that I might take you on as a project.

"Again, don't flash the fire of defiance from your eyes that way. No one is disparaging you here. Your brains are not in question, I'm told you have plenty of those; it's only that you haven't been trained to use them in the way we like to see. That's where I come in: not to give you extra lessons, or coaching, or anything like that. Simply to point out new ways of approaching subjects, that you may never have encountered before, in everything from arithmetic to literature to music. I think it might be rather fun, don't you? We can wander together through all the wealth of human knowledge and culture, practising new techniques and insights—and at the same time you can give me a few glimpses into what you clearly know inside out, all the language and lore of the Raj. All I know of that, I had from Kipling..."

# CHAPTER SIX

## Into The Swim of Things

"I say, Radhika—do you swim, at all?"

"What kind of a question is that? Of course I—Melanie! I do beg your pardon, I thought..."

She didn't know quite what she had thought, so that sentence died a-borning in the heat of her flush.

Happily, the tall Head Girl was laughing rather than frowning down at her. "It's always a good idea at school, you'll find, to be sure who is calling to you before you make reply. I myself nearly fell into that same trap, and found myself teetering on the very edge of having said something quite unspeakable to Miss Leven herself, when I was a rowdy Junior. But back to my question: you do swim, then? Only I know that Maya and Samira do not, or at least did not before they came here; and I wondered if perhaps that was an Indian thing at all, and whether perhaps you might share it?"

"Oh! Oh, yes, I see. It's true, a lot of girls don't learn, even among the army brats like me. And Mama-ji didn't, only, well, Papa-ji was at Sandhurst with the younger son of the Maharaja of Sinditpoor, and one summer he invited us all out for a visit to their houseboat on the lake in Srinagar. It was so hot that year, you could really only bear it if you spent half the day in the water. As it happened, I had learned to swim already, apparently I'd insisted on it until the Tommies took me to the river when I was little; but that year even Mama-ji learned, and I swam with the boys, all the princelings and boat-boys and beggar-boys mixed together, until Mama-ji used to swear that we were half fish."

"That's splendid. In that case, you should have no trouble with Miss Whitworth's rather fiendish test, to be sure you're safe before you're let out on the water. We do try to get in as many lake sports as we can at this time of year, while it's refreshing rather than chilly. Or, of course, frozen over. Have you ever done much with boats?"

"Not really, no. I can catch crabs, but not much more."

Melanie smiled. "Well, we'll see what we can do about that, before the end of term. I think perhaps that famous fierce energy of yours could do some good on an oar, or perhaps a pair of sculls. Will you be a lone player, or one of a team? I look forward to finding out..."

"This feels ridiculous," Radhika grumbled, as the entirety of Upper Third made their way down to the lakeside wearing dressing gowns over their swimming costumes, bare feet in outdoor shoes, towels around their necks.

Charm giggled at her side. "Miss Whitworth says that every year, every single year at budget time she asks for a proper changing-room to be built next to the boathouse. She says she has a whole speech about it. how the boats enjoy shade and convenience and shelter from the weather, while we mere girls do not."

"She says that every year, Mrs Mac and the trustees promise to consider it, but somehow they never actually come up with the money," Marigold put in. "*We* think they're waiting for some generous benefactor parent to offer it instead, rather than get one more tear-stained letter from their beloved but rather chilly daughter. How's about it, Radhika— think your Papa-ji would fund the Mr and Mrs Harvey Changing Suite, for the benefit of all?"

Radhika scowled. "That's *Captain* and Mrs, thank you very much—and no. We don't have that kind of money." *Not any more.*

They marched on in silence, even insouciant Marigold understanding that she had blundered, that a light-hearted question had pierced the new girl deeply. She would have apologised instantly, of course, only that she didn't quite know what she needed to apologise for. Meantime, Radhika's unquiet mind roiled in its misery; and as always, as ever, misery expressed itself in her as fury.

Nothing in their lives had gone right for them, individually or as a family, since they left her beloved India. Papa-ji losing his money was the least of it, in many ways; he was a rigorously honourable man, quite willing to set his shoulder to the wheel and work for a living. But his honour had been ... besmirched, by what happened in Hyderabad, and he had seen nothing for it but to flee the shadow of a ruined reputation, and seek a new life far away.

And so they were here on Mars, and so Mama-ji was deathly ill, and so Radhika was here, separated from everyone and everything she loved, and—oh, she hated everyone and everything about this place, all of it, the school and the crater and the whole entire colony, more, the entire *planet*...

"I didn't realise I'd be performing in front of an audience." Miss Whitworth raised a surprised eyebrow, and regarded the small person in front of her with some perplexity. She was really not used to being scolded by a schoolgirl, never mind—as Radhika had said—in front of an audience.

Yet here they were, at the far end of the landing stage, with Upper Third lining both sides, all of them gazing in fascination, those close enough to hear in fascinated disbelief.

"My dear child," Miss Whitworth said faintly, "your friends are here to support you, to urge you on to greater effort. This school is a community; your form is another, as is your house. We believe in mutual endeavour here. They also serve who only stand and cheer, as Milton might have said instead. Besides which, this is by no means a performance. This is a serious assessment, and my eyes on you are the only ones that matter here. Now stand properly, please, and take that scowl off your face, I won't be lectured by a pupil."

"Yes, Miss Whitworth."

At least the child had some basic notion of manners, unfolding her arms immediately and standing with her hands behind her back, adopting as neutral a pose and posture as she could manage, when she was clearly seething inside. There was a fierce spark in her eyes, and the games mistress wondered quite what devils lurked therein—and quite how they would manifest today. Perhaps the imp's already-legendary performance on the cricket field would not prove to be a singular occasion.

"Very well. Now: first, how many strokes do you know?"

"Um, I think my breaststroke is quite decent, and I can thrash about at backstroke, but mostly I just, sort of, swim?"

Miss Whitworth sternly suppressed even the hint of a smile. "Very well. Do you see the rowing boat out on the water there?"

"Yes, Miss Whitworth."

"Can you swim that far?"

"Yes, Miss Whitworth."

"Very good. Go out with your breaststroke, come back with your backstroke. Concentrate on style, rather than speed; performing a stroke properly will always get you further and faster than slapdashing it. Are you ready?"

"Yes, Miss Whitworth," with that ferocity informing her face again. This should be interesting.

A blast on Miss Whitworth's whistle, and Radhika was away, with a running dive off the end of the landing stage that was not perhaps in the true spirit of the breaststroke, but she thought she heard a cheer from her classmates before her body sliced neatly into the still lake water.

One long pull underwater, then a second before she broached the surface. Once again she blessed that long summer in the houseboat. The Tommies might already have taught her to swim in their own rough fashion, but officer cadets learned proper strokes and had cheerfully inculcated her into all their secrets. So: head out of the water, reach and pull, kick like a frog, reach and pull, smooth and wide...

The boat, when she got there, proved to contain Rowany, similarly swimsuited, the long bright glory of her hair tucked sternly into a rubber cap in school colours, an exact match to Radhika's own.

"Good girl," Rowany called down. "Very neat, and barely a splash. You should expect to be told off for that running start, mind you. *Not* quite according to Hoyle. What's next, back?"

Radhika nodded, and caught hold of the boat's gunwhale to tuck up into a starting position.

"Right. Good hard kick-off, now." Rowany produced a whistle of her own, and blew; Radhika kicked, arching her back in her best reverse-dolphin leap before again the waters closed over her head and she could steal a couple of strokes underwater before rising into the discipline of the backstroke.

This was harder work, and not as polished; she'd learned it because she was being taught it and it seemed a shame to pass up the chance, but she didn't much enjoy it, so she'd rarely practised since.

Still, it carried her through the water at a fair rate, even if not quite straightly; she had to twist her neck to look ahead and adjust her line a couple of times before she touched home at the piers of the landing stage.

"Good," Miss Whitworth called down to her. "We will work on the orthodoxy of your strokes later this term. For now I'm more concerned with your stamina and agility, and how comfortable you are in the water. Not winded yet? ... Very good. Why don't you do that again, then, only this time showing me whatever your 'just swimming' stroke may be? Get set, and—"

The whistle sent her away; and this time she gave not a thought to style or grace or proper motions. There were no proper motions, there was only propelling herself through the water as fast as might be; and oh, it felt so *good* to cast all other considerations aside and just drive herself forward, burning out all her pent-up rage, and—

—and she reached the boat too soon, far too soon, long before she was ready to stop; and Rowany grinned at her over the side and said, "Well, I don't know what you call *that*, and you should probably not teach it to your little friends, but my word, it's effective. Tell you what," sliding effortlessly over the gunwhale and into the water, "let's test it against my Australian crawl, shall we? A race back, yes?"

Oh, yes. Very much yes.

"One hand on the gunwhale, then, so that we start fair. Ready? Go!"

Radhika went.

This time, she was sure about the cheering. It felt like she was swimming into a rising tide, except that the tide shrieked her name and lifted her, claimed her, carried her in.

Her hand was first to the pier, there was no doubt of that, either above the landing stage or below it. Rowany trod water, and held out a hand; Radhika shook it solemnly.

"Well done, youngster. Melanie herself couldn't do that to me in a straight race. I don't remember the last time anyone could. You're going to be quite an asset on the sporting field, I deem, if not quite yet in the classroom. Just put that kind of energy and focus into your schoolwork too, though, and you'll get there, sooner than anyone expects."

Of course there was more to Miss Whitworth's notorious test than simple swimming. There was getting into and out of a boat, from the water; there was diving, "though we've already seen your running dive, Radhika, so we won't have you do that again unless you want to," which of course she did, for the sake of another cheer; there was swimming around an obstacle-course of boats and buoys, and more besides.

And then, finally, up on the landing stage again, wet wood underfoot and her sodden costume clinging to her in a way that was not quite comfortable:

"This is not an official part of the test," Miss Whitworth said, "so there is no penalty for failure, or not at least for you; myself, I have to apologise to Mrs Bailey every year for losing yet more of her teaspoons. But here is today's sacrifice," a spoon from the dining hall, held high to catch the sunlight. "Your task, Radhika, is to save me from Mrs Bailey's wrath if you are able, by playing kingfisher and retrieving the spoon before it is lost forever in the silt of the lake bottom. Are you ready?"

To the wonder of all, Radhika turned her back to the lake and took several slow, deep breaths before nodding. "I am now, Miss Whitaker."

"Very well, then. When it reaches apogee and starts to fall, then you may go; not before."

She flung the teaspoon high with a practised hand. Radhika kept her eye fixed on it as it climbed; when it seemed to pause in the air before heading down towards the water, she bent her legs, arched her spine and dived—backwards, so that she could watch it all the way into the water and know just where it had fallen.

Following it in, she thought for one heartstopping moment that she had lost it after all, but no: there it was, turning end for end as it dropped through the water, still high enough to catch the last of the sunlight at every rotation. Radhika kicked, stretched, seized.

And made ready to swim up into the light again, arm aloft in triumph—and hesitated, thought again, made another choice. She still had plenty of air in her lungs, so why not...?

Up in the bright light of day, Miss Whitworth was growing anxious. Some of her pupils were already dropping their towels and peeling off their dressing gowns, ready to jump in and save their classmate if she was in trouble, if they could locate her in the deep. Rowany was there in a moment, telling them not to be little idiots, to calm down and be patient; but Miss Whitworth was already halfway to calling the tall girl back and sending her on that precise mission. It seemed unlikely to the point of impossible that as strong a swimmer as Radhika should have found trouble on a simple dive-and-retrieve—but she had been down a long time now, and all Miss Whitworth's training and experience wanted to cry out that it was too long, that the girl needed help, that Rowany must go in search of her now, right this very—

There! A sudden disturbance in the lake, a dim figure rising from below—and an arm thrust up, the hand clenched around the spoon!

Cheers echoed back from the crater's rim as Radhika swam back to the landing stage one more time. She was using a curious kind of sidestroke, keeping one arm underwater at all times, and Miss Whitworth just found time to worry that she'd met trouble after all down there, and come back to them hurt in some manner.

Then Radhika was there, but not climbing out of the water quite yet. Hooking one elbow around a rising timber, she opened that hand so that Miss Whitworth might reclaim her spoon.

"Thank you, Radhika," said that worthy, bending to take it from her. "And well swum, well swum all around. Come out of the water now, dear, and—"

And that was when Radhika drew her other hand from beneath her, and let loose a positive shower of spoons, all over the decking.

"How did you do it, though, Radhika? How could you possibly stay under that long, is there a trick to it?"

The swimming lesson was over, and the still-damp mob that was Upper Third was hurrying back up the hill to their various houses, to dry off properly and change back into their gym tunics for lunch. All of them, though, every single one of them was intent on hearing that question answered, before they split off from the pack.

Radhika was buoyed yet by their enthusiasm, as she had been in the water by their cheers and yells of encouragement. She had a rare smile on her face as she said, "No trick. Well, none except practice, and breathing deep to get plenty of oxygen into your blood before you go. But there's a place in Benares where the Ganges has dug itself a deep, deep pool, for rivery reasons all its own; and all the local urchins gather on the rocks there, and the Tommies used to love tossing pennies into the water, just like Miss Whitworth's spoon, to see the kids dive after them.

"Of course they wouldn't let me join in, I was a mem-sa-hib and an officer's daughter, I couldn't possibly mingle with the likes of them; but I'm afraid I may have behaved quite dreadfully, quite quite dreadfully, until the men gave in and started tossing pennies for me in our own private river-pool. So that's a game I know inside-out and backwards, as the saying goes."

"How long can you stay under?"

Radhika only shrugged, suddenly a little embarrassed by all the attention. She had thoroughly enjoyed her time in the water, and had been feeling very much better since; but now this conversation was abruptly only one more vivid reminder of everything that she'd lost, everything that had been taken from her.

"Here's Stokes now," she said gruffly. "We'd better run, if we're not to be late."

# CHAPTER SEVEN

## Some Most Peculiar Noises

According to legend and lore, a girl needs Actual Magical Powers to study a musical instrument at the Crater School. As has been noted by every generation, the ordinary school day is hectic and demanding, so that there is never ever time enough spare to catch your breath; and yet, a musical girl is expected and required to find half an hour's practice time per day, in addition to all the regular lessons and supervised prep and games and other activities, and woe betide her if she tries to negotiate her way out of any obligation, including meals and bedtimes and rising times too. It is quite clear that all of that requires them to be in two places at once on a daily basis, or else sneakily adding unused time from some other dimension into their day; and yet, not only do they contrive to keep up with that rigorous timetable, they also somehow contrive not to miss out on any of the fun, frolics and downright mischief of their unmusical or uninterested cohorts. Hence, clearly, Actual Magical Powers are involved.

Two of these acknowledged magicians—violinist Janna Silverstein and cellist Elana Grey—had just compounded their reputations by adding their practice times together, thus stealing an entire hour to work their way through one of Mozart's lovely horn concertos, arranged for their own instruments, with Elana dancing between alto and bass clefs as she went. It had been enormous fun, if just a little fiddly, and they were feeling somewhat confident about the notion of performing it before actual people before term's end. They ceded their practice room to the next impatient player, and were walking along the corridor debating tempi in a pleasingly adult manner when they heard some most peculiar noises emerging from another room.

They were notes, to be sure, and perhaps sometimes they were even chords, though neither listener could quite entirely swear to that. And they thought that perhaps those notes were issuing from a guitar, except that surely no guitar in the history of humanity had been tuned that way?

They stood still to listen, rapt, intrigued—and then they heard another noise, another kind of noise, even less comprehensible than before. The two girls gazed at each other in wild surmise.

"Is that—?"

"You know, I think it is! But..."

Like the classrooms, the practice rooms had glass panels in their doors. It was commonly supposed that this was for the convenience of Authority, that a single glance might tell them who was getting up to what in the absence of proper oversight. That being so, the girls tended to frown on any of their number "spying in", as they called it, choosing to leave such behaviour to the prees and mistresses.

On this one occasion, though, in these particular and peculiar circumstances, our two were helpless to resist the temptation. Two heads sidled up to the glass, and peered through.

They were right!

It was indeed Radhika Harvey in there, and she was really, truly laughing!

She had rather a lovely laugh, too, lilting and musical. Upper Third and Stokes House had not supposed until this that she had any kind of a laugh at all; certainly no one among their numbers had ever heard it.

"Eavesdropping, girls?"

The voice came out of nowhere, cold, with a nasty edge to it. Janna and Elana gasped in tandem, flushing as they turned. Spying in was a social sin, mostly of their own creation; eavesdropping went far more strictly against the school's moral code.

"P-please, Miss Llewellyn"—of course it would be their own beloved music mistress who had caught them at it—"we, we only stopped because there was the strangest kind of music coming out..."

"Indeed, Elana? And yet I hear no music at all, but only two girls talking. Two girls who should be listening to an apology from you, I believe. Come along."

She opened the door and stalked in, two miserable youngsters dragging at her tail.

There was Radhika, yes, still a little slow to get to her feet when a staff entered the room; and her companion was Lois Shannon, who was holding her own guitar. It was of course impossible that she had been the source of those first extraordinary sounds, for Lois was a musical genius who could turn her hand to anything, and would never have so mangled the very name of music; just as it was equally impossible that Radhika of the Rage—that term had caught on, rather—could have been the source of that rippling laughter. And yet that last was certainly true, so...

"I believe these children have something to say to you," Miss Llewellyn snapped to the startled twosome she had interrupted.

81

Janna took a slow, unwilling breath and said, "Please, we're terribly sorry, but I'm afraid we were listening at the door, it was all so..."

That was as far as she got. Once it was clear that she would be going no further, Lois moaned, laid down her precious instrument and sank her head into her hands. "You mean you little wretches actually *heard* that, that cacophony? My life is over, my reputation ruined, my hopes are in tatters, oh woe is me forever!"

The older girl was clearly taking advantage of her status to try to lift the mood in the room a little. Perhaps she succeeded; there might have been the briefest twist of a smile to Miss Llewellyn's mouth before she stifled it. "And what, exactly, was the cause of this ... cacophony? Do please enlighten me."

"It was all my own doing," Lois confessed. "I asked Radhika to retune my guitar in one of the modes she knows from India, but I can't make head nor tail of it, I'm afraid."

"May I?" Miss Llewellyn held out her hand, as one who never expects the answer *no*. Lois meekly passed her the guitar, and she ran her fingers lightly over the open strings.

"Hmm. That is ... curious. I should not like to find my way around that in the dark. Radhika, could you enlighten us a little, play us something that you know?"

"Yes, yes, of course," said the flustered Radhika, flushing darkly. "But, please, may I sit? I don't think—"

"Yes, yes. Perhaps we should all sit. Even you two miscreants," frowning ferociously from one to the other. "It ... is not impossible that I might have paused too, hearing inexpert hands on such a peculiar tuning."

An invitation to stay meant that their scolding was over. Janna hurriedly fetched a chair for the music mistress, while Elana took two more from a stack in the corner and placed them at a sensible, tactical distance, quite out of Miss Llewellyn's eyeline.

Radhika settled the guitar on her knee, strummed it lightly, adjusted a tuning-peg and strummed again. Satisfied, she said, "Mama—I mean, my mother used to sing this to me as a *lori*, a lullaby, when I was a baby. It's almost the first thing I learned to play on a *veena*. Which is a plucked stringed instrument, and almost exactly nothing like a guitar, but I think I can make shift..."

The fingers of her right hand danced across the strings, while her left slid up and down the fretboard according to no pattern that even musical girls could read. Sweet, gentle music flowed out, utterly strange and utterly entrancing.

"Sing the words, Radhika," Miss Llewellyn said softly.

Radhika closed her eyes, and her voice melded with her music. Of course they couldn't understand the words, and their classically trained musical minds puzzled much over her technique and tuning, but the effect was remarkable. As Janna said to her friends later, "If I'd been a baby, I wouldn't have dared stay awake a moment longer. It was something like magic, just a different kind of magic than we'd ever heard before."

Her heart like a stone in her mouth, so cross she was almost sore with temper, Radhika rapped lightly on Rowany's door. Charm and co had gone skipping off down to the stables for evening chores, to see the ponies settled; she meanwhile had been summoned here, and she resented it bitterly.

"Come in!"

She opened the door and stepped through into a charming little sitting-room, neatly furnished with anything an inquiring mind might desire: bookshelves, a desk, a magazine rack, a comfortable-looking sofa. There was a vase of fresh flowers on the coffee-table, and—

Oh.

Rowany turned from the leaded-glass window she was opening wide, and laughed at the expression on Radhika's face.

"Ah, I see you have spotted your doom for today. Yes, that is indeed the essay you wrote for Miss Harribeth about the Roman invasions of Britain. Now, come and sit down next to me," patting a sofa cushion invitingly, "and we'll make our way through it together, shall we? We'll do this Oxford-style, which means that you read it through aloud, and I will comment as and where necessary."

Radhika was abruptly furious at herself for flushing, but more so at Rowany for putting her through this torment.

"I know, girlie, you're hating me rather a lot right now, aren't you? Don't worry, it won't last long; you didn't actually write very much, did you? Just enough to squeak by, by the look of it, in your largest handwriting. Which is quite remarkable, by the way, but perhaps a *little* ornate for a schoolgirl essay. Come, sit, read. The sooner you start, the sooner it's over."

As it turned out, Rowany didn't interrupt once during Radhika's stumbling, embarrassed read-through. She didn't need to.

"Yes, well," she said into the silence after. "I think you can tell for yourself what a shoddy piece of work that was, can't you? Reading something out loud even without an audience, hearing it yourself, is always a good test for the quality of writing. Or the lack of quality. What you gave Miss Harribeth is basically just a list of dates, Roman emperors, British tribes and battles. It shows you spent half an hour in the library with Britannica, but it's pretty dry stuff, Radhika. There's no life in it, no interest. Didn't it occur to you to wonder *why* Caesar wanted to invade Britain? Or why he did it a second time? Why the Romans would keep trying to come back, time after time, until Claudius finally made it stick?"

There was no point in denying Britannica, so Radhika simply said, "The, the encyclopaedia didn't say anything about that."

"I don't suppose it did. That's why it's important to read more than one article, to get behind the mere facts of an action and into the motives that drove it. Even more important, you need to *think*, to consider your subject from every angle, and most particularly the human. What happened is never as important as why it happened."

"But, but if the books don't *say*..."

Rowany gazed at the baffled little face before her, and sighed. "All right, let's try this another way. Your father was a military man, I know, like mine. I expect he was in the war?"

On Mars, there was only ever one war, Radhika understood that. It was much the same in her own head, despite long years on Earth. Only the last one mattered, perhaps? "Yes, of course. When the Tsar's men tried to come down into India through Afghanistan, his regiment was sent to hold them back, until reinforcements could arrive."

Rowany whistled softly. "Part of the Khyber Push, was he? Hard fighting, over hard ground."

"I suppose so, yes. He, he's never really talked about it much."

"I should imagine not. He likely doesn't want to relive it, any more than he wants his daughter dwelling on it. Mine is much the same. I suspect all soldiers think that way, that Martian women as a whole may be tough and self-reliant, but their own daughters are precious little flowers of femininity to be protected from nastiness at all costs." As it happened, this was a grotesque slander against General de Vere, who had in fact raised his only daughter to be just as strong in body and mind as he did her three brothers; but Radhika wasn't to know that, and the appalling untruth did at least raise a giggle from her, which had been all of its intent.

"Even so," Rowany went on gently, "you must have wanted to know what the war was all about. Any girl with half a brain would have to be curious about something so all-consuming, and I know full well that you have both halves of yours, young Radhika. Did you or did you not pester the poor man with questions, until he surrendered in the face of an irresistible force?"

Another giggle, and a confession: "Well, I did, a bit. He got, um, 'cut up a bit' in the fighting, that's how he says it, he was in hospital for a long time after, and his doctors told him that swimming would be the best sort of exercise to keep him in shape. I loved to swim too, so he used to take me along to the public baths. I, I got to see... He has these horrible purple scars, all over his body. So I had to ask. He wouldn't tell me about the fighting, but he did say how this one was a sabre cut in Kandahar, and that one was a bayonet outside Peshawar, that sort of thing. He'd make up funny stories about what he was doing when he got them. Only, sometimes I wouldn't let him distract me like that, because I wanted to know how it all happened, how my Papa-ji ended up all hurt and cut about..."

"Yes, of course. So why do you think the Tsar did send his men into Afghanistan?"

"Oh, but he's always wanted India, ever since the old Company days." On Mars, they speak of the Tsar as though he were one consecutive figure, rather than a succession of individuals. Miss Peters would debate with you about whether this is an example of metonymy or synecdoche, but Radhika would have nothing to say to that, she'd only picked up the habit during her years in Marsport. "That was even before the aetherships came. He looks at us and sees all the wealth and splendour of the Raj, Papa-ji says, and he wants it all for himself."

"Yes, and after the aetherships came?"

"Well, that only made it worse. The Tsar got Venus, which may be full of, of minerals and ores and things," rueing for a moment how scanty her education in planetology had been at St Dymphna's, "but it's—well, Papa-ji says it's a hell off Earth, though he does also say that I shouldn't say that in polite company." She peered a little anxiously at Rowany, as though trying to decide how polite she might be. With an effort, Rowany kept her face neutral. "*Any*way," Radhika went on hurriedly, "it's so horrid there that he uses the Venusian mines as his new Siberia, for prisoners and rebels. It's barely habitable, and even the guards are lucky to come back alive.

"Meanwhile, of course, Farmer George got Mars, and poured all his energy and effort into making a viable, self-supporting colony here; and the Crown has supported and continued that work ever since, the Empress particularly, and it's like a slap in the face to the Tsar, Papa-ji says, every time he sees the two planets in conjunction, in the sky together. He's hungry for the Raj—and for Constantinople, that was another of his war aims, why he went to war with the Ottoman Empire as well as us and our allies, the silly man— but he *aches* for Mars. That's why his nickname in all the newspapers is Envious Casca..."

"Mmm. Do you know where that reference comes from?"

"Yes, I do, actually. I didn't understand it, so I asked Papa-ji, and he showed me where Mark Antony says it in *Julius Caesar*, and then he took me to see a production of the play given by the officers in Bow Barracks in Calcutta. It was awfully good."

"Don't say 'awfully' in that context, the staff don't like it at all—but your father is a good man, Radhika Harvey, and that little gem about the Tsar's nickname would have earned you an extra point from Miss Harribeth if you'd used it in an essay. You still might get the chance, so hold on to it. She loves little sidelights like that. She would have wanted you to go on to say that it isn't only about the wealth, from either India or Mars; the Tsar's envy reaches further than that, to the power and prestige that they confer. He hates it that ours is seen all through the worlds as the senior empire, his the junior. His wife is the granddaughter of our Queen Empress, you know, which also leaves him feeling junior, perhaps even inferior. Every time the Prince Regent calls him 'cousin', you can see him gritting his teeth; he wants to hear 'sire', and he never will."

"Yes, Papa-ji explained some of that to me as well, how all the royal families of Europe are woven together, and the Queen Empress is right at the heart of that web."

"Quite right, may she live for ever. But that was extremely well thought out, Radhika—"

"Oh, but I was only quoting Papa-ji!"

"No, you had listened to your Papa-ji—I do rather love that name you have for him, by the way—and absorbed what he was telling you, understood it, and passed it on to me in your own words."

"Well, not really."

"Close enough. You will never be reprimanded for quoting from an authoritative source, and no one is more authoritative than a soldier who was there. Now, let's turn our minds back to the Roman emperors, shall we, and see if we can uncover their motives for aiming over and over again at British shores?"

"Well..."

It was a hard-wrestled debate, with Radhika learning to take a position and defend it, standing firm even when Rowany offered to undermine her. After an hour, the older girl cried *pax*, and grinned at her triumphant opposite.

"There, now! You enjoyed that, young Radhika, and do not even think of telling me otherwise. Also, you made some telling points; and I think you understand now, don't you, what Miss Harribeth expects of her pupils? You don't have to rewrite that," a gesture at the scorned original essay, "but I think you'd be delighted by her response if you did; there's nothing she or any staff enjoys more than enthusiasm for their subject. Meanwhile, arguing out the strands of historical motivation is hot and thirsty work; and here—oh, thank you, Anneke!—is our tea and biscuits, come most carefully upon their hour. Which is Shakespeare again, if you didn't know; has your father taken you to see Hamlet yet? No? There are several excellent repertory companies in Marsport, I know, and a host of amateurs as well; you might try to inveigle him. Some fine *grande dame* observed that the play is nothing but a string of old and very well-known quotations, but even so, there is some virtue in it yet..."

# CHAPTER EIGHT

## The New School Hand

Whenever Upper Third filed into the art room, there was always a murmur, an undercurrent of speculation as to what Mrs Buchanan would have them do this week. She was a delightful teacher, unpredictable and challenging and fun, full of unexpected wisdoms, seeming often as excited by their work as they were themselves. They had long since forgotten to be in awe of her fame, finding much more to love and be awed by in the person herself.

This particular Monday afternoon, they trooped in after lunch to find a new set of posters, all around the room. Isobel smiled a greeting and said, "Don't take your seats yet, girls. Spend five minutes looking around, soak yourselves in a different kind of beauty. Talk among yourselves if you want to, but keep it to the subject at hand. Shout out if you recognise a particular piece. Charm, you've seen all these before, I know, so don't butt in yet."

"My lips are sealed, Mam-Mrs Buchanan."

Her mother wafted her away with a wave of the hand, and she skipped off to join her particular friends, which meant about half the class, so even without a contribution from her, the noise level from that group rose quite alarmingly. Isobel was on the verge of calling them to order when a slim, tentative arm rose up from the throng.

Isobel came to her feet, and the class fell quickly silent.

"Yes, Radhika?"

"Please, Mrs Buchanan, I think I know this. I think I've seen it. This is Mohammedan calligraphy, isn't it, from the Moghul Empire?"

The mistress smiled at her. "Are you asking me, or telling me?"

The slight figure hesitated, then stood firm with a curious little shake of the head. "Please, I'm telling you. It's, it's in Lahore, on the wall of a mosque. I can't remember the name of it, but it's near the Delhi Gate. Wherever we were stationed, Mama-ji and I would always explore, and she'd explain things to me, and..." Her voice caught a little at the memory, and she fell silent.

"Go on, dear. You're doing excellently well so far. What more do you know about it?"

"Well, I know that, that Mohammedans aren't allowed to paint pictures of people because it's, it's idolising...?"

"It would be better to say 'idolatrous', but yes; they believe their holy book, the Koran, forbids the portrayal of human figures. Carry on, tell us about what you see here."

"Well, because they can't paint people, they concentrated instead on patterns and, and words. Calligraphy," repeating the word, simply for the shape of it in her mouth. "Mama-ji was a St Thomas Christian from Kerala, so she couldn't read it any more than I could, but I think she said it was verses from the Koran?"

"Yes, indeed. This is a formal, stylised version of Arabic script, which has followed the spread of Islam all across the worlds. You can see how the designs are rich with colour, while the actual letters of the text are spare and reserved, not to elevate the artist, or to set any hindrance between God's word and his adherents' eyes. Very good, Radhika. Now, can anyone tell me anything about these other images?"

Another hand, this one waving wildly.

"Yes, Cate?"

"This illuminated manuscript, Mrs Buchanan—I can't quite read it, but I'm sure it's a page from the Bible. Could it be the Book of Kells?" Cate, or more properly Agatha Hecate St-Clair, had Irish blood somewhere in her complicated family history, and was always alert for an opportunity to parade it.

"Well, I suppose it could have been, though in fact—well, you tell her, Charm. You've been containing yourself long enough, you may as well let something out."

"It's from the Lindisfarne Gospels," Charm said, "produced on Holy Island in honour of St Cuthbert, though I think it's in the British Museum now, isn't that right?"

"It is," her mother confirmed, "much to the chagrin of a great many people who feel it properly belongs where it was made, or thereabouts. Durham Cathedral would certainly have a claim, since that's where the saint's body lies. It was originally buried at the monastery he founded, on Holy Island or Lindisfarne, but the monks were forced to flee when Vikings started raiding that stretch of coast, so they dug Cuthbert up and took him with them. ... Yes, I thought you'd like that little detail, you ghoulish creatures. It is said that his body was found to be uncorrupted; whether it is still that way, we cannot know unless we dig him up again, and the Dean and Chapter of the cathedral are not likely to—yes, Agnosia? Ah, yes. The Dean is the senior official at a cathedral, the man in charge of its administration, and the Chapter forms his supporting body. Like the Chairman and the Board of Governors at a company, you might say, but these are all men in Holy Orders, the Chapter generally being canons of the cathedral.

"But come, we are straying—however interestingly—from our point. As I've no doubt you've all spotted by now, all these posters, the examples we've discussed and every one of the others too, which Charm will be delighted to introduce you to after class, are examples of writing used as art; and the significant factor for today is that beautiful as the results are, that is a long and a slow process. I don't know how long the Wazir Khan Mosque took in the decorating, once the shell of the building was erected, but it's believed to have been seven years in the making from start to finish. The Lindisfarne Gospels took longer; at least ten years, we believe.

"Art and time are old friends. However, schoolgirls and time are not, as I suspect you are all very well aware by now." Groans of recognition and agreement, from all around the room. She laughed, and went on, "Now it occurred to me that I might be able to help a little, to buy you a touch more time in your day."

Now they brightened; now they sat up and looked interested. "Yes, I thought that might strike home. The point is, girls, that a number of you have been taught a very pretty copperplate hand," *which is bad enough, but one of you has been taught something worse,* "which looks fine once it's on the page, but takes an age to get there. When my own two were little, and starting to struggle up the slopes of Mount Literacy, I was constantly on the move, shifting the poor creatures from hither to yon with barely any warning. That meant they were being bumped from one school to another, sometimes two or three times a year, when they could go to school at all. And all those schools taught different styles of penmanship, and different ways to approach it, so as you can imagine, my girls' handwriting was getting worse rather than better, they were so muddled by it all.

"I needed to take things in hand. They were too young to leave behind, which would be the only way to give them a consistent, steady schooling at the time when they needed it most; so for a few years I took them out of school altogether, and taught them myself. We covered a lot of ground then, didn't we, Charm?"

"Those were the best years, Mamma," with a beaming smile, relying on her fond parent to overlook the forbidden word, just this once.

"What, better than now?—Marigold, sit up straight or you'll have your whole desk over, inkpot and all. I do understand that my tactless daughter's pigtails make a very tempting target, but none the less: if you insist on pulling them, do it in your own time, please, and not in my artroom. Thank you.

"Anyway," she went on, "one thing I did for my girls was to devise and train them in the use of a simple, legible script that is swift and easy to write, once you're into the way of it. It'll take a little work on your part, but you should be comfortable by half-term and fluent before the holidays; and I promise, it will save you a lot of time in prep and class and all through your life going forward.

"So: you all have paper, pens and ink in front of you. I am going to write each letter on the board here in both its capital and lower-case form, and I want you to copy my lines as neatly and accurately as you can. Then, I'm afraid, it's simply a matter of practising them again and again, until you can write them without thinking. You'll find they join up quite handily, when you feel ready to try your hand at cursive—oh, a new word? Well, it just means joined-up writing: from the Latin *currere*, which means—well, what? Yes, Lauren? 'To run', quite so. I know we don't actually teach Latin here, somewhat to my chagrin, but there is a tutor down in Terminus who is happy to take individual pupils, and might be tempted into coming up here perhaps one day a week, if there were enough demand. Think on it, girls; a little classical education is an unexpectedly useful thing, in a surprising number of ways. Those of you who want to go on to university, of course, will absolutely need it before you can even matriculate, never mind graduate.

"But I am straying from my course. For your prep this week, girls—yes, yes, I know, the art mistress does not traditionally assign prep, but this is an exception—I want you all to do one piece of work for another mistress in this hand I am teaching you today. All the staff know this, and are ready to expect it. Concentrate on neatness and accuracy, as I say, and you will find that speed will come, sooner than you expect it. Also, my daughter is a resource in this, so do make use of her. It may be that she's picked up a few shortcuts through the years, eh, Charm, that I of course can know nothing about...?"

"Isobel, you are a fiend in human form. Every girl in this establishment, from the most junior to the Head Girl herself, is inveighing against your name and lamenting that ever you should have come to these shores."

"Well, every girl but two," Isobel said complacently. "My two are fine."

"Three," from the corner where Rowany was inclined to make herself comfortable, when she chose to spend time with her elders in their Staff Room. "*I* don't care what you put the little darlings through; and I'm half inclined to have a go at it myself. I can see the use of a plain swift hand, at need."

"You see? Thus am I justified! But seriously, people, just give your victims lighter writing tasks for a few weeks, and I promise, by term's end we'll have a schoolful of legible literates fit to go out into the world and show what they are made of, in clear simple prose. Speaking of which, Miss Peters—?"

"Yes, yes," that worthy groaned, half on a laugh. "I am duly following your example, and encouraging every year in turn to trim their more fanciful turns of phrase, to reach for the Anglo-Saxon in preference to the Latin where possible, and generally to produce more workmanlike, less elaborate pieces of work. Asking for shorter essays is a great help in that campaign also, I might add. Though I still say it seems quite some length to go to, in order discreetly to correct one girl's tendency to overabundance of decoration, both in line and word."

"Oh, poor Radhika may have been the trigger for this, but trust me, the powder was ready for the spark. If that's not a mixed metaphor. If it is, I apologise. *Why* so many people who presumably have the child's welfare somewhere at heart should feel that formal Imperial copperplate is the only way to go, I simply cannot imagine. It's cruelty to dumb animals, is what it is."

"Oh, if only they were dumb," murmured Miss Fanshawe, who taught Areography and had a lifelong habit of expecting long screeds of text from her pupils, and had consequently been fielding a lot of complaints and pleas for mercy. "However, even I am not made of stone, whatever the rumours may be. I have adopted a policy of asking for a number of paragraphs, rather than pages. That requires them to condense their thoughts, of course, and make their points more briefly: again, no bad thing, if only they weren't all so woeful about it."

"Cats and schoolkids: creatures of habit," Miss Tattersall opined. "They abhor change, even where everyone must change together. Which is why it is our duty to force it upon them. I don't suppose anyone has any bright ideas on how to upset them further, by turning their mathematics lessons upside down...?"

"I swear, I thought I had left my days of pothooks and hangers far and far behind me."

Thus the exalted Melanie Fitzwalter in all her glory, gazing discontentedly at a sheaf of remedial exercises, amply illustrating her struggle to convert her former well-established writing style into something approximating what they had taken to calling the New School Hand. On occasion that phrase might come with adjectives attached, for Martians are a forthright people when no one from Authority is listening.

"Be of good cheer," quoth Arie Bunker consolingly. "I've just had a squad of second-years in literal tears over this, because they simply *cannot* unlearn what has been beaten into them over years, *years*, and *please* could I plead them into some remission? I ruthlessly pointed out that it was the same for all of us, except harder for those of us even more ingrained into our ruttish ways than their fresh-faced and flexible youth; and then I took pity on their woes, and spent this last hour trying to help them over the hump, which of course meant that I have missed my own chance to practise and must expect to be hauled over the coals tomorrow when I turn my prep in for scathing commentary. Why did I ever think it would be such a grand and freeing thing to be a prefect? I'll tell you what, Melanie my love, why don't we fling down our whitewash and our brushes, cry "Bother spring-cleaning!" and go out on the lake instead? Because after all, there is nothing—"

"—Absolutely nothing—"

"—Half so much worth doing—"

"—As simply messing about in boats!" they concluded in defiant, delighted chorus.

Melanie flung down her pen in lieu of a whitewash-brush and rose to her feet, tucked her arm through her friend's and steered forth into the corridor and beyond, leaving all her wretched exercises behind her.

"Look, isn't that the curious Radhika Harvey child?"

"Now that you mention it, I believe you're right. But why do you say 'curious'? I haven't had many dealings with her, as she falls just a little outside my purview, notwithstanding her newness and all." Arie's particular charge and interest were the little girls, the Juniors. There was something about her that they loved and responded to, to the point where their small troubles could eat up half her free time if she allowed it, which she usually did.

"Oh, I've barely rubbed up against her myself, but it's the privilege of my position that I hear all manner of things, from staff and girls alike; and I dislike to tell tales out of school, as it were, but there are—well, let us say mutually contradictory stories about young Radhika's behaviour. She is a budding genius, apparently, in various different ways, and yet she is a fiend from hell and hates us all, etc."

"Oh, one of those! Just give her time, Mel my love. This school will sand her edges down, you know we will."

"Perhaps. Per-haps. And yet my soul misgives me. I fear we may see some particularly dramatic outburst from the girl, before she mellows. She seems the type."

"What type? Small, quiet, mild-mannered, a little shy...?"

Melanie snorted. "I thought you said you'd had little to do with her?"

"And so I did, and so I have; but I too hear things. The little girls like her, rather. She's not remotely condescending to them, despite her Middledom and somewhat exotic past."

"Mmm. I say it's the quiet ones you need to keep an eye on. They bottle things up, you know, and then—ka-boom! But speaking of matters curious, that is a *very* curious rowing stroke she's trying to adopt. And she appears to be alone in the boat, which is so very thoroughly against the rules, I think we must make a nuisance of ourselves..."

98

A few swift strokes brought the prefects neatly abeam of where Radhika was struggling to make any progress at all through the water.

"Radhika!" Melanie called. "You must know you're forbidden to bring a boat out on your own."

"I am *not* on my own," Radhika scowled back. "It's only that my ever-so-helpful sherpa is helpless in the bilges, and being no help at all..."

Melanie peered over the gunwale, to see that Charm Buchanan was indeed curled up tight in the bottom of the boat, breathless and useless with laughter.

"Charm! Pull yourself together, for goodness' sake! This is no place for hysterics!"

The stinging prefectorial snap in her voice brought Charm scrambling up to her knees, hastily wiping tears of mirth from her cheeks. "I, I'm sorry, Melanie. It's only, oh, it was so *funny*..."

"I don't see much humour in a girl struggling to learn an art that's new to her, while her friend does nothing but mock her." It was the redhead's curse, of course, that her pale skin should flush suddenly to fire. Radhika's complexion bespoke her origins, but she too was abruptly darker than before, and scowling with it. "Do I need to take your boat in tow?"

*"No!"* That came from both in tandem, as she had hoped it would. Charm scrambled up onto the thwart beside the other girl; Radhika ceded her an oar; Charm muttered, "On three, then, and this time remember to feather your blade, or you'll just turn us in circles again..."

Melanie spared her juniors any more of her mind, and sat quietly watching them as they pulled rather awkwardly back towards the landing stage.

"Hmm," Arie said. "There does indeed seem to be some fierceness there, which my little'uns had missed. I wonder what's the why of that?"

"I have not yet been able to discover. But something there is, upsetting her equilibrium; and I still say we'll be lucky if it doesn't upset us all, before term is out."

# CHAPTER NINE

## A Blow to the Heart—

"**A**h, Radhika! Just the girl I was looking for!"

"What may I do for you, Miss Whitworth?" It was hard, she was finding, to keep up even a façade of reserve, never mind active dislike, when people kept complimenting and encouraging you.

"As you know, dear, we play host to St Emelia's cricket team this weekend. The First Elevens will play on Saturday afternoon; but we have another game on Sunday, somewhat less formal. They always bring a few reserves to try out, and I like to give some of my hopefuls a run, to see what they can make of a real match. I'd like to play you as an all-rounder, batting in the middle of the order and bowling your absolute fastest."

"Oh, Miss Whitworth! I'd love to—but I'm so sorry, I simply can't. Not on Sunday." Two Sundays, two full weeks had come and gone, with no visit allowed to Mama-ji in the Sanatorium. Miss Hendy had pressed the issue on her behalf, with the powers-that-be on both sides of the crater, as a result of which a reluctant consent had been given to a very short, quiet visit this coming weekend.

"Can't?" Miss Whitworth was not accustomed to being told that a girl—and a new girl, at that!—had better things to do than represent the Crater School in a match. Her eyebrows rose almost to her hairline. "And what, pray, might be more important than playing for your school?"

"My, my mother's in the San across the water, and I haven't been allowed to see her yet, but I can now, and I'm to go on Sunday, so I simply can't, do you see?"

Miss Whitworth's eyes softened. "Oh, my dear child, I thought you must have been told already. There's been an outbreak of fever among the staff, quite half the nurses are down with it, and until it's been identified and treated, the whole Sanatorium is in quarantine. There are to be no visitors allowed on the grounds for any reason whatsoever. So you see, Sunday is your chance to shine, with the whole school watching."

"But, but, I was *promised...*"

"Oh, come now, Radhika," Miss Whitworth said, sharpness in her tone again. "You must see that it's quite impossible. The welfare of staff and patients—including, as you say, your own mother—must take priority, not to mention the risk of your bringing infection back to the school. I am sorry, but there is no help for it. The two teams will eat Sunday lunch together, so change into your whites after Chapel, if you please."

"I hate Miss Whitworth. I *hate* her!"

"What, because she's offered you a chance that any other Middle would give their eye teeth for, to play in a Senior side, when neither you nor she could do anything about the situation at the San?" Charm regarded her mentee a little askance.

"That's if it's even true, about the San," Radhika muttered darkly.

"Wait, so now you think you're important enough that a staff would lie to you directly? My dear goop—"

"We're not allowed to say that," Radhika growled, wondering if now she was going to have to hate Charm too. It seemed a shame, when she was turning out to be such good company, but needs must.

"So we're not. I amend: my dear nincompoop, no one in this school, no one on this entire crater would want to stop a girl seeing her mamma, as soon as ever it's possible. But no one is going to take any chances whatever, with our health or with theirs."

"That's just what she said."

"That's because it's true, and you know it."

It seemed wise to abandon that angle of attack; so, "And to make matters worse," Radhika muttered, tucking a bottom sheet in so savagely tight that Charm almost expected to hear it rip, "now we have to make room for this extra girl, too."

"Oh, this always happens, when a team comes from far away," Charm said, with all the wisdom of one whole year's experience. "No house has a spare dormitory, so we squeeze them in where we can, by ones and twos. She'll be our responsibility to take care of, too, when she's not with her team-mates or our own Seniors. I'm looking forward to meeting her. Aren't you?"

"I am *not*." Radhika straightened her back and glared across the mattress. "As far as I'm concerned, she's just making extra work for us," a wave of the hand at the bed they were making up for their visitor, "and I don't suppose she'll have anything to say to a couple of third-years anyway." At St Dymphna's, Seniors did not mix with their juniors even one year below them, never mind three or four.

"Oh, no, St Em's isn't like that at all. They're the friendliest bunch of girls you could hope to find. You'll see. Just don't sulk at them, Radhika." Charm was worried; the new girl appeared to be closing up again, just when she'd seemed about to flower. *Radhika of the Rage.* "That'll just make all of us look bad..."

St Emilia's had hired a steam-charabanc to bring their girls up from Terminus. They arrived on the Friday afternoon, bringing a splendidly early end to the school day, because of course guests must be greeted and welcomed and toured all over, and who could possibly concentrate on schoolwork when all that was going on? Besides which, it was a Craterean tradition that visiting teams should be given their money's worth, sportswise, to thank them for coming all that way. After tea the First Elevens would meet in a tug-o'-war, to see the festivities started, and then there would be races and jumps and games of all sorts, before cleaning up and quietening down to make an orderly supper.

Miss Whitworth, flanked by Melanie Fitzwalter and Alis Rasmussen the Games Captain, stood ready to receive their visitors as the charabanc drew to a whistling halt. All the school else was packed about, staff not excluded; they lived and worked so far from any notion of Martian civilisation, these visits came few and far between, and not a moment would be wasted.

A woman stepped down to shake hands all around, presumably St Emilia's Games Mistress; a tall senior girl followed, probably their team captain. Then the rest of the visitors trooped out of the vehicle and stood in rank behind: fifteen or so, Radhika estimated. The First Eleven, a twelfth man, plus an assorted few for the Sunday game.

That tall girl raised a hand. "St Emilia's! Three cheers for the Crater School! Hip hip—"

"Hooray!" There were so few of them in contrast to the gathered throng, but they did their best, three times over. Then Melanie raised her own arm to return the call, and the Castle echoed to the cry of two hundred voices joining together to welcome their guests in proper fashion.

"Ah, here they are now. Charm, Radhika, thank you for coming so promptly. This is Capri Demetreu, one of St Emilia's reserves. Her elder sister Sophia is the team captain, and I'll warn you now, watch out for her twisters! She can put a wicked spin on a ball. If you two will take Capri down to Stokes, please, and see her settled, then show her around until it's time for tea."

"Yes, Miss Whitworth."

Polite handshakes all around, a broad grin of welcome from Charm and something of an effortful grimace from Radhika, a quiet smile that might have been shyness in return.

They quarrelled politely over who should carry Capri's weekend-case, Charm emerging as victor by dint of merely seizing the handle and marching off with it, leaving the other two to scurry after.

"This is the main school building, of course. Everyone calls it the Castle, obviously. We'll find time later to show you everything, but I expect you'll want to see the cricket pitch first, yes?"

"Oh, yes, please—Charm, is it? What a pretty name! Or is it a short for Charmian, or...?"

"No. It is all my own, and all that I have. Though Capri is lovely too, I think. What does it mean, do you know?"

Capri laughed. "It depends whether you ask my Greek father or my Italian mother—and it isn't really pretty either way. To the Greeks it means wild boar, and to the Italians it means goats."

Even Radhika's eyes widened a little at this.

"Which is why," Capri went on, "we don't speak Greek *or* Italian at home. They can argue perfectly well in English, both of them—and they do. Constantly. Sophia and I are the no-man's-land in an eternal war of words. Maybe that's why we spent so much of our littlehood out in the park, playing games. Do you bat or bowl, Charm?"

"Oh, not really very much of either, yet. Levity—that's my sister—and I have only been at school for a year, and we never did much at sports, only having each other to play with. If you're looking for a dark horse to bet on, though, try Radhika on Sunday. She's only just a Middle here, but she's to play in the Senior game. She's a demon bowler and a famous bat already, for all that she's new this term. All our year is turning out to watch her, and we're hoping for fireworks."

Capri regarded the silent Radhika with interest. "Ohh, I know—your father's a military man, or else an Empire-builder of another sort, and you were raised on Earth but overseas, yes?"

Radhika's nod may have been a little short, but Charm made up for that, as so often. "We call her Radhika of the Raj. But how did you guess?"

"Earth-raised would give her the strength, of course, and India would give her both the time and the practice. Everyone's cricket-mad down there. We have a couple like that ourselves, and you'll meet them later, on the field and off. I'm looking forward to seeing your play, Radhika. And as Charm and I have been exchanging compliments, that's a very pretty name you have, too..."

Between Charm's relentless cheeriness and their guest's easy charm, Radhika found some of the tension easing out of her as they walked. She hadn't *quite* liked the phrase "dark horse", though she understood that Charm had no intention of referring to her skin colour, and would be mortified if it ever occurred to her that she could have been heard that way. Also she didn't *quite* like her upbringing—and probably her parentage too, though Capri hadn't said a word about that—being assessed so speedily and so accurately, as though she spoke about the breeding and the training of a racehorse. A *dark* racehorse, that was to say.

But there was no point louring over petty grievances her companions had no idea about; and it was a beautiful day for a walk, and boded well for the weekend to come. So she made a conscious effort to pick up her mood, chatting a bit as they helped Capri unpack in the improvised little cubicle squeezed between their two beds.

"See, there really isn't room for another dresser, so Charm and I cleared out one drawer each to take your things, and you are privileged to come into our cubies to fetch them, which is strictly forbidden otherwise."

"Oh, that's so kind! Thanks, both! Now, where can I hang my whites...?"

They were far from the only threesome later to make their way to the cricket pitch, with its sacred square roped off until tomorrow: "Mr Marks the groundsman guards this turf with his life, all around the year, so we lose this whole field in winter. Luckily we do still have a couple more for lax and hockey, and the *en-tout-cas* tennis courts, and there's always the lake to skate on—I forgot to ask, Radhika, *do* you skate? I don't suppose you had much chance in India?"

"Not a whiff of a chance, no—but of course I skate, numpkin. My first Marsport winter, that was pretty much all I did."

"Oh yes, of course. Numpkinnity confessed. As I was saying, though, it's such a shame you can't just roll up a good cricket square and put it away for the winter, don't you think, to leave the ground free for other games? Anyway, you've got an idea of the size of it now, Capri, and where Mr Marks puts the boundary rope. Actually I think he's brought it in a bit for this, to let more of us stand around the edge and cheer. Did your sister tell you, half of us will be cheering for you? We draw lots after lunch, to make it fair, as you couldn't bring your own supporters with you. The pavilion will be locked till tomorrow, alas, so we can't show you that. How's about a walk down to the Sculpture Garden...?"

But the Sculpture Garden had already been invaded and occupied by more senior girls and their guests, so they contentedly passed the time before tea in a knock-up game of Knock-Me-Down Peg, where Capri had her first sight of Radhika's lethal left arm, sending the single stump skittling half a dozen times from different angles and distances.

"I don't think she ever misses," Charm groaned, having been given out one more time by acclamation. "And what's more, she's not even left-handed, not properly. She does bat leftie, but she bowls right, and writes right too. She just says it feels proper to her, this mix-and-match, and it always has."

"She's going to be something to face on Sunday, and no mistake. Oh, I do hope Miss Terry—I mean, Miss Fellany, but her first name's Theresa so of course between us she's Miss Terry, because it sounds so like 'mystery', do you see, and she is a *little* bit of a dark horse herself, honestly—but I do hope she'll pick me to play. I shall point out that I have seen your girl in action, and can provide vital tips on how to face her. Which is a lie, of course, because I haven't a clue, she's had me out as often as she has you; but I shall say it anyway."

Healthy exercise—and, let us be honest, the taste of some notable triumphs—followed by a pleasant meal at a table full of cheerful, excited girls had lifted Radhika's spirits somewhat further. As a result she was perfectly amenable to being buoyed along in the crowd—Capri pinioned arm-in-arm-in-arm between herself and Charm, not to let her get lost—as the whole school now swept down the hill to the playing fields.

Mr Marks had already brought the tug-o'-war rope out of storage and laid it across the centre line of the lacrosse court, a brilliant white handkerchief tied around its midpoint for the umpire to ensure that the game started fair. High-jump and long-jump pits were ready too, as was the running track around the hockey pitch. Girls with particular interests would divide up between the various competitions as time wore on, but to start the evening off, everyone wanted to see the tug-o'-war. They formed up three or four girls deep, and the traditional cry went around: "Little'uns to the front! If the big'uns won't let you through, well, that's why God gave you elbows!"

Nobody in the Middle School likes to be thought of as "little", but Radhika and Charm were both Earth-born, with all that that implies in terms of disadvantage height-wise. They glanced at each other reluctantly, then shook their heads together—of course they must stay with their visitor, even if it meant seeing nothing of the game!—until the tall members of the Sixth who happened to be standing in front of them glanced around.

"Come on, Charm and—ah, Rhadika, isn't it? Looking forward to seeing you in the middle on Sunday, young'un. But little'uns means you, so squeeze on through. You'll make convenient chin-rests when we've tired ourselves out with cheering."

"Please, Fidelis, we can't, we—" Charm gazed meaning-fully upward, at the undoubtedly not-little Capri.

"Oh, you're sherping an Em! Why didn't you say so? In the circumstances, then, all three of you—and welcome to you, stranger!—may wriggle through, and sit at our feet as our eminence deserves. Don't even think about using our legs as a back-rest, we are not public leaning posts. No," laughing now, "don't be shy, I'm serious. Come on through."

The Sixths had taken up their position right on the line itself, so their three juniors had a perfect view as the two First Elevens made their way to the rope. Both games mistresses accompanied them, each equipped with the inevitable whistle.

"Girls," Miss Whitworth called out to the audience, "you will each support the team on your side of the line, regardless of any opposite allegiance. Am I understood?"

"Yes, Miss Whitworth," in a grand chorus.

"Splendid. Now I want to hear a lot of noise, if you please. I will be refereeing St Emilia's, while Miss Fellany does the same for the Crater School, to watch for any infractions. Team captains, you know the rules?"

"Yes, Miss Whitworth!" in an answering bellow from the anchors at the back of each team.

"Very good. Lift the rope. Take your positions; take the strain. Craters, one step back; no, no, that won't do, one more. There," as the handkerchief hung precisely above the line. "Ready! Heave!"

R adhika had attended many a festival in India where the crowds and the noise had simply overwhelmed her, in all the best possible meanings of that word. It was the simple volume of sound that she remembered particularly, and that she mourned; she had heard nothing like it anywhere on Mars, and never expected to. Now, she thought perhaps she had finally met its match. They might number only two hundred or so, but the girls of the Crater School and their handful of visitors threw heart and soul into cheering on their side, whichever side that might happen to be. The roar of "Come on, St Em's!" was at least as loud as its counter of "Heave, Cratereans, heave!"

Caught in the middle, our three abandoned any thought of favouritism and merely cheered for each side in turn, as that handkerchief went this way and that, back and forth between them, for they were quite evenly matched.

Once each, the mistresses blew for an infraction, though Radhika had no idea of the rules or what the offence might have been. Each time, the teams resumed their starting positions, the rope exactly straddling the line.

Later, dark mutters suggested that perhaps that had been strategy, that St Emilia's had deliberately infringed in order to bring them back to the line again, even though at the time they'd had a couple of feet advantage over the Crater School. Be that as it may, and rumours notwithstanding, the official record of the game in that term's *The Craterean* records that at the cry of "Heave!" after the final restart the visiting team employed a tactic not yet seen, backpedalling with many brief timed steps rather than the slow steady heaves of before. The Crater School was taken by surprise, losing ground and then more ground, not quite certain how to respond. Instructions were called urgently from their captain at the back, the indefatigable Melanie Fitzwalter, but it was too late: they couldn't hold up the rush until the heels of their own first tugger had crossed the line, and thus was she eliminated.

Eleven against ten: advantage, St Emilia's. And so it went on: another Craterean eliminated, and another. At this point, as the rules apparently allowed, the visitors turned their backs to their opposition, took the rope over their shoulders rather than under their arms, and simply charged towards the screaming spectators.

It was a riot, a rout, Melanie Fitzwalter herself being dragged face-down over the line after she refused to let go of the rope. She rose up filthy, laughing, and ran to shake her opposing captain's hand, to clap her on the back and congratulate her, to exclaim over her tactics and promise to be ready for them next year.

Radhika was surprised to find herself quite hoarse from shouting, and quite unclear which team she had finally been shouting for. She was still abuzz with the excitement of it all when Miss Whitworth came up to her scoldingly: "Radhika Harvey, there you are! Why don't you have your running shoes on? No, never mind now, you can run perfectly well barefoot in the circumstances; but I thought I had been quite clear that all members of my squad participate in the Friday games? No? Well, never mind, then. Hurry and join your teammates in the lineup for the four-forty. I haven't seen you jump yet either, so I'll want you at both high and long. It's such a pity about the shoes, jumping barefoot is never—"

"Please, Miss Whitworth," Charm said, "I could run and fetch them?"

"Yes. Good. Go. Radhika—oh, you're hosting one of our visitors? I do beg your pardon, I hadn't intended for a moment to deprive you of both your guardians."

"Oh, never think about that, Miss Whitworth; of course I'm going to follow Radhika around faithfully, to see her compete. What could be more fun, with a new friend?"

# CHAPTER TEN

## —And One Too Many Blows to the Head!

Radhika showed herself capable of both running and jumping at a level likely to satisfy any games mistress, even accounting for the fact that an Earth-grown physique did give her somewhat of an advantage, in the slightly lighter gravity of Mars.

On the other hand, she was competing against Martian girls who would always look more than a little ... overstretched ... to Earth-accustomed eyes; and Radhika had been reckoned short even down at Home. A somewhat-stronger build couldn't compete with simple length of limb, when it came to passing out advantages at the running track or the jumping pit. Radhika was doing well for her age and her size, but would surely never be outstanding in any of those events.

"You were jolly good, though," Capri assured her, after she'd been eliminated from the last of those, the high jump. "And if they gave out points for determination and effort, you'd be way ahead of everyone. I've never seen someone so, so *concentrated* on a sports field."

If there was a gracious way to receive a compliment, Radhika had never learned it. Instead she offered the traditional schoolgirl blush-and-mumble, and looked to Charm to turn the conversation hastily elsewhere.

And was betrayed, utterly: "You wait till you see her on the cricket pitch," quoth that worthy, "in a proper match, I mean, not knockabout. She's a fiend in human form, especially if she gets her gander up. Then, look out: bowling or batting, that ball comes at you like a rocket. You hardly have time to see it before it's on you; and then you're either chasing it hopelessly all the way to the boundary, or else you're trudging back to the pavilion with your stumps in shatters."

"Oh, stop it," Radhika grumbled. "It's all rot, anyway—"

"Slang, Radhika?" Of course there was a prefect coming up behind them; and of course it was Mary Holmes, who was perfectly nice in and of herself, but took everything in the most literal way imaginable, which unfortunately included school rules. It would never have occurred to her to look the other way, even though the trespass happened in conversation with a visitor and might easily have been passed over in the moment, even if it led to a scolding later. "Penny in the jar, please, when you get back to your house."

"Oh, —!" Radhika got no further in her first response, because Charm stepped quite heavily on her toe, to let her brain catch up with her temper. She squeaked, and scowled, and took a breath, and said, "I'm very sorry, Mary. Of course I'll pay the fine."

All the words were right and proper, but she was clouding up as they watched. Like many a schoolgirl, her pennies were precious to her, and painfully few in number. Every house collected fines from their more sinful children—generally, that is to say, the Middles—and used them to buy pretty things for their common room, voted for by the girls themselves from a shortlist drawn up by prefects and housemistress.

"Well, see that you do. That's all." Mary dismissed them with a nod, and went her way, with no notion of the glower that Radhika was directing at her back.

"Oh, *bother* Mary Holmes!" There was a consensus, at least among the younger girls, that "bother" didn't quite count as slang, and hence could not possibly be punishable. Even so, they were careful to look both ways before they used it, just in case.

"Well, you were asking for it," Charm said, with a measurable absence of sympathy, "slanging out here where everyone's milling about all the time. Someone's bound to overhear."

Even her friends, even her sherpa was turning against her now. Radhika scowled, but managed to bite back any response, as a courtesy to their guest.

Nothing seemed to go quite right for Radhika, all the rest of that day. Whatever she did, she was scolded for being too late or too slow or out of turn; and Capri was always there at her elbow, so she simply had to swallow her temper and fume inwardly, no more.

Even more infuriatingly, Capri seemed really nice. Radhika thought she might have liked to make friends, if only her insides weren't seething all the time. She knew she was coming across as sour and disagreeable, so in the end she gave up any attempt at being mannerly, and just let Charm carry all the weight of their conversation. Bedtime came almost as a relief to her, when she could pull her cubicle's curtains closed against the world and everything in it, and fester in silence and solitude.

It is not to be supposed that a girl taking such an unhealthy state of mind to bed with her should enjoy a night of restful slumber, or anything remotely like it. Poor Radhika tossed and turned and couldn't sleep, while her mind churned over and over; and when at last exhaustion did finally carry her away, her dreams were dark and angry and offered her no rest.

It was a sullen, weary girl, then, who rose to greet the morning with a snarl. The stark shadows under her eyes made more than one of her housemates enquire if she was feeling quite well; her answering growls made more than one of those shy away from her, and steer clear all morning long.

It was a long, long, very long morning. Even breakfast dragged; Chapel seemed endless, and had any sermon ever been so dull?

So thoroughly out of sorts was she, she even glowered at Melanie Fitzwalter her very self, when that worthy came to call her out of the room during letter-writing.

"So fierce!" Melanie laughed. "Bring something of that mood to the cricket pitch this afternoon, will you? But in the meantime, tidy your hair and go to the study for a minute; Miss Hendy wants a word with you."

M iss Hendy needed only one glance to see that something was severely amiss with her wayward charge. However, she knew enough to tell temper from temperature, spite from sickness; and she knew also how easily a schoolgirl of Radhika's age could be twisted awry, and how an afternoon's exertions under the sun could readily lick her back into shape again.

So she did nothing more than remind Radhika to go to Sister Anthony if she had the headache, and to take a friend with her; "we don't want you ailing and off your game for the match this afternoon, dear. We owe St Emilia's a good licking, after yesterday's unhappy performance."

Then, coming straight to the point, "I have news for you, which I hope won't come as too much of a shock. No, no— it's nothing to do with your mother," as the little face was wracked with fear. "Rather, your father has been called away on a matter of business."

"C-called away?" She looked bewildered. "But, but he's not here, and all his business is in Marsport, so..."

"I mean he was called away to Earth," Miss Hendy explained. "He telephoned the school, to say that he boards an aethership this very afternoon. Of course, there is no telling when he will be able to return; you know, I am sure, that passage through the aether realm is wholly unpredictable in its duration. His absence may not make very much difference to your daily life here—except," with a smile, "you may be excused writing your weekly letter to him," *oh yes, child, we do notice*, "until his return—as of course you were expected to stay with us through the holidays as well. Nevertheless, I thought you should know right away. He says he has put a letter in the post for you, which may explain more; I cannot tell. Some men prefer not to trouble a daughter," *or her mistresses either*, "with their business affairs. That's all now," with a friendly nod. "Trot along and make use of your freedom to write to a friend instead."

Radhika would have liked to hurl herself out of the study, and slam the door with all the fury her body could express. However, she was learning the temper of the school, just as the school was learning hers; so she left the room as gracefully as she could manage when her limbs were literally shaking with rage, and closed the door quietly behind her.

There was no prospect, no possibility of going back into the common room and resuming her seat, starting another letter. None at all. Instead, she sat on the polished wood of the stairs and stared down at her fists, where they had clenched themselves in her lap.

The night manager of the Blue Heron hotel had no business interests on Earth. Their coming here had been a deliberate separation, a parting of all ties. Papa-ji had made that clear, again and again.

And Papa-ji had a wife here on Mars, who was desperately and perhaps fatally ill, whom he had not seen for months on end; and he had a daughter, whom he had simply ... packaged away, somewhere she would be kept safe and no trouble. No trouble to him.

His sole excuse, his only argument had been that his job required too much of him; he couldn't take the time to visit his wife in her hospital bed, he couldn't take the time to raise his daughter, his whole focus had to be on his work, in order that he might keep a roof over their heads. Three roofs, now: hers and her mother's and his own.

And yet, and yet he had simply abandoned that work and both of them, all his obligations, to go swanning off to Earth on a trip of necessarily indefinite length?

She couldn't, she could *not* remember having been this angry at anyone, ever.

"Hullo!"

She looked up, reluctantly, and there was Melanie again.

"Bad interview, was it? Or—I hope it wasn't bad news from home?"

She didn't seem able to unknot her fists, but she used them as they were to scrub at her eyes anyway. Rising to her feet seemed only polite, so she did that too, hopeful that her knees might hold her up. "Oh—no, not really. Only, something I hadn't expected, and..."

And there were no words to take her any further, so she stopped there.

"...And you didn't know how to deal with it, so the stairs seemed the most immediate option? Trust me, Radhika, you are not the first. I'd be surprised if any girl has passed through her time at Stokes House without needing to utilise that convenient stair at some point or another. I certainly haven't. No, don't worry, I won't pry. It's none of my business, unless or until you care to share—though please do remember that I am Head of House, and you may bring your troubles to me at any time, that's one of my functions. But you're a Middle, of course, so keeping things bottled up is one of yours, I know. Anyway: you needn't go back into the common room, if you'd rather not just now. Why not take a spell in the garden, or walk down to the cricket field, have a look at the square? You'll be having a bowl on it later, or my name's not Melanie Lorraine Fitzwalter, which as a matter of fact it is. Just remember, change into your cricket whites before lunch, and you'll be sitting with our visitors. With that charming Capri girl, I expect, as you've been one of her chosen companions all weekend. I'm looking forward to seeing her at the crease, too, I'm told she has quite the eye, and a very pretty late cut. You might want to be on the watch for that."

The Crater School players were interspersed between the visitors at table, so that Radhika had Capri on one side and a stranger the other. Capri already knew that she was moody; perhaps the stranger would think she was simply shy? It didn't matter, anyway. She didn't care what anybody thought, never mind someone she'd likely never see again after today. So she stared at her plate and moved her food around and actually ate very little of it because being this angry for this long had left her feeling sick, and let the rest of the table think what it might, until:

"Nervous, Radhika? No wonder, your first appearance for the school, so young, and such a big match too!"

Melanie's voice startled her, murmuring close by her ear. She hadn't seen the Head Girl abandoning her own seat at the far end of the table, to come down at talk to her.

"Oh! Um, nervous? No, not really..."

"Not? Well, good for you—but you give every appearance of it, and if you don't buckle down and eat your lunch
instead of playing with it, trust me, you won't be playing
cricket this afternoon, you'll be in San under Sister Anthony's
thumb. She sees all and knows all, and you can't hope to hide
a loss of appetite on such an important day. You're looking
peaky already, I might add. Eat up, kid; you're going to need
the fuel."

So warned, Radhika hurriedly choked down as much as
she could. The very last thing she wanted was to be whisked
away and interrogated by the school's honestly rather terrifying matron. She didn't expect to be able to hold out under
question—legendarily no Crater School girl ever had, not
even Rowany de Vere!—and she dreaded confession. She'd
far rather bottle up and swallow down all this anger inside
her, even if it soured her stomach, sooner than let it all come
out in a flood of bile. She'd been raised by a soldier, and a
British soldier at that; she meant to keep her upper lip stiff,
her emotions in check, and her problems to herself.

Lunchtime took for ever, but at last, at long last it was
time to accompany the St Emilia girls down to the
cricket pavilion, and the glorious pitch itself. All the school
filed down in their wake, ready to cheer both sides indiscriminately, as was their wont; but Radhika distinctly heard
her classsmates call her name as she took her place in line.
She blushed, feeling uncomfortably that she hadn't quite
deserved to be celebrated, so far this weekend. Charm must
have told them how she'd been behaving, but they seemed to
think that a girl from the Upper Third playing with a senior
team was reason to cheer regardless.

Well, at least she'd do her best to keep them cheering till
the end. It was true, she did seem to play better when she was
furious; and oh, she was furious today.

Alis Rasmussen was captaining the Crater School team, to help settle the new picks with some solidity and experience. She tossed the coin high, and the visiting captain Heidi called "Heads!"

Miss Whitworth bent over to see where the half-crown had landed.

"It's tails, I'm afraid. Alis, will you bat or bowl?"

"Oh, bat, please," Alis said promptly. She knew this pitch of old. It should bounce high and true at the start of play, Mr Marks had prepared it so lovingly; but it had seen hard play yesterday, and all the rolling in the worlds wouldn't keep it smooth for long. By the time their innings was over, she could fairly hope it would be breaking up, to provide a grippy bed for spinners.

Heidi nodded, a little thin-lipped. She had played here yesterday and in previous years as well, so she too had some knowledge of what to expect. The two captains shook hands and wished each other luck, then Alis led her team back to the pavilion, while St Em's scattered to their fielding positions and their opening bowlers started pacing out their runs at either end of the pitch.

Two minutes later, the Crater School openers came out to the wickets, padded up and gloved against some anticipated belters. The two schools loved each other extremely, and therefore gave no hint of quarter on the playing field. That ball in Miss Whitworth's hand would be coming at them with all the speed and craft and guile at St Em's disposal; they might hope to be striking it far and wide in response, but not for nothing are the bowlers on a team known as the attack. These opening overs would be a testing time, with both sides striving their utmost to seize the momentum of the day.

The two games mistresses, of course, were standing umpire. Miss Whitworth set the bails on the stumps at the non-striker's end, holding one arm out to keep all things in abeyance until her counterpart had done the same at the other end and then walked out to take up her position at square leg.

A moment's breathless hush, that seemed to encompass all the players and all the girls around the boundary rope and the sun, the chasing moons, the very afternoon itself—until Miss Whitworth dropped her arm and called "Play!"

Momentum is a fickle beast. "Who's winning?" is the stupidest question ever asked at a cricket match; advantage can swing this way and that, and a single bad over from either side can change the entire course of a game.

The bowlers of St Emilia's were fit and trained and eager for the fray. They came pelting in from either end, each sending down six balls bowled fast and straight and true before the cry of "Over!" came and they must cede the ball to their colleague.

For a while, the opening bats stood firm against that onslaught. But alas, one nicked a flyer straight to the wicket-keeper, who made no mistake in gloving it one-handed and holding tight. It was the last ball of that over; and with the very first ball of the next, as so often happens after a determined stand is broken, the survivor stepped back to a ball when she should have stepped forward, the bowler appealed, and Miss Whitworth had no hesitation in raising her finger: out, leg before wicket!

Alis put herself in next, to steady the ship. She was a steady and reliable bat, but a slow scorer; spin bowling was her passion, and she only really sparkled with a ball in her hand. She played out the rest of that over without scoring a run. At the other end was a nervy left-hander in her first game for the school. Seeing that Alis meant to drop anchor and occupy the crease, that meant—to her mind, at least—that it fell to her to get runs on the board. In vain did Alis warn her to play defensively for an over or two, to get her eye in before she started striking out. Lefties often have an advantage, facing right-arm bowlers; she meant to take every opportunity to exploit that, before the bowlers too could get their eye in.

The very first ball she faced, she stroked elegantly to the long-on boundary for a four. The school cheered lustily; she gazed around the field, tapped her bat in the crease, and waited for the next delivery.

It came off-line for once, and bouncing high; she swivelled on her heel and hooked it higher yet, to fly over long leg's desperate leap and into the crowd. A six!

"Don't let it go to your head," Alis warned again, as they waited for the ball to be returned by the excited Juniors it had fallen among. "You don't need to score off every ball."

Her blood was up; she barely heard her captain. The next ball, the bowler gave a little more air to; it was that deadly ball known as a yorker, pitching just before the crease and eluding the bat altogether, striking the batsman's toe with a cruel thud. Out for ten, lbw again!

From the pavilion verandah, her team-mates watched glumly as she trudged back to join them. Melanie Fitzwalter clapped the next bat on the shoulder: "Out you go, Felicity— and for Heaven's sake show a little discretion, before you start flailing wildly!"

"Yes, Melanie. I'll try."

Melanie watched her go, without too much hope in her heart, and said, "Better get padded up, Radhika. You're next in, according to Alis's list."

She might deny being nervous, and her brain might still be seething over matters nothing to do with cricket, but even so there was something of a tremble in her fingers, as she buckled on the pads and sat with her bat between her knees, watching the play. Her heart wasn't in her mouth at every ball bowled, every ball survived, not exactly, not to say in her *mouth*—but it did seem to give a little flutter at the sound of leather on willow, as if something had worked a little loose down there.

Ball after ball, over after over, the two batsmen did survive; but there were precious few runs coming to trouble the scorers. A one here, a two there; no boundaries at all, with the St Em's fielders every one of them on their toes and chasing after everything, hurling the ball back to their keeper before the Cratereans could even think of stealing another run.

Time was ticking away, and stumps would be drawn at four o'clock, for tea. That would spell the end of the Crater School's innings, however many girls they had left yet to bat.

"Oh, thank goodness, that's the end of their quickies," Melanie murmured. "About time, too—those girls look quite blown. Slow bowling for a while now. As I recall, though, Felicity doesn't quite like spin...?"

Felicity did not. She survived three balls, missed the fourth altogether, and heard the fatal rattle of her stumps falling at her back.

"You're in, Radhika. I wouldn't normally say this even to an old hand, never mind a new girl—but do try to get the scoreboard moving, if you can. We can't afford to lose more time just blocking everything."

Radhika nodded, and trotted down the white-painted steps to the boundary rope. She nodded at Felicity as they passed, then put the older girl entirely out of her mind. Spin, was it to be? She didn't mind spin at all. Indeed, she relished it. Growing up on the dusty, hard-baked, cracked-earth pitches of India, she had probably seen more spin than all the other girls on both teams put together...

124

*India.* She was suddenly heartsick, more than homesick, for the life there that she had loved, that she had had to leave so cruelly.

And Papa-ji has gone back, for his own private purposes, leaving his wife and daughter in the lurch, the absolute lurch...

There was almost a literal red mist abruptly in front of her eyes, as all her stoked anger surged to life again.

Alis wanted to speak to her; she shook her head, thin-lipped, and stalked to the wicket.

"Ready, Radhika?"

She nodded, and Miss Whitworth's arm dropped again. "Play!"

The St Em's girl skipped a few short paces to the line, and her arm came over.

Right-arm, leg-spin. Very well.

All the wise counsel would say to step forward and smother the ball, kill the spin, drop it at her feet. Learn the temper of the pitch, take the measure of the bowler before cutting loose. Radhika did the opposite. She stepped back, watched the ball bite turf, watched it turn as it rose—and clattered it to the square-leg boundary, almost knocking St Emilia's games mistress off her feet as she hastily scuttered out of its path.

A roar of approval, from all around the ground. Radhika shrugged, and readied herself for the next delivery.

This was pitched further up. Quite properly she stepped forward to meet it with the full face of her bat, before the spin could twist it away from its line—but far from the defensive block that any cautious batsman would have displayed, she drove it hard back along the pitch, nearly toppling Miss Whitworth this time as it evaded the bowler's desperate dive and scuttled swiftly to the rope. Another four!

That was the end of the over. While the fielders changed position, she met Alis in the middle of the pitch.

"Well played, young 'un! It's not quite according to Hoyle, in your first real match; but keep this up if you can, we're desperate for runs. I'll tip a single, first chance I get, and see you back at the crease again. I've seen this next bowler before; orthodox left-hander, so with you batting leftie as you do, you odd creature, her standard ball will be coming in to you. Be aware, though, she also has a Chinaman..."

As promised, the first ball of the next over, Alis dropped it at her feet and sprinted for the other end. Radhika was ready, already backing up as far as the law allowed and perhaps a whisker farther. She pelted down the pitch for all she was worth, and slid her bat in across the crease before the scrambling wicket-keeper could come around the wicket and stump her out.

That worthy gave her a nod of approval. "I should have been ready for that, I suppose, after watching you despatch poor Sylvie. Something of Madras in your style, I fancy?"

It probably wasn't meant to sound sneering; it certainly wasn't even a hint at the colour of her skin; but Radhika was hypersensitive to any slight just then. She nodded curtly, and turned her attention back to the game.

Overpitched. Two quick steps made it into a full toss, which got everything it deserved, lofted over the boundary at point.

Almost inevitably, the bowler overadjusted; her next ball was a long hop, allowing Radhika to step back and cut it fiercely through the covers for four.

The cheering was all but continuous now, a steady rolling roar. Radhika was barely aware of it; all her contemptuous focus was on that ball, and the swiftest, most ruthless way of smacking it into the crowd.

After two more costly overs of spin, the captain of St Em's was forced to bring back her quick bowlers, if only to stop the rampage. But they had been tired already, and Radhika had allowed them little time to rest. The spring had left their step, the sting had been sapped from their arm; the best they could manage now was what Papa-ji was pleased to call a "military medium". Radhika had no fear of that.

The score rose up and up, as the clock ticked on and on. She had scored twenty-five runs, thirty, thirty-five. Nothing St Em's could offer was going to defeat her, in this mood. She cut and drove and hooked with impunity. Forty runs. Forty-five. A precious maiden fifty was in sight, perhaps only two balls away. Here came the first: an overpitched yorker, coming to her as a low full toss. Splendid. A swing, a crack, a cheer: forty-nine, and—

—and the school clock sounded the first stroke of four, and Miss Whitworth whipped the bails off at the other end and called time.

Radhika couldn't believe it. One more ball, she only needed one more ball! And it was her own side, her own mistress that betrayed her...!

"Forty-nine not out! Radhika, that's, that's epic! Congratulations!"

Capri seemed as excited for her as her own team was, but Radhika seethed with resentment. All through the twenty minutes allotted to tea, she ignored Mrs Bailey's dainty sandwiches, sausages and hard-boiled eggs, and devoted her time to glowering across the room at Miss Whitworth. She could have let them play out the over, rather than snatching the bails at the very first stroke; or she could simply have let all four strokes ring out before calling time. That would have allowed for one more ball, all Radhika had needed. It was deliberate, she was sure: an act of sabotage, to stop the new girl, the coloured girl from getting uppity.

Enragingly, Miss Whitworth had her back turned to Radhika throughout, and didn't even notice.

After tea, the opening bats for St Emilia's took centre stage. Thanks mostly to Radhika—and, let it be said, her tempestuous temper—they faced a stern task: ninety-two runs to make, and stumps to be drawn promptly at 6.30, whatever the state of the game.

They made a steady start, eating away at that total by ones and twos, until at last the ball went deep into the covers and they tried for three.

Alas for them: Radhika was patrolling the covers, and her arm was as lethal as her feet were quick to cover ground. She scooped up the ball, swivelled, sighted the keeper and hurled it back, all in one swift, economical motion. The keeper caught it above her head, swung her arm down and removed the bails, with the runner still a yard short of her ground.

The crowd erupted. The Middle School in particular was almost incandescent with joy, feeling that this marvel reflected well on all of them, even those who'd never so much as spoken to the new girl yet. Her dorm-mates, her classmates, her housemates were all but floating on the glory of it all.

"Tell you what, kid," Alis said, dropping a friendly arm across Radhika's shoulders, "first change of bowling, I'll put you on. They'll be expecting a change of pace, a little spin, a chance to catch their breath. They don't know we have a miniature demon in our midst."

She didn't quite like "miniature", but never mind. Let it go.

Next time the ball came her way, there was no glory to be seized, only a long hard chase to the boundary. A long hard unavailing chase, as it happened; and the Junior who snatched the ball as it bumped over the rope threw it back over Radhika's head and not very much further, which is always infuriating to a fielder.

As she went to retrieve it, already aggrieved, she heard a clear voice rise among the crowd: "I say, have you heard? False alarm, over the water at the San. That fever they were worried about? Turns out to be nothing worse than the Martian flu, and everyone's had that. They're wide open for visitors again, as soon as you like."

A false alarm. It was a false alarm. She could have gone to see Mama-ji this afternoon after all. She could have said no to Miss Whitworth, with the perfect excuse at hand; she could have avoided all that dancing about with Capri, because the St Em's girl would have been billeted in another dorm altogether, with another member of the team. She could have told Mama-ji about Papa-ji's latest betrayal, and they could have talked it over between them, and...

"Radhika! Pay attention, for Heaven's sake! You're on!" She startled around, fumbled the ball that an irate Alis had just tossed to her, had to stoop to pick it up again.

Feeling that dark flush on her cheeks that she hated so much, she stalked to the wicket and paced off her usual run. Scratching a mark with her heel to guide her, she turned to face the pitch—and realised that it was Capri taking guard in front of the stumps. Another wicket must have fallen, and she hadn't even noticed.

She didn't even care. She'd greet Capri with her very best, her very worst, her very fastest bowling, and see how the St Em's girl liked that.

"Play!"

A little skip to get going, and she fell into the familiar rhythm, the long swift run, the leap at the end as her arm came over. The ball left her hand with all the ferocity she could put into it, flying straight and true—and straight at Capri's unprotected head!

Her bat came up too late, too slow. She tried to twist aside, too slow again. She hadn't seen it in time, because no one looks for a beamer at all, never mind at head height.

Exactly at head height, to poor tall Capri. It caught her on the brow, with all the venom Radhika had put behind it, and it felled her like an ox. As she dropped, she broke her own wicket, but that was incidental. No one appealed; no one spoke at all as Capri lay across the stumps, still and lifeless and apparently quite dead.

The whole ground was eerily, dreadfully silent, except for one small, appalled voice: "Oh! Oh, no! Oh, what have I done...?"

# CHAPTER ELEVEN

## Aftermath

"I don't believe for a minute that the child ever meant to do it."

"Oh, great heavens, no! The ball slipped from her grip, that's all. She's been in floods of tears ever since. One thing to be said about Radhika, she does *not* indulge in half-measures. All her moods are extreme, where it's fury or remorse that has her in its grip at any given time. I'd ask Sister Anthony to give her a dose, just to quiet her down, except that of course the good sister has gone over the water with her poor patient."

An urgent consultation on the telephone had resulted in the still-unconscious Capri being stretchered to the water's edge by four prefects and then rowed across the lake—a shorter, smoother journey than the coach road—to the doctors of the great Sanatorium, with her own games mistress at her side, as well as the Crater School's matron.

Just as urgent, just as critical, but far less easy to resolve was the matter of Radhika. Miss Leven had convened a panel of senior mistresses—herself, Miss Hendy, Miss Whitworth, Miss Harribeth—and two supernumeraries, in the persons of Isobel Buchanan and Rowany de Vere, to talk it over. The latter two brought different perspectives with them, arising out of their very different experiences; they had proved both inventive and helpful in previous crises, and Miss Leven turned to them these days almost as a matter of course.

"Even after the weeping-fit passes," she said now, "as in the end it must, I still feel that Radhika will need some days out of school. Also, perhaps, the school will need some days absent Radhika, to let the shock of today fade into memory, till only the fact remains."

"Yes," said her housemistress judiciously. "She would hate to be the centre of attention in that way, stared at and whispered about—and much as I dislike to admit it, it is beyond the capacity of a teenage girl to refrain from staring and whispering, in the immediate aftermath of high drama. Shall we send her to Sister Anthony?"

"I dislike to use our own San as an isolation ward," Miss Leven said slowly, "though we have of course done so at need. Sister Anthony, I know, dislikes it even more, especially when she has other girls under her care and has to police the ward to keep them all apart. Besides, the San may be a particular, specific element of the school, but it is still school, in every sense of the word. I would send Radhika home for a week, if I could; but her mother of course is here, and her wretched father has chosen this time to go swanning off Home, about some business of his own. Which leaves her orphaned entirely; she has no other relatives on Mars, and as far as I am aware no close ties to any other family that might have been implored to help us in our hour of need."

Isobel Buchanan stirred thoughtfully. "I could take her down to my house in Terminus, if it came to that. The current tenants are artists, friends of mine; they'd welcome company, and I could promise a thoroughgoing distraction to a young girl's mind. Extremely thorough; she'd have no chance to dwell on anything, under their care and my own.

However, I do have another idea. Looking back to last term and Mary Ellen's crisis, or one of them: is it possible that Mrs Mackenzie might take Radhika in for a few days?"

"My dear, the very thing! Evelyn keeps busy in any number of ways, but I happen to know she does repine a little, over her necessary separation from the school. I shall telephone her immediately, to put the question; but I already know what her answer will be. It may be that she can give us news, too, about poor Capri."

So saying, Miss Leven bustled out of her study, towards her secretary's office where the Castle phone was kept. In the sudden silence caused by her departure—Isobel, like Nature, being no friend to a vacuum, and feeling somewhat responsible for this one—that worthy said, "Miss Fellany, of course, will stay with her pupil, until Capri is well enough to be escorted home. Has any thought been given to who will escort the other girls from St Emilia's?"

"Oh, that's quite settled, yes. They will escort themselves, or each other. They're all relatively senior; half of them are used to making their own way to and from school, quite alone; they have their Head Girl to look to in any matters arising, and there is always the telephone if they need more adult advice or assistance." Miss Harribeth smiled at her less-experienced colleague and added, "I know you've always kept your own girls close, and no wonder in the circumstances, no blame to you for that; but the average Martian schoolgirl is as independent as they come. Fifteen of them together? That's a war band, if they meet any kind of trouble."

"Oh, of course. You'd think I'd know that by now, wouldn't you? Some Earthly attitudes are insurmountable, it seems. Shame on me. I shall show remorse by passing this plate of biscuits around one more time—and lo, they are all gone, thanks to my sacrificial generosity."

Miss Hendy snorted, and touched the bell to summon Miss Leven's devoted maid. "Ah, Mary: a fresh pot of tea, please, and another plate of biscuits. Thank you, dear. Whatever news Evelyn brings back to us," after Mary had closed the door behind her, "it'll require more planning and discussion, you all know that; and never a discussion was born, that didn't go better with another round of refreshments."

So it was that when at last Radhika roused from the bewilderment of misery and nightmare into which her tempest of tears had flung her, she found herself in her dormitory bed and the sky not even dark yet outside the window, which was strange enough. Stranger yet, there was a kindly seeming, motherly type of woman there in her cubicle with her, neatly and efficiently packing Radhika's own night-case with Radhika's own things.

"I, um—*oh!*" as it all came back to her, the deeds of this dreadful day and hers the worst, the worst by far. "Am I, am I to be expelled, then, must I go—?" That thought, that dreary expectation cut itself off mid-word, as she remembered that she had no place *to* go, quite. Perhaps Mr Garrard would take her on as a chambermaid after all, if she flung herself on his mercy, in the absence of her father.

"Expelled? What nonsense you children do come up with, to be sure! Expelled, forsooth! We never have, and I hope we never will; I hope we take better care of our girls than that. No, no. It's only that you've worked yourself up into quite a state—I expect your head is aching quite dreadfully, isn't it?—over a simple accident, and Miss Leven quite rightly felt that you should come to me for a day or two, to catch your breath and set your thinking straight. My name is Mrs Mackenzie and I live across the way, across the water. Now trot along to the bathroom, dear, and splash a little cold water on your face, you'll feel better for it."

Radhika had been at school long enough to understand that as an instruction to wash, to groom, and to put herself in order. She hastened to obey, muddled though she was at meeting nothing but kindness where she had fully expected, where she had surely deserved stern censure, punishment, removal.

When she made her way back to the dormitory, her case and apparently her hostess were standing ready for her, outside the door.

"Yes. I'm sure that feels better, doesn't it? Come along, then. Hoist up your things—I don't suppose you're feeling remotely strong right now, but there's no weight to it, you won't be needing much—and follow me. Another day I might have rowed over, and we might very well bring you back across the lake when you're ready for school again, but on this occasion I borrowed the gardener's boy to stoke for me, and brought the steam-car. We call him Percival: the car, I mean, not the boy. The boy is Ixaka, and I believe he loves Percy better than any of his proper work. I had intended to find him a place on one of the local farms, where he could stay close to his village and his people; but now I think perhaps I should look further afield, perhaps to the railway-yards below, if he yearns this much for machinery and grease. You do know of our work among the Basques, I expect, how we give the youngsters work here on the lake when their families need it, and help them move on when the time comes...?"

Afterwards, Radhika could remember only snatches of that journey around the lake. She remembered Ixaka, who made her say his name three times before she had it right. He was a cheerful youth, with a smear of oil on his cheek and redcoal dust in his hair, more of both on his ill-fitting dungarees. She remembered Mrs Mackenzie's voice all the way, though hardly anything of what had actually been said. She remembered no scenery at all, though surely there must have been views all across the valley and further yet. Mostly, she remembered her own dizziness and confusion, that feeling of being neither quite on her head nor quite on her heels, as unfamiliar and unpleasant a sensation as she could ever recall.

At last, though, they came to a small, very solid-seeming house on the water's edge, in the shadow of a long, high building that was only one among others, a complex of red stone and mysterious meaning.

She was far beyond asking questions, about anything at all. She could barely fumble for words in the back of her mind, never mind give them voice. She just let Mrs Mackenzie draw her out of the car and over the hearth, into a warm, pleasant, comfortable home. She followed orders, because nothing else could ever have occurred to her; and so soon enough she found herself tucked up in bed in an attic room, with a mug of rich, meaty broth in her hands and firm instructions to drink it all, yes, every last drop, and then let Nature take her kindly course and ease a sore and suffering child over.

It may be that Mrs Mackenzie too keeps a dose or two on hand in case of need, courtesy of her husband the celebrated Dr Mac of Crater School lore and legend.

Whatever the truth of the matter, the fact is that Radhika slept deeply, long and late. She roused in the morning to the sound of curtains being drawn, and a fall of summer sunshine across the bed. Blinking, she squinted up to see, once again, a stranger smiling down at her.

"Good morning, miss. My name's Verna, and I'm the cook and housekeeper here. I've brought you up a nice tray of breakfast, so see you do justice to it, now; and then you're to have your bath, get dressed and come downstairs in your own time, if you please. No hurry in the worlds. Everywhere else may be all hurry, hurry, but I won't have that, not here. Sit up, now, and eat up."

She offered to lay the steaming, tempting tray across Radhika's legs, but, "Please, may, may I get up, and sit at that window there?"

"Fussy about crumbs in the bed, is it? Yes, of course you may, you silly goose. Just mind you put that pretty robe on— Indian silk, is it?—for the breeze off the lake is still too cool for pyjamas at this time of day, so it is."

Radhika did as she was told, robe and slippers too. Then she sat in the window-seat with the tray on a side table, conveniently to hand, and nibbled toast and sipped milky tea as she gazed across the lake. There was the school, so much smaller and less overwhelming at this distance; and there were fishermen out on the water, and other traffic going this way and that, to speak of a world beyond hers, far broader and far deeper. There was a lesson there, she was sure, only that she didn't much want to be thinking about lessons just at this time. She didn't much want to be thinking at all, she'd rather just look, and feel the sun on her face, and eat that boiled egg right out of its shell, holding it warm in her hand here, in a way she'd never be allowed at home; and then perhaps some more toast, with butter and some of that delicious-looking honey...

When she came shyly downstairs, the housekeeper Verna took the tray from her with all its empty dishes, nodded her approval and added a gentle scold, "Don't you be doing my work for me, now, young lady. You leave dishes where they lie, you hear me?"

"I, I don't think I could, honestly."

"Brought up better than that, were you? Always doing for yourself, and others too, I make no doubt? Well, and there's no fault to be found with that—but you're here to rest and ease your mind, as I understand it, so just you let me do for you, this one chance. Now go through there," a nod at a French window standing ajar, "and you'll find Madam busy in the garden. You'll never find her anything else but busy, mind, wherever she is, so don't you go making more work for her, I won't thank you for it."

The words might have been stern, but the little nudge at her shoulder was gentle, and just enough to get her started. She stepped out onto flagstones, a patio with garden furniture, plants in pots. Beyond was a lawn, or perhaps a long bank of grass said it better, running down irregularly to the water's edge. It was lined with flower beds, and shaded by old trees; and there was Mrs Mackenzie, yes, on her knees with a trowel and a trug.

"Radhika! There you are! Did Verna roust you out? She does not believe in letting young bones lie abed, that one. But I know she'll have fed you properly, and that's the main thing. I want you eating like a horse, you hear me? You're far too thin. A Martian girl is robust, above all else. Honesty and clean living and all the virtues we try to inculcate in our girls all stem from good health and a sound constitution, and so my husband will tell you, when he sees you later on—oh, don't look so alarmed, child! He's not an ogre. Actually, I find him rather nice. I do want him to give you a once-over, just to be sure you've taken no harm from your ... passions yesterday, but I promise, it won't be a terrible experience. Now, you sit on that tree-stump there—it's quite clean—and talk to me while I chase out the last of this redwort, vile stuff that it is. Did you sleep well?"

"Well, yes, I did, awfu—I mean miraculously well, to tell the truth. But please, Mrs Mackenzie, before we talk about anything else, may I know how, how Capri is doing?"

"Ah, now." Mrs Mackenzie sat back on her heels and nodded approvingly. "Nicely done, that girl. Just the right question, at just the right time. And as a matter of fact, you may. I am pleased to be able to tell you that Capri has woken up at last, and survived a relentless battery of tests. I'm told she has a monstrous headache, and something of a concussion too, which means she'll be staying with us a few days longer— why, Radhika, what's the matter now?" as Radhika stared a little wildly over her shoulder and up at the house, wondering quite which window concealed her suffering victim.

She didn't have the words to explain her sudden panic, but then she didn't need to. Mrs Mackenzie took a moment to compose herself, and said, "Radhika Harvey, do you not understand where you are? What all ... this," with a broad sweep of her arm to encompass those looming buildings at her back, "what all this actually is?"

"I, I—oh. *Oh!*" Once again, she was dumbfounded. She hadn't thought about it all, but of course; that complex could only ever be one thing.

"Yes, dear. This is the Sanatorium, and my husband is its founder and leading light, for his sins. Which is why we live ever in its shadow, because he keeps himself permanently on call, available day or night, every day and every night of the year. He has perfectly competent colleagues and eager juniors ever ready to carry some of that burden for him, but— oh well, never mind. He would be less himself, if he listened to them. Or to me, come to that. At any rate, that is that, and you are here. Capri is somewhere in there," again that wave of the arm, "receiving the very best attention, I make no doubt, with the younger doctors dancing attendance on the poor frail maiden—"

"I, I really thought I'd killed her," in a small voice, her absolute confession.

"Oh, nonsense, child. I told you, Martian schoolgirls are robust. She will be perfectly fine, and able to tell you so herself, in a day or two. Before that, though—well, has it not dawned on you yet, Radhika? Not even yet?"

Mrs Mackenzie was teasing her. Actually teasing, when Radhika had been so solemn and baring her soul, and, and—

"Ohhh... Mama-ji! I can see my Mama-ji!"

"Indeed you can. Day in and day out, so long as she is strong enough and you are our guest here; but not before Dr Mac has checked you out, and read you all the awful warnings about not exciting her and not troubling her and so on and so forth. She remains desperately ill, Radhika, and so I warn you. The doctors are doing everything possible, and even now that may not be enough. But, yes, you will be able to see her, at long last. I know it's been an age—and you will find a clean handkerchief in your blazer pocket, I know, because I put it there last night..."

# CHAPTER TWELVE

## Many Meetings

"Come to see the little mother, is it, dearie? I think she's sleeping now, but of course you may sit with her till she wakes. I know the doctor said you could only have ten minutes, but we don't count that until her eyes open, so…"

It was a long, long walk down to the end of the ward. There were beds on both sides, seemingly in endless number; and every one of them occupied, and their curtains tossed high over the bars at this time of day, so that Radhika felt every patient's eyes on her for every step of that walk. She knew that her hair was neat and her shoes polished, she knew that she looked quite trig in the Crater School uniform, green and gold, a quite unexceptionable schoolgirl—and yet she felt her cheeks burn darkly under that scrutiny. What would they be thinking of her, all these curious women? Perhaps they would find her exceptionable after all. An Earth girl, all too clearly, no natural or native Martian; and a half-caste at that, her bloodlines clear to be seen, neither one thing nor the other. There was a horrible word for that, she knew: *miscegenation*, that was it. Once heard, never forgotten; and she had heard it more than once, a great deal more. No one would ever tell her what it meant, they just sneered it quietly between themselves in the officers' mess whenever she was guesting there. In the end she'd had to root it out of the dictionary herself, hitting on the spelling at last after many trials, many errors. Was it any wonder that she preferred the company of Tommies, or her Hindustani friends? Papa-ji had taught her to ignore the officers' contempt, just as he did himself, but the fury had burned in her long and long, and still did.

She glowered sullenly left and right, silently daring any one of the patients to make any comment they chose, to speak their mind. Why not? Only a schoolgirl, after all; what would she know, what should she care about manners...?

All that walk, all that way, and she knew perfectly well that she was distracting herself, teasing herself into a temper, simply in order to avoid thinking about what waited at the end. She had yearned for this moment, yes, and pleaded for it, argued for it, and raged when it was denied her; and now almost she dreaded it. Dr Mac's face came back to her, his eyes kindly but his expression solemn, his words clear and to the point, no equivocation: *You must understand, Radhika, you should prepare yourself to find your mother much changed. She has been very ill for a very long time, and she is ill yet, far from out of the woods. For every step forwards, she seems to slip another back. Whether we will save her in the end, or whether this dreadful disease will take her at last, as it has taken so many others before her— as to that, I cannot say. Some treatments seem to show promise, but there are no true promises in this work, no guarantees.*

The very last bed in the ward was the only one curtained off for privacy. Radhika felt a lump in her throat the size of—well, it couldn't actually be the size of Olympus Mons, that was just silly, but it surely felt that way. The ward sister smiled down at her in understanding, twitched the curtain aside and peered in.

"Yes," a soft murmur, pitched not to disturb a sleeper, "she's not roused yet. She will soon, I expect. Trot along in and sit with her awhile, let yours be the first face she sees when she wakes."

Radhika nodded nervelessly, and still needed the sister's gentle shove on her shoulder to urge her on, between the curtains and into the dimness beyond.

O h. No. It was the wrong bed, the wrong ward, the wrong patient. How terrible to be standing here staring at, intruding on a stranger as she slept, caught in all her vulnerability...

*You should prepare yourself to find your mother much changed—* but not this much, surely? Not so much as to make her unrecognisable, a shrunken shadow, grey and wasted, the skin stretched over her skull, every bone and sinew in her arm clear to be seen, where it lay revealed on the coverlet.

Radhika let slip a gasp, she couldn't keep it in; and half turned to leave, half believing that first desperate notion that somehow a mistake had been made, that no, this really wasn't Mrs Geeta Harvey, wife and mother and...

No. Of course it was her mother. Only for a moment had the ravages of illness confused her eyes, and the shadows of the cubicle. That was her mother's wedding band, on a saucer beside the bed with all her other jewellery, her finger too reduced to bear it now. It was her mother's hand all the same, though there was no flesh left to it now. That was her mother's face, for all its stark exposure.

There was a chair beside the bed, and just as well, because Radhika fell into it more than sitting down, her knees abruptly treacherously trembly. For a while she only gazed at her mother, holding her own breath until she saw the faint rise and fall of the coverlet, all that she had to tell her that her mother still lived and breathed. She had seen death, more often than she should have done, perhaps, certainly more often than her parents knew; but Mama-ji herself had taken Radhika to her grandmother's pyre before it was lit, to let her speak her final, private farewells to her beloved Nani-ji. It had and had not been the elderly woman of her lifelong memories, the skin waxy and all the humour, all the experience, all the wisdom fled away.

Now she looked at her own mother and saw the same, or something close akin. This was not the vibrant, lively, tender woman who had made her and raised her and taught her so much about the world. She could barely even be called a shadow of her own true self, so diminished she was, and all her living qualities absent. *The little mother*, the ward sister had called her, and she had been little enough before; she was smaller now. Radhika almost felt grotesque in her youth and strength, her heedless native health.

Tentatively, she reached out a hand to touch her mother's. There was no response except in herself, a soft sigh, almost a sob of relief to find it warm beneath her fingertips. Seemingly lifeless, but warm yet: surely that had to be a good thing, a sign of promise, a breath of hope? She slipped her hand under her mother's, not daring to grip for fear of breaking those fragile bird-bones beneath the parchment skin. This was enough, simply to be palm to palm, to have the touch of her, to feel a tremulous pulse.

"Radhika, child, is that you?"

It was only a whisper, but it startled her quite out of the reverie she had slipped into, so that she gasped again, and gaped to see her mother's eyes open and frowning at her. For a moment she could only make breathless, meaningless sounds, so that Mama-ji went on, "Why are you here? So far from your father, who cares for him...?"

*Not I*, she thought in English, defiant, dismissive; but her mother was speaking Hindustani, as they always had between themselves, and the double meaning didn't fit.

"He, he sent me here," she said slowly, picking her way delicately between one truth and another—*under no circumstances are you to excite her in any way*, another of Dr Mac's warning precepts—"to be close to you. There is a school, across the water."

"I have seen it, the girls in their uniforms, yes, as you are now. But your father—"

"My father is gone Home," Radhika said. She would choose her truths, yes, and skirt some of them as she must, but she would not lie. "I don't know why, but he, he said it was important. And I am here," and never mind in what order those two truths had occurred, "so now we can see each other, and I can watch you get well while he is gone."

"Child—"

"You must," Radhika said, suddenly fierce. "You *must*, Mama-ji. For me, and, and for Papa-ji too. How are we to live, how get by without you? He sent me here to watch over you," not quite a lie, not *quite*, "to make certain of you. You dare not fail me now."

Her mother made an odd, croaking sound, something halfway between a laugh and a sob, it might have been, in a throat too dry for either. "I will try, little one," for all the worlds as though she was still the Mama-ji of yore and Radhika an infant at her knee, "but all the doctors on Mars have not found a cure yet, and Papa-ji, you must promise me to look after Papa-ji when, if, I cannot..."

Just now, Papa-ji's welfare was the last and the least of her concerns. She felt that bitter, familiar rage roil in her stomach, and swallowed it hastily down; Mama-ji need not and must not see the least hint of *that*, above all. She well knew her daughter's temper, but this latest festering fury would distress her beyond measure, never mind what it had led to, another patient in another ward.

Another time, Radhika might have worried that keeping all that to herself was just another kind of lying, lying by omission; but on this occasion she was under strict and explicit orders. Mama-ji was to learn nothing that might remotely upset her, and that was that.

Very well, then. Radhika called up the spirit of her younger self, that self that had run wild through city streets with disreputable friends and babbled cheerfully about her adventures after but never quite let her parents learn the extent of her doings, never let them plumb the worst of what she had seen and experienced.

"Let me tell you about school," she said artlessly. "It's called the Crater School, because, well, here we are on the rim of Lowell Crater; and it's nothing like any school I've been before, so very much nothing like St Dymphna's. The staff—we're supposed to call them mistresses, but mostly we just say staffs—are really, well, demanding, but not in a *strict* way, 'zackly. They can be Tartars if you cross them, and the prees, I mean prefects, are even worse, but mostly they're quite friendly and helpful, so long as they think that you're trying. They keep us on our toes, anyway, from rising-bell to bedtime—and woe betide you if you haven't made your bed as neat as Papa-ji always insists on, because Sister Anthony will come down on you like a fall of rocks. She's the matron, and I don't know why she has a man's name but she does, and she's taller than Rowany, even, and as thin as, as thin as," *almost as thin as you,* "well, anything, really.

"And they have this system where a girl in your class, your house, your dorm is told off to look after you when you're new, and they call them sherpas, like the men who help us climb mountains in the Himalaya, because it really is steep at the start. My sherpa's called Charm, and she's the daughter of the art mistress, who's famous somehow but I don't think we've seen any of her work, it's all here on Mars and, well," they hadn't kept up their habit of seeking out art and beauty since they emigrated here. Life had been too hard, too much of a struggle, once they'd lost all that they had before.

"Charm's lovely, though. She has this fierce red hair, but no hint of a temper to go with it." *Not like me.* "She says her mother called her that, and her sister Levity, just to be certain they never grew that way. *Naming calls*, Charm says, and it works for virtues as well as the bad things. I don't *think* she's serious, 'zackly, but you never can tell, really, can you?

"Anyway, they take their cricket really seriously here, and I," *I knocked a girl to Kingdom come,* "I made forty-nine not out when the stumps were drawn for the end of our innings, and in a Seniors match, too, though I'm only a Middle here and a junior one at that. So that was good. And I wrote Miss Harribeth—she's History—an essay about the Roman invasions of England that she really, really liked," and no need to mention the first version that she really, really didn't, "and even the music mistress is baffled by all the tunings I know from Home," where *Home* meant *India* of course, and never England, "but there are some girls who are really keen to learn about them, so that's fun..."

She chattered on, steering further and further away from anything she very much didn't want to say, and found it easier than she ever would have expected, to paint herself as a happy schoolgirl in a happy school. Her mother barely spoke, but that didn't matter, so long as Mama-ji's palm lay atop Radhika's own, and her eyes were open and her mind was following along, so very alive after all; and when the ward sister came to call Radhika away, Mama-ji's fingers tightened at last into a firm grip of her daughter's hand, and something very much like a smile touched her wan, worn, exhausted face.

Ordinarily, Radhika could not bear to be idle. Her body grew as restive as her mind, if she lacked tasks or objectives or simply something, anything to do.

Here, though? This little house was like an island out of time, an oasis in a desert, a place to rest and breathe and let the world go by. She sat in the charming garden and read storybooks, or else she simply sat and watched the traffic on the water, hikers walking the lake path, birds and clouds overhead. Sometimes she would see a party of Crater School girls; they always waved as they passed, and she made a point of waving back, though she didn't really think they were waving to her. She didn't really think they'd seen her, honestly, in the shade beneath the trees. All their concern was the great bulk of the Sanatorium, and the patients who might be out on their balconies or on the lawns beneath.

She tried to explain it to Mrs Mackenzie once, how she hated having nothing to do, except that here it felt perfectly fine, permitted, even encouraged.

"That's because you're not doing nothing, dear," her hostess had replied, gathering up the tea-things and gesturing her to stay in place, in the comfort of her deck chair. "You're healing. It's a task, like any other."

And then she was gone, before Radhika could object that she wasn't the one who'd been hurt, and had nothing to heal from.

Light suppers and early to bed were the order of the day, come its ending. She didn't even mind that, somehow. Her bed was comfy and her room was snug, and for someone who had sat idle all day, she always did feel ridiculously weary when she got there, and was swiftly away.

Even her dreams seemed kinder in this kind house, and she woke more hopeful every morning.

"Now then, young lady. I'm going to talk to you like a Dutch uncle. Are you ready?"

"Um, yes, sir."

It was the evening of—was it her third day here, or her fourth? She wasn't sure, entirely. Nothing marked a change, really, from one day to the next. She might be reading a different book, she might go to visit Mama-ji at a different time of day, Verna was safe to put different meals on the table, and even so: everything blurred together into an idyll of peace, that she treasured if only because she knew it couldn't last.

She'd known that this time would come, too. Dr Mac had called her into his study and sat her down with pen and ink, a fresh sheet of paper. She didn't really understand that, but she had no doubt that this was the long-delayed retribution for what she'd done. Perhaps she was to write an apology to Capri? She was endlessly willing to do so, only that she'd rather not do it under adult supervision, and that she'd not been allowed so much as a pencil or a scrap of paper ere this.

"When we've been troubled," Dr Mac said musingly, steepling his fingers, "especially when we've been troubled for a long time and carried it all with us inside, all the story of that time tends to get twisted up with our emotions, our desires, our frustrations. It makes such a tangle, it comes hard to sort out what actually happened, and how you actually felt about it before the next thing came along, and the one after that.

"So what I want you to do," he went on, pulling a pipe from his jacket pocket and beginning to fiddle with it in the way of the dedicated smoker, "is to start at the top of the page there, and make a list of everything that's happened, everything that's gone wrong for you since your mother fell ill. No need to write that, I know all about that already; but whatever else there's been preying on your mind, please, in a nice clear list. In order, with numbers. Take your time, take the opportunity to practise the New School Hand; a man and his pipe may never be hurried, and it's an hour yet till supper."

One thing Radhika had learned in her time at the Crater School: it was useless to appeal an order of this nature. She wasn't quite sure if it counted as a punishment, and this house didn't really count as school—Dr Mac wasn't even a teacher!—but even so. She was still wearing the uniform, and still felt the entire schoolgirl, even under his benevolent gaze.

She sighed and reached for the pen, trying to organise her thoughts, as he disappeared into a cloud of fragrant smoke.

It was a hard task, harder than she'd expected. She felt that she was exposing herself with every word on every line, and she didn't much like the picture it painted of her attitudes or behaviour.

Nevertheless, she persisted; and when at last he tapped out the dottle from his pipe and left it upside-down in the ashtray to cool, she had a list that she could slide across the desk, mute and anxious.

1. Papa-ji sent me away, when I didn't want to come. Marsport is all I've known of Mars, all my friends are there, and Papa-ji needs someone to take care of him, but he wouldn't listen to me. I was so angry with him, I knew I was going to hate the Crater School.

2. Miss Hendy said she'd arrange for me to see Mama-ji as soon as possible, and then it didn't happen and it didn't happen, so I was angry with her and with the doctors here.

3. Then there were little things: Miss Hendy spoke to me about my English, and about my accent, and I felt hurt over that. Those. I think "slighted" is the word, perhaps?

Nothing about me seemed quite good enough for the Crater School, so I was resentful.

4. I was scolded for writing to Mama-ji instead of Papa-ji. That rankled too.

5. None of the mistresses were satisfied with my work, and I had to take extra tuition from Rowany. That was humiliating.

6. And then Miss Whitworth told me I couldn't go to see Mama-ji AGAIN, even though I'd been promised, and I was so furious. And we had to look after a girl from St Emilia's, and so I had to bottle everything up, and everything was going wrong for me just then and I kept getting into trouble, which was ~~awful~~ most unpleasant under the eyes of a stranger.

7. And then Miss Hendy told me that Papa-ji had up and left for Home without a word, leaving Mama-ji and me both, and I was rageous about that.

8. And then I heard that the infection at the San was a false alarm and I could have gone to see Mama-ji after all, and then I was livid about everything.

"Ye-es. You have been stewing, rather, haven't you? This is quite the confession, young Radhika."

"Please, though, that isn't all of it."

"Not?" He raised an eyebrow.

"No. You said to start after Mama-ji got sick, because you knew all about that; but I think it really started before then, years before. I never wanted to come to Mars at all, you see. It was like being sent to school here, only worse: leaving all my friends, and all the life I'd ever known, the way that I'd grown up, barracks and camps and Tommies and, oh, everything. Papa-ji loved the army, and then they made him leave it; and, and we lost all our money too, so he had to take the best job he could find when we got here, and I know it humiliated him; he was so proud of being an officer for the Empress, and now he was just a night manager for a rather seedy back-street hotel, where things went on that of course he didn't want me to know about, though of course I did. It embarrassed him, that he couldn't do better for Mama-ji and me. He thought he'd let us down entirely, though that wasn't true, it *wasn't*, he was doing the very best he could when all the worlds had turned against us..."

There needed a little pause there, while her handkerchief was put to use, and then his too. His smelled of pipe-tobacco, which reminded her of the officers' mess and all the mixed emotions which that called up within her, so that there was something more of a delay before she could sit back in her chair with damp linens in each hand, and raise woeful eyes to his, and wait to learn what came next.

"Hmm. I'll tell you what, Radhika, I think perhaps you need to tell me what happened in India, why your Papa-ji had to leave the army, and how it came about that you lost all your money. I know these things ought to be private to a family, but this is a deeper mess than I knew, and not just one little girl in a bit of trouble."

She sighed. Papa-ji had said she wasn't ever to talk about it, that they'd left it all behind them back on Earth; but that was never really true. It still knotted itself about them in their Martian lives, affecting the kind of jobs he could get and so the kind of life they could live, above all keeping them far and far away from anything military, which had been all his love before. Here he couldn't bear the sight of a stray Double Red, never mind the company of his own kind. *His own unkind*, she thought.

"Well," she said, "it was all in the papers anyway, so I know you could find out if you wanted to. So I suppose I might as well say. Papa-ji would have been cashiered, with a dishonourable discharge, if he hadn't resigned. They gave him one chance to do that, and he snatched at it, to spare us whatever shame he could."

"But why, Radhika? What had he done?"

"They said," she growled, "they *said* that he'd stolen, that he'd misa, misapp—"

"Misappropriated?"

"Yes, that, and other words. *Embezzled*, I learned that one too. Mess funds, it was, so all the officers were up in arms against him. He didn't do it, though," passionately, "he did *not*! He told us so, he swore it, and Papa-ji has always been a man of honour, a man of his word. It's what matters to him more than anything. That's why this broke him so deeply, to be accused of something he'd never done, he'd never dream of doing.

"The truth is, his colonel had always been against him, because, because of Mama-ji, and because of me. A native wife and a half-caste daughter: we revolted him, and he never tried to hide it. This was his chance to be rid of us all, and he took it.

"And then, and then, the story was in all the papers, and none of them accused Papa-ji outright but it was all there between the lines—and the colonel threatened to sue him for the missing funds, and Papa-ji couldn't stand to have us all dragged through the courts and through the gossip and the press all over again. I said, he's a man of honour; and his honour meant that he paid back all that was missing, all we had, so that we could walk away with no one at our heels, even though he'd never touched a penny of the regiment's money in the first place."

"Oh, my dear. Oh, my very, very dear. What a tale that is; and no wonder that you're so at odds with all the worlds together. Well, well. We must mend things one step at a time, as we can, as it falls to us to do so; which is why I'm going to have one of our people here spend some time with you for the rest of this term, an hour or two a week, to teach you ways to practise keeping your temper, even when everything seems to turn against you. You've had a rough time of it, no question, but you can't go on fuming and fuming until you break out in a passion, so I want you to take this seriously, yes?"

"Y-yes, Dr Mac. I, I don't *like* being angry all the time..."

"Of course you don't; no one could. So we'll show you some tricks to diffuse it when it comes upon you. Which it will; there's always something at school that's going to trigger a temper like yours. We just need to direct it into other channels. Though not perhaps quick bowling, hmm?"

Radhika shuddered. "I never want to touch a cricket ball, ever again."

"Oh, I think that's a little extreme, don't you? You're a demon bat, and I've never seen your like as a fielder; we'll get you back in your whites soon enough, I fancy. I believe Melanie and Alis have some ideas about that, as it happens. However, on the matter of slinging balls about, confession may be good for the soul, but I tend to feel that apology is better; so I'd like you to do something for me tomorrow, before you go to see your Mama-ji, yes...?"

She had wanted to do it, every day she came here. Her courage had failed her, every day till now.

This time, though, Dr Mac had asked her to do it. Somehow that gave her the impetus to quell all her hesitations, to find the room, to tap—lightly!—on the door, and then a little more firmly.

"Come in!"

The voice was firm, robust, adult. Radhika swallowed, found that she had quelled all her hesitations but one, and overcame that in the face of necessity. She opened the door, and stepped across the threshold.

There was Miss Fellany, the games mistress from St Emilia's, just rising to her feet with a nod.

"Good. I'm glad you came, Radhika. I'll leave the two of you alone for a while."

So saying, she stepped past Radhika and out into the corridor, drawing the door closed at her back.

Radhika stared at the patient in the bed; the patient stared back at her.

"Please," Radhika began, "I just wanted to apologise, I never—"

"Oh, I know you never meant it, you goose. I never supposed that you did. It happened, that's all. Cricket balls are hard, and you bowl like a fiend possessed. I'm sorry we never had the chance to face each other properly, I'd have enjoyed that. But Radhika, please—forget the past, and please, just tell me what I look like? They haven't let me near a mirror since I woke up."

"Um." Radhika gazed at Capri, and said, "Honestly?"

"Honestly, yes. As God is your witness."

"Well, most of all, right now, you look like something risen from the mummy's tomb."

It was true. Capri's head was all wrapped about with bandages, only her eyes, nose and mouth visible at all. Radhika's heart was sinking once again.

"Will you, will you be much scarred, have they said...?"

"What? Oh—no, no, not at all. All this," a waft of her hand towards her head, "it's mostly just to hold the pads of witchhazel in place, to bring down the bruising. They tell me no mirrors for a week, though, even after it all comes off. Can you see anything of actual me, anything at all?"

"Well," a deep breath, and, "I can tell you that you have two of the juiciest black eyes I've ever seen. Even just seeing the rims of them, I know that."

"Oh, glory. At least there's time for all of that to fade, though, before my brothers see me. They would never let up with the teasing, you know."

"Well, I don't, really."

"No brothers?"

"No sibs of any sort. I'm just an only."

"That sounds heavenly," Capri said with a sigh. "I'm number three of four, girl boy girl boy, and it's a nightmare in school and out. I'm so glad Sophia felt her duty lay with the team rather than her kid sister, to see them all safe back to school. I'd rather pass the journey with Miss Fellany any day."

"Really? I always thought it might be rather fun, to have sibs."

"Oh, it can be—but when you have boys on either side of you, it's a trial and a tribulation too. It's why we both grew up sporty, Sophia and I, so that we could run the edge off them and bring them home at least half civilised. Look, for Heaven's sake, Radhika, come and sit down, will you? I can't be doing with you looming over me like that, looking all guilty and stuff. Here, try some of these chocolate caramels your Rowany brought me, and tell me more about her while you're at it. She's quite the thing, isn't she...?"

# CHAPTER THIRTEEN

## The Book of Common Sins

"The trouble," Marigold declared, "is that we have been having far too much fun remembering and recording all the mischief of our predecessors. What we have not been doing," frowning around at her gathered circle, "is coming up with any ideas of our own, never mind actually doing them."

Alas, it was all too true. As scholars, they had proved themselves exemplary, quizzing their elders about misdeeds of yore, drawing the more sociable mistresses into reminiscence, even luring gruff Mr Felton into telling legends of long ago, for he had been there from the school's very earliest days, when the school roll amounted to barely a baker's dozen. The girls of that time, all but outnumbered by the staff, had felt it incumbent upon themselves to lay down some prime examples for their juniors to follow. Those had long been spun into Crater School lore, of course, and the girls of the Upper Third had mostly heard them many times already; but some were new at least to some of them, and there was nothing like hearing them from the horse's mouth, from a man who had actually been there at the time.

So their archive flourished, having been diligently written up in half a dozen different hands; and yet, they had advanced not one whit further towards their goal of conjuring up some scheme for wickedness that had never ever yet been thought of by all the generations who had come before. The Upper Third—and in particular this covey, this gang of girls who yearned to outshine the Crew two years above—needed to make their mark, to leave an indelible story in their wake, and they had not one idea to pick up between them.

It was a great shame, it was disgrace in their own eyes, eventually to be recognised by all those who came after: what, a whole year that failed to leave a single memorable act behind them, that contributed nothing to the record, to the legend...?

No, it was unthinkable. Brains were racked, nights were sleepless; and yet, and still, nothing came.

"Rowany, a word?"

"Sister Anthony, of course! What can I do for you?"

"Solve a mystery, perhaps, I hope. Of a sort. As you know, I frequently conduct a search of bedside lockers—"

"Oh, I do know. Much to my chagrin, in years gone by. Wait, you haven't been—?"

"No, of course not. You no longer fall—quite—under my aegis. Though now I'm curious as to what you might wish me not to have found?"

*Well, there's a set of lockpicks, for a start...* Rowany smiled brightly and said, "Oh, nothing terribly sinful, I promise." The lockpicks had been a gift from a man she hoped would prove to be her future employer, after all. A man high in the confidence of government, at that: not a sin in the world, simply tools of the trade. "But if you haven't caught me out in some disgraceful misdemeanour, then—?"

158

"Yes. I was looking through the things of a girl who has *not* earned herself a reputation for tidiness, and one particular drawer seemed far too suspiciously neat; so I pried a little deeper, and found ... this."

*This* was an exercise book, standard issue in every class. Any Crater School girl would have a dozen of them, and more as she advanced through the years. This one, however, bore neither pupil's name nor subject on its cover, though that was always the first rule when they were given out. *Officially* given out, that was to say. Of course some were ... abstracted from stock, for purposes not remotely to do with any lesson. The stationery cupboard was generally kept locked, to prevent more outrageous losses; Rowany thought again of those picklocks, and half wished she'd had possession of them during her own Middle years, as well as the skill to use them. It would have made things so much easier.

Curious, she flipped the cover open. The first page was a simple list, apparently of traditional schoolgirl mischiefs, midnight feasts and the like; but when she turned a leaf the handwriting changed abruptly, and she found herself reading a description of one particular incident, almost a story chapter in itself. Over the page another, in another hand; and so on, through quite half the book. A number of the tales she remembered directly, either as prefect calling perpetrators to account, or else as perpetrator herself, often sole initiator. Others she had only known as legends, passed down from before her time.

The individuality of the various hands vanished abruptly, some number of pages in. "Oh, you good girls," she murmured, briefly delighted with them.

"*Good* girls?" Sister Anthony repeated, a little acidly.

"Well, yes. They're using the opportunity to practise their New School Hand, do you see? They'd have felt themselves to be cheating, else. And—well, there's nothing particularly wicked going on here, is there? This isn't plotting, this is reportage. It's like a miniature history of the school, told through memories of mischief-making down the years. It needs putting into chronological order, of course, and a little editing for style...."

A snort issued forth from Sister Anthony, of that kind that most people felt was as close as she would ever come to laughter. "More than a little, I fancy. And for spelling, too. How those imps have found the time to compile all of this, on top of their schoolwork and all their other activities— well, it quite defeats me. But the thing is done, and here it is. Now, what do we do about it?"

"...Redirect it, I think," Rowany said. "It seems to be semi-official already; you see where some of the narratives have initials bracketed at the end? That must be a citation, acknowledging the source, and I believe they are mostly staff. 'Mr F' must be Mr Felton, at any rate. They might not know his initial, but I'll tell you one thing, they've got a lot more out of him than I ever did...."

"Hullo! Here comes your sister, Charm. She looks awfully serious. Any squalls in the family recently?"

Charm considered the question from every angle, then shook her head firmly. "None that I know of. Who's that with her, Mary Ellen?"

"I believe she prefers Mae these days, or rather the Crew preferred it for her, and so it was. But yes, that's her. That's she? No, that sounds so wrong...."

The niceties of grammar had to be set aside then, as the new arrivals made a beeline for the bench they were currently occupying, all too clearly intent on conversation. The somewhat-younger two came to their feet, out of some vague notion of manners towards the elderly, but Levity just laughed at them.

"Fie on you two! Are we not all Middles together? Sit, sit! Mae and I will perch on the arms, thus," suiting the action to the words, "so that you may blink up at us in admiration and wonder. Yes, good; just like that, Marigold. Now, let me start by telling you that you're a disgrace to your dormitory, your year, Stokes House and the school at large."

She didn't seem very cross about it, but even so: blinking and wonderment were indeed the order of the day, for Marigold knew of no particular sins in her recent past, and Charm was taken aback simply to hear her slightly-elder sister speak that way to her best friend.

"I say, Liv—"

"No, Charm, let me finish. For crying out loud, Marigold Elizabeth Kettle, have you no better sense than to hide your contraband in your cubie dresser? You *know* Sister Anthony is always poking about among our things up there, making sure that everything is just so."

"But—ohhhh..."

"*Oh*, indeed. Possibly even *oh dear, all is known, fly at once*, except don't you even think about flying. Why on earth didn't you think to conceal the wretched thing in the Middles Common Room, if it had to be concealed at all? Safely anonymous if found, it could have been anyone's; and highly unlikely to be found, in any case. Even Sister Anthony has given up trying to impose any kind of order in that mare's nest of a room."

"I, I didn't think..."

"Of course you didn't. That has been the cry of every schoolgirl, every *discovered* schoolgirl, since time immaterial."

Mae frowned, and made her first comment of the encounter. "Immemorial."

"Oh, is it? I suppose it must be, if you say so, O everybody's editrix. Bother, I thought I was on a good run there. Anyway, here it is, you two. Sister Anthony found your book, and read it frowningly; she passed it on to Rowany, who read it delightedly; and Rowany has passed it on to us. Well, to Mae, really, that she may read it editorially."

"I don't understand, Liv. I don't think either of us does."

"Oh, don't you see, you goops? Mae took one look and dictated your future for you."

Two puzzled pairs of eyes turned to the other end of the bench. Mae flushed a little, under their concerted gaze, then spoke determinedly.

"Some of these are lovely stories, with some very lively storytelling. What you're creating here is an alternative history of the school, through the eyes of girls dreaming up things to do outside the classroom. I think it's going to be a genuine resource for historians of the future, to see how notions of mischief alter over time. At any rate, you can't keep it to yourselves, I won't allow you. Marigold, you're still likely to get a lecture on using your dresser for its proper purposes only, and not trying to hide things from the staff; but I've begged you all off any trouble else, on condition that each girl who's written one of the stories in this book"—and here she produced from inside her blazer and handed it back to its original author, with something of reluctance in her manner—"copy it out fair and bring it to me. I'll revise as necessary and pair similar stories together: all the midnight feasts, that is to say, and all the trespasses out of bounds, and so forth."

"But, Mary Ellen—Mae—I still don't understand. What *for*?"

"For publication, of course. In *The Craterean*, term by term. I'm giving you your very own regular column. I thought perhaps I'd call it "The Book of Common Sins", if the chaplain doesn't think that's treading too close to holy ground. Hustle everyone up, please, I'd like to have these in as soon as possible. Oh, and once you've all copied out your own work? I absolutely want that exercise book back, for the archive."

She looked quite unexpectedly fierce as she said that, so that both her auditors gulped as they promised that of course she should, they would do that, absolutely. They didn't perhaps quite understand what an archive was, or why Mae needed or wanted one, but—like *genuine resource for historians of the future*—it did sound very important.

The older girls nodded a farewell and went about their business, leaving their juniors gaping at each other in some bewilderment.

"A *column*? In Mary Ellen's blessed *Craterean*?" Again, that notion had a most imposing ring to it. "When all we were doing was..."

"Was listing all the things that had already been done, so that we didn't just repeat them. I mean, we did get a *bit* carried away," Charm mused, "scraping up every last detail that anyone could remember, and writing it all down as excitingly as possible, like in the books." Charm was a devotee of boarding-school stories, and by now something of an expert. Not only her own cohort was prone to turn to her for recommendations from the library, where she was held already to have read every single example on the shelves. Indeed, it had been her inspiration to write out their catalogue in the same style; her friends had simply been following her example, for fear of sounding plain or dull in comparison.

"A *column*, though? Coo!"

A little lost in wonder, they sat and considered the notion for a while, until a crisp voice interrupted them in mid-contemplation.

"Idling your time away, girls? Have you never heard that Miss Hendy finds work for idle hands to do?"

They had indeed heard it, often and often. They leaped to their feet, assuming that they would be yoked in to spend half an hour pulling weeds and deadheading roses. It wasn't a chore they particularly minded, because she would stay to work beside them, and tell them all kinds of fascinating things along the way.

Today, however, she wasn't carrying a trug and a trowel, nor wearing gloves or her ancient disreputable gardening hat. Rather, she had a trig little beret perched atop her head, and a basket in her arms. A large and somewhat promising-looking basket.

Of course, they both stepped forward as one to relieve her of that burden.

"Thank you, girls. Take a handle each, and we'll get along splendidly. How fortuitous, to find the two of you ready and waiting for me! I'm just going to pull across the lake and collect Radhika, to bring her back to school. I was hoping to find company for her, as a mistress alone can be a little daunting. You two will be just perfect. We may not be back in time for supper, so Mrs Bailey's put up a picnic we can all enjoy by the waterside, before we head for home..."

Not for the first time, Charm was glad that her friend was the chattiest small person imaginable, undaunted by mistress or prefect or even Rowany de Vere. It meant that she could safely leave Miss Hendy in Marigold's hands, while she did her best to emulate her more thoughtful elder sister.

She gazed at the water, watched the lake's banks going slowly by, and thought this through, more deeply than she was accustomed to do.

She didn't for a moment believe it was fortuitous, that their housemistress had happened on the two of them on her way down to the water. It was hard to isolate quite how they had ended up on that bench, with time on their hands for once in a vary rare while; but however it had been managed, managed it had been, she had no doubt of that. Radhika's own sherpa, plus her inseparable friend? It couldn't conceivably be a coincidence, that they were there and available when wanted.

Of course, Miss Hendy might simply have told them to be there; but then they'd have known why in advance, and—well, there were a lot of complicated thoughts and feelings about Radhika. The girl was nice enough, when she tried to be; and of course she was a brilliant sportsman, as well as being fascinating in all sorts of other ways; but mostly she seemed to have gone out of her way to be grouchy and difficult. Of course there were all sorts of stories about girls who'd never wanted to come here in the first place—Liv's friend Rachel being a prime example—but those stories, like the ones in the books that were Charm's constant reading, always ended with reconciliation, chips knocked off shoulders, contented schoolgirls at term's end already looking forward to the next.

Charm could not quite see how that could happen, with Radhika. It wasn't only that she'd sent the St Em's girl to the big San across the water—deliberately, according to the most blood-curdling versions of the story, *attempted murder* some of the girls had taken to murmuring, so long as no prefects were about—though that was bad enough, even if it had been entirely accidental. Rather, Charm worried that a foul temper was something inherent, a character flaw that couldn't actually be corrected by any means a girl's school would dream of attempting.

That was the case in her favourite reading, at least. It was a well-established theme, that a girl's violent nature would always break out again, however hard she might try to suppress it, under whatever discipline or persuasion. Commonly their parents were asked to remove them, often before the end of term. It had never seemed fair to Charm—and should she ever write school stories of her own, a private dream of hers not yet shared even with her sister, she meant to address this very problem in fiction, rather better than she felt her favourite authoresses had done so far—but as Mamma so often said, life was not fair. Certainly it didn't seem to have been so to Radhika. It was Charm's fear that the circumstances of her upbringing, particularly everything that had happened between her leaving India and coming to the Crater School, that all those unfortunate happenings and misguided decisions by grown-ups who should have known better had broken something in the girl's mind, to leave her in a permanent state of furious resentment. Radhika of the Rage, indeed—and Charm could conceive of no way to mend something so fragile, so internal, and so horribly damaged.

*Just be her friend, girlie, and trust in Providence.* That's what Mamma would have said, if Charm had taken the problem to her; and that's exactly what she meant to do, insofar as she was able. She was just dreadfully afraid that it wouldn't be enough, that she couldn't be enough and nor could anyone or anything else, and that more and worse trouble lay ahead.

"There's the landing now," Marigold called, "and I can see one, no, two girls waiting for us!"

Two?

Two, indeed. One to take the bow rope, one to take the stern. One was Radhika, of course, nimble and adept as always, albeit looking somewhat abashed at the awkwardness of this reunion. The other was tall, a stranger—or rather no, not a stranger at all, just not a Crater School girl. The girl from St Emilia's, of course! Charm blinked a little at the sight of her, having assumed her long departed. But here she was, in the somewhat pale but nonetheless quite solid flesh, holding a courteous and wholly unnecessary hand out to help Miss Hendy step ashore.

Miss Hendy took the hand in any case, and held on to it for a moment or two while she looked Capri up and down with the experienced eye of a biologist.

"Yes, good. You'll do," for all the world as though she might have known better than the famous doctors here at the Sanatorium. "I'm glad your people chose to keep you here for these extra days, mind you. I expect you're aching to get back to your own life now, though?"

Capri smiled, and nodded shyly. "Everyone here's been wonderful, Miss Hendy—but truly. Papa's sending an airship to whisk us away in the morning, and I honestly can't wait."

"An airship, indeed? That's better than a long day on the trains, for someone only recently recovered from concussion. Your papa is a wise man. I expect Miss Fellany will be glad of it too. Speaking of whom, come along with that basket, girls, I see the rest of our company waiting in the tree's shade, there on the lawn..."

# CHAPTER FOURTEEN

## One Surprise After Another

It is a truth universally acknowledged—at least in Miss Peters' English classes—that the opening lines of some few favoured books have been parodied to exhaustion already, and the practice should be put a stop to forthwith.

However: equally universal is the truth that four girls who may be feeling slightly uncomfy with one another can be splendidly distracted if simply tasked to unpack one of Mrs Bailey's picnic hampers.

One girl per side, they took scrupulous turns reaching in and lifting out whatever item next came to hand, declaring its contents, and placing it reverently on the tartan blanket laid out to receive.

"Ooh, sausage rolls! Wait till you try these, Capri, Mrs B makes her own sausagemeat from our own pigs and everything."

"Oh, poor porkers!"

"Yes, I know. It'd be horribly sad, if they weren't so horribly delicious. We're strictly forbidden from giving them names, so of course we do. I think we're eating Percy at the moment."

"Morbid creature! My turn. It's a jar, and it seems to be labelled "Curtains Chastity," which I don't quite think can be right?"

"Ah, Mrs Bailey is a wonder, but deciphering her handwriting is an art that demands a lot of practice. Someone should teach her the New School Hand, except that nobody would dare. That's her Christmas Chutney, which goes down just as well at midsummer, especially with sausage rolls."

"Oh, marvellous! Who's next?"

"Me!"

"The first thing you touch, remember. No groping about for something interesting."

"Oh, but they're all interesting! Here we go. Now what's this? Golden, crispy, wrapped in a napkin—ooh! Baby pork pies!"

"Good old Percy. Me again. Oh, yum—I do love hard-boiled eggs."

"Who doesn't? I suppose that's salt and pepper, in the twist of wax paper?"

"No, that'll be Mrs B's magical stardust. Go lightly; it leaves your lips all tingly and your tongue a little startled, first time of trying. Sort of a gentle burn in your throat, too."

"Okay, we're down to the sandwiches now. I love these neat little packages, don't you? This one's egg-and-cress."

"Jam... Jam-bone, no, that can't be right... No, wait, I've got it. Jambon beurre!"

"Lovely. There'll be mustard in that pot too, for those who prefer their ham English-style. One more pack of sandwiches—honestly, she doesn't expect us to eat all of this, does she?—and this one's beef and horseradish, as solidly English as they come."

"Oh, bless her: she's given us little individual marmalade cakes!"

"And slabs of fruit cake to follow."

"With icing, or marzipan?"

"Both, of course!" in a chorus that made them all giggle, and everyone was friends all around.

"Ahem! If you gaggle of gluttons would care to stop ogling and pass plates around, perhaps we might hope to start our meal before it gets dark. Scurry, scurry!"

There were long hours to go before dusk—the "long hour" or "Martian hour" is one Earth hour, plus one minute and thirty-nine seconds long, which adds much joy to astronomers' calculations on all three worlds, and therefore to schoolchildren's also—and yet of course they scurried none the less.

Soon enough everyone was equipped with plates, napkins and cutlery, courtesy of Mrs Mackenzie's bountiful supply from her house nearby. There were jugs of ice-cold lemonade from Verna, who might perhaps have been heard to grumble that she could perfectly well have put up such a picnic her own self, no need to put Mrs Bailey to all that bother. There were choices to make, what to eat and in which order: "Why must one always eat bread before cake, savoury before sweet, I wonder? I mean, I don't mind, these sandwiches are delicious; but it feels like a rule, more than just etiquette, and I don't quite see..."

Conversations about the origins and oddities of manners died away, as so often, in the face of other ingrained manners, such as not speaking with your mouth full. There was a lot more to eat than to say, and for a while it seemed more urgent. Even the grown-ups said little more than "Pass the mustard, please," or "Do take another of those sausage rolls, they are so very good."

At length, though, even teenage appetites were satisfied and the remains of the feast were ruinous, little more than crumbs and spills. Pioneer-trained, the girls quickly packed up all stray wrappings and any food worth taking back to the school, shook out and folded the blanket, carried that along with the used crockery and so forth back to Verna at the house, and returned to find Miss Hendy glancing once again at the sky, and at the boat.

"Oh—please, Miss Hendy, mayn't we walk back? It won't take above an hour, we'll be back well before dark, and we would just like a little more time with Capri, before we have to say goodbye." *Time without grown-ups* might not have been spoken, but was absolutely understood by all parties.

"I can't see how, Marigold. Of course we'd trust you on the lake path, now that there's no naiad in the water or nymphs raiding the shore to find her food, and you couldn't possibly get lost; but we couldn't let Capri come back here on her own, and one more pull across the lake will be plenty enough for me. I can't undertake to return her when you're willing to let her go."

"I could volunteer to walk the girls there, and keep Capri company for the homeward leg," Miss Fellany murmured, "but—"

But kind as the offer was, her presence would totally undermine that whole *no-adults* bid, which was the point and purpose of the proposal. She knew it as well as any of them, and shrugged herself to silence.

"Oh, but please," Capri put in with a sudden urgency, "mightn't I spend just one more night at the school? That way no one has to see me back, and, and..."

And I don't have to spend my last night here in the company of adults, again unspoken, again heard by all present.

Miss Hendy's lips twitched, but she said only, "Mrs Mackenzie, Miss Fellany? Will that put you out too much?

It's quite unmannerly of me to steal your guest away, and frankly quite ungrateful of her to plead for it so passionately, but she'd be no trouble to me, and welcome, rather."

"Indeed, it would probably be a good thing," their hostess agreed solemnly, "to let the girls see her alive and kicking, at breakfast tomorrow morning. I've no objection. Miss Fellany?"

"None in the world. In fact, Miss Hendy, I'll scull across and join you for breakfast, if I may."

Thus, their guardians shed like a fond old coat, four joyous girls set off along the path that ran all the way around the lake; and if they chose to go the slightly longer rather than the slightly shorter way, no voice hailed them back to change their course.

Aware that they were being indulged, at least a little, they took advantage of the rare opportunity every way they could; which of course included setting all notion of manners aside, and grilling poor Capri for every gruesome detail about her injury and treatment.

"I mean," Marigold said judiciously—for of course Marigold had taken the lead in this—"we can all see there's still something of a bump on your forehead, and shadows under your eyes, but—"

"Oh lordie, you should have seen me when they finally took the bandages off and let me bathe in a room with a mirror!" Capri said, laughing. "I swear, I shrieked loud enough to bring the matron bustling in all ready to save my life. Instead she gave me a terrible scold for vanity, and threatened to take mirror privileges away again if I couldn't behave like a decent Christian girl and not go disturbing other patients. But oh, there was a bump on my head the size of a goose egg, almost the size of the cricket ball that put it there; and half my face was black and blue, and swollen so badly my own mother wouldn't have recognised me. I barely recognised myself, except that I have this fortuitous gap between my teeth, there, do you see? I always check that, if I'm in any doubt that I am actually me. Which happens more often than you'd think, I may tell you. You wait, you're young yet," quoth the sixteen-year-old philosopher.

There was a little quiet time, while the Upper Third thought that through, those of them who were present for the occasion. Then, hesitantly, Radhika: "Please, I'd like to say something."

Sensing an uncomfortable solemnity in the offing, Charm and Marigold both tried to head her off, but Capri was having none of it. "No, you two let her speak. I've an idea what might be coming, and I do think it needs to be said. Go ahead, Radhi."

Wait, *Radhi*? These two, who had seemed so much in total opposition a few days before, and now they were on nickname terms? Charm and Marigold blinked at each other, tried the taste of it on their tongues, decided that they liked it, rather, and should probably introduce it to their cohort. Along with this seemingly new, curiously changed girl who wore the name.

"Well, I'm afraid it's all rather obvious, really. I've been vile, horrible, ever since I came here. I came in a terrible temper, and I've let it be stoked by absolutely everything and anything I came across that I didn't like. There's been a lot of things happening, to me and around me, and not all of those are my fault—but the way I reacted absolutely was my fault, and I need to confess it now, and say sorry. Probably I should apologise to the whole school at assembly or something"—here the cries of horror from her two compatriots were enough to break that brief solemnity, and make even Radhika giggle for a moment—"but don't worry, I don't intend to do that. Unless Miss Leven asks me to, I mean. I'm sure I should speak to Miss Hendy, and she might want to take this higher, I don't know.

"But what I do know, I know that you two have borne the brunt of it, being in my class and in my house and sleeping either side of me and sherping me between you and so on and so forth; and Capri's had the worst of it, of course, just because I was in such a fury when I let go that dreadful ball..."

For a moment her voice faltered at the memory, but then she collected herself and went on determinedly. "Anyway, that's it. I am truly, deeply sorry for everything I've said, done and thought about you and the school and, and, everything. Even about my father, maybe, a bit. But Mrs Dr Mac has talked to me these last days, and so has Dr Ed; and, well, they've helped me see that while I may have a beast of a temper when things don't go as I'd like, I don't need to give way to it every time, or any. That's, that's just selfishness, and it's wrong. Another doctor there has shown me ways to stop it, to trip it up before it runs away with me, Dr Ed says, and I'm counting on you three to help me. If you spot me stewing over something, tell me so. Take me somewhere quiet if you can, and help me talk it through."

Capri chuckled lightly. "That all sounds splendid, Radhi, and I'm impressed as anything that you managed to say all that, to bare your soul without howling about it—but I don't think I'm going to be much help to you, honestly, half the province away from here."

"Oh, you're going to be the most help of anybody," Radhika assured her, slipping her arm through her tall new friend's elbow. "Talking about things is hard, and writing's easier. I'm going to write to you every week, and work out all my rages on paper. And you're going to write me back quiet, calm, considerate letters full of wise thoughts and, and..."

"And modern instances? Well, I'll do my best. Though my letters will probably be more about cricket and exams, if I'm honest. We've got a beastly set of exams at the end of this term, and I may need shoulders to cry on."

Three shoulders were of course instantly on offer, and there was a certain degree of dignified, courtly ceremony as they shook hands all around, making vows each to help the others.

Then, much relieved, they marched gaily forward through the lowering evening, wondering if perhaps they might even make it back to the school in time for tea after all, if they put their best feet forward.

"Honestly," Miss Hendy said somewhat testily, "I vow, I am never allowing a Stokes Middle out of the house unsupervised, ever again. Those girls should have been back by now, and they're not even in sight! I wouldn't have let three Middles loose on their own anyway, but Capri's sixteen, and seems to have a good head on her shoulders. I suppose I trusted her to crush any particularly wild flight of fancy that Marigold and co might come up with, but—"

"Hullo! What's to-do here, I wonder?"

"Why? What do you see?"

They were standing atop one of the Castle's towers, for the best possible view of the lake path. Miss Hendy had fetched Rowany along, with the excuse of borrowing her younger, sharper eyes. They'd been taking turns with the binoculars; right now, Rowany was delicately adjusting the focus without shifting her gaze one iota.

"I see one, two girls. Two of your missing lambs, I fancy; that blaze of red hair is diagnostic. Yes, Charm and Marigold. *Not* coming along the path, though. Scrambling down from the crags as best they can. At least the cliffs are a little more kindly on that side, but even so... What on earth can they have been doing, wandering that far from their proper way?

And what, I wonder, have they done with their blazers and ties? And their companions, come to that...?"

"We'll find out soon enough," Miss Hendy said grimly. "Come with me, please. Don't worry about the binoculars, just leave them here. I'll collect them later. Heaven help those children if they lured Capri into some rash idiocy and she's had a setback, or hurt herself again..."

Down from the tower, through the Castle courtyard and out over its drawbridge; through the Mistresses' Garden, and down to the lake path.

The two girls were plain to be seen now that they'd won the path, pelting home as swiftly as ever they could. Rather than run to meet them, Miss Hendy elected to stand on her dignity, a figure of authority, four-square in their sight. Rowany perforce remained with her, a little to the side and a little behind, not to seem quite so intimidating.

The two youngsters were too urgent to be intimidated. Whatever had impelled this haste, it was snapping at their heels like a demon from hell. Rowany half thought they might plunge into Miss Hendy full-force, if she didn't move aside.

Happily, they both found brakes from somewhere, skidding to a breathless halt right in front of their housemistress.

"Well?"

"Please, Miss Hendy, we have to hurry! We need a stretcher, and people to carry it, and—"

Rowany's heart sank, and so she suspected did Miss Hendy's too. If Capri really had had a setback, while she was under their care...

"Why, child? What has happened?"

Marigold had offered all she could, for the moment. Charm had caught her breath just enough to take her turn.

"There's a boy up the slope, he's badly hurt. We, we saw the vultures..."

That was enough, for now.

"We'll take a boat," Miss Hendy snapped. "Easier for all. Rowany, run and fetch Sister Anthony, will you, and perhaps one more Senior? Melanie, if you can find her; she knows her way around those crags as well as you do. We'll be ready at the boathouse by the time you get there. Girls, come along with me. No, don't try to run any more, Marigold. It won't gain any time, and you two need to cool off, you've had a hard go of it. You've both done very well. I don't want to hear any more from either of you until you're quite calm and recovered."

They took one of the school's longer boats, to allow for a patient on a stretcher and extra hands besides. Rowany and Melanie took the bow oars, the two grown-ups the stern. Marigold was on the tiller, as having rather more experience, which left Charm to tell the tale of their adventure to a number of very interested ears.

"We were walking along, just chatting, only then Capri looked up and said, 'What's that?" So we all looked, and there was an absolute *kettle* of vultures circling over something. We don't often see that this side of the ridge—well, I never have, nor Marigold either, 'cos I asked—so we were wondering if maybe a stray sheep or a goat had found their way over from the pastures and got hurt. Only then one of the vultures stooped down like a hawk will, or an eagle; only it sheered off halfway, and I thought I'd seen a stone, and Marigold swore she'd heard a voice yelling. So then of course we had to go up and see.

"It wasn't too hard, more of a scramble than a climb; and we were absolutely right when we came to the ledge, because there was a boy there, one of the shepherd boys by the look of him, and there was blood all over his leg. I don't know how long he'd been there, days, I think, he was hardly conscious at all and his lips are all cracked and bleeding. Capri thought vultures only took carrion, but we knew the black vultures around here will attack anything living as long as it's weak. And we couldn't get him into any kind of shelter, there isn't any, so we bandaged him up as best we could with our ties, gave him our blazers for a blanket, and left Capri and Radhika standing guard while we came for help. Well, Radhika was standing guard with a stone in her hand, while Capri scouted for more ammunition. We thought we could see a quicker way down," she added a little ruefully, examining a torn and bloody elbow, "only it turned out to be much harder than it looked."

"Often the way, kid," Melanie said, with a sympathetic grin. "It's always best to go down the same way you came up, if you can. Now, keep your eyes on the slopes ahead and point us towards your easy scramble up. Marigold, you too; it's not always easy to spot landmarks from the water, especially with the light going, and we want to be sure of our goal."

N either of the Middles was in any doubt when they came to it, even without the helpful draw of the vultures, who must have gone home to their evening roost. The two girls led their seniors confidently up and up and higher yet, to a ledge where indeed they found Radhika still on watch—"in case a sandcat came," she said darkly, tossing a stone in her hand—and Capri on her knees with a boy's head cradled in her lap, some small relief against the ruthless rock.

He seemed barely aware of anything about him, though he sucked eagerly at a cloth moistened with water. Taking command as to the manner born, Sister Anthony left Capri in charge of that while she peeled away the girls' improvised dressings and made a brisk field assessment of his hurts.

"Yes, well. He'll come back to my San tonight, at least. That leg's broken, and badly so. It'll need setting, but not this night. I'll speak to a doctor in the morning, and see what other hurts the lad has taken. Meantime, Rowany to the head and Melanie the heels, please, while Miss Hendy and I take the midportions, easy up and over onto the stretcher on my word. Radhika, abandon those stones and stand by with the blanket, please; you other two, the straps."

The boy safely strapped in, it proved easier to have two in control of the stretcher rather than four, for the steep climb down. The grown-ups gladly left that to the two older girls, as being younger and nimbler, while their juniors trooped down behind.

Pulling easily back towards the school, Miss Hendy said, "What I'd like to know is what the wretched boy was doing our side of the rim in the first place? They don't usually let their flocks stray past the Devil's Teeth, and what else could have brought him?"

"Oh, I can tell you that," Rowany said. "They have a, a tradition, I suppose, unless it's a superstition, that when they want something really profoundly, if their grandmother's sick or there's a girl they want to notice them, they'll bring an offering to the chapel on the far side of the lake. They never have money, of course, so it's usually a bunch of wild flowers they've picked or a fresh cheese they made in the caves there, perhaps a whistle they whittled, something like that. Father Ignatius does nothing to discourage it; he likes the chapel to be remembered as a place of hope, even if the boys don't actually pray as such. Also, I believe he's very fond of cheese."

Back at school, four stretcher-bearers took a handle each, with four tired schoolgirls at their heels. Straight upstairs to the San they went. The girls were chased away to hot baths, with hot soup to follow; the boy was washed and dressed and dosed by Sister Anthony's own hand, then laid asleep on the truckle in her own austere room.

The weary girls were bedded down quite firmly in the ward, despite their pleas for their own homely cubicles in their own homely house. They'd been too late out and too much excited; Sister Anthony had known nightmare, sleepwalking and worse to follow such an adventure, and she wanted them under her own strict eye until morning. Nobody else would plead their case for them, not even Rowany, though there was a glint of amused sympathy in her eye as she bade them goodnight and steered Melanie away by the elbow.

"Sleep well, girls—and don't even think about talking after lights out. Sister Anthony has the ears of a bat."

"I heard that, Rowany de Vere!"

"Of course you did. That only proves my point."

# CHAPTER FIFTEEN

## Drama in the Morning

"Well, but he's our boy, isn't he? I mean, we *found* him..." Many strive, but few can actually achieve the levels of indignation that come naturally to nearly-four-teen-year-old schoolgirls who feel deprived of what is due to them. The Upper Third all felt as one in this, that their whole year was being snubbed. Peak protest, of course, belonged to the three prime movers, the discoverers, but their class would back them to the hilt if they could only come up with some way to make it right, with or without the law on their side.

"We *saved* him," Charm asserted, in support of Marigold, and not a voice was raised against her. That was as close as any of them cared to come, but *he would have died without us* lay unspoken in every girl's mind, whether she had been there or not.

Radhika absolutely shared the common outrage, but she was trying to hold back for once, and let the others rant. Her return to school might have been uncomfortable for everyone; her coming back as she did, as part of a heroic rescue mission, had wholly eclipsed any sense of wariness among her cohort. Her welcome was as genuine and vociferous as any girl might have hoped for, never mind one as shy as Radhika had always pretended not to be. She'd found it somewhat overwhelming, and was still hoping to fade into the background, in defiance of everyone else's determination to thrust her into the limelight.

"Even Capri was let have at least a glimpse of him first thing, before she left; but not us, oh no, we're too lowly..."

Capri's promised airship had come buzzing over the lake just after breakfast. The three young adventurers had been allowed to accompany their fourth down to the waterfront—passing her case between them as they went, so that each shared the privilege of labour and the duties of hosting—and wave her off. Before that, though, Sister Anthony herself had loomed above them as they chatted over their eggs and sausages, whisking their guest away. "Only for a minute, mind, and not a sound out of you, for he's sleeping still and much in need of it. I thought you might like to take home the memory of his resting comfortably, rather than the state you found him in." And then, to the Stokes Middles at large but specifically to our somewhat stunned threesome, "The rest of you are to keep away, am I understood? I don't want sight nor sound of you, anywhere near the San. He needs rest and quiet, while it's determined what's best to do with him, and I mean to see that he has it in full measure."

Hence, of course, the growling discontent all through the Upper Thirds, as Stokes passed it on to their friends in other, lesser houses. Was he not their boy, their very own, theirs by right of salvage and by dint of curiosity and courage and exertion, all the qualities so highly esteemed in Pioneer lore? They couldn't—quite—begrudge Capri her glimpse in the circumstances, and they were careful to show no hint of resentment until she was well away, the neat little airship soaring over the rim and gone. Once they had waved it out of sight, though: oh, then they could give vent to all their fury at being so unfairly discriminated against.

They were venting even now, among their fellow-suffering sisters; or at least, as noted, Marigold was venting, Charm was supporting her loyally, and Radhika was marching quietly in support as they led their troupe of supporters into Miss Peters' English room, for the first lesson of their day.

Any Crater School girl learns early on the one way a mistress is supposed to find her class, when she arrives to teach them: each girl quiet and prepared at her own individual desk, rising to her feet in greeting at first sight of any staff.

Any Crater School mistress learns early on the first signs of a thoroughly disturbed class: girls gathered in knots around ringleaders, voices raised, many with their backs to the door, utterly unaware of the arrival of Authority.

"Girls! Girls! CLASS!"

Thus with a bellow did Miss Peters finally attract Upper Third's attention. There were squawks of alarm and a hasty scuttling to their proper places; there was a mighty tugging of uniforms into something somewhat approximating order; there was a murmur of "Good morning, Miss Peters," rather more muted than usual, for she was one of the mistresses more accustomed to being greeted with broad smiles and good cheer. On the whole, girls tended to enjoy her classes thoroughly.

Not a girl in the room was now expecting to enjoy this one. For a full minute, their beloved Miss Peters only surveyed them, one by one and top to toe, standing beside her desk in grim silence.

Then she drew breath.

"You blocks, you stones, you worse than senseless things!" Her voice reverberated throughout the room, astonishingly powerful for one so slender and ordinarily so soft-spoken.

"I bite my thumb at you!" and promptly did, to the utter astonishment of one and all, even as several were filing that particular gesture away for later use. "What, you eggs! Young frys of treachery! Let's meet as little as we can. You minions are too saucy. Your abilities are too infant-like for doing much alone. I wonder that you will still be talking! No one marks you. You speak, yet you say nothing. You have no more brain than I have in my elbows! You are not worth another word, or else I'd call you knaves."

And then she turned her back on them entirely and swept out of the room, leaving all the class agape.

"...Do we, should I,"—as form captain, Elana Grey felt it necessary to take the lead, at least in asking for help—"should I run after her, to apologise? For us all?"

There was too much shell shock still in the room for any coherent answer to emerge from the class as a body; and then it was too late, for the door opened and Miss Peters made a second entrance.

This time, it all went perfectly. The girls rose to their feet, chanted "Good morning, Miss Peters," albeit still somewhat more subdued than ordinarily, and she smiled upon them with all her usual beneficence.

"Yes, much better, girls, and a very good morning to all of you, too. Let us work towards making it so, yes? I'm not even going to ask what was the occasion for all that ruckus; I will assume it's no business of mine, and move on."

As one, the whole room breathed a sigh of relief.

"On the other hand, my response was very much your business, today and going forward to the end of term. Who can tell me quite where I plucked those ripe and ready phrases? ... Yes, Radhika?"

It had not, it had absolutely not been her intent to put herself forward today, in this or any other class, for this or any other mistress. No one else was volunteering, though, and it did seem politic that someone at least venture a guess. Besides, one of those lines was sounding echoes in her head, raising memories of a stage in the open air, in all the heat and dust of a Calcutta summer, her father at her side sharing the same bench, thrilling as she was to the sheer power of words as they flowed forth from men who looked ever so much more comfy in their togas than their audience was in uniform.

She came slowly to her feet and said, "Please, Miss Peters, I think, I think they might all have been Shakespeare? Not all from the same play, perhaps, but..."

"Good. *Very* good, Radhika. Can you say more? Something in your voice suggests that you can."

Did it? Oh, dear. Still, she was fully committed now. "I've heard 'You blocks, you stones, you worse than senseless things' before. I think I have. Isn't it from right at the start of *Julius Caesar*?"

"It is indeed, which is one reason it tends to stick so readily in the mind, besides the common tendency to relish insults more than compliments. 'Home, you idle creatures, get you home'—those are the very first words of the play, and I might have used those too, but for worrying that you might take me literally and all troop out back to your houses. So tell me, Radhika, how do you come to be familiar with *Caesar*, and have you seen other of the Bard of Avon's work?"

Poor Radhika found herself obliged to tell again the tale she had already told to Rowany, and to confess that having uncovered her delight in theatre, Papa-ji had delighted them both with other trips, to Shakespeare plays as well as those of lesser mortals.

"Splendid. You interest me strangely, young Radhika. Have you ever felt the lure of the stage yourself, any interest in treading the boards?"

"Oh—oh no, Miss Peters, I couldn't possibly..." The usually well-buried shyness was showing itself in full force now, burning her cheeks to char and ashes, as it felt.

"And yet I say you shall, or at least have a stab and see how you like it. You see, girls, there is method in my madness—which is another Shakespearean quotation, or close enough. Unsurprisingly, it comes from *Hamlet*. Here's a little shortcut for you, that I share from my own schooldays, when occasionally there was in fact a thing I did not know: if someone asks the source of a quotation, when in doubt, say *Hamlet*. You'll be right more often than not. Some Victorian lady is said to have swept out of the theatre in disgust, declaring that the whole piece was just a string of clichés, one after another—and if there is some echo of a modern truth in there, the reason for it is that he created every single one of those clichés in that original text, and they have come down all these centuries to us still intact. In a word, girls, Shakespeare is simply impossible to overrate; he was and has been better than everyone else, before or since.

"I hope to show you that more clearly, as this term progresses. Later in your school career, you will have the opportunity to study certain of the great man's works in depth; and I feel an earlier introduction will do you no harm at all. I've always felt that having our Speech Day at the end of Hilary Term as we do, for reasons lost in the mists of antiquity, we rather miss the chance of calling a significant end to Trinity, before we all go away from each other for two months and more.

"This year, I've decided to do something about that. We've been established long enough to hold a formal Old Girls' Day. Pupils of years gone by, parents and friends of the school are to be invited to a far less formal occasion than Speech Day, a day of fun and frolics, with no solemn prizes awarded and no reputations at stake. There will be stalls and games of many kinds; a cricket match pitching School against Old Girls, perhaps even a round-robin tournament if enough willing parents should come to field a third team; and a pageant, presented by myself, in which I intend that each year of the school shall perform a piece from the Shakespearean canon.

"Oh, don't look so terrified, you cream-faced loons! Yes, Radhika, that is indeed another insult lifted directly from the First Folio, and I *don't* want to hear it bruited abroad. Be assured, I'll not ask anything beyond your abilities to deliver. The little girls will be content with tableaux, costumes and narration; the big girls will act their hearts out on the full text of a famous excerpt, or I'll know the reason why; which leaves us, of course, with you in-betweens.

"Each year of the Middle School will read their way through this, in class," a book, flourished significantly at them. "'Scenes from Shakespeare,' edited for the classroom by Milton Hall, one of the great modern Martian scholars of Shakespeareana. I will tell you more about Professor Hall on another occasion; I have the privilege of being acquainted with the gentleman. Meanwhile, I want you each to take a copy of his book as you leave the room today—Janna, Agnosia, if you two would hand them out when the time comes, yes? Thank you, girls—and read the scenes through, find which ones thrill your collective hearts, and if possible which in particular you can all agree that you would like to perform. You will have all the help you need in matters of dress and scenery, from Miss Tarleton and her sewing classes in the former case and Mrs Buchanan and her art room in the latter. I will be on hand at all times to direct, to advise, to console and encourage. Not everyone has to act, but I hope that everyone will contribute in some wise. Now, having set you all abuzz with excitement, I'm going to damp you down by talking for the rest of the lesson while you sit quiet, while I tell you more about Master William Shakespeare, and the influence he has wielded over our language, our theatre and our culture for lo, these three hundred years and more..."

Indignity, as it seemed, was quite forgotten. The boy—their boy!—was not so, or not quite so; but in the thrill of this latest unexpected turn, the Upper Third would reluctantly allow that the right care of an injured lad lay with Sister Anthony and the wise doctors of the Sanatorium across the water. It was known that Dr Ed had driven around the coach road to see the damage for himself. His verdict, and hence the boy's fate, were not known to the girls, or at least not yet. There had been no stretcher sighted, though, no ambulance or steam-yacht, no transfer by land or water. For now, at least, the school possessed him yet, and the Upper Third possessed him most, in their most acquisitive of hearts.

What possessed their tongues, however, and their eager minds? Why, this new excitement, this total treat. Every year since the school's founding, a number of girls new and old had petitioned for a school play; every year, reluctantly, they had been refused. The school was simply too remote, in Authority's view, to draw a decent audience.

By now, though, every corner of the province could boast its population of Old Cratereans, many of whom remained devotedly loyal to their school, and—it was hoped—would love the chance to come back, catch up with staff and local friends, reunite with their own cohort, marvel at the school's growth and the new generation of girls. Which being so, drama could at last be introduced to the curriculum, at least in a limited way. If the day was a success, it could be an annual affair, and perhaps more ambitious projects might be tackled. For this first step, a pageant was challenge enough.

"Now, has everybody read all these scenes?"
    "Well, not to say *read*, exactly..."

There was general sympathetic laughter, among the Upper Thirds. Cate St-Clair was known to be—well, whatever was the opposite of a bookworm, and any class preparation that involved reading even a chapter, never mind a whole book, was anathema to her. On the other hand, she had three generations of actors in her blood, had practically been raised in the wings of a dozen different theatres across the province, and knew all of Shakespeare's plots off by heart, not to mention many of the famous speeches.

"That's all right, you're a special case, Cate. You're excused. Anyone else not caught up?"

They had annexed an empty classroom, and were holding a council of war. As though by nature, Marigold had taken charge, with her loyal lieutenant Charm on one side, and—somewhat to her own surprise, never mind everybody else's—Radhika on the other.

"Right, then. Off we go. Who has an idea, which scene we should pick, from which play?"

There were various cries: the assassination of Julius Caesar, "easy to dress, all we'd need is bedsheets; only we'd need some kind of fake blood that would wash out easily, or Sister Anthony would have our heads"; Henry V at Harfleur, "except that there's really only one part there, and then a whole mob swarming the breach"; a scene from The Tempest, "with Ariel and Caliban and everything".

"I'll tell you what we could do," Cate called out above the hubbub in her clear, carrying voice. She being a renowned expert in the matter, everyone else fell silent to hear her wisdom.

"We could do a scene from The Taming of the Shrew," she said sweetly. "We've got the obvious person to play Katherine, after all," and her smile fell brightly on her victim. "Radhika of the Rage!"

Nobody so much as let a pin drop, till Marigold drew a much-needed breath and said, "Agatha Hecate St-Clair, you will apologise for that remark right now, or, or—"

"No, it's all right, Madame Chairman." For once, one girl alone could override even the indomitable Marigold—but only because that girl was Radhika herself, rising to her feet to meet her accuser eye to eye. "For one thing, Cate's absolutely right, I'd be a natural for the part; I wouldn't even need to act, would I? And for another, well, I thought that was pretty funny, honestly," her lips twitching at the smile she was still trying valiantly to suppress. Apparently she wasn't the only one; a light ripple of laughter ran around the room, now that she'd given her consent to it.

"And for a third thing," Radhika went on firmly, "none of you supposes that Miss Peters would actually *allow* us to do scenes from that particular play, do you? She'd think it most unsuitable, mostly because it is. I say we should do something violent, from the Scottish play. Bloody murder is much more appropriate, for girls of our age and breeding."

This time the room laughed aloud, in clean relief. Marigold jumped on the mistress's desk and danced a dance of frustration, until they subsided; then she said, "Well, but we can't, though. The Juniors have all got together and decided to make a joint effort. I think it's a really good idea, because Lower Third can help the littl'uns no end; only they've snagged Macbeth already. I think Mary Ellen McKay is going to help them with a narration, and they've got that Fiona kid from Inverness to read it for them in that incomprehensible accent of hers, while the rest of them mime the action along. It'll be great; but we need something different."

Debate ran long and hot, as such debates will do. At the last, it was quiet little Tabitha Pierce—putting her hand up as she would in class, waiting to be noticed and called upon, which did mean rather a long wait, so that she had to swap arms a couple of times, because of growing tired—who came up with an idea that pleased them all.

"Why don't we do the Pyramus and Thisbe scene from A Midsummer Night's Dream?" she said. "The one where they perform the whole play, I mean, for the court. I think it would be fun. And the audience could be the court, so that our Theseus and Hippolyta and the rest could sit among them making all their rude remarks, and sniggering to their neighbours."

There was a pause, while they all thought that over; then, "Marigold could be Bottom," Cate said diplomatically. "Can I be Wall? I always wanted to be Wall."

There was a clamour of other voices, too many candidates trying to claim too few parts; and by the time the racket had subsided, it was clear to all that the question had been quite decided.

# CHAPTER SIXTEEN

## Rowany Takes Charge

"Well. It seems we are to keep our problem child with us for at least some while longer."

"To be fair," Fräulein Grüber murmured, peering at Miss Leven over the top of her spectacles, "that particular soubriquet might be applied to any number of the children here; but I am not to tease, I find. I assume you mean the boy?"

"I do indeed. Dr Ed—excuse me, I mean Dr Penberthy—had so much trouble setting that leg, or 'reducing the fracture' is I learn the correct medical terminology, he doesn't want the boy moved even an inch until the bones have had a chance to knit. Which means we have him as our guest for the next several weeks at least, assuming that all goes well and that he obeys doctors' orders implicitly, which in an active boy of that age—"

"He will obey my orders," Sister Anthony observed grimly from her corner. As often before, the staff had gathered in their own room, inviting Miss Leven and the school matron to join them there, to talk over this latest disruption to the even flow of their days.

A slightly uncertain chuckle rolled around the room, as no one was ever quite sure whether Sister Anthony had actually intended to raise a laugh. Bolder than most, Miss Harribeth stepped up: "Of that, my dear Sister, I stand in no doubt whatever. On the other hand, youths of any age are prone to forgetting even the sternest of instructions, under sufficient provocation; and with a schoolful of young demons to tempt him—"

"Which they will not, for I will not allow them anywhere near. I have him against the end wall in the San, and I have already discussed with Mr Felton the feasibility of building hardboard partitions with a wooden frame, to close off the open sides and provide a more secure separation from the rest of the ward than cubicle curtains could ever offer."

"Great heavens, Sister! You can't mean to wall him in like an anchorite! There must be some kinder way to keep the poor boy safe. Besides, what will he ever do for sunlight and fresh air?"

Sister Anthony had lived some years more or less as an anchorite herself, in a lonely stone cell high on the crater wall. Now, though, she scoffed at Miss Hendy and said, "Of course I mean no such thing, Katherine. There is a window between his bed and the next; if the partition encloses that much space, he will have all the light and air a healing patient needs."

"I don't see that we can deny the girls all access to him, though," Miss Leven said thoughtfully. "It wouldn't be healthy for anyone. He will need the company of his own age-group, if he's to be cooped up unmoving for weeks on end, a boy who's accustomed to living his life out of doors, roaming the sheep-pastures and sleeping in caves; and the girls will fret each other into open rebellion, if they're to be kept away entirely."

"Upper Third is halfway there already," Miss Hendy added. "Since three of their number—three of my own Stokes bairns, I may point out—were directly responsible for his rescue, they seem to feel they have some claim to his person, an inalienable right to visit. Oh, not all of them, of course," seeing Sister Anthony about to interrupt again, "and certainly not all at once; but a delegation, surely they can be allowed that much?"

"To what end? The boy barely speaks a word of English, and those amiable fluffheads certainly have no trace of Basque about them."

"I don't think you're quite right about that, Sister." Rowany's voice, softly from the background. "About Eder, at any rate. When I've been interpreting for him between the doctors and yourself, he sticks to Basque just to be safe, to be clear in his meanings; and of course he speaks nothing else with his family, which is all the visitors he's had so far. But he does already have more English than you'd think, and his letters too. That's Father Ignatius' doing, of course; he has all those children through his little school before he'll allow them out to work. They all think he's a monster, of course, but their parents listen to him. He's sitting with Eder now, and I can promise you they're speaking English. He won't allow anything else, for all that his Basque is immaculate after all this time. He'll use that with the older generation, but never the kids. It's for their own good, he says—which is why he'll marry his voice to Miss Hendy's and my own, to have some of the girls let in to speak with Eder. Daily, for preference. Good practice for all concerned; it'll do our girls no harm to spend some time talking to a boy who has lived a life so very different from their own. As I have cause to know, from my own adventures here."

"Don't remind me," Miss Leven said, with a shudder. "Oh, I'll allow that they gave you a broader base of experience, and appear to have done your morals no more harm than your person; but your parents sent you to us to keep you securely within our ambit, not to see you gallivanting all over the crater at any hour of the day or night. Many of my greyer hairs have your name written on them, young lady, so don't hold yourself up as an example to be followed, I beg you."

Rowany chuckled comfortably. "Oh, you knew you never had to worry about me. I always came safe home, didn't I?"

"Providentially, you did. I should *not* have liked to face the General with news of your untimely demise. But come, let us return to our muttons. Strictly limited and regulated visits from selected girls, yes, I believe we might be able to manage that; I can see some good in it. But how are we to keep young Eder amused otherwise? Weeks in bed, unable to move: to a boy like that, it's the very definition of misery."

To nobody's surprise, it was Rowany who claimed that particular task. "Leave him to me. I'll speak to Father Ignatius, and to his family, and his friends on the slopes. He can't be the first boy from the village to be laid up with a broken leg. I'll find some way to distract him, or my name's not Rowany Angelica Marten de Vere—"

"Which, as a matter of fact, it is," came a murmured chorus from all across the room, that had Rowany choking with laughter as she made a hasty exit.

Father Ignatius had overseen the welfare of his congregants, both here on the crater and down in Terminus, since time immemorial, or so rumour had always had it. He was old, to be sure, though he never seemed to grow any older; he was as bent and as tough as a moorland tree, and as impervious to time.

Rowany was not of his faith, but that had never mattered to either of them. She met him on her very first day at the Crater School, and had treasured him in her heart ever since; whenever possible, she crossed the lake early of a

Sunday morning to attend Mass in his little stone chapel by the water, in company with patients and staff from the great Sanatorium and Basques from the village below. He had the same welcome for all comers, and the same little wisdoms to offer from his pulpit, commonly more human and spiritual in nature.

He came to the school at need, and sometimes simply to visit old friends on a Sunday afternoon; whereby Rowany had of course learned his weakness, as she learned every-one's sooner or later.

Today, then, she waylaid him as he slipped quietly out of Sister Anthony's San, managing a tolerably credible cry of soft delight. "Father Ignatius! Just the man I'd hoped to see!"

He gazed upon her as cynically as an old man may, when confronted with a sinner he'd known since she was an imp of eleven years' standing. His hands made shushing gestures; "Peace, peace. Eder is sleeping now."

She nodded her understanding, took his arm and steered him gently along the corridor, in her own preferred direc-tion. "I have quarters to myself here now, did you know? Just as if I were a staff! Would you honour me with a visit?" And then, when he made no swift reply, "As it happens, I can offer you English tea..."

He was not, he hoped, a greedy man. Certainly that particular sin never figured in his confessions to the bishop, when that dignitary came to visit this most remote of par-ishes. English tea, though, afternoon tea: it was his utter downfall, and wicked Rowany knew that all too well.

"None of my doing, I'm afraid. Well, I'll make the tea," as her kettle began to splutter and sing on the spirit stove, "but all the rest I have begged from Mrs Bailey, in the realms below."

He was familiar with Mrs Bailey long since, aye, and all her works as well. Experienced eyes—we will not say *lascivious*, when speaking of a priest—saw plates of sandwiches, of course; they saw little pork pies and leek tarts; they saw scones and jam and clotted cream; they saw slices of cake. Nothing little about those. Mrs Bailey knew and loved the father on her own account, and well understood the trajectory of his appetite.

Rowany went through all the tender motions of a proper pot of tea, aware of an expert watching every move. She had set out her prettiest tea things, a gift from her grandmother which she'd left at home until she was a Senior here, when at last she felt grown-up enough not to ruin it with stains and breakages. She poured and passed a cup just as he liked it, strong and milky and sweet; she handed him a plate and gestured towards the sandwiches, because the proper order of a proper tea must always be observed.

*No shop in the mess.* That was another rule absorbed young and transposed from military to civilian life. One did not interrupt a pleasant meal with talk of business, however urgent that business might be.

So they ate, and talked somewhat of his life and somewhat of hers, as much as either of them felt able to share, without ever seeking to test the other's boundaries. His acquaintance was broad, and so was hers; they shared news of mutual friends, and caught up with doings at the school and in the valley.

Then, at last, when he had reluctantly pursed his lips and shaken his head at the last possibility of cake, he allowed his cup to be refilled one more time and fixed her with a dark and beady eye.

"So. Tell me what it is that you want."

"Father, what I wanted most was to spend this hour in your company." Her protest was so earnest, she could almost have believed it herself, if she hadn't gone on to say, "However, there is also a matter connected with young Eder, and I would welcome your wisdom."

He nodded noncomittally, and waited.

This was the tricky bit. She said, "I know these boys come to the chapel with gifts and prayers, for what their simple hearts most desire."

Another nod.

"We believe that Eder had done just that, and was on his way home when he fell. I have chosen not to ask him directly, but rather to come to you, his spiritual father"—a snort, as though there were very little that was spiritual in his relationship with that particular or any other boy—"to ask if you know anything at all of what he might have been asking for, in his heart of hearts?"

Father Ignatius was quiet for a time, for quite a long time, for long enough to start a seed of worry in Rowany's not-quite-easy mind. Then he lifted his head, pierced her with his gaze again and said, "I am not to be tricked into breaching the secrets of the confessional."

"No, no, Father, of course not! I would never—!"

"Quite so; and neither would I. What the boys ask in my chapel, they ask of God, and not of me. I am not there when they come, and they leave no notes."

Rowany nodded her understanding, while still holding to a shining thread of hope.

"However," the old priest went on slowly, "I do know what the boy holds most precious in his hopes, for he has told me, time and again. It is hopeless, he knows, but he hopes none the less. And there is no seal on this; these are conversations we have had in private, yes, but not under the strictures of God. Under His eye, to be sure—He sees all, hears all, and knows all—but this would not be a matter for the confessional, unless ambition be a sin. Perhaps—it is not my place to say—but perhaps this fall, this confinement, they may be Providential after all?"

She might have run to Miss Leven there and then, with what the old man told her; but Rowany was wiser, or else perhaps ambitious in her turn. She wanted more.

Out she went, then, down the path that led between the playing fields and so eventually onto the open moor, the smooth fall of the sheep pastures down to the valley below. With her back to the school, she clambered up a long-familiar rock, cupped her hands about her mouth and view-halloo'd, as the General would have called it, except that this was no hunter's cry in pursuit of a hapless fox. This was a very ancient and particular call, safe to be heard and understood by any shepherd boy in hearing, safe to be passed on to those who weren't.

Now all she needed do was sit and wait. So she did that, and soon enough, sure enough, here came wild-looking figures running to find her.

Lean, ill-barbered youths, all rough and greasy clothing, bare feet, tangled locks, dark compelling eyes. She greeted each of them by name, and asked formally after their families and their flocks, as was only proper. When all the news of the season had been shared—and shared again for those who had been further off, the last to come—they shrugged away their manners and crowded about her, squabbling amiably over squatting rights on this particular ledge or that one, until she laughed and offered to cuff them quiet.

They shrugged then and subsided, abruptly boneless, sprawling all over each other in a kind of intimate disregard.

"That's better," she told them sternly, all the while their eyes sparked laughter at her. "Now. You all know that Eder has been badly hurt in a fall, and we have him in the school sanatorium, yes?"

Solemn nods, slow blinks. Of course they all knew that.

"Very good. Now then, I want two things from you, to ease his time of pain. In the first place, I want you to visit him, in pairs perhaps, one pair a day—"

Sudden alarm, an awkwardness of elbows, all comfort gone. None of them would meet her eyes, and she knew exactly why.

"Idiot boys! Sister Anthony hasn't eaten Eder, and neither will she eat you, I promise."

Eat them, no—though that was as far as she was prepared to promise. In the school holidays, Sister Anthony was prone to go down to the village and inoculate each and every child, willy-nilly. Then she'd strip them bare and bathe them against fleas and ticks and lice, examine them all over, treat anything she didn't like the look of. These boys maintained a healthy terror of Sister Anthony, to the point where they wouldn't willingly come near the school buildings, just in case.

Perhaps that was wise. It was certainly not beyond the realms of possibility that any of them who dared venture the sanatorium would find themselves enduring the same treatment yet once more. Still, it would do them no harm in the long run, and possibly some good; and he was their friend, in many cases their cousin, absolutely their flock-brother in need.

She said all that, lightly scolding, and won shy glances, reluctant nods. That was as much as she would ask for, today; except,

"Two things, you said."

"Yes, Xabier, I did. Now, this is the second…"

"Ah, good. I'd hoped to find you two here."

It was a Saturday afternoon, devoted at the Crater School to activities of all kinds, so long as they were not schoolwork. The playing fields were busy with girls dashing this way and that, under the eye of whichever mistress or prefect they had persuaded to oversee their game; but sport was by no means the only choice on offer. Mrs Buchanan had her Printing Club; Miss Hendy helped green-fingered girls to manage the school's extensive gardens, when she wasn't leading a nature walk instead; other members of staff had their own interests, through which to guide the young and curious.

Out in the stable yard, patient steeds were being prinked and preened, their manes plaited and their coats brushed to a shine, and all of this before their adoring Pony Club tenders had so much as saddled them up, never mind ridden them anywhere. Rowany had squeezed her way through the throng, greeting girls and animals indiscriminately as she passed, until she came at last to a particular outhouse, the province of yet another pursuit.

Next term, she knew, the sign on the door would read *Engineering Club*, and any visitor could expect to find themselves breathing air dense with motor-oil and other fumes. Today, though, the sign was still reversed, to show the side that said *Carpentry Club*; Rowany had been greeted by the pleasant scents of linseed oil and fresh sawdust, as well as two cheerful voices and a grunt.

Until last year, this structure was known as the timber store, and the name bespoke its usage. It still had all manner of beams and boards stacked against the walls, and slotted overhead between the open rafters. At the pleading of two of the more unusual pupils at the school, though, space had been cleared for a workbench and a set of old but still practical tools.

Those had come courtesy of Mr Felton the school care-taker, and the grunt from the man himself, for no one was going to allow a pair of Middles to play with chisels and saws unsupervised. He had a chair in the corner, and a carving in his hand which he was filing carefully smooth. The two girls in question—Pete, who only wanted to be a boy, and Elle, who had been raised as one regardless of preference—stood side by side at the bench, dovetailing two lengths of wood together.

"That's a very neat joint," Rowany observed. "Which one of you cut it?"

"We both did," they said together, and grinned at each other before tall Elle gestured little Pete to take the lead, which she would have done anyway.

"I cut one side and Elle cut the other, but honestly I barely remember who did which. It is rather neat, isn't it?" Its complacent co-creator gazed upon their work with a smile, then glanced up at Rowany enquiringly. "Did you want us for something?"

"Yes, as a matter of fact I did, and do. I have a commission for you."

"Ooh! That's a first! What can we make for you?"

"It's not actually for me, only at my behest. You will know by now," all the school would know by now, "that our unexpected guest in the Sanatorium will be staying with us a while yet. He's going to need a mountain of things to do, but he can't get out of bed, so the mountain has to come to Mohammed. If you're willing, I'd like you two to design and make a, a bed-table: something that can sit across the mattress and safely above his legs, and give him space and a solid surface to work on. It'll need a book-rest that can be raised and lowered, and an inkpot that he can't spill. A place for pens and pencils would be useful, and, well, I'm sure you can think of other conveniences. I hope Mr Felton will keep an eye on things, and help out if you run into trouble"—another grunt confirmed it—"but I'd like the two of you to do all the work, if you will. Yes?"

"Yes. Absolutely yes. We'd love to, wouldn't we, Elle? We'll need to go up and measure the bedframe, of course, to get the dimensions just so; but oh, this is going to be fun. I wonder if we should paint the wood or varnish it, what do you think, Elle? Varnish would give it the look of a school desk, perhaps, or an artist's drawing board, something more serious than paint..."

One of Eder's aunts had worked in Mrs Bailey's kitchen for some number of years, and several of his cousins were employed here and there about the school, so that Rowany was no longer obliged to hold herself in readiness to act as interpreter when needed.

This time, though, she felt the need to be there in person; and so it was she who accompanied Charm, Marigold and Radhika, the first pupils authorised to visit the patient.

Mr Felton's promised partitions had yet to be realised. It occurred to Rowany that the Carpentry Club could be practising joints to some purpose, though neat dovetails might be gilding the lily just a little. For the moment, the boy's domain was still no more than curtained off from the rest of the ward, though those curtains were of a dense, heavy fabric, far more severe than the other cubicles'. Sister Anthony was making an emphatic point here.

The girls had been excited at first, when Rowany collected them from Stokes House. Now they were quieter, as the moment approached. She took the lead, then, drawing back one curtain and ushering them through.

"In you go, girls. See, there are chairs enough for everyone, and room to be comfy, not all crowded around poor Eder's bed."

Indeed, to include the promised window, Eder's allotted space was at least twice the width of the standard cubicles. Room in plenty, a light and airy bedroom, probably more spacious than any the boy had known thus far; and the bed turned around from the normal arrangement, so that he could see out over the flat gatehouse roof and all across the lake.

He'd been doing just that when they arrived, gazing out of the window, perhaps for want of anything else to look at. Now he turned his head, and tried a greeting smile.

It wasn't a great success. If anything, Rowany thought, he looked even shyer than the girls, for all that he had to be at least a couple of years older. Also, he was shockingly pale beneath a robust outdoor complexion. He was in a great deal of pain, she thought, and boy-like determined to hide it. It was the set of his lips that truly betrayed him, too thin and stiff to support that attempt at a smile.

Making a mental note to ask Sister Anthony—or perhaps Dr Ed—if they might be a little more generous with his medications, Rowany smiled brightly on her own behalf and said, "Eder, here are Marigold, Radhika and Charm. These three girls have been desperate to see you better. They're the ones who found you after your fall. I can translate if you need me to, but I think perhaps you can talk with them in English?"

"Please. I will try." It called for a frowning focus, apparently, but he seemed quite determined. "I should thank you in words you can understand, yes?"

"Oh, please. There's no need to—" It was an interesting phenomenon, watching three girls colour up at once, all across the palette from a redhead's pallor to a half-Indian tan.

"Yes," Eder said. "I must. You save my life, yes? My mother says so. I must thank you each."

And so he did, one by one, repeating their names to remember them, while the girls squirmed in a turmoil of social discomfort. Rowany didn't interrupt, despite their agonised glances in her direction. Not till he was done did she steer the conversation another way.

"Thank you, Eder; that was very sweetly done, and very proper. Now, I need to have a serious talk with you, and I'd sooner do it in English so that the girls can follow what I say. If there's anything you don't understand, I want you to stop me and ask, yes?"

He nodded solemnly. The three Middles glanced at each other, puzzled; what part could they have, in any matter that serious?

"You know you will be here, in this bed, for a number of weeks. You can't suppose that we would let you lie idle and dull; that is not the Crater School way," with a smile, "and I don't imagine that you would want it yourself. Am I right?"

"Yes, of course; but," a shrug, a gesture at his splinted leg below the covers, "what can I do? I will run mad, I think, except I cannot run."

"Don't worry, we'll find plenty of things for you to do. You will have visits from different girls each day, and I'm sure some of them will teach you games or bring you puzzles and other pastimes. More than that, though: Father Ignatius tells me that you are always asking him to tell you more about the worlds, to teach you more. He says you never wanted to leave his little school, except that you had to, to help your family. Isn't that right?"

"Yes. I like to learn."

"Exactly so; and now here you are in a school, and we are going to help you learn. Girls, the best way to know your topic is to teach it to someone else. Eder can read and write in English, but only slowly. I want you to help him practise. Bring him exercises, bring him books. Read to him, and have him read to you." *Take his mind off his leg, and that abyss of pain that seeks to claim him.* It might be better than poppy, if they could overwhelm him with distraction. "Remember that he's never left this crater; show him pictures, and talk to him about the places you've been, the different lives each of you has led. Do you understand?"

Three grave nods took on the responsibility, as she had known they would.

"Good. You won't be alone, of course. Only a few of you can come in here at once, and for now we can't stay long; but tell your friends, make plans between you. They'll have their turn, and so will girls from other years. Ask the staff for anything you think Eder might need, anything at all..."

# CHAPTER SEVENTEEN

## Knitting, and Spinning, and More Between

"**K**nitting?"

Upper Third might be willing—a little reluctantly, let it be said—to share their very own boy with other years, but they did very definitely feel that any new developments were theirs to witness as by right, theirs to share as and when they chose. It was particularly galling, therefore, to overhear those two idiots Hilda Rathe and Christine Elphinstone giggling with their friends about this strange manifestation. And given that Hilda and Christine were idiots of the Lower Fourth and therefore senior to themselves, school etiquette ruled against the remarks that should have crushed them utterly. Besides, eavesdropping was anathema at any level, even if said idiots were regaling the tale at the tops of their voices, so that one really could not help but overhear.

Nothing to do, then, but march silently and disapprovingly by, noses in air, utterly ignoring the creatures who were so convulsed by their own wit that they didn't even notice how thoroughly they were being snubbed.

"No, I swear it! We were to read to him from that history book the kids love so much, all about Ancient Egypt and

Rome, though why a shepherd boy should need or want to know any of that, I simply cannot imagine; and it was so hard to keep a straight face, because there he was, sitting up in bed, and *knitting*...!"

The whole school knew, of course, that two of his own kind had turned up at the school gate, too shy to cross the threshold until Mr Felton came out of his cubby to see them standing there. He took pity on the poor lads and escorted them himself, a comforting masculine presence, first to the study to make their duty to Miss Leven and thence up to the San and past the looming threat of Sister Anthony.

One of them had a large pack on his back, when they went in to be closeted awhile with their friend. Neither of them was burdened by it when they left.

Comforts from home, the school presumed, in some kind. His mother's cooking, perhaps—though that would be an unimaginable insult to Mrs Bailey and all her works—or a musical instrument, if Sister Anthony would ever allow music in her ward, which no one could actually quite imagine.

Now, apparently, here was the mystery resolved. Knitting needles, skeins of homespun wool, half-completed projects: the kind of workbag you might find in any rural Martian home—but not in a boy's room, never. The women of the province might have a reputation for being more independent than their Earth-bound sisters, but there were still some tasks that fell by immutable tradition to the spear side of the family, and others to the distaff. It was especially true in the countryside, where people tend to be more conservative by nature, and hold to the customs of their forebears. Knitting was women's work yet, as it always had been; no boy of Mars would dream of taking it up.

Except, apparently, Eder. And perhaps his friends, too? They had brought the bag to him, after all, and not mocked him brutally for it either. Nor did he seem remotely embarrassed about it, by all reports, rattling away with his needles whenever his hands were free.

It was a puzzlement, among the younger girls at least. In the end, the Stokes Trio—as they were beginning to be known among their cohort—took it to their housemistress, as Miss Hendy was held to be the sole authority on all things native and natural, and there was nothing after all remotely more natural than a boy.

The easiest way to approach her, all knew, was to find her at work in a garden, and quietly join in. This was what they did, then, helping to weed a long border by the Castle moat; and eventually, when they felt they had sufficiently laboured to have earned the right to a question and a response, Marigold presented the problem as gravely as she knew how.

"Miss Hendy, do you know Eder, the Basque boy up in the San?"

She allowed that she was acquainted with his presence there, and had indeed talked with the lad herself.

"Well, please, is it, is it quite *normal* for him to be so interested in, in *knitting*, of all things?"

Wise in the ways of girls, she had known for a while that there would be a question coming, and that it would very likely be related to their unexpected guest. She hadn't quite expected this one, though.

Matching Marigold's gravity with her own, sternly suppressing even the least twitch of a smile, she said, "As a matter of fact, while many of Eder's interests are frankly very far from normal among those boys, knitting is something they take completely for granted. It's a custom, indeed, that goes all the way back to their homelands in the Pyrenees. You must consider, they're out with their flocks in all weathers, rain or shine, snow or ice. They have their caves to shelter in, along with their sheep, and a bad storm can often pen them in for days and nights on end, for weeks together. They have rough beds and blankets, mutton-fat lanterns, a fire to cook over, a store of food and fuel; but they're going to need something to do during those endless hours, something to occupy their minds. They play card games and pebble games, I know—but they also have a long tradition of handi-crafts. They whittle sticks into whistles and toys, they cut and sew sheep hides into leather goods, and, as you have learned, they knit. They knit for their own comfort, warm clothes for the winter; they knit for their families and the village as a whole, anything that might be needed; and there's still some work left over that can be traded or sold, again for the welfare of the village. They're swift and accurate with their needles, and there's quite a market now for Basque knitwear in fashionable circles. Some of the patterns they know are positive works of art, and I mean that quite literally. You can find them in galleries and museums, as well as adorning the upper echelons of society. Talk to Eder about it, don't be shy; he'll know a lot more than I do. Perhaps he could even teach you a stitch or two, or one of their simpler patterns. If you wrote that down in proper notation, you'd be doing the worlds a favour. There's no record else, it's all passed down from one generation to the next, and it's always a terrible shame when any knowledge is lost, never mind something as beautiful as that work can be."

Upper Third spread the word joyously, far and wide, so that the idiots of the Lower Fourth—their natural ene-mies—were humiliated for their unkind mockery of ancient customs and wonderful skills.

It was quite wonderful, they found, to watch Eder while he knitted, or *knat*, to use their own preferred form of the past tense. His fingers were a blur, he was so fast; and he never looked down, and he could be talking with them or listening to them read or working out a puzzle in his head but he never missed a stitch, he never made a mistake in his pattern, and the wool almost seemed to twist itself together in his hands, so that every day he was working on a different piece.

Rowany had decreed it to be their task to teach him the New School Hand, rather than the awkward old-fashioned script he had learned from Father Ignatius. Also, he was required to read to them, rather than the other way around. Neither of those activities lent themselves to watching him knit, but they were little daunted. They swapped tasks with willing Juniors—who would much rather be read to than read aloud, a chore universally abhored among the younger set—purely for the pleasure of seeing those magic fingers at work, watching the work grow almost of its own volition, pouring forth across the bedsheet.

Despite their own irrefutable claim to Eder's person, their absolute possession, even Upper Third allowed it to be totally fair and reasonable that Rowany, who had conceived and arranged and organised this new life of his, should be the first to flaunt a genuine Eder piece around the school. It was a scarf even longer than she was tall, in muted colours fading one into the next, with a positively textural pattern to the touch. The weather was still too warm for such a garment, and yet she wore it anyway for sheer love of the thing, draped loosely around her neck and flowing out behind.

In her role as art mistress, Mrs Buchanan sent for magazines and catalogues from Marsport and Cassini and New Victoria, and gave each class a slightly different lesson on the ways that high fashion can batten onto a frankly peasant culture, take what they want for as long as they want it, and offer nothing back. Older girls were invited to write essays on the irony of the wealthiest sporting the selfsame clothes as the poorest in the province; as a matter of honour, Isobel did the same herself in a somewhat more technical manner, and submitted it to a highbrow arts journal with photographs of Eder's work attached. Some months later, that was to appear under the somewhat garish title—not her own—*Is It Art, or Is It Theft?* That would cause a ruckus through several inter-locking circles, art and fashion and high society. It would also prove Isobel's point entirely, by provoking numerous offers to buy Eder's pictured works and any others he might have for sale, his entire output even, "Let us make you famous..."

Fortunately, by that time he had learned a little more of the worlds, courtesy of the Crater School and its happy adoption of his cause, and he felt no qualms in turning all such offers down in favour of his own preferred future.

All that was yet to come. In the meantime, Eder knitted, yes; but he also whittled, once he had learned to send his ancient belt-knife downstairs every morning to be whetted by a kitchen maid under Mrs Bailey's critical and eagle eye. Marigold was gifted a sleek and subtle otter, Charm a dolphin: neither creature one that he could ever have seen in his life, solid evidence that this late and somewhat ramshackle education was already yielding results, stretching his young and willing mind.

Radhika the musical received a whistle, cut and carved from a hollow reed. She could make nothing of its tuning, and so took it to Lois Shannon, who was by way of becoming a friend, albeit senior in both age and tenure at the school. Lois was just as baffled, and insisted that they take it in their turn to Miss Llewellyn, "Yes, of course together, you clown; it's your whistle, you have to be there."

Miss Llewellyn played the full sequence of the whistle's notes, and then a few experimental trills. Handing it back and nodding in satisfaction, she said, "Yes, I've met other examples of this. We have a few in the school's museum, I believe. The Basque language has held together as a creature entirely of itself, with no traceable relationship to any other. The same is not in fact true of their music, thanks to constant trade and pilgrimage passing between France and Spain and hence by definition through the Basque country too, but at its core it is still something alien and unique. The urge is there, the drive to music itself, to cadence and rhythm; but they have made their own path and found their own destinations. This is called a *txistu*, a three-hole whistle. It's as simple as can be, and profoundly unusual to our ears. As far as I can tell, Radhika, working from memory, this is pitched exactly as it ought to be. What you do with it hereafter—well, that is entirely up to you. I would ask Eder to teach you some tunes, if either of you can find the time. It's a lovely gift."

It was, and she did; and she shared what she learned with Lois, so that they could delight together in exploring new pathways, new notions of a tune.

After one such session, when they tried to follow such a pathway and became hopelessly lost, to the point where they were both of them too breathless with laughter to be able to blow another note, Lois cocked her head to one side and said, "You know, you were an odd duck when you came here, Radhi, but I swear you're even odder now."

Radhika frowned, sobering in a moment. "How do you mean?"

"Well, you were such a little cloud of fury when you came, you know you were. Dark and doomy." She swivelled around to the piano and played a few melancholy, illustrative chords. "And then something broke inside you—no, don't worry, I'm not going to ask what happened—and you went away for a bit; and now you're all light and curiosity and..."

And she ran out of words there and had to substitute notes, a quick and quirky tune in the piano's upper register; and then she stopped and said, "Oh, wait, there might actually be something there, and Miss Llewellyn says I have to write everything down or I'll never remember it, even if I think I will, so could you just pass me that manuscript paper and a pencil? Thanks... There. Got you, you winsome little thing. Now, what was I saying...?"

But the moment had passed. Radhika shook her head, *it doesn't matter*, and it really didn't. She knew exactly what Lois had meant, and exactly what the older girl was seeing in her now. No better than Lois did she understand quite how the change had been effected, but she did know how deep it ran. Oh, she still had a hair-trigger temper, and she supposed she always would; but the urge to control it was far stronger in her now than the urge to give way, to let it all spill out. It was hard even to remember how willingly she'd given it sway, allowed it to govern her life. Well, no more. Not her temper was in charge now, but herself; and she was more and much more than a snarl and a spit, she'd show the world that—

She was startled out of introspection by a sudden rap at the practice-room window. She and Lois both twisted round, to see the Head Girl herself beckoning imperiously. As the junior there, Radhika ran to open the glass, expecting Melanie to want something of Lois. Instead, it was herself that judicial eye fell upon.

"I've been looking for you, young Radhika. Your practice hour is over, isn't it? Long over, by the written schedule... Yes, I thought so. Well, enough of this; shimmy up to your dorm, change into your whites, and find me on the cricket field. Hop to it, now."

R adhika hopped. Indeed, she ran, where she was allowed to—never in the corridors, but open air was safe ground for any kind of hurry, so long as you kept alert for other traffic, especially traffic in any way senior to yourself—and so came to the cricket ground in fair time. There she found herself awaited not only by the Head Girl, but by the Games

Captain Alis too, and also the third of that long-established triumvirate, Rowany de Vere herself. All of them in cricket whites, with an improvised pitch, or at least two wickets set the proper distance apart, set up in the outfield.

"Oh, don't mind me," Rowany said, in response to what might possibly have been described as a gape. "I'm just here to keep wicket. Gloves and pads, see? In case Alis lets anything by her. Melanie is going to stand as umpire and *beau idéal*, which is to say exemplar, to watch your motions and offer counsel. Obviously, if Alis actually hits anything, it's your task to chase it. Here, catch," and she tossed a cricket ball casually underarm.

Radhika caught it instinctively, gazed at it in her hands in bewilderment. "I, I thought I wasn't allowed to bowl any more...?"

"Oh, not your slingers. Not till  you learn better control. We'll work on that, too. But in the meantime, with all your experience in India, it's a crying shame that you haven't tried your hand at bowling spin. Given how well you play it, and all of that."

"Oh, but I did, and I just didn't, I didn't have the knack."

"You mean that bowling fast came easily to you, so you never learned the knack. It takes work, Radhi—I understand that's what the smart set is calling you now?—and we, we three are here to work you. As you can see," a gesture at her whites, "we're all taking this seriously. Now, you stand as umpire for an over, while Melanie bowls her wickedest twisters. Observe her hand, and how she spins the ball; pay no attention to how much trouble she puts Alis in. That's for later. The craft begins at your end, with the hand."

Radhika duly observed, and felt immediately that this craft was far and away out of her stars. Nevertheless: she wouldn't have been allowed to cry uncle without even trying, so try she did. Under Melanie's exacting coaching, showing her exactly how to grip the ball and what twist to apply as she released it, she bowled over after over at an empty wicket. Some balls went wildly astray; some hit an ugly tuft of turf and bounced unpredictably; both kinds sent Rowany lunging this way and that to keep the ball in bounds. Neither, of course, was what was wanted. Her every decent release she watched with pleading eyes, begging it to pitch and then turn offline, even just a fraction, just enough for everyone to see. On and on they went, until at last,

"There, you see? I knew you could do it! All it takes is strength and a supple wrist, and of course you have both of those, from your music. After that, it's just practice. Which means that we practise until you get it right, which you just did; and now we go on practising until you can't get it wrong. This time, I really will take bat against you; and I really will have you chasing that ball all over the field, if you don't wrangle it past me one way or the other. Up to you, kiddo."

# CHAPTER EIGHTEEN

## Matters in Flux

"**N**o, no, Chrissy! You can't say your line till *after* you hit the ball!"

"Well, don't make it so hard to hit, then!"

"But that's the *point*...!"

"If the point is to learn our lines, then wouldn't it make better sense to say them every time we *miss* the ball? That happens a lot more often, and repetition is really the best way to learn."

"I still think that grinding over the line internally, again and again, till you finally get the chance to say it..."

It was a new game, and the rules were still somewhat in flux. Arguing was half the fun, though, along with trying out new ideas to see what worked best.

Apart from fun, the purpose of the game was twofold. Radhika needed to practise her new bowling; they all needed to memorise their lines for *Pyramus and Thisbe*. Threefold, if you counted batting practice against the demon spin. It was a highly economical usage of their time, they felt; they were very pleased with themselves for coming up with the notion.

They stood in a wide circle, with a roughly measured radius of twenty-two yards, the length of a cricket pitch. The centre point was Radhika's; the girls in the circle had one cricket bat between them, which belonged to the girl whose line came next. Under the current regulations, Radhika bowled at her until she managed to hit the ball. Then she might say her line, pass the bat to whoever's line followed her own, and then lurk behind her as wicketkeeper, in anticipation of many misses. Radhika's skills were developing swiftly, driven by her own determination and the support of her peers; it follows, then, that the scene was progressing slowly.

"Hurry up, Chrissy! It's my line next, and I can feel it oozing out of my head already. If I don't say it soon it'll be gone for good, and I'll have to ask for a prompt again."

"I am trying, I promise! It's just that wretched ball, which is never ever where I think it ought to—oh, red riminy, do you see? It positively *swirled* around my bat, and I'm sure I would've been bowled."

"Middle and leg," Maeve confirmed, as she retrieved the ball and tossed it back to the bowler. "That was a juicy one, Radhika! Try to watch her hand, Chrissy, as she releases; you should be able to see the turn she's putting on it. You'll never see it on the ball in flight."

"I *am* trying! I just—oh, what's the point?"

A sympathetic Radhika sent down a particularly slow ball, making no attempt to disguise her action. At the same time, a frustrated Chrissy threw all caution to the winds, and danced over the grass to meet it before it could bounce and turn. There was nothing wrong with her cricketing eye, in those circumstances. A slow full toss deserves to be cracked to the boundary, and duly was.

She stared after it for a moment, seeming more aghast than satisfied. Then she turned to her friends and said, "I, I'm sorry, I know that wasn't really the point. But it was making me so, so *rageous*..."

"Oh dear, was that my fault? I'm sorry." Radhika dropped down onto the grass, while fleet-footed Charm chased after the ball. It was going to take her a while. "That was a lovely stroke, though—and a gruesome ball. It's a lesson for me, not to feel sorry for your victim."

"I should think not, indeed!" Marigold followed Radhika's example, and the others recognised this as a general signal for a break. "Spin bowling is all about the art of torture, tying the poor batsman into such knots that in the end they get themselves out. Miss Whitworth taught us that, our very first term here."

"Miss Whitworth never said anything about *torture*, Marigold!" Chrissy objected. "You know she never would!"

"Well, not in so many words, p'raps. But I divined her inner meaning. Now, are you ever actually going to say your line?"

"Well, not till Charm gets back. 'Twouldn't be fair. It's her line next, and she needs to hear the passion I put into mine, so she can reply in kind."

Thwack!
"'A very gentle beast, and of a good conscience.' There! Your turn, Elana. Here's the bat."

Thwack!

"'The very best at a beast, my lord, that e'er I saw.' D'you know, Radhi, I think we might be getting the hang of these."

"Oh, do you? Wait till your next line, I'll bamboozle you all square up and you'll never get it out..."

"**O**oh! I spy strangers!"

It wasn't true, of course. Their unexpected audience was a solitary figure standing outside the boundary rope, and they all knew perfectly well who she was. They had recently learned this traditional cry, though, from a lesson about imperial governance in general and the Houses of Parliament in particular, and had adopted it forthwith as being far preferable to "Cave!" as a warning of impending interruption.

Cate's call brought the game to an abrupt halt, as they all turned to look. Mary Ellen—who generally went by Mae these days, but was inclined to forget more often than any of her friends did—took that as an invitation, stepped carefully over the rope and strolled out to greet them.

"I'm sorry, but I do have to ask: what in all the worlds are you *doing*?"

A babble of voices tried to explain it, all at once. The resultant cacophony was no help to anyone, let alone poor Mary Ellen, who had to shush them with her hands when her own voice wasn't able to rise above the throng.

"One of you, please? Just the one?"

Marigold took charge, as ever. but not to hog the limelight. "Agnosia, you say. It was your idea."

Agnosia laid out the rules of the game in a few crisp, clear sentences. Her audience of one laughed aloud.

"How ... original! And how appropriate, too, in a way: Shakespeare and cricket, you couldn't find two more quintessentially English subjects if you searched with both hands for a fortnight. And here you come up with a way to combine them, in our little outpost absolutely as far from England as you could conceivably get, except that I suppose we always take a little bit of England with us, wherever we go. Even those of us who've never actually been Home, we're still cast from the same mould at heart, I do believe." Her voice

220

dropped lower yet and her face took on a sort of inward look, all humour falling away. She waved an absent-minded fare- well and wandered off, pulling a notebook from her pocket as she went.

"Well!" Marigold exclaimed. "What was *that* all about? There she was, being all interesting about things, and sud- denly she's gone in her head, even before she takes her body with her!"

"Oh, I know what that is," Charm said. "Liv says she does this all the time. She's just been smitten by a notion for a poem, or an essay, or a story. P'raps we'll see it in *The Craterean*, and know that we've inspired an actual piece of literature. Liv's much the same way, honestly, when she starts thinking about making art. It's no use trying to talk to her then, never mind anything else you might want to have done. Mamma used to say, 'Not now, darlings, I'm work- ing,'—well, she still does, honestly—but Liv doesn't trouble with that, she just scowls and shakes her head at me and goes back to mulling whatever it is she has to mull."

The manners and habits of genius occupied their minds and conversation for another minute or two, before the summons of the school bell overrode all thoughts else. They squawked, and dashed, and more than one of them had the charity to hope that Mary Ellen was not so deep into her idea as to miss that imperative call, or worse, simply ignore it altogether.

Come Sunday, Radhika wrote her duty letter to her mother, all the news of the week that she judged fit to share with an ailing and beloved parent. Under those restric- tions, it didn't take too long, though she practised the New School Hand throughout, trying for what Mrs Buchanan liked to call "flair". When she had sealed it and stamped it, she still had plenty of time; so she took a new sheet of notepaper, headed it and dated it carefully, and began her other, her self-imposed duty letter.

*Dear Capri,*

*As I promised, (sorry!), here is my confession for this week. I think I ought to call it A Tale of Two Tempers. You'll see why.*

*I am still furious with my father: not for sending me here, in the circumstances, but absolutely for going off on his own, about his own mysterious affairs, without a word to Mama-ji or me. I know she feels as abandoned as I do, though of course she wouldn't ever say so to me. That's the worst of grown-ups, the way they try to keep so much from us, when it affects us just as much as it does them.*

*However! There's nothing I can actually do about being angry with Papa-ji; I can't even shout at him in a letter, as I don't even know where he is and it might take months to get there anyway. Not even the Imperial Mail can make the aetherships run to any kind of schedule whatever. They come when they come, and they go when they go, and that's all there is to it. Oh, and they take as long as they take on the way, that too. People say it's different every time, though how they can tell, I do not know. I had no idea of days or weeks, when we came up; and of course our cal-endar is wildly out of synch with Earth's, so dates had nothing to say about it.*

*Anyway, apart from that, which is just a silent sputtering lava-pool in the back of my head, the good news is that everything else I was angry about this week, everyone else was too, and we were absolutely right. U3 was late for tea on Tuesday, every man jack of us, because Miss Whitworth had taken us out boating on the lake and she kept us too long and it's simply impossible to put everything away tidily in the boathouse and then pelt up to the Castle and make yourselves neat and tidy when there aren't enough basins or mirrors for everyone in less than ten minutes, which was all the time we had. It can't be done. But the prefect on duty wouldn't listen to us, despite reason being on our side, and she gave us a dressing-down in front of all the school and fined us all our cake besides. Everyone now officially hates Mary Holmes, and we shall be revenged. One way or another. It's quite decided.*

*And then Charm and Marigold and I—you'll remember them, of course—got into trouble with our housemistress. Ordinarily she's the kindest person alive, but perhaps she had the toothache or some such on Wednesday, if grown-ups get such things, because she was grumpy all day, in school and out. And perhaps we were being a little too noisy, maybe, in the hall, but that's no reason for her to come boiling out of her study with a face like thunder and the default book ready in her hands. Anyone who's written up through the week has to give up their Saturday club and go to Sister Anthony to hem sheets and darn socks and the like. And Miss Hendy put asterisks by our names, which means two weeks running for us; and it was all so unfair, even if we were maybe sliding on the parquet in our outside shoes—which she had not seen us doing, anyway—we were so seething mad with her, I'm still amazed that we all managed to keep our tempers in check. Yes, even me! I didn't say a word, where she might have heard it. We changed our shoes like good girls, and then stayed in the boot-room to agree with each other about how rageous we all were.*

*It did seem to help, somehow, that we all felt the same way. It's nice, sometimes, not to be alone even on the inside. Anyway, I haven't really been stewing about it since, the way you'd expect me to, knowing what you know about how awful I am at that sort of thing. We served the first half of our sentence yesterday, and there were maybe a dozen of us altogether, even a couple of big girls, fifth-formers, who must've done something truly dreadful to be punished with us kids. One can't ask, of course. But we could talk, so long as it was softly and what Sister Anthony calls "non-contentious", and it was nice to get to know some of the girls we haven't run across before. There'll be a different batch next week, and it's weird, but I'm almost looking forward to it. Is that weird?*

*Anyway, that's it for this week. Do write back and tell me all about yours. I know you're a fifth-former yourself, so I don't expect you get into trouble at all, but tell me what the other girls get up to, because that's the most interesting part of school, don't you think...?*

"Kathy, are you *sure* you don't want to take some leave? Go to Cassini, see your brother off this final time? He'll be going in style, you know, and well deserved: the service in the cathedral, all the pomp and majesty the Double Reds can achieve, and the Archbishop on top; and then his interment on San Michele itself, in the family tomb, where you'll go yourself when your time comes..."

"Thank you, but I'm quite sure, yes. I said my own good-byes to Robert some time since, when we learned that this was coming. How could I conceivably leave, at this end of the term, with so much going on? I've girls preparing to sit School Certs and Highers, and they need me on hand, never mind the rest of my classes, and my house besides."

"Kathy, we would manage." Miss Leven poured coffees for each of them, and passed the plate of biscuits, but Miss Hendy only shook her head. "We've managed before, at such times. You know that. You left your own classroom when Miss Harribeth's mother died, to teach Martian history in her stead; you stepped up to take charge of Butler House when you were almost a new girl on the staff yourself, when Miss Tattersall needed to spend a term away to see her own sister through her final illness."

"Oh, I do know—and I know how much strain it puts on everybody, having to fit themselves around an absence. Robert had the strongest sense of duty I've ever known in a man; he would absolutely understand my staying here. If I could ask him, he'd insist on it."

Miss Leven gazed at her colleague thoughtfully. "Is it that you don't want to go?"

"No—oh, but perhaps. Perhaps it is. Is that odd, I wonder? We raise our girls to be tough-minded, to face whatever life may throw at them and meet it with a will; and when it comes to seeing my last living relative, my baby brother being laid away—well, you may be right. I still don't think so, and I hope I'm right; all my reasons seem valid to me, here and now. But then they would, wouldn't they? If I were simply rationalising? I'd need to convince myself, before I could even hope to convince anyone else. Never mind you."

"Well. You do as you see fit, my dear. There's time yet, to change your mind. They won't delay in case an aethership comes in, I know, the way they might for a Viceroy; but there will be people heading to Cassini from all across the province—including, I believe, the Viceroy—for your baby brother's funeral. Colonel Hendy is a public hero, and a famous name. Which is one reason why I feel that perhaps his only living relative should be there in the place of honour, first mourner, walking behind his coffin all the way. There are private goodbyes, Kathy, and there are public proclamations. Oh, I know," as Miss Hendy shuddered visibly, "the very idea appalls you; we schoolmistresses are a retiring breed, the very last to want to thrust ourselves forward into the public eye. It might do the world of good, though, to our whole profession, if one of us marches in the vanguard—in your scholar's gown, yes, proclaiming your DPhil, not simply *sub fusc*; all the men will wear their uniforms and decorations, so why not you?—at the very head yet, on such a day, to declare our particular primacy. Let the press and the people all see the generals making way for you, saluting you, as a representative not only of your family but of our particular, peculiar calling..."

225

# CHAPTER NINETEEN

### "Oh, *Bother* Rowany!"

The news of Miss Hendy's abrupt departure ran around the school like a sand-rat in a cage, around and around in "an orgy of speculation," as Melanie Fitzwalter would refer to it in an epic scold at teatime, when prefects supervised the meal and no staff were present. "Dishonourable" was another word she would use, as she moved to crush this unpleasant manifestation.

To be fair, there was some excuse for all the gossip and guesswork. Not a girl would be unaffected, from the youngest Junior to Melanie herself. Unusually for such a school— but then, the Crater School was of course somewhat unusual in any manner of ways—Natural and Native Sciences was an obligatory class, from first to last. As with Areography, it was felt that the better the leavers knew and understood their world in both its human and its alien aspects, the better they would get on as adults, the better lives they would be equipped to build for themselves and others.

In Miss Hendy's absence, though, who could, who would step up to fill her exemplary shoes—it was commonly held that she knew everything, but *everything*, about this their home planet—and take her classes? No one knew, no one could guess with any likelihood of proving right. That didn't stop anyone from trying, of course, given the shocking paucity of information coming their way from the Powers That Be.

As it happened, the unrelenting, unforgiving, almost-sacred Timetable decreed that the first Natty-Natty-Sci class on that enlivening day should fall to the Upper Third. They had assembled as usual, as instructed, in Miss Hendy's normal teaching space, "half classroom," Rowany had once dubbed it, "half laboratory, and half museum."

The room was abuzz with wonder, until the watcher-of-the-day, peering through the dimpled glass of the door, cried "I spy strangers!" as her task was, and every girl scattered to her own stool, at her own given part of whichever bench she shared with a handful of others.

There wasn't even time for the watcher-of-the-day to advise them of who was coming, if indeed she'd been able to make it out through the distorting glass. The door opened; the girls rose to their feet and chorused "Good morning, Miss—" and promptly fell into a chaos of confusion, as the figure who marched in was known to them all but not as a member of staff, not to say the *staff*, not a *teacher* at all—and, come to that, not even a "Miss" anybody.

A few bold souls scrabbled after correction, "uh, I mean, Mr Marks," but most of them simply stood mute, rapt in horror and fascination combined.

Mr Marks it was: Mr Marks the groundskeeper, the terror of the cricket square, supervisor of the dreaded Litter Patrol for defaulters. Mr Marks, whom rumour said—had always said, that is to say, until this actual moment—was never to be sighted within the Castle, living as he did in permanent exile in his own little cottage in the grounds. Forbidden to enter here, rumour said, this being the undisputed territory of Mr Felton the caretaker, and the two of them sworn enemies from time immemorial...

Here he was, though, and quite unassailed: dressed in a wholly unfamiliar suit and tie, stepping up onto Miss Hendy's dais for all the worlds as though he had the right to.

"Good morning, girls. Do sit down." His voice was somehow milder than they were used to, though no less compelling. They sat "as if our strings had all been cut at once," as Marigold would later describe it.

"Now, I know you've been told that Miss Hendy is called away," though not a soul had told them why, which was a breach of the Schoolgirl's Code if ever there was one, "and so I've been asked to step in and field some of her classes. Now I'm not the scientist Miss Hendy is, not by a long chalk, nor the scholar neither; but I was born and raised in Terminus, just down in the valley there, and I've roamed this crater and the hills around all my born days. Aye, and fished the canals too, and hunted hare and grouse with the shepherd boys in my time, when I was a boy myself. It'd be a shame, a shame on me, if there wasn't something I could teach you about this land we live on, wouldn't you say? Or show you, as much as teach: I'll take you out and show you the otters' holts by the water down below, the bats in their caves. We'll take the sandkits out on leashes and teach them the scent of a rabbit.

"Other days," he went on disappointingly, "you'll have other people giving you proper lessons in here. That's not my style, except for today. This is what we call an exception. It won't be proving any rules, but just this once, I'm going to sit here," perching on the edge of Miss Hendy's bench, which all girls were strictly forbidden to do, "and we'll see if I can't answer any questions you might throw at me. And if some clever-clogs among you," he went on suspiciously, glowering around the room, "asks me something that Miss Hendy has answered already, and I answer differently, well, we'll just have to go out and find the truth for ourselves, won't we? Now, who's first? Don't be shy, I don't bite. Unless you go walking over the square, that is, just when I've mown it ready for a match, and you in those nasty square heels..."

O nce he'd chased away their shyness, it was quite the most delightful lesson of the day, and almost, *almost* distracted the Stokes House girls from their own particularly troublesome question, that again nobody was offering to answer. Stokes was Miss Hendy's own house, she their own beloved mistress; who would be standing in for her, while she was away? There were no spare housemistresses, as far as the girls knew, no one who had served in that role and stepped down and might be willing to step up again at need. Housemistresses went on and on, unchangeable as the seasons.

No answer vouchsafed itself, no one deigned to tell them until the last bell rang for the end of formal school and they trooped down the hill together, Stokes girls finding each other on the way and joining in an informal, spontaneous singularity, even scooping up Melanie herself in all her grandeur as they went. They filed in through the back door *en masse*, changed school shoes for house slippers in the boot room, oddly quiet despite the crush; then they headed as one for the common room, where they could all stay together until their doom was announced, and—

" R owany!"
If the cry didn't rise from forty throats at once, it was only because the doorway wasn't big enough to allow everyone an instant sight of her. There was something of a scrum, indeed, as those backed up in the corridor tried to bully their way in at the sound of that cry, while those at

the front were still at least a little dumbstruck, apt merely to stand and stare.

Rowany it was, though. Laughing at them, from where she sat perched on the desk prefects used when they supervised prep; beckoning them in with broad welcoming gestures; grinning slyly at her best friend Melanie when that girl scowled at her and demanded to know what was the why of this, and why, pray, had she not been informed?

"Oh, phoo—what's the fun of a friendship, if you can't keep a secret now and then? Anyway, come here," pulling Melanie down onto the desk at her side, "and be all official, because I can't. Indeed, I am most unofficial—and no, of course I'm not standing in for your housemistress. Can you imagine? But if you would all just settle down and listen," addressing the room at large now, and its cohort of noisy and excited girls, "I will tell you what's what. Pretend this is prep; sit in your chairs and be quiet. *Quiet*, I say! There, that's better. Rowany-voice still works, I find. Good to know. Now, *for* your information, your temporary housemistress is to be Miss Harribeth, until such time as Miss Hendy can make her way back to us, if indeed she manages to do that before the end of term. No," as a buzz arose again, "it's not certain. She may find all manner of things to attend to, that will eat up more time than she might wish... Yes, Betty?" for that worthy had stood up in front of her locker, clearly with a question.

"Please, if it's not, not intrusive,"—Betty Waterhouse was a Senior, and a close crony of Miss Hendy's, suffering as she did from an inexplicable beetle-mania, "may we know why Miss Hendy had to go away?"

Aware of the closeness between mistress and pupil, Rowany smiled upon Betty more kindly than she might have done with another girl. "I am permitted to tell you that there has been a death in her family. You will need to know that, in case she does return this term; she may be quite low in her spirits, or otherwise not quite the woman to whom you are accustomed. You need not don kid gloves, or gather cotton-wool to wrap her in, but a little extra thought for her welfare might be appreciated. Other than that, her business is her own, and none of ours. Satisfied?"

"Yes. Yes, of course. Thank you, Rowany..."

Rowany gave her a moment to settle, then went on. "Now, Miss Harribeth has never taken on the responsibility of a house before—which means, of course, that she has never lived in a house, and has no notion of what a horrible rabble you can be." She paused, to allow hisses and growls to die away. "As witness, I believe. I know you'll all be on your very best behaviour, to bid her welcome and make smooth her ways; and just to ensure that, I myself—who have lived in this house for longer than any of you, and know exactly everything about it—will be joining Melanie and the other house prefects, to keep some sense of order and discipline among you rowdy lot. Oh hush, hush," as the protests threatened to begin again, "you know I love you all. I *know* and love you all, which is the whole of my point. Just be as good as you can manage, yes? From now until Miss Hendy reappears, whereupon you may instantly revert to your wild and wicked selves? Please, for my sake, if not poor Miss Harribeth's?"

There was a somewhat grumpy chorus of "Yes, Rowany," which she trusted not at all, to judge by her demeanour as she gazed around the room, catching each and every Stokes girl eye to eye, or so it seemed. Then she laughed, nodded dismissal, tucked her arm through Melanie's and led her away to some more private converse.

"Well, *I* say it was really mean-spirited of Rowany to make us promise like that." Thus Marigold, holding forth on the staircase after supper. As newly promoted Middles, she and her cohort—now including Radhika as a matter of course—were entitled to a precious extra half-hour, but the juniors would be trooping up to bed at any minute.

The stairs were their favourite place to meet at this hour, as offering at least an illusion of privacy; if meetings were interrupted or curtailed by other traffic, then so be it. "She knows just how much fun we could've had, playing tricks on Miss Harribeth and, and leading her far astray."

"Well, of course she does," said Charm the peacemaker. "She'd have done just the same herself, given the opportunity. Maybe she did do the same herself. Perhaps we should interrogate her, while she's here? But anyway, she saw the danger and averted it, being as she is, ever on the *qui vive*."

"Ever on the *what*?" cried more than one outraged girl, causing Marigold to make urgent shushing sounds. Lingering on the stairs might not be against a strict interpretation of the rules, but it was very much discouraged—which was of course another reason they were so fond of doing so.

"On the qui vive. It's French, and it means, oh, being on the alert, on the lookout. Mamma uses it a lot, so." A shrug stood in for the rest of the sentence, all she needed; nods of acknowledgement and understanding all around.

"So does Papa-ji," Radhika confirmed. "When we were waiting for a visitor, he used to put me on sentry-duty, to watch for them coming, I mean *their* coming,"—as a soft warning hiss reminded her of the gerund, which Miss Peters was *very* strict about—"and he always said to stay on the qui vive. I expect he said it to his real sentries, too. He probably left a whole string of soldiers all across India who know at least two words of French."

"Well, that's all very well, and now that we know it we should use it too—but what are we going to *do*? It's a terrible shame to let this opportunity go by, it's just the kind of chance that we were looking for; and of course we can't break our word to Rowany, and Miss Harribeth is a dear anyway and we wouldn't want to absolutely *alarm* her, but—"

"Well, Marigold, I'm relieved to hear that, I must say."

The voice came from above, beyond the turn of the stair. Their startled upward stares found, inevitably, Miss Harribeth herself, descending.

They gasped as one, as soon as they could breathe again, and tremulously awaited their doom—which was, apparently, to be laughed at.

"Oh, for goodness' sake, girls, don't sit there gaping like moonstruck loons! Believe it or believe it not, I too have been a Middle in my day, with all my mind bent on mischief; and I too would have lamented the loss of such an opportunity. I owe a vote of thanks to Rowany, I learn. Not at all to my surprise, I might add. Is it lawful, by the way, to gather in a mob on the stairs?"

They rose awkwardly to their feet, pressed back against the wall or each other, mumbled something or other about there not really being a rule, not to say a *rule*...

"I see. In that case, consider yourselves officially discouraged from the practice, as being inconvenient to others. Yes, I know, it's like losing your clubhouse, isn't it? You're bright girls, by and large; find another one. In the meantime, as I gather I'm to be made safe from the perils and dangers of teenage jokesters, why don't you tell me about Miss Hendy's evening routine? I know all about sending the prefects to bed early and letting Middles sit up as late as they like, obviously, but..."

Thus did a dormitory's-worth of the wickedest-girls-to-be find themselves, somewhat to their own surprise, actively helping their new substitute housemistress settle in. They told her all about the customs and practices of the house; and when the first bell sounded and the juniors came to make their way upstairs, they stood back politely in the hallway while Miss Harribeth wished each of the youngsters goodnight, so that when that was done they could lead her around and show her where everything was kept.

When second bell rang and they lined up to be dismissed in their turn, a muttering Marigold aptly summed up all their feelings in one: "Oh, *bother* Rowany! She's, she's actually made us be *good...*!"

Miss Harribeth took up that same station at the foot of the stairs to see the Seniors off to bed when their time came. No bell was sounded for the prefects, but they followed in fairly short order, feeling perhaps an extra responsibility for their particular roomful of charges on such a night as this, even despite Rowany's preemptive measures.

Rowany herself came along with Melanie, her own particular friend. Miss Harribeth stayed her, with a hand on her arm: "Bide a while, if you will. Find a chair in Miss Hendy's sitting room—I suppose I should call it mine now but I don't believe I'm able—while I just have a word with Melanie. Don't worry, I shan't keep you late."

Rowany laughed, bade Melanie goodnight, and went through the door into the little room she'd always loved, which Miss Hendy had indeed made very much her own. Between the bookshelves, the walls were hung with engravings by Thomas Bewick, original prints from his *History of British Birds*, which of course could stand in perfectly well for a history of Martian birds as well.

Of course, Rowany entirely ignored the instruction to take a seat. The lure of someone else's bookshelves is irresistible, to any right-thinking mind; and Miss Hendy was an avid reader of modern novels, as well as a collector of any and every book that treated with Martian flora or fauna. The girls held it to be manifest that she knew it all already, and should write a book of her own. It had been noted among the staff, at least, that her regular demurrals were growing less and less convincing as the years went by; they looked forward to their colleague's definitive volume, as and when. She would, after all, be neither the first nor presumably the last Crater School mistress to share her expertise through the printed page.

When Miss Harribeth came bustling in, therefore, she found Rowany leafing through a collection of the latest short stories from Martian authors, as published in *The New Victorian Review*.

"Do borrow that if you'd like, dear. I did myself, so I know Katherine has no qualms about lending to responsible folk; and it's quite a wondrous assortment, so it is. But just now, lay it aside and sit down, will you?"

Obligingly, Rowany sat, gazing at her former history teacher with some curiosity.

"That's better." Miss Harribeth took a seat opposite, and reached into a cabinet at her side. "Now, to help see me through this ordeal, Miss Leven has kindly gifted me with a bottle of her notorious brandy. I believe it comes from a cousin of hers, and I'm not entirely sure about the validity of his licence, so we never ask about that. Take a tot with me now—and no, don't you dare try to claim yourself a schoolgirl still, and so immune to such blandishments. I know perfectly well why you're here, girlie, and you stand no more under my authority than Miss Leven herself. You may not yet be of legal age, but that means nothing in a private dwelling; and I happen to know that any child raised under the General's roof will be well accustomed to the pleasures of a little tipple now and then. You forget, I've met each and every one of your brothers down the years, not to mention the man himself. Take this," a generous measure, only made to look mean by the volume of the glass it came in; Rowany took, swirled and sniffed as to the manner trained, sipped with wonder and made no more demur, "relax, and tell me just exactly what I'm in for during the rest of this term. Assuming Kathy doesn't make it back before the end, which I am in hopes that she will, but mortals propose and God disposes, so I count no chickens at all..."

# CHAPTER TWENTY

## Shattered with Delight

"I must say, I little dreamed that our next Crater School prodigy would turn out to be a boy."

"I don't suppose any of us did—but do you truly find Eder so prodigious, Lesley? His English is coming on in leaps and bounds, I admit, both written and spoken, but I'd put that down largely to his perpetual stream of visitors, coaching him in any way they can think of, rather than an innate linguistic genius on his part."

"Ah, but mathematics is a language in a different kind, Alison, as you know full well. That boy eats and drinks numbers, and picks up new ideas and concepts faster than I ever did. I'm sure the symbology helps—he doesn't have to struggle through a page of English instruction, when he's looking at a new equation—but his progress is genuinely remarkable. He's already working through problems I normally only show to Seniors. His work is careful, clear and precise; he's a joy to teach. Also, the preparation I'm getting back from some of the Middles far exceeds what I would expect from those hoydens, so I expect he's helping them as well."

"If you want to call it 'helping', when what you mean is he works out the answer for them and they copy it out fair."

"That is exactly what I mean, and they'll be sorry for it at term's end, when I hit them with examinations. But oh, give me this boy for a year of coaching, and I could have him ready for the university."

"I hardly think we can do that." Miss Tattersall and Miss Peters could have had no reasonable expectation of privacy, speaking as they were in the heart of the Staff Room. Now they looked up to find Miss Leven herself smiling down on them. "Oh, goodness me, don't get up; you're neither of you schoolgirls any more, and I'm the one invading your territory. And without an invitation, too. I try never to do this, but as it happens, I most particularly wanted to speak with you two, and asking a child to find and summon the pair of you to my study seemed too much of an imposition on all concerned, so the mountain has as it were come to Mohammed. If I may...?"

They were swift to assure her that she might, and disregarded her orders entirely in order to pull up another chair and fetch her a cup of coffee from the table.

"So," she said, once everyone was settled, "as it happens, Eder was exactly what I wanted to talk to you about. I know he's been reading history and areography and anything else he can lay his hands on, but your two subjects are those that he has battened onto, so I thought perhaps I should discuss his situation with you first.

"Lesley, I'm sorry I can't let you keep him for an entire year, but that really would be impossible. For one thing, while we do our best to crush the first hint of snobbishness from our girls, there's not much we can do about their parents. I could unfortunately name you some few who would be outraged at having their precious flowers educated alongside a peasant boy, and a charity case at that, for his family couldn't possibly approach our fees.

"However, having given him this brief taste of academic instruction, and having seen him devour it so eagerly and look for more, it seems clear to me that we can't just mend his leg and toss him back to his sheep, however good he may be at counting them."

"Funnily enough," said Miss Tattersall, "I believe it actually was counting sheep that woke this talent within him. He has an innate sense of number; it didn't take him long to puzzle out that there was more that he could do with those figures in his head, this flock and that. He hadn't gone far beyond arithmetic on his own, of course, but I've already been able to lead him a great deal further. And no, we can't possibly let a mind like his moulder away in a cave. I'm not actually sure that university would be the best place for him, with that background, but..."

"Quite so. 'But.' There must be another solution, and I'd like the pair of you to bend your minds in that direction, if you would. There's no hurry; he won't be leaving his bed for weeks yet, nor I believe our care for months. Dr Penberthy won't let him risk that leg out on the slopes until it's good and ready to be risked, so we may as well keep him here. The long summer holiday is coming up, and I know both of you intended to stay at school at least for part of it. You might think about giving the lad some more intensive coaching—"

"Oh, I've already thought of that," Miss Tattersall assured her. "I'll chart him out a course into the deeper, stranger ways of number, and he will lap it up, I do believe. What comes to him after that—well, that may lie in the lap of the gods, but if I see any chance to give him a providential push, I promise you I'll take it."

"And I'll help you shove," Miss Peters confirmed.

"Splendid. Thank you both. Really, every term does bring its own surprises, does it not?"

The unwitting subject of this frank debate was gazing, with some satisfaction, at a chessboard laid somewhat precariously across his lap. An incautious subset of the Upper Third had taught him the moves, declaring that there had to be *something* they could do to distract him from those appalling sums and number-games he was so dead set upon; and chess was another brain sort of thing, wasn't it, so maybe he'd pick that up instead?

Which he had promptly done, with a speed and avidity that overrode all their hopes and occupations. They no longer even tried to play him individually; instead they had banded together, on the principle that many hands make light work, so surely many brains must be better than one.

Unfortunately, this was proving not to be the case. Many brains apparently only led to many arguments, and many strategies too when in desperation they tried taking turns.

At last, "We're sorry, Eder," Charm said, tipping over their king in surrender once again. "This can't be any fun for you either, you're just too good for us."

"No, it is fine," he replied good-naturedly. "I like to sit and think what other moves you could have made"—*should have made* was what he meant, only he was too nice to say so; they all knew it—"and how I could have answered those."

"Well, even so. We'll find you some better players to practise on. Mary Holmes is a fiend, I know. In the meantime," Marigold took the board away, folded it in half and spilled all the remaining pieces into the box to join their fallen comrades, "let's think of something else. Sister Anthony said you can have us till teatime—"

"Well, what she *actually* said was that he can't have his workbooks back till after tea—"

"Which amounts to the exact same thing, doesn't it? That was practically an order, to keep the poor boy amused. So what do you want to do, Eder?"

He thought for a while, and then said slowly, "I want to laugh."

They gaped at him blankly, until Charm said, "Um, how? I mean, we can't climb on the bed and tickle you, Sister Anthony would slay us all."

"No, no tickles. But you said to keep me amused. I have ... not been amused, since I came here. On the hills, with my friends and my kin, we laugh all the time, at everything and nothing. If one of us falls in the water, we laugh and laugh, before we help him out. And the same at home, during the winter. So much is funny. I miss that. Nothing is funny here."

Marigold was inclined to take offence, on behalf of the entire school; it was Radhika who saw through to the truth. "No, but he's right, Mari. Nothing is funny—for him. We get to laugh all day, outside of class and prep and so on, and sometimes even then, if the staff and the prees are relaxed about it. But that's because we're with friends, and things are happening all the time, and everyone's talking. Nothing happens here, for poor Eder. He's alone all the time we're in school, and after tea when we go back to our houses; and Sister Anthony," with a careful, theatrical look around just to make certain sure, "Sister Anthony is not exactly a barrel of laughs, now is she?"

Everyone held their individual breaths, only waiting for her to manifest in her wrath. When she didn't, they all sighed in relief, and Radhika went on, flushing a little under the weight of everyone's attention. It was still rare for her to speak out as much as this, even among her own cohort. "And when he's alone, he's always working on something, and mostly doing sums. And I know he likes that, and he's ever so good at it all, and he's got a lot of catching-up to do and not much time to do it." The Upper Third not being privy to Miss Leven's thinking on that matter, they all assumed he'd be gone as soon as his leg was well enough healed that he could go home to his mother's care. "But there's nothing funny in numbers, even if there's something *very* funny about someone who gets so excited over them," with a scolding frown at poor Eder, who really couldn't help it. "So anyway, that's it, isn't it?" She looked for his nod, and saw it. "He woke up here in horrible pain, and he's stuck here for weeks, and we're all doing our best, but in all that time no one's ever made him laugh." And then, her private moment of confession, "You all know that I came here just absolutely furious with everything and everyone. I was absolutely not going to laugh at anything, if I can help it; and I can tell you, even when you don't want to, going without laughter for that long is the most misery-making thing. It really is."

"Goodness." The new girl had found yet one more way to surprise them, as it seemed. They gave her a moment of silent respect, before Marigold rallied. "Well, then. Ladies, our path is clear; it is our solemn duty to make poor Eder laugh. What shall we do, tell him jokes? Funny stories? Some of those tales from the Book of Common Sins? Some of those are really hilarious, the way they worked out. Think up your funniest offerings. I'll go first, while you put your thinking caps on..."

They did try. They tried their best, in all the time they had. They tried this approach and that, from the corniest music-hall gags to their own misdemeanours, which last had some of them in such stitches they could barely breathe, never mind finish the tale with aplomb, or even at all.

They tried, and they failed. In all that time, until Sister Anthony came in with a tray for Eder and chased them away to their own teas and the routine endings of their day, Eder only lay there, frowning as he tried to follow when they got too excited and talked too fast, completely bewildered at the finales. Even after they had explained the jokes—which takes away most of the point in any case—he just didn't understand why that should be funny. Was it only his still-hesitant English, or was there perhaps something else being lost in translation, between languages and cultures too? Or was it that a gulf lay between girl-humour and boy-humour? Those girls with brothers tended to opt for that last—"I mean, *I* wouldn't laugh if my friend fell in the stream, before I went to fish her out! But yes, the boys would, no question!"—but Radhika for one didn't believe that all Basque humour depended on the slapstick. There wouldn't be much of that in the village over winter, except perhaps for people slipping on the ice, and that was more dangerous than funny, surely, even to a boy...?

At any rate, they were left frustrated, and yet determined, more determined than before. One way or another, they would induce that wretched glum boy to laugh!

But how, how...?

Doors, as it turned out, were more complicated than one might suppose.

It was Saturday afternoon, and the Carpentry Club was in session, but not at home: which was to say that its entire membership-in-good-standing, the two of them, Pete and Elle were in the Castle, in the San, confronting the challenge that Mr Felton had laid before them. With, it must be said, quite a nasty little smirk on his face.

In recent days, he had erected the walls of Eder's private cubicle, boxing his prisoner in with hardboard partitions that reached up as high as the curtain rails, some ten feet from the floor. The timber-framed wall fronting the aisle had a doorway set within it, tall enough to allow Sister Anthony to enter without needing to duck her head, for Mr Felton was a more considerate man than many of the girls would assume.

He had also, of course, made the door, to the same pattern: a wooden frame, covered with hardboard on both sides. This had been waiting for the girls, leaning against the bench as they trooped into their workshop after lunch, in overalls and enthusiasm.

"Right, you two. That's ready now. All it needs is to be furnished, and then hung. Hop to it, I don't have all afternoon."

"Furnished" was a new word to them both, in the context of a door. Its meaning was simple to deduce, though; on the bench were a door latch, two handles, and a set of three hinges. A wooden box beside held presumably all the necessary screws.

Pete whistled softly under her breath, as she always did when brainwork was required. She tucked a carpenter's pencil behind her ear, took up an elderly tape measure, thought some more, and then spoke.

"Stop me when I'm wrong, Elle, but it seems to me that we drill through that central crosspiece with a brace and bit, to take the shaft that joins the handles on either side of the latch. Then we chisel in from the edge, here," a quick X with the pencil, "to seat the latch in position. When we can see light all the way through from one side to the other, it's in the right place and we can screw it in. Then the shaft goes in, and the handles go on, and—"

She glanced up expectantly; Elle smiled, and didn't disappoint.

"And Ray's your uncle."

"Yes, he is; and Mr Felton isn't actually sniggering at us from his corner yet, so I don't think I said anything too terribly wrong. Let's get at it, shall we...?"

There might be nothing too terribly wrong with the plan as laid out, but the girls soon found that turning plan into process took a lot longer than they'd airily anticipated.

In the first place, everything had to be measured. *Measure twice, cut once*—Mr Felton had drilled that into them from the very beginning; and as there were two of them, they each of them measured everything. Then there was marking up, with set square and pencil, abundant caution and double-checking and perhaps a surreptitious third measure just to make sure.

A brace and bit is a fine tool, and Mr Felton maintained his with all the loving care of a craftsman; but no one has ever claimed that it is a fast worker, especially with two lightweight Martian girls doing the work. Leaning as hard on the brace as they could, it still seemed to take forever for the bit to chew through the hardboard and into the much harder timber beneath.

Elle had placed the dot on one side of the door, Pete the other. Of course they had to stop at the more-or-less-halfway point, turn the door over, change driller and go again from the other side, see how closely their two marks had aligned.

When at last the bit broke through, and despite all their care, the hole they'd carved through the door was offset by perhaps a quarter of an inch at the meeting point. Mr Felton chuckled dryly and handed them each a file, before going back to sharpening the chisels.

Cutting into the timber and chiselling it out curl by shaving curl was slow too, and effortful; and whenever they stopped to say, "Try the latch now, see if it'll fit yet," it never quite did. There was a sticking-point somewhere, or one side was sloping in while the other was sloping out, or they weren't quite deep enough to seat it properly, or there was just too much accumulated debris at the bottom of the cut and blowing didn't help, except to get sawdust in their eyes. In the end they had to turn the door upside down and shake it, to make room enough in there.

Finally, though, the metal structure of the latch did slide into the hole they'd dug; and when they held the door upright between them and both ducked down to see if it was in the right place, aligned with their holes on either side, and neither saw anything but darkness, they may have cried out in disappointment and despair, until Mr Felton kindly pointed out that each of them was blocking the light from the other.

Admitting themselves to be idiots, they tried again, one girl at a time; and not only was there light to be seen coming through, but when they tried it, the shaft that would link the two handles slid neatly into position, turning both ways and jutting out on both sides just as it ought.

After that achievement, the rest of the work seemed a breeze. They fitted the handles, screwed everything down tight, and took delight in working the handles back and forth, from one side and the other, seeing the latch move obediently in and out at their command.

That settled, they turned the door the other way around, measured and marked, chiselled and seated and screwed, until all three hinges were happily in place. Then they heaved their masterpiece up between them and carried it proudly into the school and up the stairs to the San, Mr Felton ambling along behind them and chuckling softly to himself as he filled his pipe with finest New Victorian shag.

The girls bore their triumph proudly to the cubicle at the far end, where they found that Eder's bed had been turned around with its head to the window, so that he could watch this final fitting. They waved cheerfully at him, set the door vertically so that he could admire it, first one side and then the other, showed him the working of the latch, how smooth it was, how perfectly placed—and then, they turned their attention to the waiting framework, and the task of actually hanging the door.

They looked from frame to door, and back to frame again. They looked at each other, aghast. They turned in mutual accusation to Mr Felton, who must have known and could have told them at any time, only to find him vanished. Not far: he was out on the flat roof of his own gatehouse, puffing contentedly, grinning around the pipestem as he watched to see what they would do.

Either Miss Hendy had run out of Sister Anthony's patent and potent cough medicine, or else she stowed it somewhere that Miss Harribeth could neither discover nor divine. Accordingly, with several Juniors—little pests that they were!—beginning to sound uncomfortably like the rasp of a lucifer struck against a wall, Marigold and Radhika had been sent on an urgent errand to the San to beg first a jorum of that sovereign physic, and then a visit after tea to examine the woebegone sufferers and determine whether they should be isolated in a single dormitory, or else marched up to the San itself with their night-things, slippers and robes in a sorry procession.

The two girls pelted up the stone steps into the Castle, and then again at the same rate of knots up their proper side of the divided staircase. They were taking a chance there, and breaking a strict rule about never running inside the Castle, neither in the corridors nor most especially on the stairs. They both felt, though, that their mission of mercy might excuse them from being called to order or made to march down and then up again in a discreet and ladylike manner. That was a favourite discipline from both staff and prefects alike; the girls suspected the prees particularly of loitering at the head or foot of their own staircase, purely to catch anyone trying to scuttle up or down the other.

They skidded to a halt—another crime!—on Mr Felton's polished boards, opened the San door and walked through as demurely as they might.

Sister Anthony's office and medical store lay to their left. The door was open, though, and the room was empty. That was unusual. What was startling, what was quite unheard-of was the rising cackle of uncontrolled, adolescent laughter—a *boy's* laughter, no less!—coming from the ward to their right.

The girls turned as one, gaping. They saw Eder's new cubicle, all but finished; they saw Elle and Pete standing there in the aisle, with a door propped up between them, both of them looking strangely blank; they saw Sister Anthony standing out on the roof terrace with Mr Felton, both of them somewhat bizarrely with their backs turned, as though captivated by the view. It seemed to Radhika that Mr Felton's shoulders were shaking, and then he seemed to choke suddenly on his pipe-smoke and had to succumb to the matron's hard hand between his shoulder-blades until he could catch his breath again.

Bewildered, and more than a little indignant, Marigold and Radhika marched down the aisle, past the other girls, and into Eder's space.

Where indeed they found him, just as they had suspected, racked with laughter, howling with it, gasping for air only to lose it again in an immediate new guffaw.

Assuming that this wasn't some new Martian disease that no one had encountered yet, they stood silently glowering at him until he had recovered enough to draw breath and hold it this time, to find his voice and his English words, to say, "They, they, they have put the hinges on the wrong, the wrong edge of the door. Now they are arguing about how to fit it upside down, or back to front, or opening out instead of in; and Mister and Sister are being no, no, no help at all..."

And he was off again, hugging his pillow in wild delight, in a way that surely couldn't be good for a boy with a shattered leg.

# CHAPTER TWENTY-ONE

## An Upscale Adventure

"I say, Rowany..."

Rowany might have sighed inaudibly—at least, she hoped it was inaudible—as she slid her bookmark into place and looked up enquiringly. Of course the Stokes girls would bring their questions to her instead of their temporary housemistress; for one thing, she was readily available, sitting in a comfortable chair in the common room, rather than forbiddingly behind a door that must be knocked upon. But oh, they did seem to have so *many* questions, and how she was ever to read any further into this fascinating collection, she simply couldn't imagine.

"Marigold." Of course it would be Marigold, with her two faithful lieutenants at her flanks. "Yes?"

"Radhi has something she wants to ask you."

That was unexpected: not that shy Radhika would pass the task to her friend, but that Marigold would immediately pass it back again. Maybe the girl was beginning to develop some sense of what was rightly someone else's, that she didn't need immediately to possess whatever came her way.

"Radhi? Ask away."

"Well, it's only that Miss Llewellyn mentioned something in passing to, to Lois Shannon and me"—the grammatical sticking-point safely navigated, Rowany suppressed a smile and simply nodded—"and neither of us knew anything about it, and nor do we," with a nod of her own to her fellows, "so…"

"I'm intrigued. Something that nobody knows? Do tell."

"Well, Miss Llewellyn said, or, or *suggested* I suppose might say it better, that there was, there was such a thing as a school museum…?"

Of all the things that she hadn't been expecting, that must certainly come close to the top of the list. Rowany took a moment to wonder at the never-ending novelty of schoolgirls, before she said, "As it happens, there was indeed. Technically I imagine there still is, although it's been moribund for more years than I have seen here. You do all three know what 'moribund' means, yes? … No, Marigold, it's nothing to do with 'morbid', except that the roots converge. Moribund means in terminal decline, on the point of death. Seriously, I who know everything, I couldn't even tell you where the exhibits used to be displayed, never mind where they're being stored now.

"However," she went on, rising to her feet as dramatically as she knew how, "I know exactly the right person to ask, to relieve our ignorance. Come along, ye seekers after knowledge long hid from mortal ken!"

She strode out of the common room and across the hall, to rap firmly at the door to the housemistress's study. The three younger girls followed somewhat reluctantly, glancing at each other, agreeing in silence that Rowany was—well, she was an astonishing human being, taken for all in all, but, well, she could really be a bit *much* sometimes…

"**C**ome!"

Miss Harribeth looked up from where—not *quite* liking to disturb Kathy's desk, with all its chaos of papers and fossils and bones and only its right possessor could know what more—she was marking essays in a chair by the fireplace, lamenting a little that it wasn't cold enough to call for an actual fire. Oh, winter was surely on its way, but as usual taking its own sweet time about it.

Rowany opened the door, and ushered in three somewhat abashed Middles. Yes, those three; of course it was. Still, they weren't exactly acting guilty, any more than Rowany was looking grim. More curious, perhaps, and a little stimulated. She prepared herself for a surprise, only hoping that it might be a pleasant one.

"Do come in, girls, and make yourselves comfortable." The three youngsters, of course, would squeeze onto the settle; that left another easy chair for Rowany. "Now then, what can I do for you?"

"Indulge us in a little history, if you will. *School* history."

"My favourite kind." Miss Harribeth set aside the fifth-formers' thoughts on the development of intellectual life across the colony, with something of relief. "But I thought you knew everything already, Rowany?"

"Oh, so did I, once. So did I."

Rowany's sigh was worthy of an ancient. Ah: in *that* mood, was she? This promised to be fun. "Do go on."

"Well, I oughtn't to steal someone else's thunder. Radhi, would you—no? Well, we'll teach you to claim your own before you leave this place, but very well, I'll be your runner on this occasion. Miss Harribeth, from something that Miss Llewellyn let fall, Radhika understands that the school has or used to have its own museum, and I was hoping that you might enlighten us, for I truly have never seen hide nor hair of such a thing, though I do confess to having heard a rumour or two."

"Oh, good heavens. Yes. Yes, indeed. Let me gather my thoughts a moment... Rowany, in my little kitchen there you will find a jug of milk and a plate of biscuits, if you would be so good...?"

Thus did three somewhat awed Middles find themselves leading a staff far and far down Memory Lane.

"We won't concern ourselves with the year, this isn't that kind of history; but Miss Hendy and I were both young, both new here, eager to make our mark on the school. We looked about, for something lacking; and came up with this between us, and took it to Miss Tolchard, as she then was.

"The school was relatively young yet, but the crater of course is ancient; the canals and then the railway hatched Terminus between them; and the Basque community doesn't even remember when their forebears came here, following their sheep. Before the railway, though, that much is certain. We felt, Kathy—I mean, Miss Hendy and I," with a scowl so stern, it made the younger girls giggle, "that we could assemble and host a little museum of local culture and history: she of course to oversee the natural history, and I the human development. Later, as the school flourished, it could become a record of our own history too.

"We were young, as I say; we had the energy and the enthusiasm, and few responsibilities outside our own classrooms at that time. The Castle absolutely had the space; the school stood at little more than half its current enrolment. Jopling House was still a-building, and Stokes hadn't yet even been imagined, if you can believe it, girls."

The girls, who had clearly imagined all houses to be even more ancient than any mistresses, looked suitably aghast. Gratified, Miss Harribeth went on.

"We made our interests known, as far and wide as we could achieve. In general, I believe our neighbours thought us slightly cracked, as schoolmistresses so often are taken to be. By their pupils too, if I am to believe what I hear." Another glare, another giggle. Good; they were enjoying this as much as she was. "At any rate, people began bringing us all manner of things, that had been gathering dust before. Works of art and craft, skulls and bones and birds' eggs, taxidermy of … variable quality, other offerings of deeply dubious provenance. We had a ball.

"Of course we engaged the girls to help in writing labels, setting up display cases, giving tours on Speech Day and on other occasions that brought visitors. That was most of the point, to engage their interest in this area and its peoples, its history, how very much it's changed since the earliest pioneer days. I'm pleased to say that it did work, or seem to. Miss Tolchard was very complimentary; we were secretly delighted."

"I'm sure you were," Rowany said, with a smile. "But—well, what happened? Where did it go?"

"Ah. The time went first, unless it was the energy. We took on more and more work for the school, in and out of class hours, in and out of term-time. The more senior we became, the less we had to offer the museum. For a while we had a Museum Prefect, in hopes that that would be enough to keep things ticking over, but it never really was. The collection … staled; people stopped offering new donations; everyone had seen everything, and no one wanted to go around it again.

"Eventually, when Kathy expressed serious interest in taking charge of the new house—we hadn't even settled on a name yet—she and I agreed it was time to call a halt. Nothing was discarded, of course, but it all got packed away. Only Mr Felton could tell you where, I fear."

"Then Mr Felton shall," Rowany declared. "We will bring it all out into the light of day—won't we, girls?—and see what's what. With your permission, of course, Miss Harribeth? I'd ask Miss Hendy too, but..."

"But. Quite so. You know, Rowany? You give me an idea. And as it came from you, I shall burden you with all the work of it. Oh, don't look so disappointed, girls; I am morally certain that she will burden you."

"The old museum, is it?" Mr Felton chuckled, and scratched the back of his head. "Now there's a thing I haven't thought about in a long, long time."

"You did keep it all safe, though?"

"You do know where it all is, though, don't you?"

"Aye. That I did, and that I do." He puffed on his pipe, and gazed thoughtfully at his young interrogators. "What's this all in aid of, eh?"

"We mustn't say."

"It's a secret."

"Well," Rowany amended, "at the moment it's only an idea. We need to take a look at what there is, first, to see if the idea can become a plan. Where do we need to dig, Mr Felton?"

"Oh, not dig." He smiled the contented smile of a man passing an uncomfortable chore to someone else. "Climb. I'm sure you remember the way up into the attics, Rowany, m'girl."

"I'm sure I don't know what you mean," she said haughtily. "We were always most strictly forbidden to go up into the attics."

"Aye, that you were, and with good reason. The things I've found up there... Well, ne'er mind it now. You'll find everything you're looking for packed up in tea chests and labelled in ink. Put on your overalls first, before you go up for a look-see."

Radhika and Charm had plaited each other's long hair, the red and the black, to keep dust and spiders out; now they tucked the plaits firmly down the back of their necks, inside their overalls. Marigold donned a school beret over her glorious golden pagebob and yanked it most unbecomingly down over her ears, tucking stray wisps up as she would under a swimming-cap.

"Come to think of it," she said, "I could just have worn my swimming-cap, but that's not the sort of thing you do come to think of, is it? Not on dry land, you don't. I'd feel silly."

"You look ridiculous as it is," Radhika said promptly. Being a quick study, she had picked up the outstandingly rude ways good friends talked to each other here, and adopted them wholeheartedly. "And I dare swear that poor beret will never find its proper shape again."

"No matter. T'ain't mine," quoth insouciant Marigold.

"Mari!" Charm was shocked. "You can't go about taking other people's things!"

"No, but that's the thing. T'isn't anybody's. I was *looking* for mine, rummaging in the lost-property box"—Marigold was an inveterate mislayer of her personal effects, especially those most easily discarded from her person; she always kept a supply of halfpennies to hand, for the inevitable fines—"and I found this one, and I looked in the band, and it doesn't have a name-tag at all. So I dropped two halfpennies in the jar and took two berets back to the house, so's I'd have a spare for the next time I lost my own."

"But how can it not have a name-tag? Sister Anthony always checks, always."

"I know! It's a mystery!"

It was a mystery that had to be examined, obviously. Marigold plucked the remarkable object off her head again and passed it around, so that each of her friends could confirm the truth of it.

"There's no sign of stitching being cut out," Charm said, turning the beret inside out and squinting at the band. "It's almost like it's never been owned before."

The Mystery of the Baffling Beret occupied their minds and their tongues for long enough that an exasperated Rowany, who had been waiting downstairs in her own overalls for some considerable while, appeared abruptly in the dormitory doorway. Marigold hastily jammed the much-mistreated beret on her head again, her friends performed some necessary tucking-up around the edges, and at last they were ready to go.

"You know," Rowany said, leading them away at a determined pace, "you might just as easily have worn a swimming-cap, Marigold. It would have been much easier to wash, too, afterwards."

The way to the attics—they had had no idea there were attics!—lay behind one of Mr Fulton's mysterious doors, labelled "No Entry" firmly in his own hand. Some held that they were magic, or else somehow under the control of his mind. Whenever a girl wanted to sneak an illicit peek behind one, just to see, it would always prove to be disappointingly locked; whereas on the rare occasion that entry was in fact authorised, as now...

"Did Mr Felton give you the key?"

"Key? No need. The Crater School trusts its girls."

The door opened readily to her hand, just as though it had always been unlocked.

The three Middles glanced at each other in a kind of mute wonder. He hadn't known they were coming, so he couldn't have left it open for them beforehand, so...

That was a thought leading nowhere, a simple acknowledgement of the mystery that lay so often at the heart of life, especially here at school. Rowany reached around the jamb to turn on an electric light, and they saw what seemed to be an empty cupboard, except that one wall wasn't a wall at all, but rather a set of steep wooden uncarpeted steps.

Radhika sneezed; her friends blessed her as one, then cried "Snap!" at each other and had to link little fingers and make a wish, while Rowany sighed over their heads with a pointed patience.

Then, "I did warn you about the dust. It'll get worse, believe me. Follow at your own speed, troops! Do try not to fall, and not to imperil each other."

Bare and dusty wood, steep steps with nothing to soften them, no handrail to hold on to and a drop that only grew deeper at their backs: they scaled that hidden staircase with a caution rarely to be detected amongst the young of Mars, who are an adventurous and often heedless breed, by and large.

At the top at last, they found Rowany waiting on a narrow landing, where there was just room enough for all four of them to stand. Beyond her was another door.

"Ready, mes enfants?"

They assured her that they were indeed, and she flung the door wide with an extravagant gesture and a bow of invitation, crying "Behold!"

All three girls gasped aloud.

They knew about attics, of course they did. Who didn't have an attic? Attics were dark, musty places, full of hidden corners and ancient cobwebs, holding broken lamp-stands and chests with exotic labels bearing witness to travels all across the Empire and further yet, *Manchester via Staly-bridge, Sydney, Rangoon*, before at last they all bore the same dull ending to their journey, *Marsport Only. Not Wanted On Voyage. Custom Paid.* Nothing on Mars could ever be truly exotic; it was all too new, too purposeful, too planned. To an Earthling's eye, it might perhaps seem different, but to a Martian? Here was merely home, where Earth was Home, where all glamour dwelt.

Rowany knew very well where their expectations lay, which was why she made such a happy little drama out of the revelation. A flood of light framed their astonished faces; they hesitated briefly on the threshold, like the apostles at the tomb, not quite daring to claim any right of passage, so that she had to shoo them in.

Then she closed the door behind them, and explained.

"In Victorian times, as I'm sure Miss Harribeth has told you, the custom was to bed the live-in servants up in the attic, in poky little rooms where the ceilings sloped down to the eaves with mean little windows and as like as not bars over them, because who knew what the lower classes might get up to if they could slither in and out at all hours of the night? Well, the Castle was built as a hotel, and a hotel needs lots of servants; but the gentleman who built it was an enlightened soul for his time. Like Sister Anthony, he believed that light and air were crucial to a person's health; and servants were after all people too, and a sickly servant is no use to anyone. His edifice was to have a flat roof, with no eaves to make a nuisance of themselves; and he had world enough and time, and money to spare; so he built his

servants' quarters high and wide and handsome, with generous windows all the way around the outer wall," a gesture to
her right, where glorious sun beat in through glorious glass,
"just below the parapet—I'm a little ashamed of you for not
noticing those and pestering people with questions, as I, I
myself did—and the same on the inward side, all around the
courtyard. There was a central aisle, do you see, and rooms
on either hand, but everyone had a window they could open
at will. It was really quite revolutionary, and probably at least
a symptom if not a contributory cause to the hotel's failure.
He may have been a very nice person, but I'm afraid he was a
terrible businessman.

"It was the army, I believe, who knocked out all the internal walls when they took this place over during the war, and
made this single stunning space, for reasons of their own. I
know that Miss Tolchard always intended to find a use for it,
that wasn't simply storage; but it's too low for a gymnasium,"
her hand touching the ceiling in evidence, "and too difficult
of access for dancing-classes, we'd have half the girls out with
damaged ankles before we knew it, on those stairs, and no
one has ever yet come up with a solution. So, as is traditional,
Mr Fulton just keeps  everything up here that has nowhere
else to be. Including, apparently, a museum.

"Scatter, children. Interrogate the labels, until you can
find it out. As you see, we have no need of torches."


*Tea chests*, he had said. But tea chests are the most common storage crates on three worlds, and Martians grow
and drink a lot of tea. The original dividing walls might be
gone, but there were tea chest walls everywhere in their
stead, stacked in blocks and avenues according to some
method known only to Mr Fulton. He might know the exact
coordinates of what they sought, but if so he had not shared
them.

And of course there were items too large to fit in tea chests, pieces of furniture and a pyramid of school trunks and other things wrapped in dust-sheets that defied diagnosis, unless one took a peek. And of course one did, and that only slowed the hunt even more.

At last, though, Charm's voice rang out, echoing strangely in this strange space: "*H/H, artefacts, mixed.* Might this be it, do you think? There's the same label on more than one chest."

"It might very well be." Rowany came striding over, with the others hot on her heels. "*H/H* is Miss Harribeth and Miss Hendy, of course, or at least that's a decent guess. And these have all been set together in an island, as it were, separate from anything else. Well, there's nothing more to be learned by staring at the outsides. Let's have a look within."

So saying, she reached up and lifted down the topmost chest.

"Hmm—lighter than I feared, but of course any sensible creature would save the lightest loads for the highest layer, and I do believe the Misses H & H to have a tolerable quantity of sense between them. So, without further ado..."

Alas, there was further ado, because the chest's lid had been nailed down rather more firmly than the girls felt the situation called for. Certainly far more firmly than fingernails alone could pry up, though the Middles would happily have made that sacrifice—and faced the inevitable interview with irate prefects, housemistress, possibly even Sister Anthony— if it could only have saved them more delay.

Happily, though, Radhika reached into a pocket in her overalls and produced a solution.

"Um, Papa-ji gave me this, long and long ago. He told me always to carry it with me, so I always have. Um, I didn't really know if it was allowed, but..."

"Meaning that you knew perfectly well that it wouldn't be, and so you never asked? Quite so." Rowany hefted the pocket knife in her hand, unfolded the blade, and whistled softly. "Army issue, I take it?"

"Well, I don't know about *issue*, exactly. All the Tommies carried one, but they weren't exactly regulation. I think they came from the bazaar, because they were always a little bit different, from one camp to the next. The sergeants never said anything, though, because they all had one of their own too, and the officers knew just exactly how useful they were, so..."

"So, unofficial issue, then? I see. Certainly this is a lovely piece of work. Solid as a crowbar, and," testing the blade with a cautious, a very cautious thumb, "sharp as a scalpel, too. You keep it well, young Radhika."

"The armoury sergeant, he showed me how. And I hardly ever use it anyway, it's just..."

"Handy in case of need, quite so. Well, if you don't mind my using it now, I think it should be sturdy enough to lever out these nails, though you may need to put your skills with the oilstone to use after, if I nick the blade. I don't believe there's any danger I might break it."

She worked her way around all four sides of the chest, worming the blade beneath the lid and pressing down, levering up. One by one and little by little, the nails yielded their grip, until at last she could take hold of the loosened lid—carefully, mindful of her fingers and those sharp little nails—and tug it away.

The watching girls cheered; four heads endangered each other and blocked out much of that wonderful light, all trying to peer in all at once.

"Ohhh..."

260

"It's all right, ninnyhammers. Were you expecting gold and jewellery, gleaming up at you? These are museum exhibits; of course they're individually wrapped. I confess, I hadn't quite expected pages of the *Arean-Messenger*, but we're thrifty folk, we reuse what we can. I tell you what, let's take one package each, unwrap them in turn, and then we can all see what we've got..."

# CHAPTER TWENTY-TWO

## Like Presents at Christmas

On the long staff table at the top of the dining hall stood a small bell with a high, clear tone that could cut through any amount of girlish chatter. Commonly it was used for exactly that, to ask for less noise, when one table or another was becoming particularly shrill or rambunctious.

This morning, though, the girls were all standing in their places, waiting for the duty prefect to say grace before they could drag out the benches and sit down, when the staff's bell chimed unexpectedly.

Two hundred startled heads turned as one, to be surprised for the second time in as many moments. The headmistress herself was rising from her chair, to capture their attention. Miss Leven rarely attended school breakfast, preferring to start the day more quietly in her own small house, either alone or with a few invited colleagues, occasionally one or two Sixth Form girls in their final years under her guidance.

The hum of murmured conversation died entirely, as they waited to learn what exactly had occasioned this most unusual of mornings.

262

"Thank you, girls. I won't keep you a minute: only to say that when you have finished your meal and cleared your tables, please remain in the hall. Go quietly to the table you would sit at for luncheon, so that you are sorted by forms rather than houses. That is all. Mary, if you would say the grace now?"

Speculation ran rife, of course, all through the hall. The Sixth Form knew what was up, that quickly became clear; but not one of them would divulge the secret, under whatever threat or inveiglement. "Only wait, and you'll see"—those infuriating words were probably uttered more often and in more variations than at any other gathering in school history.

Never had Mrs Bailey's porridge and bacon rolls been relished so little, swallowed so hastily; never her excellent coffee slurped down so fast that more than one girl burned the roof of her mouth. Infuriatingly, it was all to no avail. The prefects and seniors ate at their normal pace, chatting blandly, pretending to notice nothing amiss; and not a girl could leave her seat in any case until the staff had risen and departed. There was an unusually high number of staff present, for a weekday morning; that too was noted and discussed, but led to no useful conclusions.

At last, at long last, the bell sounded again, and Miss Leven rose for the second time.

This time, she was blatantly laughing at them. "Oh, don't mind us," she said. "We're staying this morning. Clear your tables, girls, and find your places among your own year groups. No talking now, please."

In silence, then, aside from the odd hissed whisper from someone who simply could not swallow it down until she was glared mute by the nearest prefect, the girls carried their cups and dishes, their cutlery and napkins to the trolleys and baskets waiting to receive them. In silence they shuffled themselves about by age ascending, with the first years directly beneath the gaze of the staff table on its dais, and the Sixth Form down at the far end of the hall. Those worthies settled themselves down in comfort to watch the fun, while all the school else jigged and jittered in frustration.

"All done now? Hurry along, Lorraine dear, you're the last... Good. Now, then, the news. As I'm sure you all know by now, a few intrepid explorers—*with* permission, I might add, so don't give each other any ideas—have unearthed our old school museum from its storage in the attics. What we haven't tracked down yet is the catalogue, so carefully drawn up by Miss Harribeth and Miss Hendy. I'm afraid this means that all the exhibits must be identified and dated again. To make this more fun and less of a chore, it has been decided that each year—excluding the Sixth Form, that is, who have public examinations ahead of them and are therefore excused from all fun for the rest of term—shall take charge of one division of the old museum, one aspect of its collection. Don't look so alarmed, you young ones; you won't be called upon to research the items and their provenance. Yes, Katie? I said "provenance", dear. Look it up later, and explain it to your friends. What we do want you to do is to clean and prepare everything for exhibition, again under guidance, and write out signs to explain their origins and uses, once you understand them yourselves. Mr Felton is kindly making display cases, so you can design your exhibits to those measurements; and of course you can make dioramas or other illustrations to show your finds in use.

"Yes, I know, it does sound like a terrible lot of work, doesn't it? And just when you were getting down to work on Miss Peters' pageant, too, and all the other arrangements and displays for our first-ever Old Girls' Day. Daisy, do you know another word for 'old girls'?"

"Um, 'ancient Craftereans', Miss Leven?"

She let the inevitable laughter roll around the hall for a little, before quelling it with a gesture of both hands. "That'll do, thank you, school. Daisy, I was actually hoping for 'alumnae', which wasn't really fair of me, as we don't teach Latin here; but I thought you might have come across it, as your own mother is an alumna of ours, and very pleased to be so. I expect she'll be coming on the day, won't she? Excellent, excellent. How many others know they have relatives or friends of the family intending to come? Hands up, please— ah yes, that's most gratifying, isn't it, Miss Peters?

"You see, girls, the point of all this is that I do most especially want the old museum ready to put on show in all its new finery, for the Old Girls to appreciate. We've a special reason for this, which I won't elaborate just now, but we are asking you all to put your best foot forward to make this happen, and the day a very special one indeed.

"Now, we'd never ask you to give up your precious free time, to labour on the school's behalf—yes, yes, I know the most of you would volunteer without a second's thought, and that's very kind in you, but no, that's not how we want to approach this. Instead, we are going to break with long tradition, and put our sacred Timetable into abeyance, ah, which is to say suspend it, for the time being, to give girls and staff together some time to really knuckle down on these new projects. Yes, of course we staff are going to be joining in! Did you think we'd let you have all the fun?

"At any rate, we are still deliberating what time may be allocated to the museum and the pageant and so forth, and how much lesson-time is really essential, though I daresay some few of your lessons may be related to whatever it is you're working on here. Also, we will of course be keeping up our regular sessions of inter-house matches and other exercise, while this weather holds. Your health is the most precious thing you have, girls, and we will not allow you to squander it under our care, however keen you may be to knuckle down to work.

"In the meantime, senior girls and staff have given up their own free time to sort all the artefacts into five general areas of interest. First Years, I know Miss Harribeth has been teaching you about the pioneer years this term, the earliest history of our colony, with all its triumphs and disasters. We felt it only fair that you should have the chance to see and handle everything we have collected from that time, and write up all you learn for our visitors. You will of course have help; Miss Harribeth herself will oversee your work, as well as the project in general, and I understand that Melanie and Mary are quite determined to lend you a hand as well, when they can be spared from their own studies."

The two named prefects came down the hall, grinning encouragingly at their juniors, each bearing a tea-chest whose contents was annoyingly hidden from view. Miss Harribeth quietly left the staff table and went down to join them with their assigned flock of youngsters.

"Second Years, we'd like you to look at the history of life on the water here, both the canals and our very own lake, in the time since the first surveyors came." Miss Fanshawe, who taught Areography, stepped up to take them under her wing, with the able support of Alie Bunker and Alis Rasmussen.

"Third Years, please remember to breathe. To put you out of your misery, we feel that you should tackle everything we know about our Basque neighbours on the crater here. Thanks to our close relationship with the village, we have quite a collection of their crafts and clothing; and, of course, you have, ah, a captive resource here under our roof, whom I understand some of you consider to be your own personal property, so I suggest you make as much use of him as you may."

One or two girls looked somewhat puzzled, until their quicker neighbours whispered "She means Eder, idiot!" into their ears. The rest were too busy beaming to notice.

The Fourth Years had the school itself, and the Sanatorium, and the whole history of development up on the crater rim; "which leaves only the Fifth, who we felt would be the fittest to handle the skeletons and skins and taxidermy of the natural sciences, as well as being hopefully the most knowledgeable, in the ongoing absence of Miss Hendy. No, no: I have no news to share, as to whether or when she will make her return this term. That decision rests with her, and her alone. Now, you all have your tasks ahead of you; you have your supervisors and their assistants; you have your artefacts at hand. I suggest you start unwrapping."

Once it was clearly established that no, the nasty ghouls of the Fourths would not be permitted to swap with the Fifths, however much they pleaded, each table turned to examining the contents of their chests, or at least peering at them hopefully, trying to guess what might be inside.

"Patience, girls! You'll see it all in a few minutes." Mrs Buchanan had come to take charge of the Thirds, with Fidelis Carpenter and Elise van Buren in support. Those two were rarely seen apart; they were known to holiday together, alternating one family home with the other, turn and turn about. Charm, meanwhile, began an inward chant, as she often did: *she's Mrs Buchanan, she's Mrs Buchanan...* Her friends and classmates were used to it, but she was entirely determined not to slip up today and call her "Mamma". Not in front of the Lower Third; why, those children were mere *Juniors...*!

"First, Upper Third, I want you to lift your table—when I give the word, Marigold, and not before, thank you— between you and carry it over to adjoin Lower Third's, to make one long table of the two. Lift it, don't drag it, please.

Let's not leave scrapes on Mr Fulton's polish, he wouldn't like that at all. Ready? Lift!"

The table was sensibly heavy, to prevent accidental or deliberate tipping, but it was no trouble for a robust classful to pick it up, shuffle sideways, set it down again end-to-end with its neighbour, nestling the two together with an accuracy so painstaking that it made the girls at that end giggle at each other.

"Very well. Now, I know how you like to gang together with your own class in general and your special friends in particular, and make believe you're at war with the other class, but for this you have to work together, so I'm going to mix you all up ruthlessly, by alphabetical order across the whole Third Year. Take two steps back from the table, please, all of you." She produced a list from her pocket, while Fidelis and Elise moved to either end in a prearranged manoeuvre. "Annabel Adams!"

"Present," that particular girl answered automatically, as though this were a normal rollcall. Realising, she blushed as a laugh—a tolerably friendly laugh, because any one of them might have done the same, and they all knew it—rolled around the table.

"Thank you, dear. Go and stand at the far corner. please, next to Fidelis. Charm Buchanan!"

Charm startled slightly, had no idea quite what to say, and so said nothing. Her mother grinned at her. "You stand next to Annabel, that's all. No need to answer, just move. Shoo! Maeve Denney...!"

Charm at least had one of her particular friends to stand beside her. Radhika, being a Harvey of that ilk, found herself positioned between Pen Harrington and Feste Hughes, neither of whom she knew from, well, from Annabel Adams.

Mrs Buchanan ran down through the list, all the way to Yolanda Zenobia, who was already standing in her place opposite Annabel on Fidelis' other side, knowing full well there was no one to come after her. Not for nothing was she known universally as the Brain, though generally referred to as Laney.

"Good. Now, you can get to know each other, side to side and across the table, as you work—but don't start chattering yet, girls. First, you have to play a game of Lucky Dip. Fidelis and Elise will carry these tea-chests down either side of the table, and each girl may put a hand in—without looking, thank you; as it happens everything is wrapped in any case, but I don't want anyone hesitating over a little piece or a big one—and draw it out. Just set it on the table before you for now, and no peeking. Don't worry, there's plenty for everyone and to spare. Fidelis, Elise, if you would..."

Fidelis and Elise duly did. Some girls closed their eyes; some ostentatiously turned their heads away and used their other hand as a blindfold, just in case; Radhika was morally certain that some just peeked regardless, or else fumbled around until they found something interesting. Herself, she played the game straight, but Marigold had apparently landed very lucky, drawing something out that was the largest of all, and intriguingly shaped within its newspaper wrappings.

"Very good. Pull up your benches, girls, sit down, and unwrap your artefact. Let's see what each of you has. One by one, as you do at Christmas, so that everyone gets a look. Annabel, we'll start with you again and go down and up the line in order."

Annabel's mysterious object turned out to be a handle-less drinking cup, cut from a single bole—"that's b-o-l-e, dear, for when you come to write it up, not b-o-w-l"—of scragthorn, dark with age and very finely whittled. There was even a pattern of ridges and crosscuts, still to be made out around the rim.

269

"Oh, that's very nice. Very nice indeed." Mrs Buchanan was known to have a passion for old handicrafts; she turned it lightly, wistfully between her fingers, before passing it back to the waiting girl. "I wouldn't care to venture how long ago he made that, whose name and story we'll never know, but at least he left us something of his life. Charm, you're next. What do you have?"

Charm had an iron sheep-bell, complete with clapper. It made a dull clanking sound when she tried to ring it, but she seemed happy enough. "I like sheep," she said. "And look, you can still see the hammer-marks left by the smith."

Maeve's was another piece of ironwork, long and thin, with a wooden handle at one end and a hook-shape at the other. When Maeve professed uncertainty, Mrs Buchanan encouraged guesses, from up and down the table. Marigold asked, to general laughter, if it might be a device for taking stones out of the hooves of *really big* horses; others opted for something the smith might have made for himself, for his own use, as they'd had a lesson on how early pioneers had to make all their own tools, barring the few they'd been able to bring with them.

Shy Radhika lifted her hand at last and, when called upon, suggested that mightn't it be a, well, a fairly ordinary house-hold poker? She'd seen dozens over the years in India, all hand-made, and just like that...

Some girls groaned, at their own idiocy; others were quite indignant, insisting that no, it had to be something more exotic than a mere poker!

In the end, Mrs Buchanan fetched Miss Harribeth herself to adjudicate. She took one glance and said, "Oh yes, I remember that perfectly well. Certainly it's a poker—and not Basque work at all, as it happens. It was made down in Terminus; you should be able to find the maker's name burned into the handle, if you squint at it from the right angle. I thought it belonged in this collection because it did come to us from the Basque villagers, and it shows that there was trade between town and country, right from the earliest days..."

Radhika's own artefact, when it came her turn, was something soft and heavy, intriguing to the touch even through layers of newspaper. When she unfolded those, she found a piece of leather—suede-like on one side, furry on the other—with laces dangling. It was quite lovely to the touch. She turned it over and over in her hands, until at last it made sense to her.

"Oh—it's a hood! A hood for winter! I'm right, aren't I?"

Indeed she was proving it as she spoke, fitting it over her own head and trying the laces beneath her chin.

Mrs Buchanan laughed. "Quite right, I'm sure, Radhi"—not all the staff did the same, but she was always careful to keep up with how the girls chose to shorten or occasionally to lengthen their own or one another's names—"though there's a lot more than that to be said about it. Anything you'd like to add, before I throw it open to the house?"

Radhika took it off again, now that she'd answered the most important question. "Well, it's marv—I mean, it's excellent work. The stitching's so neat, and look, there's that kind of patterning again, tooled in around the rim. That must have taken hours."

"Days, I should imagine," quoth the experienced artist. "Days, at least."

"Yes, but—it's odd they didn't dye it, don't you think?"—for the hood was clearly the natural colours of its material. "Given how much care they took with it otherwise?"

"A simple lack of resources, I should imagine. Lambs come in a rush, remember, and at any time of day or night. The boys can't conceivably leave their flocks at such a time.

Yes, Cate, I'm absolutely sure this was a boy's work. Lambs that don't survive"—that was the kindest way she could put it, for there were many paths to a young lamb's death, if they were born alive at all, and some of her auditors were gentle souls—"need to be skinned and their hides processed quickly, if the community is to have any use from them. Dyeing is a complex process; there wouldn't be the time."

"This, this is definitely lambskin, then?" Radhika stroked the suede tenderly.

"Oh, I've no doubt of it. It's so soft, inside and out. This is called shearling leather, where the fur is trimmed into neatness, rather than being soaked away; it would make a splendid warm hood for him, through the most brutal of winters. Perhaps that's why he put so much fancywork into it, as a token of gratitude."

"Perhaps he made it as a gift," Agnosia put in. "For a sister, or his mother, or—"

"Or a girl he liked." That proposal came from Lauren, ever inclined towards the romantic.

There was something of a groan, from the far end of the table. Charm's elder sister Levity was currently walking out with a boy from the town, and in Charm's opinion could be very dull about the matter, and at length. "'Rian says..." were fast becoming her two least favourite words, being the most common ones out of Levity's mouth just now.

Their mother suppressed a smile, and moved on.

# CHAPTER TWENTY-THREE

## Radhika in a Rage, Again

They worked all morning on their museum exhibits, excited by something wholly new: learning more about their own pieces and others up and down the table, seeing how one might be a part of another's story, squabbling amicably—for the most part—when their ideas clashed, either about the history or else about the display.

Everything had to be tidily packed away again at noon and the tables moved back to where they belonged, so that the maids could make ready for lunch. After washing their hands clean of newspaper-ink and other debris, the girls were chased outside, to take whatever exercise they cared to during this free hour. Once they'd eaten, the afternoon was to be devoted to preparing for the pageant, one way or another.

For the Third Years, this meant two hours spent in the sewing room with Miss Tarleton, cutting out and sewing their costumes according to the patterns she'd drawn up. When this news broke, Radhika heaved such a dismal sigh that everyone around her laughed aloud.

"Oh, go ahead, mock me if you want to," she growled. "I just hate sewing, that's all. With a passion."

"We know you do," Marigold crowed. "You tell us, every week!"

Radhika had learned to take the teasing of her friends with good grace—for the most part. It had been weeks since she'd lost her temper with any of them, or even felt more than a little cross inside. Today, though, was apparently a different matter. With the prospect, the inevitability of a long and dreary afternoon ahead of her, and the almost-certainty of a scolding from Miss Tarleton for making a poor job of her seams, she scowled and turned away from them without a moment's thought, walking off by herself.

Any other day, one or another of them would surely have run after her, linked arms, tried to jolly her back into a proper schoolgirl frame of mind. Today, though, there were no hurrying footsteps at her back, just another burst of laughter, which only served to deepen her scowl further. The odds were good that that second round was actually nothing to do with her—as a group they laughed freely and often, sometimes finding the most peculiar things hilarious—but it couldn't help but sour her mood even more.

Voices called her name, wanting her to join an impromptu cricket game, apparently for both sides simultaneously. Any other day, she would have gone along, giggling. Today she hunched her shoulders against them and offered no other response, mooching along the path at a rate of knots to get away from any other invitations that might come her way, her whole body expressing the fact that she wanted to be left alone, and it would be in everybody's best interests if she were.

A stone lay in her way; she kicked at it moodily, and it wasn't a loose stone at all, but rather the tip of a rock embedded in the gravel. That didn't move an inch, not a fraction of an inch. The pain of contact made its way from Radhika's toe all the way up her leg. She cried out at the shock of it, and was left limping after. Any other day, someone would have noticed that and insisted on accompanying her to the San for Sister Anthony's attentions. Today no one heard, no one noticed.

By the time the bell called her back for lunch, she had learned to disguise the limp, at least enough to pass muster. On the way into the dining hall, someone did ask if her shoes were pinching her; but she didn't even see who it was in the crush, and felt safe simply to ignore them.

She wasn't free to choose her table, but by long custom she was free to choose where at that table she should sit. Her friends tended always to gather at one end; she made her way determinedly to the other, even though that meant sitting next to the prefect taking charge.

"Is there something wrong with your food, Radhi?"

"N-no." Of course not; the very suggestion bordered on heresy, when that food had emerged from Mrs Bailey's kitchen. "I just, I'm not very hungry."

Any other day, any other prefect, that would have resulted in an ultimatum: make a proper meal, or I'll march you straight to Sister Anthony as soon as we've cleared away.

But this was Arie Bunker, who knew her juniors better than most, and cared more too. She eyed Radhika thoughtfully, diagnosed something wrong with the girl rather than what lay on her plate, and said, "Well, try to eat as much as you can."

"Yes, Arie."

Radhika was actually doing that, chewing on something—she wasn't quite sure what, her mind was so distracted—to be sure that Arie would notice her efforts and let her be, when her neighbour on the other side nudged her sharply. She glared around; Laney the Brain merely jerked her chin

275

suggestively towards the head of the table. She didn't say a word; she didn't need to. It was the task of whoever sat next to the duty prefect to make conversation throughout the meal. Radhika's opposite had been doing her best to hold Arie's attention, but she was running dry; help was far and far overdue.

Radhika scowled momentously, trying to think of something, anything to say. She liked Arie normally, everyone did; people would commonly fight to sit next to her, those days she took their table. Thanks to her pals' tendency to cluster at the other end, Radhika hadn't taken a turn for weeks. That was the only reason that Laney had begrudgingly made space for her.

Speaking seemed as impossible as eating, though. She chewed on, racking her brain, finding nothing that she remotely wanted to say.

At last, despairing, Laney leaned forward and spoke to Arie directly herself, asking a question about how the Sixth were preparing for the pageant. The prefect hesitated a moment—it was a solecism of the worst order, to speak across your neighbour—but she answered pleasantly enough.

Any other day, caught in the same hopeless situation, Radhika might have understood that they were both trying to help her out. Today she burned with humiliation, laid down her fork and merely stared at her plate, no longer making the least effort at pretending to eat. Or to talk, either. Why should she? If they were going to pretend she was simply not there, then so would she. She didn't want to be there anyway. Any more than she wanted to spend the afternoon in the sewing room...

Any other day, they would have been allowed half an hour to their own devices, after lunch. Today, though, they'd had that full hour to roam and run about before; accordingly, they were only granted five minutes to get themselves to their required destinations, neat and tidy and ready to start work.

"Radhika, dear, you're slouching. Don't slouch."

Radhika snarled something thankfully incomprehensible in response, a Hindustani expression that even her soldier father would have been shocked to hear coming from his daughter. Only then, belatedly, did she recognise the voice that had addressed her.

"I, I beg your pardon, Miss Leven, I didn't see you there..."

"Hmm. Well, try not to slouch in the future. A Craterean always seeks to meet the world eye to eye, her step firm and her demeanour certain. And I'll pretend I didn't hear the rest of it, shall I?"

There was something of a twinkle in her eye, at that last sally—her brother had served in India before the war, and she was not as wholly ignorant of worldly matters as her pupils tended to assume—but her face was grave as she passed by. Was the wretched child about to break again, when she'd been doing so well for so long?

In their presentation of Pyramus and Thisbe, complete with comments from the audience, Radhika had been cast among the Greeks, to play Philostrate.

In theory, this fell out well for her. Her costume was to be a simple tunic with a cloak thrown over, the *chiron* and *himation* of recorded history. Those could be sewn out of old bedsheets, to keep stark contrast with the colourful over-complications of the rustics' dress, and even her needlework ought to be up to the seams and hems required.

There was still a lot of fabric to manage, though; and oh, she did hate this task so much! She had it all bundled up in her lap as she sewed two lengths together, one stitch after another, on and on and...

"Radhika, let me see, please... Oh dear, no, this won't do at all. We are dressing the Athenians plainly, yes, but this is still your wedding gown; I really must insist on fine stitchery, not these clumsy bastes. And, and what have we here? Stand up, please."

Obedient to command, Radhika stood. In front of the class, two whole classes, those stark white sheets tumbled to the floor—except where they didn't, where they clung inexplicably to the skirt of her gym tunic.

"Radhika Harvey, you have sewn your costume to your everyday clothes!"

The laughter was abrupt, immense, overwhelming. Radhika felt herself flush as dark as it was possible to go; she clenched her fists, felt the fire rising in her blood, felt the brute humiliation of being so exposed before not only her own classmates but Juniors, *Juniors* too—

And suddenly a very worried Charm was there with her embroidery scissors, "It's all right, Miss Tarleton, I'll have this cut free in no time, and I can help Radhi after that. I don't have a costume of my own to make, so..."

And Marigold was at her other side, on her knees, lifting the weight of the fabric to give Charm some slack to work with, to make it easier to snip the threads away; and Radhika was so unused to anything like this, to having people step in and rescue her, she somehow lost connection with her anger. She started to shiver violently, as all the tension rushed out of her body at once; her head felt strangely dizzy; the room seemed to spin away as she crumpled.

"Honestly, Radhi, if only you could have seen yourself! You turned as white as, well, as white as these sheets," holding up the evidence, "and fell all over me. It's lucky you're so small, because otherwise I never could have held you. I passed you down to Mari, and we laid you out between us like a corpse. It was quite a sight to see. Mari asked Miss Tarleton if we should slap you, to bring you around, but she said no. I think Mari was quite disappointed, weren't you? We were only allowed to pillow your head, while Cate ran for Sister Anthony."

"Who bent over and picked you up wholesale," Marigold interrupted, determined to have at least some share of the tale, if she couldn't have it all, "and positively carried you all the way up here, no help needed, thank you very much, though of course we offered. So we asked if we could come with you, only they weren't having that either, worse luck. Sister Anthony said you'd only fainted, and you'd probably been overdoing things, and an hour or two in bed would set you all to rights again, and we could see you then. Which is now."

Which it was indeed. Radhika had passed from her faint into a natural sleep, rousing to the sound of the school bell chiming the hour. She'd been a little bewildered to find herself in bed and in the San, and had to spend some time thinking back over her day, to sort out the progression of events. Then she'd faced Sister Anthony's interrogation, and found herself confessing fully. Expecting a severe scold at best, she was surprised when nothing of the sort occurred. Sister Anthony listened, and nodded, and said not a word, beyond the fact that good friends are a blessing indeed. Then she examined Radhika's foot, daubed something stinging and mysteriously scented on her toe, and made her swallow a tonic. "Your housemistress will give you another dose every morning, before breakfast. Miss Hendy knows the routine but Miss Harribeth does not, so mind you remind her if it slips her mind."

After that, she was told she might read a story-book if she truly had no headache to speak of, but she didn't trouble. She just lay gazing out of the window and across the

279

water, thinking of poor Eder in his cubicle at the far end of the ward, doing much the same for days and weeks on end. Surely there was something more they could do to entertain him, beyond bringing him yet more work to do...?

And then Charm and Marigold had slipped in, Charm with Radhika's costume rolled up neatly under her arm and a hussif in her hand. "I can sew and talk at the same time, and Miss Tarleton said I might. I think you scared her, honestly, Radhi, with all that drama."

Thus the tale of her collapse was told to the collapser, unless she was the collapsee. That important question amused them for a while, before their talk moved on to other things. When the bell rang for tea, Sister Anthony took her patient's temperature once again, and counted her pulse, and pronounced her fit to return to her regular day, "so long as there is no more of this nonsense."

"Yes, Sister Anthony. No, Sister Anthony. Thank you, Sister Anthony..." and they were gone, hurrying down to the hall to claim their tea and buns while any yet remained, and whatever Mrs Bailey had elected to offer in the way of cake today.

"I *thought* we'd made it *clear*," Agnosia said frostily, "that there were to be no more of these ... disappearances, Radhika?"

"It, it was only for an afternoon..."

"Yes, which handily got you out of the sewing, which you despise. Highly suspicious activity, I call it."

"Aggie!"

The outcry was general, from all around the table. They might sit where they liked for their prefect-supervised tea, but naturally most chose to be with their pals, from their class or their house or often both. Radhika herself had been delighted to be steered directly to their regular gang, who had saved spaces on the benches for all three of the latecom-ers—for late they had been, with the concomitant necessity of then apologising to the senior prefect on duty, and hear-ing the inevitable lecture on the pleasures of punctuality, which certainly included the best of buns and cakes.

Still, there had been enough left to fill their plates, of course. No Crater School girl had ever yet left Mrs Bailey's table hungry, except when she herself was off her feed. And as mentioned above, there were those seats reserved among their particular friends, and all had been well, or seemed so, until this.

Agnosia held up her hands in surrender, as everyone rounded on her. "I was only teasing! Well, mostly. And the little bit that wasn't was envy, not really an accusation. I don't much like sewing myself. And don't, do *not* call me Aggie."

"Well, don't rile us up, then," said Lauren.

"I love that we all did it deliberately, and all at once," Mar-igold put in. "But honestly, Ag-no-si-a," drawing each syllable out to its full value, just to make her point, "we've got to call you something. We've been playing along on the whole thing all this time, and it's wearing out our tongues, not to mention our patience. I mean, what do they call you at home?"

"Agnosia," quoth Agnosia. "I mean, what else is there to call me?"

"Nosy, perhaps?" Radhika suggested, with just a hint of spite.

Agnosia glared at her—then giggled, and held her hand out across the table. "Oh, pax! Pax? You're too nice to fight with, and far too smart on top. Just promise never to call me Nosy, and it's pax."

Radhika promised solemnly, and they shook with an equal solemnity, watched with approval by all their cohort. Thus should all quarrels between them be settled, from now until the end of time, with a formal and gentlemanlike courtesy on both sides.

"Sia?" Charm offered abruptly. The others stared at her, and she went on impatiently, "For Agnosia's new name, obviously. If the first two syllables are both out, then there's nothing left but the third, or a total nickname, and you know the staff are really down on those. Pete Thorogood gets away with it, but I'm not sure there's another in the school."

"How's about it, Agnosia?"

A dubious shake of the head, and "No-o—but when my gran says it, that hard 's' gets softened, and I, I think I could live with 'Shea', perhaps. Spelled with an 'e', of course."

"Oh, of course." Her friends nodded in chorus. They tried it out, up and down the table, and decided that they liked it, rather. Certainly it would save time, and effort too.

"And," the newly rechristened Shea observed with some satisfaction, "with any luck I can stop explaining how I got my name, and what it means."

It was obvious that everyone else knew the story and sympathised entirely with this point of view. Radhika took a vow of pax very seriously, but even so: she still felt entitled to ask. "What does it mean, Shea, and how did you get it?"

She groaned theatrically, but perhaps ceded the justice of the exchange. "All right, this one last time. Mummy had a terrible time giving birth to me, and we were both of us deathly ill afterwards. The hospital chaplain suggested baptising me there and then, for fear that I'd not survive long enough for them to do it properly at a christening. Daddy was more or less out of his mind with worry about us both, and went along with it, just in case. There was a little font in the hospital chapel, just for reasons like this. The chaplain called in a matron and a doctor to be my godparents, and when it came to the bit where he asks for the child's name, of course they didn't know; so they looked to Daddy, and..."

"And what?" It was an appalling place to pause, and Radhika knew she was only doing it for effect.

"And that's when he realised that, what with all the fuss and bother leading up to the birth, he and Mummy hadn't talked about it at all. He hadn't even thought about it, till this moment. And he's a professor of Ancient Greek, you know, and he looked at me in all my frailty and innocence—those are his words, not mine—and he said the first word that came into his head."

"Which was Agnosia," Marigold explained, helpfully.

"Yes, but why? What does it mean?"

There were grins and giggles all around the table now, but even Marigold left it to Shea to cap the tale.

"It means 'ignorance'," she said wearily. "There I was, knowing nothing of the world, knowing nothing of Mummy's peril or my own, an absolute blank slate that had never yet been written on; and that's what he came up with."

"What, what did your mother say? I mean, assuming—"

"Oh, she survived. She's been left an invalid, but she gets by, with Daddy's help. That's one reason they sent me here, to lighten the load a bit at home. And neither of them has ever told me what she said when she heard, when she understood. I don't know what kind of debates they had or for how long, what to do about it; but they both ended up resigned. They always have called me Agnosia, and I grew up being quite fierce about it, for some reason. It's my *name*, and I won't give it up. Even now, I won't. But you may call me Shea for short," she added graciously. "Now, please, enough about me. Radhi, just promise me one more thing: next time you, you faint with fury, please don't do it in front of a gaggle of Lower Threes? They'll be talking about it from now till Doomsday, and it, well, it doesn't reflect well on our dignity."

Radhika promised, with a weariness of her own; and wondered just how she was going to explain this sudden lapse, this loss of control in her weekly confessional letter to Capri.

# CHAPTER TWENTY-FOUR

## An Unscheduled Matinée

"I've been thinking."

"Oh, dear."

"What a pity."

"Did it hurt?"

"I thought you weren't yourself today."

"Ha," Radhika enunciated carefully, "ha, and ha again. You all think you're so funny."

It was true, they did; they entertained themselves and each other enormously. Radhika might be growing accustomed—slowly, slowly!—to their level of teasing, but it did still grate on her sometimes, especially when she was trying to be serious.

Charm had perhaps picked up on that. "What about, Radhi?"

"About Eder."

That sobered the group quickly. "What about him?"

"Well, it must be so dull for him up there. I mean, even with as many visitors as Sister Anthony will allow, he's still

285

alone most of the day and all the night; and even with all his books and exercises and so on, there must be times when he literally has nothing to do but lie still and stare out of the window."

"Well, it is a lovely view," Lauren murmured.

"It is; but this is the land he grew up on, the land he's lived in all his life. I doubt he even sees it as a view."

"Well, but what do you think we can do about it?" Marigold asked, ever practical, ever going straight to the point. "We can't exactly change the landscape."

"No, we can't—but we can give him something else to look at, for a bit."

Various expressions of puzzlement came back to her, along with frowns and the cocking of heads. Now she really did have their attention. She straightened her back, took a breath, and told them of her idea.

If there was one major disadvantage to converting an old hotel into a school, it was the lack of large open indoor spaces. Really, the dining hall was the only option, so it had to serve numerous functions besides seating two hundred girls at breakfast, lunch, tea and supper.

The fine clear air at the crater rim afforded the very best atmosphere for young lungs, so the school took its exercise out of doors summer and winter, as often as might be. At times, though, the weather closed in hard, often for days and occasionally even weeks on end, making their usual sports impossible. Then the long tables and benches of the dining hall all had to be stacked against one wall after breakfast—by the girls, who constituted the only available source of labour—so that the hall could become a makeshift gymnasium for the day. Lunch on those days would be sandwiches, collected on enormous trays and eaten in formrooms, with an urn of tea or coffee to wash them down.

At the end of school, Miss Whitworth's final gym class would haul the tables out again for tea, while all the mats and vaulting-horses and so forth took their turn against the wall, ready for tomorrow.

At Christmastime, the hall played host to the traditional concert of carols gathered from far and wide; at Speech Day and other festivities too it had a formal role to play. Whenever many heads needed to be gathered together in one space, that duty fell to the dining hall.

As now, towards the end of the Trinity term, when all school leavers on Mars sat down to their dreaded public examinations, that could well determine the path of their adult lives to come. By law, these had to be worked through by everyone at once, at the same time on the same date, all across the province, with senior staff to invigilate.

Accordingly, after the tables had been cleared and wiped down, the Seniors fell to carrying them across the hall and stacking them in tiers, while the Juniors took care of the benches. The Middles were marched to their own form-rooms, where each seized hold of her own desk and carried it bodily back to the dining hall, where prefects supervised their setting out in neat and scrupulous rows with ample space between one desk and the next, then sent the Middles back to fetch their chairs.

"Do we have to do this every day?" Radhika asked, as she shuffled along in line astern.

"No-o," judiciously, from Marigold ahead. "Most days we do, though it's not always the whole hall; sometimes there's only half a dozen people sitting one exam or another. Occasionally we do get a day off, if nobody's doing physics, say, or Russian literature this year. The first few days are always English language, English lit, and maths, though, and everyone sits those, they're compulsory."

"So what do we sit on? Our bottoms, on the floor?"

A giggle from Charm, bringing up the rear of their own particular threesome. "No, we just have our formroom lessons wherever's available. Last year we had French in the chemistry lab, I remember. Mlle Latour taught us all manner of new sciency words; not that I remember any of those, mind you. It's hard, when you don't understand what the science actually means. And lunch will be a picnic, at the cricket pavilion."

"Oh, fun!"

"Come on, hurry up, there," called a stern Melanie. "Then get changed, quick as you can; Miss Whitworth wants you in your whites, down at the nets for practice."

"Sometimes," Marigold sighed, "life just seems to be always changing out of one set of clothes and into another. It's, it's wearying, is what it is. I mean, these things we wear," with a sway of her hips to draw attention to the flaring skirt, "why do they call these things gym tunics, given that we're never actually allowed to gym in them?"

"That may well be a question for the ages, Marigold," snapped Melanie, who was not in the least looking forward to her test papers today, "but it is absolutely not a question for now. Put that chair straight, please, and then flit. Fleetly, if you don't want trouble at the other end."

Flit they did, and fleet they were, and trouble there was regardless, for they were the lastcomers of their class, and examination-time put everyone's nerves on edge. Even though the school clock struck the hour even as they were being scolded, thereby proving conclusively that they absolutely were not late, the scolding continued. They should have been present and ready to play five minutes ago, apparently, because last-second arrivals just delayed everybody, besides being discourteous to staff and class together. Others had arrived in good time; so too could they, so too should they. Order-marks all around; give them to Melanie, as head of your house, before the end of the day. Et cetera.

It wasn't fair—indeed, it was the very definition of *un*fair—but Authority's word was law. Technically they could appeal to Miss Hendy, as their housemistress; except that Miss Hendy wasn't there, and wouldn't have been likely to remit the punishment anyway, and Miss Harribeth certainly wouldn't do so in her stead. Staff and prefects always took one another's word in such matters. Which was another great unfairness in the world, which seemed to Radhika entirely constructed for the purpose of tormenting schoolgirls.

"Radhi? Are you all right?"

They weren't supposed to talk while they waited for their turn on the practice pitches, they should have all their focus bent on those in action before them; but a low murmur could often be got away with, as could a nudge of the shoulder to attract the attention of the murmuree.

Radhika glanced sideways at an anxious Charm. "Yes, of course. Why wouldn't I be?"

"Shh! Keep it down! But you, you've got that look on your face, the one you get when you're seething inside."

"Well, I am seething inside. Aren't you?"

Charm shrugged. "Not really. It's just school. These things happen," said with all the acquired wisdom of her nearly-four-terms'-worth of experience, "and—"

"Radhika! Charm! Take a second order-mark each, for talking! I don't know what's got into you girls, but I won't have it!"

Radhika's lips tightened, as though to hold in the ferocious response she could feel building inside. Charm took her hand, and squeezed it tightly; Marigold manifested once again, on her other side, with a muttered, "Just breathe. That's all. Breathe. In and out, nice and slowly..."

It had been one of the pieces of advice she was given at the Sanatorium. She could recall the doctor talking her through it, making her practice, making her write it down on her list of strategies for keeping her temper caged. Both her friends had copies of that list now, and were ever on the alert like this.

Radhika snorted, but then drew a long and steady breath in through her nose, feeling them doing the same on either side, in time with her, as they had all practised it together. She almost wanted to laugh then, but that would be a very bad idea, with Miss Whitworth's ire aroused and her eye still on her wayward charges. Just the idea of laughing seemed to be enough, though. Much to her own surprise, she could feel her rage dissipating, drifting away from her, as she distracted her mind with this simplest of exercises.

And then at last a cold Miss Whitworth gave her the nod, and she could take her bat to the wicket and start flaying the ball far and wide, driving it back past the bowler as often as she could so that it would escape the netting cage and need to be chased and thrown back, drawing other girls into the action. That was more fun than simply clobbering it into the net on either side of the wicket; then she'd have to pick it up herself and toss it back to the bowler, as an act of courtesy. She wasn't feeling particularly courteous, just then.

Miss Whitworth had perhaps picked up on that. She left Radhika at the wicket longer than any other girl, giving everyone else a chance of bowling at her for an over or two. At last there was less brutality in her strokeplay and more style, more grace. Something of an ache in her shoulders, too; she was quite glad when Miss Whitworth eventually called her away.

"That was very good, Radhika; you show excellent form, when you think about it. There's no need to be quite so, so *hectic* at the start of your innings; take some time to play yourself in."

"Yes, Miss Whitworth."

Then, the surprise: "I have already told Marigold and Charm that I am setting your order-marks aside, on this occasion. I was perhaps a little hasty myself, given that you were not in fact technically late."

"Thank you, Miss Whitworth! I will try to be earlier in the future, I promise I will. Um, does that include the extra one you gave Charm and me...?"

Astonishingly, Miss Whitworth actually smiled. "Yes, it does. It occurred to me that the second offence derived directly from the first, and should therefore be disregarded also. Just this once, you understand. Now get back in line; I want another look at those twisters of yours. I think I see a flaw in your action, that were best addressed immediately, before it becomes a habit."

Punishments imposed and then lifted away lighten the heart far more than mere time spent without any punishment earned or received. The three of them practically skipped back to their house to change—again!—and hurry up to the Castle. Again.

There was a notice pinned to a board set up on an easel by the stairs, listing the adjustments to timetable and room allocation.

"French next. Mam'selle Latour usually comes to us, so we need to grab our books and get up to 6B, pronto. Don't linger, Radhi! We won't get lucky twice. Whatever that is, you can read it later..."

What it was, in fact, was a list of all the examinations faced by their seniors in the coming weeks, and which staff would be invigilating. Radhika didn't need to read it all, or again; she had already seen everything she wanted to know.

Accordingly, even Radhika plied her hated needle with an unaccustomed vigour, in the days that followed. So did everyone in their little band, all the actors from their pageant-piece. They even begged Miss Tarleton for permission to take their costumes back to their houses, so they could work on them in any stray minutes that might come their way.

Thus, when the end-of-school bell rang on the Friday of that week, all was in readiness. Stern prefects stood in the hallway, warning people to hasten by and not make noise, not to talk at all, for an examination was still ongoing in the dining hall and would be for another hour or more. Happily they had no need to speak, nor any cause to linger: not at all!

They duly hastened up the lawful side of the divided staircase, the other being sacred to staff and prefects and not to be sullied by any lesser shoe, though sixth-formers were usually safe to ignore that rule with impunity. Marigold led the way into their abandoned formroom—and promptly skidded, squealed, and fell asprawl, for Mr Felton had taken advantage of the emptiness to polish the floorboards to a lethal mirror shine.

The others came in more cautiously, helped her up, checked her for hurts and the corridor for anyone coming to investigate the noise. Fortunately it was negatives all around, so they stepped warily over to the big stock cupboard, and retrieved all the finished costumes they'd cached there the day before.

"Everyone set?" It had been Radhika's inspiration, and in large part they had her to thank for the preparation too, but she was quite happy to let Marigold take charge now. "Let's go!"

Sister Anthony never raised the matter herself, of course— it would have been beneath and far beneath her dignity—but she was generally understood to be one of the foundation stones of the school: the first official employee, indeed, as in those days Miss Bartlett had been retained as the then-Miss Tolchard's personal secretary, not on the school's books yet. That made her, by definition, very senior staff indeed; and she would never dream of making the point, but it was believed that secretly she rather enjoyed taking her turn as invigilator of the examinations.

Her scheduling was always contingent, necessarily, an asterisk by her name. Miss Leven would always have someone—often herself—standing by to step in if there were an emergency, or merely a busy San upstairs to make Sister Anthony unavailable. That had never happened yet, and the general feeling in the school was that it never would. No one facing an examination, of course, would dare to be sick that day, with so much dependent on it; and every girl else seemed to take her cue from that, so that the hours of Sister Anthony's absence were often the quietest of the year, in her particular bailiwick. She had taken to leaving a girl on watch in her stead, no more than that, with instructions to fetch her at a run should anything—"and I mean *anything*"—untoward occur, that might demand her presence.

Today, the excited Thirds slipped quietly into the San, all but tiptoeing past the sister's office door, for all that they knew the dragon was not in residence. Coming into the ward, they found Izzy—that is to say, Isidora Dolores Ibárruri Gómez in all her Basque pride and glory—and her inseparable friend Brigitta sitting on sentry duty, talking quietly, waiting for them. Seniors they might be now, but co-conspirators they also and absolutely were, lured in by Radhika's urgent pleas. Izzy's dark eyes were dancing with the fun of it.

Otherwise, the ward held only two girl-patients, a Junior with a tummy ache and a Middle with a badly sprained wrist. Both were sitting up in bed with their dressing-gowns on, prepared earlier for what was to come.

"You're both up for this?" Marigold asked. "You're sure?"

They nodded confirmation. Indeed, even the Junior scoffed at the notion that she might stay in her cubicle and miss out on all the wickedness ahead. Not that it was particularly wicked, exactly, but, well, it was unauthorised, and the general feeling held that what was not compulsory was probably forbidden.

"All right. You lot hop along, then, while we get changed."

All four girls thus addressed made their way—a little cautiously in two cases, each one claiming a Senior arm to help them—down to the end of the ward, and thus into Eder's private cubicle. The actors hastily shed their quotidian uniforms and donned their costumes, helping each other when they could; then they filed out through the French windows, onto the flat roof of the gatehouse below.

In Eder's cubicle, they knew, Izzy would be explaining to Eder what he was about to see. She was the only girl in the school with fluent Basque, as far as any of the company knew; she was their narrator, there to describe the action, because they could of course perform only in mime. Eder's English might be coming on in leaps and bounds—indeed, Izzy had sworn to tell the tale in English as much as she could, only slipping into her native tongue if the boy became obviously confused—but no one was going to challenge him with Shakespeare yet awhile.

"All set, everyone? Here we go..."

From Radhika Harvey's weekly letter to Capri Demetreu, at St Emilia's:

*...so with those confessions over, I simply have to tell you about Friday. I wrote to you before, I know, about poor Eder, the boy who's stuck in our San until his leg mends. It's a dreary life for an active boy; we do our best to keep him distracted, but even so.*

*So, we gave him a play to watch! We took our pageant costumes and acted out Pyramus and Thisbe, hamming it up hugely, all dramatic gestures and no words, while Izzy talked him through what was going on, in case he got completely lost. It was the best fun, and now I wish we could do it that way for the pageant too. I had the idea from the Juniors, who are doing Macbeth for the pageant, but like that, miming the action while someone narrates what's actually going on.*

*By the way, it's just struck me: do you think Pyramus etc is just Shakespeare reworking Romeo and Juliet? If he wrote them in that order, I mean? It is the same exact story at heart, it's just funnier. Just as tragic at the end, but still funnier. I wonder if this is common knowledge, or if I'm some kind of undiscovered literary genius, the first ever to see the connection...?*

# CHAPTER TWENTY–FIVE

## A New Day Dawns

Radhika roused slowly, luxuriating in the warmth of her bed, the warmth of her friends on either side. Marigold was snoring softly; to judge by the sound of turning pages, Charm was reading a book. That was allowed, if you woke before the rising-bell and there was light enough not to strain your eyes. As visiting between one cubicle and the next was very much not allowed, she thought perhaps she'd do the same.

Only then she remembered what day this was, and left her book to lie on her nightstand unregarded. Anticipation and nervousness together caught her up in a whirlwind of fancy, trying to guess just what the day might bring.

This was the Crater School's first-ever Old Girls' Day, and no one knew quite what to expect, except that it was going to be busy. Word in the corridors—never reliable, of course, but always interesting—suggested that somewhere between a horde and a host of former Cratereans was due to descend on the school, if the mountain of acceptances piled up in Miss Bartlett's office was to be taken at face value. Several girls had vouched independently for the height of it—"honestly, I could barely see over the top! And Miss B is *inches* shorter than me, so..."—and it was certain, of course, which is to say that the girls were certain, that all of them were indeed acceptances. Old Girls' Day was safe to trump any other engagement, be it prior or subsequent. Craterean blood runs rich and deep; old girls were looked on as family, their offspring the school's grandchildren.

Indeed, some few old girls were *in situ* already, the vagaries of Martian travel having washed them up on these shores one or two or in a couple of cases several days early. Some had brought their children with them, to the delight of staff and girls alike.

This was the great official day, though. Swarms of people were expected, by rail and steamcar and airship alike; Mr Marks had grudgingly sacrificed his playing fields—all but the sacred cricket square, naturally—to the needs of harbouring and refuelling a multitude of vehicles.

The best part was that the early comers without family in tow were allowed to sleep in their old houses, in whatever dormitory could best squeeze them in. They had humbly asked permission to tell stories after lights out, for half an hour only. Radhika's dormitory was blessed with the presence of a Miss Prenderville, who was a professor now at the university in New Victoria, specialising in something complicated to do with electricity and the making thereof. That didn't sound too thrilling, but as it turned out, Penny Prenderville had been something of a live wire of a different sort in her schooldays. When Miss Harribeth loomed in the doorway to say that she had quite overrun her promised time and there must be no more talk now, the girls protested as one, begged for just ten more minutes, five...

"Absolutely not," was the stern reply. "How*ever*, if you settle down and go to sleep like the obedient children I know you all yearn to be,"—snorts from several cubicles, and they could hear the laughter in her voice as she went

297

on—"tomorrow night I will come in here myself, sit on Penny's feet, and tell you some stories about her that I can guarantee she has not told herself."

Cries of acclaim, oaths of silence, a remarkable stillness all through the dormitory, their prefect not excluded.

All the current pupils had tasks assigned to them, from meeting the special trains that would be running all day, to serving refreshments, to escorting old girls wherever they wanted to go, helping them to see how the school had changed since their day, and how much it had remained the same. Radhika and half a dozen other Third Years were to spend the morning in the dining hall, laying out their museum pieces on their assigned tables and showing them to the visitors as they came, telling the best stories they had learned about the Basques and their long occupation here. Also, they had a surprise in store, one exhibit not listed in the catalogue. Not even Miss Harribeth knew their secret; the only adult who did had been sworn to secrecy by blood-curdling oaths, the very strongest they could manage to come up with.

The afternoon would be devoted to Miss Peters' Shakespearean pageant, which would take place in a great marquee erected on the hockey field, the only decent-sized patch of grass to be spared the burden of tires and tramping feet this day. Radhika wasn't quite sure how she felt about that. Their as-it-were dress rehearsal on the gatehouse roof had been nothing but fun, simply hilarious; but this would be the real thing, where every word mattered, every gesture. Would she have stage fright? She didn't know, but she wouldn't be surprised. She knew herself to be shy, when she wasn't raging. Perhaps she'd freeze, at the prospect of speaking out among all those people—and she and her fellow Athenians would be sitting right there in the audience, which could honestly only make things worse. Perhaps she'd spoil the whole show.

Almost, she wanted to ask Charm to step in for her. Charm had declined a part, thank you very much, and would be working backstage, helping with costumes and makeup and the like. Everyone assumed—well, everyone hoped— that Levity would turn up at her little sister's side to offer her own help. She was the one who'd inherited the artistic eye from their mother; Charm's gifts and interests went quite another way.

The rising bell was a comparatively quiet affair, courteous to sleepers. You learned to rouse to it in moments any- way, because what followed was cacophony, every girl leap- ing out of bed and racing to complete her dormitory chores, take her bath, dress and groom herself before everyone was marched downstairs and up to the Castle for breakfast. It was somehow worse than ever, with a grown-up guest in the middle of it all; in trying to be polite and considerate to her, they ended up tripping over each other in what was usually a well-practised and well-oiled machine, while she—who would be breakfasting with Miss Harribeth and others, and was under no time-pressure whatever—merely sat on her bed and laughed at them, and tried to stay out of their way.

"Was it like this in your day?" Charm somehow found breath and time to ask, between tidying her dresser and tossing her cubey curtains up over the rail to let the room air out.

"Oh, absolutely. I think perhaps we might have been a little shriller, even."

As they marched up to the Castle at their commonly brisk school pace, drilled relentlessly into them by Miss Whitworth at her fiercest, she having no time for dawdlers, Radhika watched a newly arrived airship moor up at the quay. One passenger aboard spurned any notion of waiting for a gangway before he disembarked; he merely set one hand on the gunwale and vaulted ashore.

Radhika gasped, for a moment seeing her father entire in that figure, in that action, that impatience to be getting on. That was Papa-ji to the core; except that this of course was not Papa-ji, only a man who stood and moved and acted much like him. She couldn't make out a face at this distance, but that man wore the crimson-and-madder uniform of the Double Reds, Mars' own regiment, the Queen's Own Martian Borderers. She hadn't been made Empress yet, the one time she visited; of course they kept the name that she herself had given them, though she would always be the Empress otherwise.

Anyway, Papa-ji would never, could never be seen in that uniform, or any. He was a hotel manager now, he wore a suit to work; and besides, he was on Earth, for whatever reason of his own.

And besides again, this man stepped down into a waiting boat and sat impatiently in the stern, while the hired oarsman rowed him away, across the lake.

Not only in Stokes House was the level of excitement—and hence the level of noise—more elevated even than usual. At breakfast the staff on duty, the commonly easy-going Miss Lowe of the science wing, felt herself obliged to call the girls to order twice. She was entertaining more of the earlycomers at the staff table, and the second time she struck the bell, she protested that she couldn't hear herself think, let alone what anyone else was saying.

The racket was at least a little more moderate after that, and besides, there was chewing to do, as well as talking. Even so, it was something of a relief to all concerned when the majority of the girls tumbled en masse out of the hall, leaving behind only those on museum duty.

At least they needn't move the tables much today, just end-to-end for each year's display. The benches, they had found, could be deployed atop the tables, as a kind of elevated shelving running their full length. That had been Charm's notion, or at least Charm had put it forward; some few suspected her elder sister's hand in that, as well as in the artwork she'd produced for the display. No one troubled to challenge her, though. If Levity cared to help them out a little on the quiet, they would be duly and quietly grateful, nothing more.

They laid out their artefacts, their explanatory notes, their art depicting Basque life down the years; and all that time they were also watching the door, waiting, all but holding their breath.

At last, at long last, there was a shadow in the doorway bigger than any passing girl, and much more oddly shaped. They abandoned their work and ran to meet the incoming figure, now resolving in the light into two: and one was Dr Ed, and the other was Eder, allowed out of his bed for the first time, under strict medical supervision, being propelled in grand style in an ancient wicker Bath chair dredged up from somewhere in the depths of the Sanatorium's basements. His poor leg could still not be bent, never mind used to bear any weight at all. Instead it stuck out ahead of him, securely bound to a stiff board. It couldn't be comfortable, exactly, but Eder seemed ridiculously happy, merely to be out of bed and out of his confining cubicle. He grinned at everyone and waved to those he knew, which was most girls in the hall that morning. Dr Ed had to stop pushing and wave in his own turn, wave them all away as they threatened to overwhelm him and his patient in a tidal wave of welcome.

"Get back, get back! Yes, you may have Eder, perhaps for a couple of hours, if he can last that long. I shall be mounting guard over him, and the moment he seems tired or in undue pain, I'm taking him back to the ward. In the meantime, he

301

mustn't be excited, more than we can possibly help. Which means that you may come and speak with him, girls, but only in twos and threes at a time, please. I shall deposit him here," at the foot of the Third Years' table, "as he does officially constitute a part of their exhibit, being the embodiment, the very pinnacle of Basqueness as the school has always understood it. Myself I shall ensconce here," on a convenient chair, intended for weary old girls to rest themselves upon, "where I can keep watch and not let you overtire him. Thirds, you get him first, of course, but then you will need to give way and let others take their turn."

Of course, that was perfectly fine. They didn't mind sharing their boy around, now that it was quite clearly established that he was indeed their boy, their ultimate artefact. They'd even brought his knitting down for him, and he was under strict instructions to knit continuously, regardless of what anyone else might be saying or doing to him or around him. He was theirs, and they meant to show him off.

So there were two steady streams of traffic moving through the hall that morning. One was the procession of old girls, some of whom remembered the museum in its original incarnation and were eager to see it anew, while others were simply curious or else nostalgic for the life they had left behind them, the crater and the lake and the valley and all, and here it all was, distilled into a tolerably scholarly whole.

The other stream was made up of girls in their best uniforms, their hair glossy with brushing, their shoes ashine and their faces too. Some of them slipped away from their own tables, to have their few allotted minutes with Eder; some rudely or recklessly abandoned their duties as those they escorted fell into the deep waters of do-you-remember? and I'll-never-forget, in order to inveigle themselves into Dr Ed's good graces and thus into the boy's company, just for a little while.

The girls made clot enough, around that enormous chair. Soon, though, old girls too were pausing, calling to each other to come and see this extraordinary work, they'd had no idea those shepherd boys could do anything so delicate and fine...

Dr Ed was young yet, and most of the guests were not. However, his white coat and title lent him an authority that outstripped his years. Far from sitting at his ease, he found himself obliged to stand beside his charge and gently urge his elders to keep moving, once they'd had a chance to admire the speed and dexterity of Eder's knitting, all done while he talked nonstop with whichever couple of girls were allowed to crouch down either side of his chair and bask in the glory of his smile.

That smile, it seemed, was infectious. Some of the girls had been feeling overburdened with the importance of their task here, fearing that they wouldn't be up to the job; now everyone was happy and relaxed, eager to show off their assigned artefacts and the work they'd done around them, eager to draw the visitors into their own engagement with what they'd learned.

All in all, the museum was already bidding fair to be something of a triumph, temporary as it had to be in this busiest of spaces. Something else was going on, though, which—to their entire outrage—the Thirds knew nothing about. Nor could the girls at any other table help them out. All they knew was what they could see, which was that almost every old girl would end their visit by producing a wrapped something-or-other from a pocket or a handbag, and lay it on an extra table left empty at the end of the hall. Clearly this was all prearranged, and no one could decipher what its meaning might be.

Until, well on into the morning, there was something of a hubbub at the great doorway to the hall, followed by a mysterious hush. That spread rapidly all through that busy space, until everyone was standing, looking, waiting to see the occasion of all this.

Three people, walking together. Three women: and one was Miss Leven, and another Miss Harribeth, and between them was—

"Miss Hendy!"

The name rose up from a hundred throats at once, as she came clear into view; and by no means all of those were schoolgirls. All of them had been, once, but those who'd left their childhoods ten or twenty years behind them were nonetheless moved to call their beloved teacher's name, at this most unexpected sighting.

She looked tired, Radhika thought, unless perhaps *drained* would say it better. Reduced, a little, perhaps. But she walked with her same crisp pace, and held her head high despite the flush in her cheeks at being the object of all attention.

"Well now," she said, her voice carrying clear from one end of the hall to the other, "this is such a wonderful surprise, our old museum risen up from the dead. I want to see and hear everything you've done, girls—starting, of course, with the very most important of you all, the First Years..."

Those wee folk were delighted to be so singled out, even disregarding that the tables were arranged in order of age, so of course theirs had come first.

Miss Hendy took her time, looking at everything, talking to everyone. Miss Leven allowed herself to be stolen away by a group of determined old girls, but Miss Harribeth stayed throughout, entirely her right as co-proprietrix and resur-rectrix of the same. The Thirds, and particularly the Stokes Thirds on duty, felt that Miss Hendy lingered longer with them than any other year—but then, probably so did every other year. It didn't matter. They were overjoyed to see her back, and quietly determined to make these last few days of term as easy for her as they conceivably could.

As he'd promised, Dr Ed wheeled Eder away before the museum had to be closed and cleared away, to make room for the Old Girls' Luncheon, a new-minted tradition that had kept Mrs Bailey and her kitchenmaids hectic for days belowstairs.

Before they took themselves away, though, to join Miss Leven in her study for sherry beforehand, Miss Harribeth steered Miss Hendy towards that table so mysteriously heaped high with wrapped ... objects. Be she girl or Old Girl, everyone held their breath to hear; and what they heard was this.

"Kathy, I asked every Old Girl who could to bring something to contribute to our museum, something sovereign of their own time here at the school. Heaven only knows when we'll get to look them over, but that we will, and find each one its proper place. We can bring the museum up to date, so that it speaks to the school's progress as much as to the valley's; and Mr Felton has moved things around so that we actually have a permanent room again, and glass cases for the displays—these tables are a makeshift only, because no room but the hall could have held the numbers who wanted to see what we had—and it's going to be glorious. It'll be like Christmas, except that the gifts matter more and far more than toys, and they will just go on and on..."

# CHAPTER TWENTY–SIX

## The End of a New Day

The girls were condemned to sandwiches in their form-rooms again, and lamented their lot in good cheer as they passed the mustard and the chutney, taking the most extraordinary care not to spill anything on their fine clean blazers and tunics.

As soon as they were finished, they streamed out of the Castle while the Old Girls were still at their lunch, no doubt making and listening to dreary speeches—or not so dreary, to judge by the gales of laughter and applause that came from the dining hall as they passed.

From most junior to most senior, they lined the way down to the hockey pitch and the grand marquee, evenly spaced on both sides, forming an honour guard. They stood at ease but in silence, hard though that was for some of them; they were on parade, and the most they could do was pull faces at their friends across the way, try to make them disgrace themselves by giggling.

Not a giggle was heard, not a whispered word—and at last, at long last there was movement, voices, footsteps on the gravel. Out of the shadows came Mrs Mackenzie, marching

306

at the brisk school pace despite the burden of her years; and the very youngest girl in the school, primed and practised till she couldn't conceivably get it wrong, called out as loudly as she might: "Three cheers for Miss Tolchard! Miss Tolchard for the day!"

That had been decided early on, that the day's chief guest should be the school's founder, and not the doctor's wife. Little Amelia hip-hipped three times, and the school roared out its cheers, making an odd rolling effect as though the sound were a boulder bouncing down the hill, as those farther away couldn't possibly have heard Amelia's call, so they only joined in when they heard the nearer girls' cheer.

And, of course, they didn't stop at three. Why would they, how could they? Following their glorious founder came the Oldest Girls there were, some of her very first pupils, marching along in time; and then those of the second intake, and those of the third and so on and on. It was a magnificent sight, everyone dressed in their best and waving delightedly to either side as they were cheered all the way.

Discipline ebbed a little as the parade moved on through time. Some girls had mothers and aunts in there, and shrieked at them as they were spotted; and a number of the Old Girls were actually not very Old at all, only a year or two gone from school. Of course they had friends still among the pupils, and some of them younger sisters too, cousins, all sorts.

After the last of the Old Girls had passed, here came all the other guests and the staff too, all mingled up together. They were cheered too, on the sheer principle of the thing, and they laughed and waved in their turn, seeming to ride on that surf of sound all the way to the marquee.

As soon as the last of the guests had been ushered in by Melanie and Alis, the girls stepped smartly to the centre of the path to march down and around that vast edifice.

Directly behind it was another, smaller, with a canvas-covered framework making a tunnel between the two.

Melanie stood at the doorway to the smaller marquee, waiting till the last girls, the youngest girls had joined their seniors. She smiled on those and said, "Year Ones and Year Twos, inside, sharp now. No one else, you hear me?" with a momentous frown at the gathered throng. "Year One and Year Two only. That's all we have room for, and space to work. The rest of you wait here till you're called."

Then she vanished within, dropping the flaps behind her so that they couldn't even see in.

"Downright mean, I call that," Marigold growled. "I wanted to see the littl'uns in their kilts and tammies, making murder."

"But you did, we all saw everyone's at the dress rehearsal," Charm protested.

"I know, and it was glorious. I wanted to see it again."

Instead, she was obliged to be content with the canvas-muffled sound of Fiona Grant's voice at its most Scottish, dwelling on all the most gruesome details they'd been allowed to include in her script. Judging by the gasps and groans that accompanied her narration, the audience was playing along delightedly.

"Pure *Grand Guignol*," Mary Ellen McKay said, with evident pleasure. She was actually talking to Levity, but the two Buchanan sisters had found each other in the crush—bright red hair being ever an advantage, except when it really, really wasn't—so Upper Thirds and Fourths were somewhat mingled together, and very much within hearing.

"Please, Mary Ellen, what does that mean?" Charm asked, as the one closest to being able to claim she was part of the conversation and not eavesdropping at all, no no.

"It means, ah, sensationalist theatre: all the blood and gore you could look for on a stage. You can read more about it in the *Encyclopaedia Britannica*, if you're interested."

"Once you've worked out how to spell it," Levity added, coming over all big-sisterly. Charm pulled a face at her, and loftily turned away.

As soon as the First Years were well away, Melanie appeared again to call the Third Years into the tent. This was their moment; they squirmed through the crowd and ducked under the flap, knowing their work already. Each year was there to help the one below with costumes and props and the like, so they'd be ready as soon as the current performers had taken their bows and departed.

The Second Years were giving an extract from *The Tempest*, and they did need the help. All their time in the tent thus far had been devoted to their own juniors, so it was a scramble now to get prepared. The main characters had heavy, courtly—or in Prospero's case, wizardly—costumes to get into, complete with fussy lacings and the like; while Caliban and Ariel were wearing the barest minimum that decency demanded, essentially their bathing suits elaborated accordingly, but both needed makeup rubbed all over their exposed arms and legs. Making Mavis Duns look brutish and Terry Avilon ethereal was a challenge, but the Thirds were willing to do their very best.

They were finished just in time, and getting themselves cleaned up ready for their own transformations, when Melanie called the Fourths in to help in their turn.

To nobody's surprise, Levity assumed charge of the operation, just as she had for the dress rehearsal. Along with her mother's eye, she had inherited also a passion for theatre in all its forms, and this was meat and drink to her. She seemed to be everywhere at once: easing Marigold into the working-man's tunic she would wear as Bottom, with

Pyramus' plate armour—actually silver paper over card-board, the breastplate embossed of course with the head of an ass—buckled haphazardly over the top; arranging Wall's brickwork so that it hung more or less level; helping Lion into mask and clawed gloves, as ferocious as they could make him.

Too soon for Radhika, who was now entirely convinced that stage fright would render her entirely mute, they were ready and called into line. Happy applause and cries of "Encore!" from the rowdier element of the Old Girls chased the Second Years out, and they were on!

Naturally for the nervous Radhika, the script demanded that she speak first, as Philostrate. Feeling utterly exposed in her short Greek tunic and cloak, she walked onto the low stage with Elana and Janna, otherwise Theseus and Hippolyta, took one shudderingly deep breath, and began.

"A play there is, my lord, some ten words long
(Which is as brief as I have known a play),
But by ten words, my lord, it is too long,
Which makes it tedious..."

As she spoke, as she reacted—no, as she *acted*—she felt new confidence stir inside her. With all the words and moves committed to memory, her path lay clear before her; and some odd, hitherto unsuspected part of her soul rather liked that sense of an audience, of having people intently listening to her. When she won her first laugh, she thrilled at it, and very much wanted more.

Alas for ambition: hers was a small part, and soon over. Instead, she learned the pleasures of watching friends and fellows carry the performance on, higher and higher, achieving peaks they'd never managed in rehearsal. She saw some of the slapstick they'd worked out and practised for Eder's mime slipping back in spontaneously, as if by nature; that even surprised a bark of laughter from Miss Peters, because of course she'd never seen it, despite having overseen all their scheduled practice.

At last, Theseus spoke the final words, and beckoned all the cast back onto the stage to take their bows and receive all the applause due, and probably more besides. The Old Girls were still cheering as they paraded down the aisle and out of the marquee, leaving by the front entrance in order not to get in the way of the Fourths, who were ready to come in behind them.

One man must have come late to the school, for he had certainly not been in the procession; unusually, no man there had been sporting the uniform of the Double Reds today. He was standing at the back, just by the tent-flap, not wanting to disturb the audience of the performers by trying to find a seat.

The moment she saw him, Radhika knew that this was the man she'd seen arrive earlier, to be rowed across the lake, almost certainly to the Sanatorium, because where else was there to go?

He had gone there first—but then he had come here, to see this. And he was a figure of shadow in the dim marquee, with the bright light of day at his back; and oh, she didn't want to deceive herself, because it couldn't, how could it be? And yet, and yet...

"Papa-ji?"

He was a tall man, her father, and he'd always struck an imposing figure, especially in uniform. "Clothes maketh the man," and somehow those particular clothes had made him seem distant, formal even with his family.

And yet, here he was on his knees in the grass of the hockey field, which was going to ruin his smart trousers that

311

he couldn't possibly be wearing, because how could he? But then, he couldn't possibly be here either and yet here he was, holding her closer and tighter than ever he had before, murmuring baby-words to her as she sobbed into his shoulder, no doubt spoiling his lovely jacket too.

He stroked her head, shifting readily into Hindi, hoping perhaps that memories of her ayah's endearments long and long ago might calm her sooner than his English could.

And perhaps that was right, perhaps they did. At any rate, her weeping ebbed away; and at length she lifted her head to meet him eye to eye, though still keeping a fierce grip on his lapels for fear that he might vanish as mysteriously as he had appeared.

"How," she said, and hiccuped, and tried again, "how can you *be* here? And wearing *this*," a uniform to which he was not entitled, with a major's crown she saw now on his epaulet, when he had retired only a captain. She had been an army brat all her life, until suddenly she wasn't any more; she knew the magnitude of these offences, and was genuinely shocked at him.

He shifted, perhaps a little uncomfortable under her stern gaze. "That ... is a long story, Radhika, and I would prefer only to tell it once. Of course you must be there, to hear it all; but so I think must some others, though it will be hard to steal them away from their festivities, I fear."

An Earthman was perhaps not to know it, but Martians in general and Cratereans in particular have always relished the challenge of what's hard. They have had to, since the first pioneers first set foot on the Red Planet; and now it is perhaps part of the provincial character, so ingrained they take it for granted.

Wiser than her father, or simply better informed, Radhika coopted the help of one Rowany de Vere, and that turned the tables wonderfully. Within the hour, there was a small committee met in the headmistress's comfortable study, refreshments to hand and expectations high, because who doesn't enjoy a good story? Miss Leven herself presided, of course, with Major Harvey—at least, that was how she addressed him, and she had never been known to err in matters of precedence and protocol—as the primary guest and storyteller. Also present were Radhika, scrubbed and groomed and back in uniform, sitting on the hearthrug where she could wrap both arms around her father's leg, because she wasn't letting him go now for anything; her housemistress Miss Hendy, also newly materialised out of nowhere; Dr and Mrs Mackenzie, who both had an interest in Radhika's welfare as well as her mother's; Miss Harribeth, who claimed her place by right of playing step-housemistress to Radhika these last weeks, but was really certainly there for the story; Isobel Buchanan, who made no claims whatever but simply chose to be there, and so she was; and Rowany, who was so much a figure of every dramatic twist and turn of recent Crater School legend, no one even thought to question why she should attend, which was of course exactly what she'd hoped.

Tea and biscuits dispensed, smalltalk dismissed, Radhika's father gazed at his hands for a moment, drew a breath, lifted his head and spoke.

"Some of you must know by now, others probably not, but know this, that I was all but cashiered from my regiment, asked to resign in no uncertain terms. I had been accused of, of stealing, of misappropriating mess funds, to quite a remarkable degree over quite a period of time. They would only allow me to resign my commission if I also reimbursed the mess for all that they said I had taken, which broke me entirely. I had nothing left, to feed my wife and daughter.

"Fortunately I did still have a few friends, who refused to believe the calumny. Between them, they financed our voyage here, with some little more to live on until I could find work. For a man with my history, a reported thief, that was no easy task, and the position I did at last secure was ... really not an appropriate environment in which to raise a child, never mind a girl-child."

Radhika pressed her cheek against his knee; he caressed her hair, before forcing himself to continue.

"That became clear, as I grew more familiar with the business, and the interests of my employer. What else became apparent was that my, my wife had contracted some illness that no doctors in Marsport could identify. They suggested that I send her here, to your Sanitorium," a nod to the doctor. "It seemed providential that there should also be a girls' school here, and one of such high repute. Again it stretched my finances to the limit, but I felt as though I were sending both my wife and my daughter into safety, into good clean air, after the murk and filth of Marsport."

This was hard for him, but perhaps more of Mars had rubbed off on him than he knew. He took a sip of tea, another breath, carried on.

"I said that I still had friends in the regiment, a few. Unbeknownst to me, they communicated with a gentleman who had recently retired to Marsport, a man with a reputation for solving cases that had baffled the police entirely.

"The first I knew of this was when this same elderly gentleman came to find me at my, at my place of work. He introduced himself as a Consulting Detective, and explained that he had taken an interest in my situation, to honour a late dear friend of his who had been a military surgeon in India. He had looked over all the documents in my case, and said he believed my protestations of innocence.

"I could make no sense of this, or of him. But he mentioned the names of my friends, and I understood at least a little, that they had somehow procured these documents and sent them to him in hopes that he might see a way through. Which he could, he said: but proving it would necessitate a trip back to Earth, back to India, for us both.

"You may imagine, I was more than reluctant. I had put all that behind me, when I brought my family here; I had little taste for revisiting the worst moments of my career, of my life. But the gentleman is ... persuasive, an extremely credible man, with an astonishing mind. If he were willing to risk the journey and the heavier gravity of Home, and it appeared that he was, then I could hardly refuse.

"Authority deliberately makes it costly, very costly, to travel to Earth, while it still remains cheap to come here. And of course I had to leave my employment, such as it was, as I might be gone for months on end. I didn't see how it could be managed. And yet it seemed that funds were in place; I supposed that my friends had clubbed together again. Good friends are a treasure, my *jaan*," his hand on Radhika's head again.

"So. We voyaged to Earth, and then from England to India in an aeroplane, which I had not looked for; again there was money working for me, in ways I couldn't quite understand.

"I will not recount the details of our time there. Suffice it to say that my companion produced conclusive evidence of my innocence, showing quite clearly that another man, a man senior to me, had been responsible all along, and deliberately foisting the blame onto me. Why he should have chosen me I cannot imagine, except that he was one of those who felt that I had cheapened the regiment by marrying out, marrying an Indian woman and she not even of the Brahmin caste. I might guess at that, but we cannot know; he was dead of malaria, a year since.

"Still, we needed no confession. All the proof was on paper, and I took that to my colonel. He might be a harsh man, but always fair; he understood what he was seeing, and accepted it immediately.

"Of course he had superiors too, and nothing is ever simple or easy with the Army in India. But at the last, they offered to reimburse me every penny they had taken, with my back pay too from then to this, reinstatement and a promotion besides. By then I honestly wanted nothing to do with that regiment ever again, but I accepted, for my family's sake. And then I took leave, and came home," said casually, but everything in Radhika's body shivered alert, "and applied immediately for a transfer to the Double Reds. Which, obviously, they granted me."

Radhika's chin was on his knee, while she gazed up at him in mute wonder, trying to understand what this would mean for his life ahead, and so for hers. "I am to spend six months at least in the barracks at Cassini, though, pumpkin," he said, directly to her now, "overseeing the regimental school; and then will likely be transferred to and fro across the province in short order and at short notice. A man of my seniority needs to know the whole of his regiment's deployment. That means we still can't have a settled home together, for some years yet. And of course your mother remains deathly ill, and must stay under Dr Mackenzie's care for the foreseeable future. Could you bear, do you think you could bear to remain here, at the Crater School, at least until things are more settled?"

She tried girlfully for a frown of deep consideration, but the underlying grin would keep breaking through, even as she said, "I think, oh, I *think* I could bear that, Papa-ji, yes. I think I could. I'll give it my best go, at least."

# EPILOGUE

"**D**o you feel as though we were living through an epilogue, at all? While it writes itself, I mean, all around us?"

Melanie laughed up at her friend. "Not remotely, no. It's the end of a chapter, to be sure, but very far from the end of the worlds, or even our worlds. We bid farewell to the dear old Crater School, and reemerge in Oxford: me a Hildabeest, you a, a, I don't know, a St Johnsian? We'll see plenty enough of each other, I'm sure. On the river, perhaps, in rival boats."

"Depend on it. But that's not what I meant, quite. For me at least, there is definitely a sense of a curtain drawing down. Perhaps it's because I've left once already, and been sent back for an extra year to do better, to learn the strangest things." She had rather thrillingly been required to sign the Official Secrets Act, before she was sent back; but there are secrets and there are secrets, and there are friends and there are friends, and some secrets have to be shared with some friends. "I thought I knew before that I'd get no second chance here, and I was wrong; but now I know for certain, I won't get another second chance. A third chance. And I was so young when I came here, and I'm so old now"—she was, in fact, nineteen—"and we're passing from a world where everything we do matters but nothing is actually important, to a world where nothing we do matters but everything is important. Um, unless I mean that the other way around...?"

"Rowany Angelica Marten de Vere, have you been at Miss Leven's brandy?"

"Alas, not. Not even the Staff Room sherry. But I do almost feel as though I might have been. Sort of floaty inside, as though the further we get from the school, the less substance there is to me, the less significance I have."

"In that case," firmly, tucking her arm through her tall friend's elbow and turning her around on the path while the waters of the lake lapped almost at their feet, "let us return instantly to school property, so you may resume your proper density, and be admired by one and all for one last night. I believe we are invited to sup with the great; perhaps that legendary brandy will make an appearance after all."

# ABOUT THE AUTHOR

Chaz Brenchley spent his childhood in Oxford, generally with his nose in a book. At the age of twelve he met J R R Tolkien in a theatre dressing room, and his fate was sealed.

He sold his first stories at the age of eighteen, and has been a professional writer ever since. His work ranges from science fiction to epic and urban fantasy, from mysteries and thrillers to romance and horror. He's published upwards of fifty books, and many hundreds of short stories.

A decade ago he moved from bachelordom to marriage, from Newcastle to California, along with 120 boxes (115 of which were books), two squabbling cats—now gone alas—and a famous teddy bear.

http://www.chazbrenchley.co.uk/

https://www.facebook.com/chaz.brenchley/

@chazbrenchley on Blue Sky

@ChazBrenchley@wandering.shop on Mastodon